Three Yards and a Plate of Mullet

Adam Gordon Sachs

Copyright © 2015 by Adam Gordon Sachs
All rights reserved.

ISBN: 1507679394
ISBN 13: 9781507679395

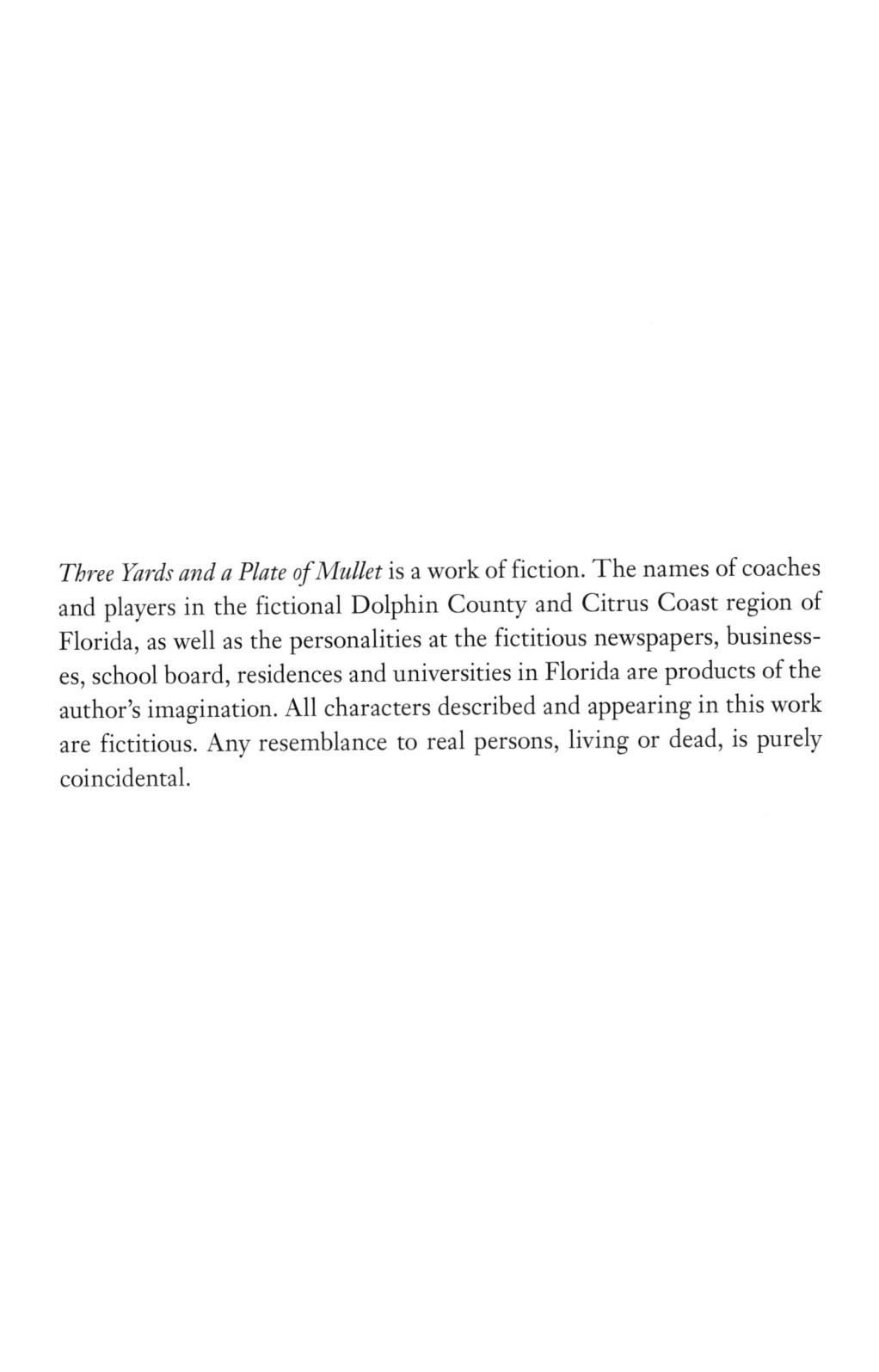

Three Yards and a Plate of Mullet is a work of fiction. The names of coaches and players in the fictional Dolphin County and Citrus Coast region of Florida, as well as the personalities at the fictitious newspapers, businesses, school board, residences and universities in Florida are products of the author's imagination. All characters described and appearing in this work are fictitious. Any resemblance to real persons, living or dead, is purely coincidental.

This novel is dedicated to the memory of my mother, Sandra Gorvine Sachs, who always believed in my writing.

I wish to acknowledge Snee G. for all the stories of the Good Ol' Days, great friendship and travels to Florida for new adventures; my wife Amy for all her love and support and encouraging me to keep writing even when I broke my leg and lost inspiration; my kids Rebecca and Daniel, for whom hopefully this novel will serve as an example (along with my other long-shot initiatives) that it is always worthwhile to pursue a dream or a goal, no matter how overwhelming it seems; my dad for his enthusiasm for this project; and the personnel at CreateSpace for guidance and making the editing and publishing process flow smoothly.

Prologue: The Sports Junkie

There are certain things from your childhood you never forget, and you don't even know why. I remember nearly nothing about kindergarten, except for the first day when I didn't know where to get off the bus and so stayed on until after the driver finished the route and drove back to the bus depot, when I emerged from my hiding place under the seat.

One other memory is seared in my brain. I'm the star, Jacob Yankelovich, five years old, a cross between a sports junkie and an idiot savant, eager to shock and entertain adults with an uncanny photographic recall and Rain Man–esque memorization of meaningless trivia and statistics.

There was a famous basketball player in the 1960s and '70s, Jerry Lucas, who won championships with the iconic New York Knicks teams featuring Walt Frazier and Willis Reed. He also happened to be brilliant.

Lucas was known for his great memory and developed a post-hoops career helping people develop their memories. Sounds boring, like diagramming the Knicks' offense, but when performed, like the Knicks' smooth-flowing weave, it astonished audiences. Lucas would make TV appearances where he would recite pages from the Manhattan phone book from memory and reel off the names of people in the studio audience in sequence after introductions.

What does Jerry Lucas have to do with me? I was Jerry Lucas, only with football cards.

I began collecting football cards when I became entranced with the Washington Redskins of the Sonny Jurgensen era, circa 1970. There was

PROLOGUE: THE SPORTS JUNKIE

something about the burgundy and gold uniforms, the Indian chief emblem on the helmet, and the bold jersey numbers that captured my soul.

So anytime I was out with my mother doing errands, we'd stop by a store to buy wax packs of Topps football cards with the stale pink gum. She probably figured it was worth the price to shut me up.

I didn't just dump the cards into a box and shove them in a closet. I sorted them by team, and then by the best-known players on each team, with quarterbacks and running backs first, and linemen at the bottom. And I studied them, maybe seven hundred cards. Players' names, positions, and teams were easy. I associated the background color on the card with the player. Then I began memorizing the statistics on the backs, not just for the current year but for players' full careers, which could stretch ten years or more. Rushing yards, touchdown receptions, interceptions—any part of the game that could be captured numerically. I memorized heights and weights, hometowns, birth dates, and odd tidbits about players' lives, like throwing the shot put in college or marrying a celebrity.

Now the unforgettable image. It was a party of adults. My father must have boasted about my photographic memory talent, because I was summoned to bring my box of cards to the table where overgrown people with too much '70s hair were waiting to see what this oddball little kid could do.

My proud father passed around the box and told everyone to take a card. They formed a circle around the midget magician.

"Cover up the front of the card, except for just a little piece," my father instructed. "You're not gonna believe this!"

I went around the circle and in rapid succession—like those master chess players who play four games at once, taking mental snapshots, and making rapid moves in each—identified the card each was holding.

A woman covered up the front of a card, except for a white cleat with three blue stripes at the bottom. "That's Jack Snow, wide receiver, Los Angeles Rams."

She uncovered the top, revealing the name. "Holy shit. Oh, sorry... That's right! How'd you know that?"

A man masked a card except for the number eight on a jersey sleeve.

"Alan Page, number eighty-eight, All-Star defensive tackle, Minnesota Vikings."

"Amazing! What are you feeding this kid?"

I felt freaky, but proud to be impressing adults.

"OK, I'm gonna stump him," said my dad's friend, Jolly Joey.

He covered all the stats and writing on the back except for one number: 1980.

"That's career rushing yards for Larry Csonka, number thirty-nine, running back, Miami Dolphins. And he has 462 carries and eighteen touchdowns."

Jolly Joey checked the numbers. "Bingo! No way!" he bellowed.

I made several circuits around the room, reading hidden cards like a psychic, leaving mouths agape and eyes bulging, bringing bewildered laughter to these adults who probably couldn't recall what they had for dinner yesterday.

But it was easy for me. It was sports, and I ate it up.

It wasn't just football that captured my snot-nosed kid imagination. My first love was baseball. Growing up outside of Washington, DC, I was a Washington Senators fan. They were terrible, they were losers, and I didn't care. The Senators had a bunch of players with anemic career .225 batting averages—stubby catcher Jim French, toothpick shortstop Eddie Brinkman—not the kind that take you to the World Series, but they were my heroes.

And players with unusual names that are etched in my mind forever, like Horacio Piña, Bill Gogolewski, and Aurelio Rodríguez, and Jewish-sounding guys like Denny Riddleberger, Mike Epstein, and Pete Broberg.

I'd listen to the radio broadcast of every game in my room, a mitt on my hand, tossing myself fly balls. I was devastated when the Senators moved to Texas and became the Texas Rangers, especially since I already

PROLOGUE: THE SPORTS JUNKIE

hated the Dallas Cowboys, like any true-blooded Washington Redskins fan.

I lived and died every fall Sunday with the Redskins of my youth, Billy Kilmer and Larry Brown and Charley Taylor and Chris Hanburger. One of the most devastating days of my childhood came in 1971 when I was seven. The Redskins led the Chicago Bears 15–9 during a late-season drive for the play-offs. The Bears scored in the waning minutes, but it appeared the game would remain tied after a botched extra point snap. But the holder, one of the great running quarterbacks of all time, Bobby Douglass, ran the ball down and heaved a wild pass from the twenty-six-yard line to none other than linebacker Dick Butkus—Dick Butkus! Only the greatest football name of all time! And what the hell was Dick Butkus doing in the game for an extra point?—and creaky-kneed Dick Butkus caught the ball tumbling in the end zone for the winning extra point. And I went nuclear, yelling at the TV and wailing at the injustice of Dick Butkus! To the point where my mom thought I was having a real mental breakdown because of Dick Butkus. Asked his best memory from his playing days forty years later for ESPN, Dick Butkus cited that one play—not any of his twenty-two interceptions or twenty-seven fumble recoveries—so maybe I wasn't crazy after all.

Luckily, I also had a couple of surrogate favorite teams. A Boston native, I also idolized the Red Sox and the Celtics.

I would play whole baseball games by myself in the backyard, going down the Red Sox lineup with Carl Yastrzemski, Carlton Fisk, and Dwight Evans. I'd toss the ball with one hand and stroke it with my bat, placing the ball wherever the situation dictated—a towering shot over the neighbor's fence if the Red Sox needed a homer late in the game against the Yankees, a line drive into the fence for a double, or a hot-smash grounder toward the woods in the corner of the yard for a two-out, two-strike single to tie the game in the ninth.

I remember when the enormous tree served as home plate, before I moved home plate to the north neighbor's fence to give me more field space as I got older. I was about seven when I cracked a shot from the base of the tree through my brother's second-floor window, the terrifying sound of glass shattering making me want to hide behind the tree but at the same time filling me with a sense of awe that I had launched a ball that far and hard. My brother was in the room but escaped unhurt. My dad didn't kill me, so I guess he was kind of impressed and proud, too.

When the weather turned colder, I retreated to the basement, where we had stored a portable outdoor basketball hoop. There I played out imaginary games, where I was the Celtics' Jo Jo White and John Havlicek, hitting clutch shot after clutch shot until the nets were frayed.

I wasn't just a geek in my own imaginary sports world. My neighborhood was filled with boys. I guess there were some girls around somewhere, but they were older and didn't even exist to me.

This was before video games, Skype, chat rooms, Facebook, Twitter, three hundred cable TV channels, and fear of unknown pedophiles and child kidnappers. We just showed up outside, ready to play ball. No need for an appointed time, and we knew the place.

We played tackle football in my neighbor's yard. Following the contours of the cul-de-sac, it sloped, and it had a hill leading to one sideline, the driveway. End zones were formed by a tree and street sign just before the curb at the cross street, and an overgrown bush fronting the neighbor's driveway. It took special skills for receivers to run pass routes up the hill and for quarterbacks to get extra air under the ball for the hill patterns.

Games often ended with someone going home crying. Teddy Beane, the oldest, strongest, and best athlete of us all, would goad two younger kids into a fight. They'd head off bawling in different directions as Teddy mocked them. Then, disappointed the game might break up, he'd shame them: "C'mon, Stevie, don't be a wuss! Game's not over, man! Aww, you little baby!"

Even when the American family who owned our football field moved and a Pakistani diplomat moved in, the games continued with their three boys, who had assimilated to American football. We butchered their foreign names, so, in an innocently racist way, assigned them the easier-to-pronounce monikers Haji, Charms Pop, and The Sheik.

PROLOGUE: THE SPORTS JUNKIE

On long summer nights, we wore a dirt path on the flat part of that lawn playing Hot Box—like a baseball rundown play when the runner gets trapped between third base and home and the catcher and third baseman play pitch and catch until they run him down—only we had a whole baseball team in the middle, hoping not to get beaned in the back of the head. With no lawn big enough, we'd play baseball on the asphalt of the wide cul-de-sac that could accommodate a diamond, only with a tennis ball in case a long drive carried over the front lawns of the houses at the bottom of the street.

The only interruption before darkness was when we heard the first faint echoes of the jingly music, our cue that in thirty seconds, Grizzly Harry, the graying, affable captain of the Good Humor ice cream truck, would come trawling up the street and stop at the top of the hill above the cul-de-sac. We'd all scatter for home and grab a fistful of loose change and rush to meet hulking Grizzly, clad in his all-whites, with his burly arms balanced on the counter and head and shoulders arched out the window, waiting to take treat orders from kids he had gotten to know by name.

In fifth grade, my buddies and I, having graduated from kickball, played soccer at recess twice a day. Adding intensity to the time-crunched games halted too soon by the recess monitor's whistle, we kept a running tally of goals we scored and recorded them at the end of the day, competing to see who would be the leading scorer on the last June day.

When a park was built in a neighboring subdivision, my neighborhood gang would hop fences, cut through backyards, and hike a mile through woods to the new basketball court. The park opened up our small world. Now we had rival neighborhoods with some older kids and good athletes to play, winner stays, loser sits.

I was about twelve, and I had finally moved up in the echelons of athletic footwear from Keds to Jack Purcells to Chuck Taylors, and finally, to my first pair of Adidas. With those three blue stripes on my skips, I knew I was coming of age.

After sixth grade, I spent the best summer of my childhood at sleepaway camp in the Berkshires. All boys, all sports, morning to night, interrupted only by the occasional play ("Ohhh-OAK-lahoma, where the wind goes sweeping down the plain...") with the nearby all-girls camp and the drunken counselors who woke us at 3:00 a.m. after their night of off-grounds debauchery with a round of Fribbles and burgers from Friendly's.

When I started Worthington Junior High, my sports world was becoming more competitive. The one team my junior high fielded was basketball, and I was determined to make it. I was a good outside shooter, my skills honed from hours of practicing alone, playing imaginary NCAA Championship games, with range to the top of the key and deep corners. I had quick feet, and I could handle the ball with either hand, something few seventh graders could do.

One thing I didn't have was height. While other boys were sprouting, I was stalling, genetically cursed with diminutive ancestors and the late-bloom gene. I was a head shorter than my competitors, and this, I'm convinced, contributed to the greatest athletic tragedy of my youth.

It was seventh-grade basketball tryouts, and there were about thirty vying for fifteen positions. I stood on the stage above the court, waiting to be called to participate in one of the pick-up games that were being evaluated. On the second day of tryouts, I didn't get called on at all. I had gone unnoticed, invisible. In two days, I had barely touched the court, hadn't had a chance to show what I could do, and was cut.

I had never been so devastated and ashamed. I locked myself in the bathroom at home.

"Jakey, what's wrong? When are you going to come out? Talk to me," my mother said.

That sparked my outburst, my fist pounding against the door. "I didn't even get a chance! No shot at all! That coach—that idiot—SUCH AN IDIOT! I hate 'im! He didn't even see me! He didn't care! It wasn't fair! Wasn't...FAIR! ASSHOLE!" With a final punch, I put a hole through the door.

In eighth grade, I tried out again. This time, it was different. The coaches conducted skills tests, which gave me a better chance to be noticed. Making lay-ups under time pressure, dribbling through obstacles

PROLOGUE: THE SPORTS JUNKIE

with either hand, canning jumpers from different spots—these were things you could quantify, things I was good at. Many of the tall boys were gawky and uncoordinated.

The coaches took me under their wings, working out with me as a ball-handling point guard. I made the team—sweet redemption. My basketball career was under way. This is where I belonged.

Then, reality set in. We sucked. When we lost our first game by twenty-five, we thought it was bad luck, must have played the county's juggernaut. When we lost our next two games in similar fashion, to teams that overmatched us physically and outclassed us in talent, we began to understand: it was going to be a long season.

I was getting some playing time, but struggling against bigger opponents. Before one game, the opposing team's manager came through our locker room, sized me up, and asked condescendingly, "Are you sure you're in eighth grade?" I tried to slug him, but my teammates held me back.

The losses snowballed. We dropped to 0–10, staring down the barrel of a winless twelve-game season and a place in Wolverine sports infamy.

Our next-to-last game was against crosstown rival Potter Junior High. Early on, we found out that Potter sucked also! Where usually we were toast by half time, this time we were in the game. It came down to the final twenty seconds. With the game tied, our center, Richie "Redwood" Mullinix, banked in a shot. In a mad scramble at the other end, Potter clanged one off the rim. Redwood corralled the rebound and bear-hugged the air out of the ball until the buzzer sounded. Then all hell broke loose.

We stormed the court and tackled Redwood, still clutching the ball like a drowning man grasping a life preserver. We formed a human pile at midcourt, surrounded by our joy-deprived cheerleaders and a scattering of students and devoted teachers, celebrating as though we had won a championship. Hell, that *was* our championship, our salvation from abject humiliation, liberation from the albatross of complete and utter Loserville.

Somewhere in the middle of that sweaty pile, Redwood's bony elbow jamming into my ribs, the thought crossed my mind: better enjoy this stinkfest with these talent-challenged goofballs for all it's worth, because it may spell the end of my scholastic basketball career. And it did.

After basketball season, I began playing tennis against our team's other short guard, Alex Weiss. Though I had had some lessons, had played at summer camps, and had a knack for it, tennis never really captured my imagination until Alex.

Alex and I went head-to-head into the twilight, when we could barely see the ball, at the neighborhood park. We wore gloves and ski hats and avoided ice patches for the rest of winter, and played through ninety-five-degree scorchers. I was hooked. I began playing tournaments, late at age fourteen.

I abhorred the culture of the tennis tournament circuit. The venues were full of overindulged and ego-driven kids, the worst of whom had full-bore, self-loathing temper tantrums on court when things didn't go their way, and high-climbing parents whose own worth and pride hung in the balance of each baseline exchange.

By summer's end, I was catching up to the early prodigies, some of whom were becoming true studs while others were on the verge of flaming out. I pulled some marathon-length upsets against seeded players, who, at some point, would wail, "How can you be losing to this guy? He's such a pusher!"

The game suited me well. My stature disadvantage wasn't as pronounced as it was in mano-a-mano sports like basketball or football. And I had some real assets that had less to do with natural-born physical prowess—quickness, consistency, patience, and endurance—tools that may not make your jaw drop but could easily frustrate opponents into a meltdown.

❖ ❖ ❖

For the next four years, I focused on this individualistic game. With growing up came the realization that I would not be a star basketball guard, rising up confidently to hit the game-winning jumper for point number forty, as I had rehearsed countless times alone at the playground. I wouldn't be

PROLOGUE: THE SPORTS JUNKIE

the unstoppable running back blazing eighty yards down the sideline with defenders diving empty-handed at my heels. I was who I was.

I was just good enough to play tennis at Colgate, a small, northeastern, liberal arts college, where, lacking an indoor tennis facility, we practiced on the slick "boards" of the basketball court during frigid winters. I rediscovered my passion for other sports by joining the college newspaper, covering the basketball team. They were the dregs of the league. But following the team as the beat writer inspired me. Eventually I became sports editor, joining a small cadre of dedicated masochists who pulled all-nighters once a week to produce an issue.

Journalism was fun. I could embed myself in the athlete's world, experiencing the highs and lows vicariously and getting to know the personalities of players and coaches beneath their stats and bios. It was a diversion from Aristotle and Russian history and international economics. It never occurred to me that it was something I could do for a living.

I was a follower. My classmates were on the verge of their first step on the ladder toward becoming professional titans of business, investment banking, law, and, for those who really had their shit together, medicine.

I took a heavy dose of philosophy and history, and so naturally, as my senior year approached, I had no idea what to do with my life. So I did what other clueless seniors did—I did on-campus interviews with big conglomerates. Rodeway, Procter & Gamble, Chase Manhattan, Chubb—I signed up for them all and was equally unimpressive and dispassionate in each conversation with the fast-climbing, real-world-indoctrinated recruiter across the table, who wasn't much older than I was. I got no callbacks and didn't expect any with my lackluster performances and lack of industry knowledge.

Finally, mercifully, the last of my scheduled interviews arrived, just weeks before graduation. It was with Northwestern Mutual Life, and I wasn't interested in insurance or annuities or risk management. I contemplated blowing it off, but I didn't want the Career Center to shun me when

I needed it as an unemployed wanderer. So I put on my student interview uniform—blue blazer, red tie, and loafers—and climbed Cardiac Hill to meet another person whom I should aspire to emulate in a take-Manhattan-by-storm kind of way.

The interview transpired much like the others. I was an actor in the sixth month of a Broadway stand, repeating my lines without a second thought, summoning my limited theatrical abilities to put a gleam in my eyes and a lilt in my voice that conveyed to my equally disinterested interrogator: "I'm the man for the job. Junior sales manager is all I've ever dreamed of. Can't you see?"

"Why do you want to work for Northwestern Mutual?" asked my upwardly mobile interviewer, Spencer Wentworth, the regional director of sales and marketing, who less than a decade earlier was probably doing beer funnels in the basement of a philanthropically and morally bankrupt Greek fraternity house, and who now had the receding hairline speckled with gray and growing paunch of a joyless, debt-ridden suburban father of two.

"I like helping people, and life insurance is a product every family needs for protection and peace of mind. I mean, everybody dies, right? It sells itself…of course, with a good salesman who can explain the costs and benefits of term and whole life and annuities," I said, blowing my whole wad of life insurance knowledge.

"I could really stand behind this product with full belief and confidence," I finished, with a confident smile.

"What skills do you have that would make you an effective sales manager?"

"I'm very organized. I can juggle tasks, prioritize them, and execute them all efficiently." (A lie.)

"I'm a quick study. I'm good at grasping concepts, figuring things out, and solving problems. I could explain Northwestern's products to prospects so they could understand how they work and turn them into lifelong customers." (An embellishment.)

PROLOGUE: THE SPORTS JUNKIE

"And I'm a good people person. I get along with all kinds of people, and I really listen. I know how to ask good questions, and I'm good at getting people to talk to me. They trust me." (Finally, the truth.)

"Where do you want to be in five years?"

"Well, what I'd really like to do is...I mean, my passion is really in the area of product development and market analysis, so I'd really like to be somewhere in Research and...um, actually, because I like working with people, I want to be in the field managing a sales team, ahhh, I think you'd call it a senior field..."

I paused to collect my thoughts and turn off my bullshit meter. I gazed over Spencer's shoulder, out the Career Center window onto the quad, transfixed by a game of touch football.

Spencer waited awkwardly for me to return. There was the unmistakable sense that something unsaid was weighing heavily in the room, and its gravity crushed Spencer's impatient, man-on-the-move instinct to push on. He may have been a "corporate tool," as we called these young slaves of corporate America (which we were destined soon to become). But to his credit, he seemed to have empathy for my angst. Maybe he had a flashback to his own experience in my seat, interviewing with his own corporate tool and evaluating whether he had ever been true to himself.

There's a moment in the symphony when the conductor walks onstage and the orchestra comes to attention. A hush falls over the audience as he steps to the podium, addresses his performers, from flute to percussion to tuba, deliberately raises his arms, pointer aloft as anticipation builds, and waits for just the right moment to drop his arms and commence a meticulously choreographed work of art, a statement of utter precision and clarity.

I returned my gaze from the quad to meet Spencer's. I felt confident, no phony theatrics required. This was *my* moment of clarity, *my* conductor's first wave of the baton. I took a deep breath, and the words that would eliminate me as a candidate for Northwestern Mutual junior sales manager tumbled out.

"Spence…Can I call you Spence? You know where I want to be in five years? I want to be sweating my ass off at an NFL training camp. I want to be in the locker room when college seniors are bawling their eyes out after an NCAA Final Four basketball game. I want to be within spitting range of spring training dugouts. Spence, I want to be a sportswriter."

Ninth Avenue Beatdown

The scoreboard clock in the sleek, blue- and gold-splashed high school stadium with the brick façade hit 1:00, and the countdown to the part of the sweat-soaked, adrenaline-fueled Friday night ritual that I loved began. I bolted from the press box as radio sports jock Whalebait Wally bellowed the final accolades on his game call on WFIN-AM and my main competitor, the meticulous sports reporter Tab Reindollar of the *Drabenville Times-Democrat*, finished adding up rushing and passing stats on his calculator.

I liked to hit the field by 0:45, so I could pick up on the mood and immediate reactions of the players and coaches before they were filtered and censored for the media to avoid giving away anything to next week's opponent. My press pass got me by old-timer security guard Lerch Lessard before the wave of blue- and gold-clad Dolphin High fans stormed the field to launch their Friday night party. I had to stay one step ahead of them for the next twenty minutes or I'd miss my first deadline and incur the wrath of preps editor Skip Blintzer.

This last Friday in September ended in a win, typical for the Dolphin Fightin' Dorsal Fins, which had regained its rightful place as one of Florida's Class 5A powerhouses since the arrival of native son Coach James "Jimbo" Bamford three years earlier. Dolphin High had a long tradition of winning stretching back to the 1940s but took a big tumble into Loserville in the late 1970s and early '80s when legendary Coach Fred Zipf fell into the grips of Alzheimer's. Luckily for Dolphin, a recruiting scandal at Northwest Florida University in 1983 had cost Bamford his offensive coordinator position just as whispers were circulating that he was a hot candidate to take over a Division I program, or at least was first in line to take the head job at NWFU from dinosaur Bubba Burnell, who everyone thought was stubbornly staving off the slow march toward death on the golf links and at 4:00 p.m. early bird dinners at Denny's, like millions of other Florida old-timers.

Bamford had left Northwest Florida in shame, but Dolphin principal George Bosley was not too ashamed to hire him and return the Fightin' Dorsals to their former glory. Bosley's reputation had taken a big hit in the community. His tunnel-vision focus on academic achievement was all well and good—as the high school on the right side of the tracks, Dolphin had always outshone the other three high schools in Dolphin County on the brains ledger—but that's not what brought bragging rights and the sense of superiority and pride to its graduates, boosters, parents, and students. Football was king in Drabenville, and Bosley knew that if he didn't recognize that, *he* would be the one out of a job.

Bosley and Bamford—they needed each other. No college programs, even Division III, would touch Bamford so soon after a scandal. But Bamford's reputation was still gold in Dolphin County, where his family had established a virtual dynasty, and where he had starred as a ferocious two-way player on a team that won an unprecedented three consecutive state championships from 1967 to 1969. So Dolphin coach Zipf was canned after an embarrassing 3–8 season in 1982, and Bamford was hired in 1983 to root out the decay that had permeated the proud program and rebuild his own reputation so he could assume his rightful place as the leader of a major college program. Back-to-back state Class 5A championships would put him back on that path, and he had already claimed one of them in 1985, the previous season.

By force of will and a legendarily ruthless conditioning program, Coach Bamford had turned the Fightin' Dorsals back into a winning program in his first year, but a 9–3 record and first-round exit in the district play-offs in 1983 and a semifinal finish in 1984 were not good enough for the locals. He needed an edge to get over the top, and he got it in early 1985 when the Dolphin County Board of Education drew new school boundary lines that redirected the low-income community of South Palmertown to Dolphin High School for the stated purpose of integration. It just so happened that many of the best athletes in the county grew up in Palmertown and developed their football prowess in Palmertown Pop Warner, one of the most renowned youth football factories in the state.

On the brightly lit field surrounded by darkness, I stole up behind the Dolphin bench as the clock hit 0:00, trying not to make my presence felt. The players slapped backs, raised fists, and whooped and hollered, "Yeah, baby!" and "Not in my house!" The Fightin' Dorsals were 4–0, an undefeated September, and that meant one thing to a bunch of sixteen- and seventeen-year-olds with raging hormones and the urge to assert their independence: it was time to party and enjoy the fruits of their labor.

But the players weren't tuned into Coach Bamford as I was. A nondominant nine-point win over the 1–3 Clear Vista Manta Rays from Mirabella County to the south—a team Coach Bamford told me was "soft as roasted marshmallows...but don't you print that"—had him in a foul mood.

"I don't know what we're yelling about; that was a sorry-ass performance," Coach Bamford said to whatever assistants were within range. When Bamford's temper got going, his assistants tried to make themselves scarce.

As the teams headed for their locker rooms, Coach Bamford kept barking at his assistants. "We don't celebrate a nine-point win over Clear Vista. We're Dolphin. We ask, 'What's wrong, and how do we fix it?' That's pathetic." He stewed for a few more strides. "That's bullshit! I'm not here to celebrate being ordinary, God dammit!"

Crossing the track, on the way to the locker room just beyond the stadium gate, Coach Bamford stopped his assistants, gathered his composure, and laid down his order: "No day off tomorrow. We're practicing at 8:00 a.m. sharp. And if any knuckleheads don't show up or come hungover, they're gone. We don't need 'em. I want the players who are as hungry as I am. That's the only way we'll be great."

I followed the coaches and players into the locker room with the giant, metal dorsal fin affixed atop the entrance. At age twenty-two, I had gotten a foothold into this world that I had admired for so long. I was a sports reporter at the *Citrus Coast Daily Inquirer*. The paper covered the Tampa Bay Bucs, the new Orlando Magic, Florida, and Florida State, and if I proved myself as the high schools reporter, I was convinced I would have a shot at those premier beats.

The air was heavy. The locker room smelled like a mildewed camper in a rain forest. The odor grew worse as the players began stripping off pads and jerseys, down to their T-shirts and jockstraps. I had to dull my senses and take bare-minimum breaths through my nose, but as a rookie reporter breaking into the world of sports journalism, there was no better place to start.

"Hey, Sammy, you got a minute?" I said to the starting quarterback, one of the Palmertown Six that had helped power Dolphin to the state championship last year. I motioned for him to sit next to me by the door, which was a little quieter than in the mob of testosterone-stoked boys where he stood at his locker. Sammy Sammons was one of those naturally gifted athletes who could run faster, jump higher, move quicker, and throw harder than other players could, seemingly without effort. I don't want to say he was born that way, but some athletes have physical talents and body makeups that the rest don't, and no matter how much the rest of us train and work to improve, we'll never match the naturals. The Palmertown Six all had that trait.

I started with a softball question to get him loose and talking; then I would follow up with observations that I expected would generate his real reaction to the team's effort.

"Sammy, nice win. How does it feel to beat your down-coast rival and stay undefeated?"

"First, Mr. Yankelovich, I give all glory to God. I play in his name," Sammons began. I had developed respect for Sammy, for he didn't just express this reverence on the football field but showed it in other aspects of his life, in his relationships with teammates and coaches, in his studies and connections with teachers, and in his community. Even though he was poor, I knew he gave back by volunteering at a church homeless shelter and coaching Palmertown youth league kids so they'd have a chance to make it at least as far as he had. Sammy knew I couldn't quote him on his devotion to God, so he kept going. "It feels great to be undefeated, but we've got bigger goals than beating Clear Vista. We're number one in the state, and that's where we plan to stay. We've got a target on our backs every game, so we just have to work harder than everyone else."

I liked it—just what the readers want to read, how Dolphin is superior and everyone else second-rate and gunning to knock out the champ. I'd use it high up in the story. Now to the real question: why Sammy's play seemed to go from chili sauce to mayonnaise compared with his first three games.

"Sammy, it looked like you were holding back. I didn't see you playing with your usual speed and aggressiveness. Do you have an injury, or was it Coach Bamford's game plan, or was Clear Vista's defense giving you problems?"

Sammy laughed at the last point. We both knew no one on Clear Vista's defense had the speed to contain him. "Coach wants us to cut down on our mistakes, so we ran a conservative game plan. It was good enough to get the W, and that's all that matters."

I only had ten minutes to spend in Dolphin's locker room, and I just spent four with Sammy. I entered the office of Coach Bamford, who had his feet up on his desk and three assistants gathered around him.

"What do you need?" he said in a gruff voice, sounding annoyed already. I knew he didn't like to deal with the media. He thought the media had given him a raw deal on his way out of NWFU. I didn't think that mattered much anyway. What Coach Bamford liked was control. His gruff and annoyed act was his way of controlling the media. It said, "I'm important, and you'd better have a damn good reason for taking my time." He had a way of bullying you to try to scare you off from asking tough questions. And he knew a twenty-two-year-old, first-year reporter new to the area and with no old-boy network connections would be vulnerable and an easy mark to bully.

Bamford was the grown-up version of the burly, buzz-cut bully in seventh grade who shoved spindly geeks into lockers and hovered over pint-sized wallflowers on the ball field, challenging them to fights.

He had the booming baritone voice of the prototypical hard-edged gym teacher, like Buzzcut, the enraged ROTC instructor–sex-ed teacher–coach who berates kids in *Beavis and Butt-Head*. When Bamford was displeased with his team's effort or concentration, he could be mistaken for Gunnery Sergeant Hartman, the high-decibel, demanding drill instructor in *Full Metal Jacket*, though physically he resembled the beefier Private Leonard "Gomer Pyle" Lawrence, who was driven to insanity by the overbearing sergeant and blew his brains out.

He still looked every bit the rugged, lumberjack-like offensive lineman that he was at Troy University in Alabama. He was considered undersized for Division I at six one, 260 pounds, so even though the University of Florida was his dream, he settled for Troy, where he was a two-time Division I-AA All-American.

Bamford's build was bulging and round—face, torso, calves, and Popeye-shaped arms. Everything he wore was form fitting—there was no way it could not be. He wore the prototypical football coach's uniform: long Bike coach's shorts, short white socks that framed his massive calves, and black "coaching shoes"—not quite cleats but certainly not sissified running shoes.

Bamford was the middle child in a family that had established a dynasty over several generations—his grandfather founded the region's premier development business; his father ran the business and headed the Dolphin County Chamber of Commerce; his older brother was the business's heir apparent and president of the Dolphin Community College Board of Trustees; his mother was president of the Dolphin County Council for three terms running; and his sister was the Dolphin County assistant State attorney. It was a family with high expectations, which translated to football as much as business and politics.

I knew Coach Bamford wasn't happy with his team's performance, but I didn't want to let on right away. "Coach, it's got to feel good to get to 4–0," I said, hoping that would get him talking.

"That's a dumb question. That's not even a question. Don't you have anything better?"

"You didn't seem satisfied with that performance when you were heading off the field. What did you see from your team that you didn't like?"

"Hey, first of all, Yank, I better not read anything in the paper about anything I said on the field. You're not even supposed to be there. I was talking to my coaches. I'll be on the phone with Blintzer if I see anything I don't like."

I didn't remember giving Bamford permission to call me Yank, and I wasn't sure if it indicated growing familiarity or disdain—OK, most likely disdain—but I decided to let it go for the sake of expediency.

"I'm going to give you what you need and then you can get out of here and let us finish our meeting."

I was actually glad to hear that. I was down to two minutes before I'd have to boogie out of the locker room to the opponent's locker room to nab a quick quote from Clear Vista's coach.

"What you saw tonight was Dolphin football at its best. Power football, smart football. We're all about winning here. Nate was hot tonight, so we let him tote the rock and carry us through." Nate Hilliard was another of the Palmertown Six, a running back built like a fire hydrant who could bowl you over or burst around you, his short and muscular legs churning like pistons.

"Clear Vista played us tough. I give their guys credit for holding us to twenty-one. But look at our records and look at our history—they're just not in our league. It shouldn't be that close."

"You got what you need?" Coach Bamford, said, wrapping up.

"Yeah, thanks, Coach," I said, flipping the page in my spiral reporter's notebook.

I made a quick run to the opponent's locker room at the other end of the stadium, just in time to catch Clear Vista coach Roy Gillingham as he prepared to lead his players to the bus. I scribbled his words as we walked together, something about being proud to play toe-to-toe with the state champions and being only a break or two away from pulling a big upset.

I yelled out to the Clear Vista quarterback, Dwayne Upchurch, another great athlete in an area chock-full of them, as he ascended the first step of the bus. Dwayne would have a chance to be all-state at a school like Dolphin, but Clear Vista just couldn't surround him with the same talent. "Dwayne, what more do you have to do to beat Dolphin?"

Dwayne turned around on the bus step. He was always good for a quote. "I did *all I can do* out there tonight, man. I left it all on the field. Get me some players from Palmertown; then we'll talk. And you know you can't quote me on that Palmertown bullshit. Gillingham would sit my ass down for that. Just say, 'We battled Dolphin even for a half; they just wore us down in the second with their size and strength. We just got to hit the weight room harder, and things will be different next year.'"

Dwayne thought for a moment. "Yeah, go with that, that's positive. Coach G. will like it. Just make me look good, my man." He bounded up two more steps and disappeared into the bus.

I scrawled Dwayne's final words in hieroglyphics that only I would be able to make out later—only by sounding out legible letters to make words that formed pieces of word puzzles that became sentences. I shoved the notebook in my pants pocket, slung the portable computer bag over my shoulder, and psyched myself for the high-pressure part of the evening.

❖ ❖ ❖

It was 10:15 p.m., a typical time to leave the stadium after a 7:30 p.m. game. The newspaper's first deadline was 11:00 p.m. Editors back in New Palm City were waiting, and if the first version of the game story from Dolphin vs. Clear Vista didn't appear on their computer screens by 11:01 p.m., my office phone would light up. First mission was the getaway from the stadium. At powerhouse schools with well-supported football programs, like Dolphin tonight, crowds would be ten thousand thick. If I didn't get my pregame phone calls completed and other weekend and next-week stories filed earlier enough in the day, or if I did anything more for dinner than wolf down a pregame sub with one hand while steering the car with the other, I ran the risk of arriving at the stadium too late—the hard-core tailgaters toting grills in the back of their pickups were there two hours early—and having to park as far as a mile away. And that's what had happened this night.

I started with a jog, then the adrenaline kicked in, and my pace picked up to near sprint as I slid by reveling fans still hanging around their cars. I broke away from the school's ozone after about a quarter mile, turning left on Thirty-Second Street with its well-manicured lawns and palms and Spanish-style stucco houses. The town was laid out in a grid, with mostly straight streets, flat as a spatula.

The bright lights and noise were fading. I felt more alone now after three hours of constant sensual stimulation—screaming fans, the thud of pads colliding, the aroma of popcorn and sweaty socks, pretty blond cheerleaders who were close enough to me in age that I didn't even know for sure if they were legally jailbait.

I broke into a full sprint, knees churning high, portable computer slapping against my back, imagining that I was a running back who had just broken a tackle at the line, made a lightning-quick jab-step to make another defender miss, and headed wide toward the sideline, straddling the imaginary barrier on my way to an eighty-yard touchdown burst. Just as I had as a ten-year-old on my elementary school field, only this time the adrenaline would help me for the rest of the night by staving off exhaustion, keeping my mind focused, and allowing the words I needed to find to keep tumbling from my mind to my fingers tapping across the keyboard until 12:30 a.m.

As I crossed my end zone, I made a hard cut to the right on Ninth Avenue West and slowed to a celebratory jog as I came to my brown Chevette parked along the curb. I had chosen to park on Ninth because from here it was just two blocks and one turn before I hit the main drag, Hernandez Avenue, which would take me downtown, past a string of traffic lights and fast-food joints, to the newspaper's lonely satellite office.

Sweat was dripping down my face and my shirt clung to my back, a condition I had become accustomed to working outside in Florida's oppressive heat and swampy air. Even at night in September, the temperature spiked at ninety. It was like living in a sponge. As I reached for the keys in my right pocket to unlock the door, I heard what sounded like horse hooves galloping closer. I turned and looked toward the Thirty-Second Street corner, the clomping sound growing louder. As they entered the streetlight's illumination, I made out two figures: football players, in blue and gold, still in their cleats, clickety-clacking over the asphalt.

"Mr. Yankelovich," one of them yelled. He was tall and angular, with a fluid, confident stride like a quarterback's. His partner looked more like a shipping container, bulky and rigid, like an undersized middle linebacker.

This was the time on Friday nights that I was used to being alone with my racing thoughts: What's going to be my lede? What catchy turn of phrase or bit of backstory can I use to introduce the game narrative? What's coming up next for these teams? What's the quickest route to my bureau? These guys, whoever they were, just interrupted that train. No players had ever followed me to my car before.

They slowed to a walk and kept coming toward me, now twenty yards away as I stood by my open driver's seat door. "Hold up a sec, Mr. Yankelovich," the stocky one said, still catching his breath.

Hearing myself addressed as Mr. Yankelovich always threw me for a loop. As a twenty-two-year-old, I didn't hear it often or expect to be called that. Mr. Yankelovich is my dad. But on this job, I did start hearing it more from the well-mannered high school athletes. So it took a few seconds even to register that these two players were talking to me.

I was so used to being around high school football players, it didn't even occur to me until they were within range for me to smell their sour breath that they were wearing the gold Dolphin helmets, which made no sense a mile away from the field. At first I thought they were two black players, but as I peered between the face mask bars, I could see blotches of white skin smeared with thick coats of eye black—like the old-school gridiron gladiators with the dark streaks under their eyes in NFL Films productions—only they were wearing too much, to the point of making their faces unrecognizable.

I ran through a mental checklist of why they would be here. Did I forget a tape recorder on Coach Bamford's desk? No, I hadn't brought it to the game. I checked my pocket for my spiral notebook, which I always inscribed with my name and contact information. No, still there. My wallet! I patted my back pocket and found the bulge. Could it be they just wanted to tell me something important for the game story? Did they want to see their names in print so they could make their papas proud?

"What do you need, guys? You got something for the story? I only got a minute."

Then it occurred to me. They were wearing the royal-blue road game jerseys, not the gold jerseys from tonight. Something was wrong.

"Yeah, we got something for ya," said the stocky guy.

The instinct to run kicked in. The open car door blocked my route away. The two guys closed in to narrow the distance between us and eliminate my other escape options. Too late.

The tall player grabbed me and pinned my arms. I struggled to break loose. Regret that I hadn't taken tae kwon do crossed my mind. The guy was strong, and he was behind me now. Even if I could get an elbow loose, I didn't know if I could connect.

"This is a message for you, Yank, and you better pay close attention," the stocky player said.

He landed a punch to my gut that made me exhale a guttural howl and double over. Then an uppercut caught me on the right cheekbone just under my eye.

As I fell to the asphalt, gasping for breath, my forehead crashed against the car door, opening a small gash.

I still heard voices, but I no longer cared. I was entering a dream state, like when I got my wisdom teeth pulled and was just beginning to go under the anesthesia.

"Take this as your warning, Yank. Don't make us come back, or we'll pummel you worse, right into the hospital. You'll wish you'd never heard of Drabenville," said the stocky guy, full of bravado.

The more cerebral one, the quarterback, added, "Stick to writing about the games and girls' volleyball, you little prick. Don't go prowling around asking questions that are none of your business, or you're gonna get hurt…bad. This was nothing…You hear me?" He grabbed me by the shirt and lifted me off the ground.

"Do. You. Hear me?"

In a groggy voice, eyes half-open but seeing only dark shadows, I replied, "I hear you…, but I don't know what you're talking about."

"Bullshit!" The quarterback was losing his cool. "Don't be stupid, Yank. Don't be a hero, you little piece a—"

I heard a door fly open and saw the flash of bright floodlights.

"What the hell's goin' on out here? What's all the racket?"

I crawled past the front hood of my car so I could see who it was. I saw a man, illuminated by the floodlights, holding a high-beam flashlight right under the barrel of a shotgun and sweeping the firearm slowly across the lawn as he scanned the street. "Don't fuck with me; I'm armed!"

This was a nice neighborhood, but it was still part of a Cracker town, full of gun lovers and clandestine Confederate flag wavers. Lucky for me, I was getting my ass kicked in front of a good ol' boy's house.

I stayed on the ground, scrambling on all fours up to the curb and into the light. My lungs had finally refilled with some air, enough to allow me to force out a garbled voice. "Sir, ahhh, I'm being, ahhh, atta…attacked. Two guys. Dolphin football uniforms. Ahhh, ohhh…over…there." I stuck up my right arm and pointed toward the back end of my car. I heard the click-clacking of cleats tap-dancing on asphalt as the two football wise guys, who must have seen the shotgun, raced back toward Thirty-Second Street so they could turn the corner into darkness before the crazy redneck could get them in his sights.

"Son, are you all right? You need an amb'lance? What the hell *was* that?"

I stayed on the ground for a minute, taking deep breaths and regaining my focus.

"Yeah…OK. Just got the wind knocked out of me…I think I cut my head." I reached for the side of my face to see if it was sweat or blood trickling down. It was blood. I leaned over and hurled my pulled-pork barbecue sandwich and baked beans dinner on his driveway from the adrenaline and shock.

"Boy, you sure you're OK? Who were those thugs?" he asked, propping the shotgun against his shoulder, barrel pointing skyward, like a Confederate Civil War reenactor.

"I dunno, couldn't see their faces through their helmets. It was too dark. Big dudes, obviously, trying to scare me, or just kids on a joyride out to create some havoc. I dunno."

"That's one helluva gash. Lemme get you somethin' to wrap it." The man headed for his open front door. On his top step, he turned. "You want me to call the cops?"

I began thinking clearly again. I looked at my watch. 10:27 p.m. It seemed like an eternity, but the whole episode had taken only four minutes. I could get to my office in six minutes by speeding and get my portable computer fired up by 10:35 p.m. with twenty-five minutes to file the first-edition story. I wasn't about to miss a deadline, not as a rookie still on probation, not for a Dolphin game, which jacks up readership by twenty thousand copies on Saturdays. Besides, who would believe that two guys dressed as Dolphin football players assaulted me? They'd probably just think I pissed off a couple of rednecks in a bar.

"Nah, I got to get going, don't have time to explain. Just get me the wrap. I'll call the police later. Thanks for everything. That would have been worse if…I didn't catch your name?"

"Haggard."

"Yeah, a little, but I'll be OK, really."

"No, Norville Haggard, that's my name. Everyone calls me Merle by mistake."

Haggard brought me a bag of frozen peas and wrapped my head with gauze and tape, like DeNiro and Walken in the suicidal game of Viet Cong Russian roulette in *The Deer Hunter*. "Mr. Haggard, I'll find you if I need a witness. I got a job…" And I screeched away, leaving the end of the thought lost in the Chevette's exhaust.

At my desk, I reviewed my notes quickly, looking for the different colors to highlight the big plays and the stars denoting the good quotes, and sewed together a seven-paragraph game story, leading off with:

Another routine win for Dolphin over Clear Vista was anything but routine for Dolphin coach Jimbo Bamford, who lambasted his team for complacency unbefitting a state championship contender.

This was the pre-Internet era of primitive digital technology. I attached the rubbery, round, black, Radio Shack acoustic couplers snugly to the mouthpiece and earpiece of the phone, dialed the transmission number, punched in some commands, and prayed that it would transmit through the phone line into the *Daily Inquirer*'s mainframe computer system in the form of words—the damn couplers were finicky, and one out of every three tries yielded an "Error" code with a bunch of hieroglyphics on the screen and an annoying buzzing sound.

Bam! The sweet sound of nothing, and within thirty seconds, a transmission "Complete" response at 10:58 p.m. Now I had an hour to tabulate all the game statistics and add more game description, quotes, and context to the story for the final edition.

The stats were time consuming on deadline but crucial. Since there was no official game statistician, my stats would be the official ones the players earned, at least for the *Daily Inquirer*'s purposes. If I made a mistake and tabulated the numbers wrong or miscoded some plays in my self-designed system of play tracking or assigned the wrong player a long run or touchdown catch or interception, it could mean the difference in earning Dolphin County Player of the Week honors, or, over time, All-County or All-Metro Team selection.

THREE YARDS AND A PLATE OF MULLET

I filed the final game story with stats at 11:55 p.m., adding this inflammatory quote from Clear Vista coach Roy Gillingham:

The state champs' reputation far exceeded their play tonight. We had them where we wanted them. In fact, the only thing that got them over was reputation. I warned our kids about giving them too much respect. We've got to learn that Dolphin puts their pants on one leg at a time, just like we do.

❖ ❖ ❖

Once the adrenaline from meeting deadline drained away, my head started throbbing, and it hurt to breathe. I slumped in my chair, pressing the defrosting peas to my head. Tonight was just a more intense variation of the way I usually felt on Fridays just after midnight—exhausted, relieved, and brain-dead, as though I had just finished a spin in the centrifugal force amusement ride. The only thing to do now was to wait for the inevitable call from stuttering high school sports editor, Skip Blintzer, for a game of twenty questions. (D-D-D-Di-Di-Did you ask Bamford about his outlook for n-n-n-next week? Wuh-Wuh-Wuh-Wuh-Why did Hilliard get all the c-c-cu-cu-carries tonight?)

Skip was a great guy, loyal, and devoted to high school sports and to giving the student-athletes the exaggerated praise and over-the-top accolades they might never again experience. The only problem with Skip was that he was annoying as hell. Part of that was something Skip didn't have control over—a stuttering problem he had mostly overcome but couldn't eliminate the last remnants of, which would manifest when things got stressful or heated, or whenever he felt he had to get on my ass to follow up on his incisive interview suggestions and brilliant story ideas.

A native of Port Huron, Michigan, at the southern end of Lake Huron, Skip was an avid fisherman and wrote the *Citrus Coast Daily Inquirer's* fishing column, "Angler's Cove," and was always bragging about his latest haul of snapper or mullet or Florida pompano. Skip had a wife who was never seen, but we prep staffers were pretty sure she existed, because who else would Skip always be arguing with on the phone over in-law visits and golf tee times, conversations that would have the poor man henpecked until stuttering became unavoidable. "Y-Y-Y-Yes, of course, I'll ch-ch-chan-change the t-t-tee time so I'll be back for lah-lah-lunch with Pops, hon-hnn-hnn-nee."

Skip not only talked fish and reeled fish, but he ate fish like a *Gilligan's Island* castaway. He would send me on late Saturday night runs when I worked the sports copy desk to The Ship's Mess about a mile down Swampbay Trail from the *Daily Inquirer's* main office in New Palm City to fetch the daily catch platter special. By the time I returned, he had unloaded his seafood cuisine drawer of packets of salt, pepper, and tartar sauce, and containers of vinegar, lemon juice, Tabasco, and Old Bay in preparation for the feast.

But on this surreal night, I couldn't focus on Skip's twenty questions ("Hey J-Jake, what did B-Bu-Bamford say about how-how come S-S-Sa-Sammons threw the ball only six times?"). All I could do was ponder what to do about my "Ninth Avenue beatdown." (In my semidelirious state, I started making up lyrics to describe my night to the tune of Bruce Springsteen's "Tenth Avenue Freeze-Out": "I'm gonna get up off the driveway a little staggered / Thanks to a shotgun-totin' dude named Haggard / With a...Ninth Avenue beatdown. Ninth Avenue beatdown.")

Call the cops? Investigate the incident myself? Tell my editors? Do nothing and pretend it was a bad dream? One thing I knew for sure: If I ever saw fully outfitted football players again that far away from the field, I was hauling ass in the opposite direction. Or getting on the Bat Phone to Haggard.

After I answered Skip's twenty obligatory and overly incisive questions, many of them with, "I don't know," or, "I didn't ask," and the paper was put to bed at 12:45 a.m., I stayed in the empty bureau office in desolate, largely abandoned downtown Drabenville for another fifteen minutes running through the scenarios.

It quickly became obvious that I couldn't call the police, unless I wanted to become part of a newspaper story myself. The *Drabenville Times-Democrat* loves scrutinizing the police blotter, and this item would pop like a Mexican jumping bean. I also had serious doubts about how much my editors would back me up on any story that made Dolphin High look bad. I knew they had to cultivate their relationship with Bamford and his posse—and all the devoted Dolphin alumni who bought and advertised in the *Daily Inquirer*—more than they needed to stand up for me, still a new and expendable interloper. I knew I would lose any battle of words with Bamford, if he ever got connected to this episode in any way, in the papers, in the courts, in the bars, in the press boxes, in the barber shops, and anywhere else it could be opined.

It was a no-win situation. I decided I'd bury it. I was pretty sure this incident was no high-schooler hijinks but an attempt to scare me off from a line of questioning I was pursuing about Dolphin players from Palmertown. I had stumbled onto inside information that the Dolphin County Board of Education's 1984 school redistricting decision that just happened to bring some of Dolphin County's best athletes from hardscrabble Palmertown section of DeVaca City, across the Blue Fin River Bridge, to Dolphin High may have been influenced by corrupt dealings extending to the county's top power brokers, including possibly the Bamford family and business.

No cops and no word to my editors, but I was going to keep digging. The stakes had just been raised, and I wasn't about to back down before my career had even started. I was now relishing pursuing the story even more. It had the element of danger and the feel of David versus Goliath. Little did I know earlier in the summer when I was applying like a scatter-armed dart player for sports-writing gigs and working demeaning and embarrassing odd jobs to keep myself afloat that I would be going head-to-head

NINTH AVENUE BEATDOWN

with the most revered man from the most powerful family in a land that was equal parts tropical paradise, suburban hell, drifter's alley, monsoon central, and last stop to heaven. I could scarcely believe I was here, and despite the black eye and aching ribs, enjoying the hell out of it.

Breaking In, Selling Out

I ENDED UP in Drabenville, Florida, and puking in Haggard's front yard, by happenstance. A few weeks after my on-campus interview with Northwestern Mutual's Wentworth, I was home with diploma in hand and no job prospects, waiting for a new life to begin.

I gathered my best clips from the collegiate *Colgate Maroon* and my internship at NFL Properties, where I profiled NFL players for stadium magazines, and set about packaging applications to sports editors around the country. I had heard Florida had a lot of good medium-sized newspapers and a year-round sporting life, so I blanketed the state.

While I was waiting for rejection letters, I had to make some money for a cheap used car, so I applied to an odd-job temp agency, the Do Anything Temp Agency (DATA). For a week, I walked a four-block square with two foam buns and a burger on my head, with an eye slit under the cheese, carrying a two-sided sandwich board advertising the grand opening of Bottomless Burgers.

The next week, I was assigned to fill in for a vacationing "employment specialist" at a sheltered workshop for people with mental retardation. I spent the week counting out beads to put in a cup for necklace production and getting acquainted with the quirky clients. It was tedious but tolerable—except for the one inevitable, cringe-inducing episode each day when some dude would blow a gasket and express his sexual frustration for all to see.

The third week, I stood just beyond the escalator exiting a subway station, passing out flyers for a blowout sale at a lingerie shop. It was a simple job and easy money as long as I could swallow my pride and keep in mind the ultimate goal of buying the shitty used car I would need as a reporter—until Mr. Kabir from Iran or Pakistan or some other ayatollah-led, angry-man nation came along.

"What da hell are you doing, lazy man?" a man with a bushy mustache, a swarthy face, and a thick mat of black hair overflowing from a cream-colored, short-sleeve shirt accosted me as I stood passively holding a flyer for Persian Leather & Lace.

"This is the fourth time I come out of the subway or walk by you, and every day you lazy, you asleep standing up, you make no eye contact, you let people walk right by you like you not there…"

Feeling assaulted and annoyed, as if standing there for $6.50 an hour wasn't already degrading enough, I interrupted this camel jockey's rant: "Why the fuck do you care, fine sir? You have stock in leather whips?"

"All these people that pass you by, these are all *my* customers, you auss-hull. Any one of them maybe want to buy something for dahr husband, dahr wife, gay lover, bitch, who give a shit who. Everyone kinky, you auss-hull. Why do I care? I'm Kabir, the owner, you auss-hull. I come here with nothing, drive a taxi like all the Muslims. Now I own business, the American dream.

"You not part of my dream. No work ethic, no pride, no nothing. I pay Do Anything Temp Agency good money to make my business, and they waste my money send me you."

With that last indignation, he grabbed my pile of flyers to demonstrate the immigrant work ethic. "Good afternoon, ma'am," he welcomed with a charming lilt, completely opposite the angry Muslim tone he took with me. "We are having an incredible sale, hope you can stop in," he said, reaching out forcefully to block the woman's path, compelling her to take the flyer.

"Hello, sir, something special for your beautiful wife today?" Kabir offered, crowding the top escalator step so the man could not maneuver away without accepting the flyer, and once he did, Kabir gracefully pirouetted to the side.

THREE YARDS AND A PLATE OF MULLET

Over the next two minutes, Kabir's aggressive approach scored a .800 acceptance rate. In contrast, my laissez-faire style, alternating between standing rigid like a pole cemented into the sidewalk and slouching against a station wall, holding a flaccid flier an inch from my hip with a spaghetti noodle arm, earned me a batting average of about .0875, a supremely non-clutch pinch hitter.

"Here, that's how you do it, auss-hull," Kabir said, shoving the pile of flyers into my belly. "Earn your money. I must go run my business. I check on you tomorrow," he said, one hand gripping my shoulder, and he turned and headed down the street.

I couldn't resist. "Hey, Kabir, why don't you go back to Cairo and look for some oil in the desert, A-rab!"

Kabir turned around on the busy sidewalk, wide-eyed, waving his fist in the air, looking every bit like the revolutionaries who stormed the gates of the American Embassy in Iran, dooming the Georgia peanut farmer/Billy Beer presidency.

"Listen, lazy man. You insult me, my family, my people. How do you say in American? You suck! You fired! I don't need you. I make American dream, and you don't!"

"You can't fire me. I don't work for you. I work for DATA." I paused for effect. "So eat shit!"

I started to sense that Kabir enjoyed ranting and arguing and swearing, as he probably did as normal discourse with his Arab hothead buddies over a crackling shish kebab grill. My anger started to dissipate. This job was boring as shit, and now I was feeling entertained and lively and engaged, thanks to this madman. I kept it going with Kabir, but now I had a business angle to pursue.

"Why should I try hard, Kabir? I get paid the same crapola wage whether everybody takes a flyer or nobody. Where's the incentive?"

Kabir furrowed his bushy unibrow and stroked his stubbly chin. "You make a good point, auss-hull. I have deal for you. You put your name on fliers. Every customer that makes purchase with your coupon, I give you 10 percent of sale."

"How can I trust you?"

"Don't you worry, my American friend. I am man of Allah. My word is Allah's word. Do your job and do not suck, or I call DATA and fire your ass. Good day, little DATA punk," he said, shaking my hand earnestly.

"It's a deal, Camel Man."

Over the next seven workdays, I put my all into this stupid job, strangely motivated by Kabir's vitriol and my need to get a car quickly so I could get out of DATA and on with the rest of my life, as soon as sports editors started contacting me. I started aggressively pressing flyers into harried commuters' hands, talking them up about improving their sex lives TONIGHT! with a salesman's flair for immediacy.

Kabir and I developed a weird friendship and an off-color street comedy shtick, berating each other with stone-faced amusement.

He'd come by several times daily to berate me loudly on the crowded intersections: "You sloppy American, you amount to nothing!"

"Go back to your 7-Eleven and make some Slurpees!" I'd respond.

Tunnel-visioned, high-achieving yuppies would suspend their workday rush to stop and listen. When Kabir turned to leave, he'd hurl a final invective: "Stinkin' Jew."

"Fuckin' A-rab!" I'd yell, oddly devoid of inhibition.

Then one more from Kabir as he got farther away: "Hebrew National son-of-a-beetch!"

"Falafel Stand turban-headed jerk-off!"

Strangely, these acerbic, profanity-laden exchanges raised interest in the flyers, perhaps out of curiosity about the sidewalk ethnic freak show. Sales spiked in my second week, and I took home an average of $180 daily in commission in addition to my $55.25 daily wages. I accumulated $2,700 to shop for a used car. On my last day, I asked Kabir if he knew of any swarthy brethren who were selling used cars, on the off chance that the Middle Eastern taxi-driver brotherhood would have car connections.

"I give you the number of my friend Quaresh El-Bhupati. He trying to get rid of Chevy Chevette. Piece of shit American car. GM...Hah! Grotesque Mistake. And fuckin' unions. Too fat and happy to make good car. In my country, we drive Fiat. If Fiat worker make shitty car, he starve in the slum. We drive Fiat on rocks, through desert, over mountain—"

"Spare me, Kabir," I interrupted. "I know lazy Americans suck. Just the number, please."

"You got it, my friend. Hey, you not a bad guy. You make me some cheese. You know, I don't mean all—"

"Say no more, Kabir. Don't change for nothin', you suicide-bombin', Gaza Strippin' fool. Now I got to go find myself a camel from Quaresh."

Kabir burst out laughing. He had been storing this one up for two weeks: "Adios, my kibbutzin', gefilte-fishin' motha fucka!"

❖ ❖ ❖

Quaresh was the opposite of Kabir—quiet, polite, and respectful. I sized him up as someone I could trust. The Chevette was the color of turd inside and out, but only five years old and with just 63,000 miles on it—reasonable usage—and in good condition. Quaresh was asking $2,450.

By now, I was in a hurry to get some wheels. Of the seventy resumes I had spread across the country to sports editors, I had received a handful of rejection letters saying there were no positions that matched my qualifications but that my resume would be kept on [circular] file, and just two informational interviews, one with the *Washington Times*, warning me against working for any paper owned by the Korean messiah Sun Myung Moon of the Unification Church and his band of Moonies, and another in Culpeper, Virginia, telling me to go somewhere else to get three years' experience to qualify for that bumfuck town. In other words, bupkis.

THE DINQY

But upon my return from my interview in Bumfuck, I received a message on the answering machine from Padraic O'Manahan, sports editor at the *Citrus Coast Daily Inquirer* (known both affectionately and derogatively as the *Dinqy*), based in New Palm City, Florida, and covering a burgeoning Quad Counties region along Florida's Gulf Coast.

On my callback, O'Manahan, also known as Paddy and "the O-Dog," told me he was impressed with my college coverage and NFL Properties features, and that their preps writer had left unexpectedly and they needed someone immediately for the start of high school football season. He asked if I could interview in New Palm City immediately.

When I exited the airport in my seersucker suit to find my rental car, I was hit by a blast of hot air that made me feel like a vase in an industrial-sized kiln. This wasn't a dry heat; it was decomposing-body-in-the-bayou heat, Vietnam-rice-paddy heat, too-many-rocks-in-the-sauna heat. When I took my jacket off in the car after a walk through a greenhouse-effect garage, I had half-moon sweat stains under my armpits, turning my light-blue shirt dark blue in perfectly symmetrical blotches. I had to crank the car's air conditioning and raise my arms for three minutes to try to dry out before I started driving.

Paddy ambled in to meet me in a *Dinqy* conference room. He was a hulking man who walked with oddly small steps. I quickly discovered that Paddy wasn't much for small talk and presented a gruff first impression. He got straight to the point, asking if I was cool under pressure, if I could make tight deadlines, how I would handle fiery and sometimes belligerent coaches, and how I would go about developing my own contacts and finding compelling features as an undermanned solo sports bureau working the home territory of the rival newspaper, the *Drabenville Times-Democrat*. Having fielded similar questions in my Culpeper and Moonie informational interviews, I had a script down pat and thought I aced the interview.

"Wait here," Paddy said. "All our editorial prospects have to meet with Chance and Alize."

That would be Chance Wellington, a gracefully aging, debonair Southern gentleman who rose to managing editor at the *Atlanta Observer-Independent* and came to New Palm City as the top dog for the swan song of his distinguished newspapering career; and Alize (pronounced Ah-lee-ZAY) Chenault, a young, ambitious Southern belle with the lean, tall, and glamorous look of a beauty contest queen transplanted from a bikini to a business suit. She was Wellington's handpicked second-in-charge and leader of the *Dinqy*'s daily operations.

I sat at the end of a table with Wellington and Chenault on either side, attempting to confirm that I had the work ethic and smarts to make their paper better. I learned that they liked to bring in non-Floridians with impressive pedigrees as they talked about how many Northwestern University Medill School of Journalism graduates they had recruited and the business editor who had come from *Forbes* and their crack crime reporter from the *Detroit Free Press* and the education reporter from the *Cleveland Plain Dealer*. They could attract these journalists because of the eternal sunshine, high quality of life and low cost of living, and the promise of working in a high-growth, dynamic area compared with the old lions of American business, industry, and civic and social life, such as Detroit and Cleveland, which were on the treacherous downward slope toward decay and obsolescence. The Citrus Coast was the New America—the popular book *Megatrends* proclaimed it so by naming Tampa one of ten "new cities of great opportunity"—and people like Wellington and Chenault were the community pioneers to lead the upstart region to the avant garde of those Sunbelt phoenixes heading toward the new millennium.

I talked a lot, and Wellington and Chenault nodded, which I took as a sign that I was saying what they wanted to hear. The one odd thing I noticed was that at certain points, both editors turned their attention away from me to glance at each other, which produced in each of them—but especially in Wellington—a shared, knowing smile and a twinkle in the eyes. They were communicating something, and my instinct told me it had nothing to do with my brilliant answer of how I once applied a strategy to solve a problem. I could have sworn I heard their shoes connect under the table, and I had the strange sense that their furtive glances had more to do with dinner plans than the midmorning editorial staff meeting.

I was home for only two days when I got a call from Paddy offering me the job of the Dolphin County bureau sports reporter and asking how soon I could start, emphasizing that the paper had already set plans for its preseason high school football coverage and needed someone in place immediately to execute them. The new reporter would need some time to meet the key coaches and players and learn about the rabid football culture during the comparatively dead days of July before being swept up in the five-month frenzy beginning in August. I did a quick calculation of how long it would take me to get to Dolphin County and commit to a first day on the job—maybe a week to secure a car, pack up my stuff, and make the twenty-four-hour drive to a fleabag motel that could serve as my temporary quarters.

Too naïve to negotiate for a better salary than Paddy's $17,500 offer and overly eager to put my Persian lingerie and other DATA jobs in the rearview mirror, I accepted Paddy's offer on the spot. "I'll start in a week," I told Paddy. "I'm excited to get going."

"Great. I'll set you up with Johnny Littleman to give you a tour when you first get down. Get your rest now 'cause you're not gonna get much once football season gets rolling. Get ready for the grind, young gun," Paddy warned with a high-pitched giggle incongruous with a man his size.

"I'm ready, Paddy," I answered, thinking there couldn't be much to it. I had been a football fanatic since I was five. I understood it. What could be so hard?

I had no idea what I was in for. It's one thing to watch football on TV. It's another thing to live it, to compete daily against well-connected rival reporters, to worry about it when you try to sleep and when you wake up, to get calls about breaking stories on your one day off, and to chronicle the men of abnormal intensity who, lacking a war to fight or a damsel in distress to save, become coaches and live and die by football through their utter dependence on their ability to mold an unpredictable, immature, erratic, and moody band of teenagers—some of whom already have maxed out their athletic potential and others whose prodigious talent is nowhere near full bloom.

Leaving for Paradise...Lost

I called Quaresh, hoping he hadn't sold the Turdmobile. Big surprise, nobody else had inquired. Quaresh added a piece of new information: the air conditioning was broken, but it could be fixed by one of his camel-jockey friends in a week. I didn't have time for that, so I dropped my offer to $2,100. Big mistake. Only a masochist drives an air-conditioner-less car in Florida. And I found out later from a mechanic that the AC repair would cost a budget-blowing $800, way too much to invest in a Turdmobile. I was stuck with a Turd.

I stuffed the Turdmobile with all my possessions that would fit in the hatchback and the front seat and headed for I-95 South.

Late afternoon on the second day, I crossed the Georgia-Florida border, and within a half hour, as I approached Jacksonville, the brilliant, blazing sun surrendered to a dark and ominous dome enveloping the ribbon of highway. With nary a warning spittle, God unleashed a torrent of water that blanketed the windshield like the inside of a car wash, splashing too fast for the wipers to clear. It reminded me of standing below the huge bucket at the water theme park that fills for two minutes before reaching the tipping point and dumping a massive sheath that leaves you breathless. Thunder cracked and lightning zapped; I thought the flimsy Turdmobile might spontaneously combust from the shock waves. The seventy-mile-an-hour traffic slowed to ten. Sick of driving, I tried to press on, leaving a line of red hazard-light-blinking quitters on the shoulder in my wake. But I couldn't see five feet in front of me. I would have hit anyone puttering along who wasn't blinking hazards, so I pulled over to wait it out with the rest of the marooned. Fifteen minutes later, the scorching, irradiant sun made an encore appearance, and it was as if the storm never happened, except for the steam rising off the roadway as if hell had taken a firefighter's dousing.

It was a resounding and dazzling performance by Nature that I would see routinely throughout the summer, sending players scurrying from practice fields to the locker room and me to the cover of the Turdmobile to protect the notes in my Sparco Reporter's Notebook from becoming blue smears.

After an eternity driving through mono-elevation Florida, I came to the Citrus Coast region south of Tampa–St. Pete. I got off I-75 on a ramp shadowed by an enormous Confederate flag waving from a convenience store / gas station and navigated the local roads to Drabenville, stopping at the first Motel 6 I found. I left the Turdmobile loaded to the roof, confident that no one would break into that junk pile, and collapsed on the beige, cigarette-burned bedspread, feeling disoriented, like a journeyman with dissociative fugue, the condition where you travel somewhere, get amnesia, forget who and where you are and how you got there, and adopt a new identity.

Stimulated by Cokes and coffees from the road and bloated from the Golden Corral all-you-can-eat, I couldn't sleep, so I left my semen-caked, cigarette-charred room and walked six thinly spaced commercial-establishment driveways down the treacherous, haphazardly planned boulevard to the Float Inn Bar, a low-slung concrete-block building beckoning lowlifes and drunkards and fellow dissociative fugue sufferers—with a hammock and plastic palm tree on the roof and two neon shot glasses forming the "B" in "Bar."

A motley crew was watching NASCAR at the bar, and two groups in motorcycle T-shirts and jeans were shooting pool in the back. I sat at the bar and ordered two shots of tequila and an Old Milwaukee chaser, hoping it would knock me into oblivion and stop my mind from racing about this unknown new life into which I had parachuted.

LEAVING FOR PARADISE...LOST

I screwed up my courage, hoping I wouldn't be pegged as a lost soul who confused the Float Inn for a gay bar, and thus pummeled by hate-crime aficionados, and asked a bar mate if he knew of any good rental apartments in Drabenville.

"Yeah, about half a mile from here, at Twenty-Sixth and Thirtieth, the Whispering Willow," said a scraggly lounger who introduced himself as Crash. "It's got everything you'd want—a pool, laundry, drugs if you're buying *or* selling, and some nice pieces of ass."

"How can it be on Twenty-Sixth *and* Thirtieth? Is it four blocks long, like a jail?"

"Twenty-Sixth *Street* and Thirtieth *Avenue*. Check it out, dude. Two of my old girlfriends live there. You can pick one. But watch out for crabs. My doodads were on fire for a month. Give me a call, and I'll hook you up real nice with my old lady and some weed."

I left Float Inn sloshed, with Crash's phone number, a Float Inn matchbox, and a Float Inn shot glass in my pocket, mementos of the first night of my life as a sportswriter. I considered adding to my Motel 6 room's collection of semen decorations on the curtains to relieve my stress but decided against it on the grounds that it would be bad karma and would put me on the same footing as all the other jerk-offs who had stayed there, and I had more pride than that.

The next day, I took my own tour of Drabenville's main commercial drags and randomly veered off into neighborhoods. I was intrigued by the lower-income, bottom-end retirement enclaves and cramped miniparks with their tiny ponds, sad fountains, and thin ribbons of grass interrupting narrow asphalt lanes. Plopped haphazardly like Dorothy's shack on Oz on winding lanes just wide enough for three-wheel bikes with metal cargo baskets to pass each other, were the boxy trailers and mobile and modular homes, with cars snug against the side panels, that retirees called their slices of heaven.

I puttered through several of these uniquely American, schlocky communities that were interspersed between strip shopping centers and industrial parks on main boulevards and plunked indiscriminately and incongruously in residential neighborhoods, a clear sign that Florida had missed its classes on zoning and New Urbanism design.

The Château Marmot Village 55-Plus Lifestyle Community featured trailer homes with Ohio State flags and "Home of the Michigan State Spartans" placards adorning the drooping carports, announcing the native lands where these transplanted retirees once toiled at monotonous if not back-breaking jobs to earn their small, prefab, corrugated-metal-and–vinyl piece of paradise, where they would live out their years on concrete shuffleboard slabs under a palm and in the sun, by God; Midwestern gloom, slush, and ice a bygone but not forgotten casualty of their reincarnation. The sheet-metal and faded vinyl homes, reminiscent of industrial metal Dumpsters or truck trailers detached from the cab, were drowning in kitsch, adorned with plastic wind-spun flowers, cat and frog and other animal figurines in tiny rock-garden plots, ceramic lighthouses and firehouses on outdoor sills, plastic lawn furniture, battered sofas and recliners that wouldn't fit inside, and battery-powered golf carts for those who could no longer drive.

Noted in large block lettering on the Château Marmot entrance sign was "A BACKGROUND CHECK COMMUNITY." I was worried, as I dawdled through, that I might get arrested and booked for snobbery. But as much as I cringed at the nightmare of one day waking up and finding myself transported to Château Marmot purgatory to live out my remaining years, I realized that parks like Château Marmot were Godiva chocolate, sweet chirping Nightingales, and sugarplum fairies for many who had led hard lives.

That's certainly why these blots on the landscape invariably carried sunny names with at least two hyphens (Shang-Ri-La, Playa-Del-Sur, Sea-Esta-Villas, Sunshine-On-My-Mind) or stately monikers with connotations of majesty (Grand Luxor, Regal Heights, Tropical Dunes, Great Palms). Somehow, the splendid names didn't match the manifestation when a car license plate hung as a greeting next to the door on the frontside panel of metal, a housing requirement when snowbirds detach their living quarters from their autos in the mobile home parks.

LEAVING FOR PARADISE...LOST

A scary thing upon leaving these communities was the proliferation of ads on the backs of street benches for funeral homes and attorneys who specialize in wills and estates. Otherwise, my aimless tour was highlighted by a preponderance of pawn and gun shops, dollar stores, taco stands, churches, all-you-can-eat buffets, and flat, straight avenues with evenly dispersed ranch houses landscaped with 2.5 palm trees and cycads with billowing crowns of evergreen leaves and driveways with motor boats hoisted on concrete blocks.

I would leave it to a *Daily Inquirer* sports staffer—most likely the flunky who gets the assignments no one else wants—to take me on a tour of the places that I'd really need to know to start working my way up to NFL beat reporter. I put all thoughts of Tampa Stadium out of my mind; I was soon to be seeing bright lights on Friday nights, but the big city would have to wait while I paid my dues.

The Haves and the Have-nots

By my second day, I was stationed at a faraway outpost, like the post office in a hick town, twenty miles from New Palm City, where everyone at the paper believed the real action was if you wanted a chance to move up. On that day, Johnny Littleman, a thirty-year Indiana-bred veteran at the paper, who had recently been demoted from sports editor to "leisure activities" reporter and was killing time until his pension kicked in, was assigned to drive me around to the county's six high schools, Dolphin Civic Center, tennis academy, racetrack, Little League complex, shuffleboard pavilion, and other venues.

Johnny had slicked-back hair, metal-rimmed glasses, a bowling-ball gut, and an easygoing manner, like thirty years of the Florida sun had baked the energy and ambition right out of him. He began a lot of his sentences with, "Well, let me tell ya…" before launching into an erudite but annoyingly drawn-out story punctuated by efforts to push his sagging glasses back to the bridge of his nose and one-nostril snot blows into a yellowing handkerchief and tying a bow around his saga with, "…that's right, yup." It was obvious that Johnny had a lot of knowledge of the region and its sporting genealogy, but I cringed at the prospect of hanging around him too much, wondering if this would be me in thirty years, driving an eager college puke around this Cracker town, snot rag hanging from the steering wheel, reminiscing about the days when I covered the Dolphin High footballers like white on rice.

THE HAVES AND THE HAVE-NOTS

To get anywhere in Drabenville, you had to take a main drag until you got to the correct numerical street or avenue, streets running east-west and avenues, north-south, with State Route 69, also known as the Flume, dividing the city into east and west, like the Berlin Wall, and for all intents and purposes, the haves and the have-nots.

Johnny turned his stodgy Buick off Tortuga Avenue onto Thirty-Fourth Street West into a neighborhood of well-manicured lawns, big-leafed palmetto trees, and sprawling ranchers, many with motorboats on trailers in the driveways.

Before we visited the top school in the county, the one attended by the children of Drabenville's most prominent lawyers, doctors, and business owners, Rotary members all, Johnny took me to the ritziest residential location in town, River Overlook Drive. Glass-backed mansions with circular driveways encompassing stone fountains spraying water up toward multilevel decks lined the twisting, scenic roadway shrouded by overhanging willows and palms. This was Drabenville's old money, descendants of the Midwestern manufacturing titans who retired here, families of the developers who built the beachfront condos and the shopping centers in the 1970s when the town was just beginning to boom from a sleepy settlement of 25,000 to a sprawling suburban city of 100,000 (175,000 when the snowbirds descended in January to clog the roads with coiffed volleyball heads peering over the steering wheels of their giant Cadillacs).

We turned off River Overlook, away from the multimillionaire set and toward upper-middle-class Drabenville on the west side of town. We came to Dolphin High School. "You got to see this campus, yup," Johnny told me, pressing one nostril and blowing into his handkerchief.

Dolphin High was a stately, historic-looking, three-story red brick building, with sleek, modern glass-and-brick additions on either side connected by canopied walkways with white columns. The main building featured steps like those leading up to the Supreme Court, and seven white columns like a Southern plantation, with ornate carvings at the tops of the pillars. Carved into the façade of the antebellum architecture edifice was DOLPHIN HIGH SCHOOL, and below that, above the doors, COURAGE, HONOR, FORTITUDE, and TRADITION.

Behind the main building, down a path lined with palms, was the new Bamford Science and Technology Center, built with donations from the foundation established by the football coach's grandparents. Adjacent to the science building was Papadopoulos Library, named after the father of the Dolphin County school board chairman, another generous, well-to-do alum.

The football field was emerald-green fescue, like Augusta's eighteenth green, shrouded in mist from the spray of the irrigation system. Blue and gold stands rose from the field on four sides, like the walls of a canyon, creating the bowl effect. High-flying, ostentatious flags emblazoned with huge dolphin fins waved from the four end-zone points. A state-of-the-art scoreboard hovered beyond the gold goalposts, topped with HOME OF THE DHS FIGHTIN' DORSAL FINS in blue lettering. Three evenly spaced palm trees stood majestically behind the scoreboard, creating an ambiance of splendor.

This was no operation where game goers would purchase tickets from a volunteer sitting behind a student desk in some school hallway. The ticket operation was its own small brick building outside Jed Bamford Field at Roop Stadium, with four glass windows like a Ticketmaster outlet. Another adjacent, larger brick building housed the concessions and restrooms.

Tall, black iron fence gates and bars prohibited anyone from entering the sacred grounds; the field was locked down like a high-security military post. The press box was an enclosed rectangle with eight viewing windows and a platform above for TV cameras.

If the home field said anything about the team, it was easy to see why Dolphin had been a dynasty.

THE HAVES AND THE HAVE-NOTS

We got back to Johnny's crusty Buick. "If you want to see a contrast, I'll take you over to East Grove High," he said, hocking snot again. "Let me tell ya, it ain't no Dolphin."

❖ ❖ ❖

We crossed the Flume—Drabenville's great divide—and the bridge over the Wallatatchie River and entered another world. East Drabenville reminded me of the rural Mississippi landscape I saw in the grainy black-and-white civil rights documentaries in high school. New to Florida, I thought of the state only in terms of white-sand beaches, palm trees, blue seas, golf courses, luxury condos, waterfront mansions, and Mickey and his Disney World pals. East Drabenville was no wish-you-were-here postcard. Sad-looking, matchbox-sized houses with peeling paint, broken windows, and sagging, loose-shingled roofs sat forlornly behind dirt driveways framed by rusted-out pickups with no license plates, doghouses, old box springs, and decaying couches. Trash-strewn, vacant lots surrounded by barbed wire fences, boarded-up houses with overgrown vegetation, and graffiti-covered cinder-block buildings, the carcasses of closed auto-salvaging and canning businesses, were interspersed throughout the residential neighborhoods.

We came to an oasis that, on this late July day in the oppressive heat, looked deserted. We went inside the East Drabenville Boys and Girls Club, and for the first time, I got an inkling how the East Grove Calusa Warriors could rival Dolphin High on the gridiron. Two half-court basketball games were going on, the preteens already displaying advanced speed and athleticism, and the older kids exploding off the floor and dunking with regularity. On the second floor, where a track ringed the court below, a coach barked out split times to waves of boys and girls running quarter miles.

Out back on a dusty brown field, shirtless and sculpted teenagers glistening with sweat were playing seven-on-seven football, working on pass plays and option runs. A wide receiver glided downfield after juking his man with a down-and-out break, looking up into the sun to locate the arching football sent airborne fifty yards away. Seemingly from nowhere, a defender flew toward the descending ball and the targeted receiver. He leaped and snatched it over the receiver's outstretched hands, tapping his feet just in front of the white chalk line before somersaulting out of bounds.

"Holy shit! Did you see that, Johnny? These guys are great athletes. Is that how they can compete against Dolphin?"

"It's not only that, Jake. Let me tell ya, they're hungry. They're born hungry. Their mamas ain't goin' to be payin' their way through college. They grow up knowing the only way out is a football scholarship. Even the marginally talented players, the wide loads and fireplugs, have seen their brothers and cousins and buddies with no more ability get to at least junior college, and once there, the opportunities open up, that's right, yup. They see their boys who didn't make it, didn't have the fire in the belly and the tunnel vision, didn't even make it through high school, now they're hanging on the streets dealing crack and running from the police, doing time in Dolphin Correctional or even dead, bullet to the head…Excuse me…"

With a huge one-nostril snort, Johnny blew a wad into his fraying rag. "Sorry…allergies. Anyway, the coaches around here will do anything to keep these kids on the right path, Pee Wee to Boys Club right on through East Grove. They're a hard-assed group but only because they care. They're not in it for their own glory. They truly want to pull these kids out of poverty and make them good citizens and successful people, and they know sports is the vehicle that will take them there, build their character and their drive and their image of themselves and their vision of something better. Just wait till you meet Coach Magnusson at East Grove. You've never met a more intense dude in your life. You'll see, that's right, yup."

Back in the clunky Buick, we drove on to East Grove High. But once we arrived, we didn't even bother getting out of the car, just cruised the parking lot and bus loop. There wasn't much to see, certainly no architectural inspiration, just a low-slung, modular, beige, cinder-block building. The football stadium down a gravel driveway was nothing more than a patchy green and brown, as yet unmarked field, with low-rising wooden-bench stands on either side that only spanned the thirty-yard lines, which meant that any fans who didn't arrive early enough sat on blankets on the man-made slopes on either side of the stands, often with a bucket of KFC. The scoreboard looked homemade in industrial arts class and had to be manually operated to change the score. Johnny told me the only way fans knew how much time was left was when the PA announcer broadcast it via a referee.

"Man, Johnny, hard to believe this is the same county. Where I'm from, everything is more uniform, not such a wide disparity in facilities, like here."

Johnny looked pensive and drew out the beginning of his response even more, as if he was debating whether to keep his journalistic objectivity intact or put on his editorial hat and risk biasing a newbie who hadn't covered one down of high school football yet.

"Well...let me...tell ya...I would never give readers even the slightest hint of this when I wrote my column...and this is just between you and me, because I could get run out of town for this, and I'm just two years from my full pension. I get the feeling I can trust you, right?"

"Yeah, Johnny, I'm just trying to learn, and obviously you know what's what. It stays right here in this Buick."

"OK then. I just love it when East Grove kicks Dolphin's ass. It's hell to deal with Bamford after that, but that dude and his ego need to be knocked from the throne every now and then or he's insufferable. I have to admit, I like an underdog, and Magnusson and his crew fit the role to a tee."

We cruised on to visit more high schools, the hucksters at De Leon Raceway, the hustlers at the Sergio Bonatelli Tennis Academy, and even the Draben Downs Dog Track and the Crevalle Jack Shuffleboard Center. There would be some time to get to know those beats. But Johnny made it clear that the centers of my universe over the next five months would be Dolphin and East Grove, dueling for supremacy like Darth Vader and Luke Skywalker.

THREE YARDS AND A PLATE OF MULLET

As we headed back to my hole-in-the-wall outpost in drab downtown Drabenville, "Wake Me Up Before You Go-Go" crackling on the Buick's radio, we passed Mudville Mike's Burger & Ale House, which Johnny told me was a local landmark watering hole patronized by Drabenville's muck-amucks and old-timers from the Chamber of Commerce, Rotary clubs, Fraternal Order of Police, Knights of Columbus, Foreign Legion, and Veterans of Foreign Wars posts. "Mudville Mike's, home of the Original Gator Burger," read the neon marquee, and just below that: "GRIDFEST JUBILEE Aug 18. Go Dolphin, Beat East Grove." Not even August, and I knew it was on.

The Nordic God

Two weeks until GridFest Jubilee, where the four county teams play one quarter against each of the other teams, and it was time for me to meet the coaching staffs to get their team analyses for the *Citrus Coast Daily Inquirer* Football Preview that would serve as the GridFest Jubilee program for rabid fans.

Based on Johnny Littleman's comments and our eye-opening visit to the East Drabenville Boys and Girls Club, I decided to visit East Grove High first. If these guys were hungry, I wanted that to rub off on me for the start of my career.

I headed east over the Wallatatchie River Bridge and into the Deep South and promptly got lost. The grid didn't hold up on this side of town. There were dead-end and realigned roads that threw me off the carefully planned route I had memorized. Two times, I had to pull over and get out my Drabenville street map to retrace my route and see where I'd gone wrong. I got back on the main boulevard, passing a string of nail salons, pawnshops, liquor stores, salvage yards, and bail bond / check cashing huts before I finally found the turnoff leading to Seventeenth Court SE, with the school at the end.

It was in the midnineties with a suffocating, swampy humidity. My wet back was plastered to the Turdmobile's seat. I got out of the car and felt a furnace blast of heat; if only there were some toucans in the trees and gorillas swinging from vines, I would swear I was in the Amazon rainforest.

A lean figure was pushing a cart down the length of the field, lining it with white chalk. He stopped at a wooden stick, performed a precise ninety-degree turn, like a soldier preparing to salute, and headed across the field, creating the goal line. At the next stick, he made another regimented turn to roll the second sideline and was now heading my way. With a closer view, I saw that this guy looked like he could put on some pads and line up as free safety for the Miami Dolphins. I got my Sparco Reporter's Notebook out of the car, slid a few pens into my side pocket, rolled up the previous year's Football Preview that Johnny had given me to study, stuffed it in my back pocket, and trotted to intersect East Grove coach Gunnar Magnusson before he covered the hundred yards.

"Coach Magnusson, I'm Jake Yankelovich from the *Daily Inquirer*. Good to meet you."

"You're late."

Oh, shit. Suddenly I started sweating even more profusely. I couldn't have written the wrong time in my calendar for my first preview interview…could I?

"Uhhh, weren't we supposed to meet at three o'clock?"

"That's right. What time do you have?" the coach asked, staring down at me with piercing blue eyes, sweat dripping off his nose and the bill of his cap.

"I got 2:58 p.m."

"So you're late."

OK, this is going like crap. If Paddy hears about it, I'm not even going to last until GridFest.

And then Coach Magnusson broke into a wide toothy smile, let out a chuckle, and put a big bear paw on my sweat-drenched shoulder. "The first thing you should know about the East Grove Calusa Warriors is that if you're not ten minutes early, you're late. But you didn't know that, so we'll cut you a break this first time. Thanks for coming by. C'mon with me to my office," he said and patted my back as if I had just come back to the bench after scoring a touchdown.

Coach Magnusson was a rock solid six three, 210 pounds, and looked like a Nordic god. I could imagine him as a Viking with a metal helmet on the bow of a wooden Viking ship, sword and shield raised. With his wavy blond hair, blue eyes, and athletic build, he reminded me of the Green Bay Packers Golden Boy Paul Hornung, whom I had seen so many times tagged as a playboy in NFL Films productions.

I discovered that Coach Magnusson was from Minnesota and played linebacker for the Bemidji State University Beavers, where he also earned a master's degree in history. After working as a low-paid defensive assistant coach at tiny Yankton College in South Dakota, he tired of the frigid weather and Midwestern doldrums and set out to become a high school head coach in football-mad Florida. For two years, he religiously followed the weekly top twenty-five national high school football rankings in *USA Today* and noticed Dolphin's customary top five spot. He wanted the challenge of coaching against Dolphin and nationally renowned Coach Zipf, so he kept tabs on openings in Dolphin and neighboring Mirabella counties.

When the East Grove job came open in 1980 after a second consecutive one-win season in which four players were arrested in a drug bust, three were suspended from school and kicked off the team for inciting a pregame brawl, and five more were declared academically ineligible midseason, Coach Magnusson went after it full throttle.

He told me East Grove's plain-talking principal, Martha Sutton, asked in his interview why on earth a college coach in a bucolic town would want to drop down a level to come to a hardscrabble high school with poverty and discipline problems that hadn't had a winning season in twelve years, coinciding with the decline of the region's agricultural economy, the growth in the drug trade, and the spread of blight.

Coach Magnusson's reply: "I'm not coming here just to win football games, and you can bet your ass I will. I'm coming here to change East Grove's next generation of men into one this school and community can be proud of. And if you don't see that change in the first group of lettermen who come through my program, you won't have to fire me. I'll fire my own ass."

With that, Sutton knew she had her new coach. In his six years, Coach Magnusson had turned a perennial loser with a well-deserved thug image into a contender for the Class 4A state championship. He had improved the varsity's graduation rate from 60 percent to 95 percent, and in his spare time helped transform the East Drabenville Boys and Girls Club from a drugs-and-craps hangout into a virtual training ground for all of East Grove's athletic teams, not to mention the school's math, mock trial, and chess clubs.

Coach Magnusson arranged to have his offensive and defensive coordinators join us in his office, which was more like a large closet across the hall from the locker room, with standard school-issued desk and chairs, a reel-to-reel film projector that evidently projected onto a sheet on the wall, pennants from Big Ten schools like Minnesota and Purdue, a poster of the Chicago Bears Shufflin' Crew, and a framed picture of Magnusson kneeling and holding his helmet in his Bemidji State green and white, with the caption, "Senior Day 1975, Gunnar Magnusson, Two-Time Captain, Defensive MVP." Above his desk was a wooden plaque engraved with a simple quote that defined his philosophy and tenure at East Grove: "Better Together."

The defensive coordinator, Hank Gamble, was a Vietnam vet who taught English and loved literature—Chaucer, Dickens, Brontë. He asked me about all them and who my favorite author was, to which I replied Steinbeck because old English literature was never my strong suit. From memory, he recited a quote from Jane Austen that he used to instill pride in the defensive unit:

> Vanity and pride are different things, though the words are often used synonymously. A person may be proud without being vain. Pride relates more to our opinion of ourselves; vanity, to what we would have others think of us.

"We want our players to think of themselves as brothers, as family," Gamble told me. "When one hurts, we all hurt. When one struggles, the rest lift him up. We take pride in our school, pride in our work, pride in our effort on the field and in the classroom, and pride in ourselves. We're teaching our kids that pride is something that is nurtured and grows inside, that no one can take away…or give to them. Once they develop that belief, they internalize this sense of pride, they stop the showboating and taunting and other crap the old East Grove teams used to do, which really was to say, 'Hey, look at me, you better respect me and be proud of me, because I'm not proud of myself.' The talent has always been here, but once we changed that mindset, you can see the results speak for themselves."

I liked Hank right away, his quiet, no-nonsense demeanor combined with friendliness, warmth, and caring. He was a high school version of NFL Bucs and Colts coach Tony Dungy, only physically more like the Pillsbury Doughboy than the angular Dungy. I would later learn that he was able to motivate his troops without bombastic threats, angry put-downs, or fire-and-brimstone motivational woofings. He treated them and talked to them like men, and just a look, a hand gesture, or a few calm and simple words, "Pride, not fear," or "Lead with your heart," or "Real men show they care," told them all they needed to do.

I asked Coach Gamble if he ever talked to the players about Vietnam.

"All the time," he said, "but only in one context. You never know when your best buddy won't be there anymore. So I tell them, love *your* family, love *this* family. Let them know how you feel about them, because someday, it may be too late. Lord knows we've seen a lot of young men succumb to the streets around here."

Zack Polansky, the offensive coordinator, reminded me of Raiders and Bucs coach Jon Gruden because of his blond hair, youthful looks, and *Child's Play*'s Chucky-like intensity featuring Gruden's clenched-teeth and rip-your-throat-out glare when he was fired up. Underneath that façade, he was a fun-loving, energetic guy, who was constantly ribbing his players: "Hey, Stanley, did I see you with a girl at the movies or was that yo mama? Julius, if I see you on your back any more today we're gonna make a trip to Mattress Discounters."

Polansky was an Ohio all-state high school player from Steubenville and a top state four-hundred-meter runner. He played wide receiver at Miami University of Ohio. He had tryouts with the Buffalo Bills and the Houston Oilers, and when he was cut, he returned to Steubenville to teach high school math and coach. But he felt himself getting soft and paunchy, like many men who hung around Steubenville too long. One day by chance in 1982, he tuned into ABC's *Wide World of Sports* and saw the Hawaii Ironman Triathlon, still in its infancy. He became glued to the TV, watching a college student named Julie Moss collapse near the end of the marathon in the dark of night, illuminated only by camera lights, get passed for the title, but still crawl on her hands and knees to the finish line. Polansky told me it was only the second time he had cried watching an athletic event, the other being the Cleveland Browns' 1970 championship game loss to the Purple People Eaters' Minnesota Vikings, ruining the Browns' Super Bowl hopes.

Afterward, Polansky put on basketball high-tops and ran ninety minutes through Steubenville. He was hooked. He joined the local Y for swimming, bought a used ten-speed Schwinn and a pair of New Balances, and became Steubenville's first triathlete. He saw more of his hometown than ever and was aghast at the abandoned factories, boarded-up homes, closed businesses, pollution, and vacant lots swallowing up the once-vibrant, apple-pie, All-American town. He knew he had to get out and go to a warmer climate for training. He remembered the fishing jaunts he'd taken with his grandfather to Drabenville, so when the school year ended, he moved there and snagged a job as a substitute teacher at East Grove, which soon became permanent. From there, it wasn't hard to get on the football staff, where Coach Magnusson saw Polansky as a kindred spirit.

Polansky helped Coach Magnusson install a dynamic offense that the Warriors ran out of two sets to confuse defenses, taking advantage of the talents of twins Ronnie and Renny Jenkins, the quarterback and running back. In the Sims set, the option formation named after Oklahoma University tailback Billy Sims, Ronnie and Renny carved up defenses with ball fakery, pitches, and speed, and for a changeup, power, when Ronny made the quick hand-off to first-option fullback Hans Czsryunkowiez up the gut. Czsryunkowiez (pronounced Zun-ko-vitz, silent "r") was one of the working-class white kids on the Warriors, who came from the rural eastern county where Eastern Europeans immigrated to work at a fish-processing plant. "The Zonk," who coincidentally bore resemblance to Miami Dolphin running back Larry Csonka, was a six-foot, 240-pound man-child with the reputation of wrestling alligators, who ran over tacklers like a steamroller.

The other set was called the Montana, after 49ers quarterback Joe Montana, and featured Renny Jenkins in the slot, two tight ends and the Zonk in the backfield, using Ronnie Jenkins's quick release and accuracy to slice and dice defenses with a West Coast ball control passing and power running attack.

I asked Coach Magnusson about his goals for the season.

"Our top goal is not to lose *any* kids to academic ineligibility or the streets. If we can do that, we've done our job, and we all can be proud," he said, leaning forward and nodding his head in conviction.

"On the field, we're aiming for the 4A championship. We've got the talent and the will to do it, and we've been close. Second, it's beat Dolphin in the Draben Bowl. Third is to have the best record in the Quad-County."

Coach Magnusson paused and looked down as if contemplating something bigger. After a few seconds, I got up from my chair.

"Well, Coach Magnusson, it was gr—"

Coach Magnusson's head lifted, his eyes widened, and a grin spread across his face. "Hey Yankelovich, one more thing," he interrupted. "This is off the record, and I better not see it in print, or the two of us are done for the season, you got that?" He temporarily replaced the grin with a drop-and-give-me-twenty look.

"Sure, you can trust me."

The grin returned. "Our kids will be more jacked about beating Dolphin in the Draben Bowl than winning the state championship, that's for damn sure. And I'm not so sure our coaches don't feel the same way. Am I right, Hank? Zack?" And all three coaches burst out laughing.

Building a Better Mouse Trap

Next stop on the Football Preview Guide tour was Great Bay High School, the school closest to the Gulf, known for its Vans-wearing skateboarders and beach skimboarders, BMXers, and pot-smoking heavy metalists, as well as academics and music and arts programs that rivaled Dolphin's. But so far, Great Bay couldn't sniff rival Dolphin's jockstrap in football. Great Bay, home of the Loggerheads, was the newest high school in Dolphin County, opening in 1982 to accommodate the booming development that had spread west toward the Gulf in the previous decade.

Great Bay drew from a solidly middle-class area—parents who wanted to be on the Gulf but couldn't afford it so purchased the next best thing, moderately priced 1970s-era Spanish and Southern-living-style homes only a fifteen-minute drive from the white-sand beaches—and from Conquista Island dwellers, although most of the islanders sent their kids to one of the two prominent private schools in Drabenville.

Great Bay gleamed with halls freshly painted in the aqua-themed school colors of teal and salmon, with state-of-the-art science labs and an auditorium built to accommodate regional performing arts organizations. I met Coach Butch Bachman in an air-conditioned, teal-carpeted coaches' lounge, equipped with a fridge, vending machines, TV/video equipment, movie screen, display case, and two couches. Being so new to Dolphin County football, the display case was somewhat bare, save for a few team photos; the principal, Warner Brix, and Bachman with the team's three all-county players from 1985; a misplaced Nebraska Cornhuskers pennant; the game balls from Great Bay's first game ever (inscribed "Start of Something Great at Great Bay: East Grove 48, Great Bay 6) and first win ever in Bachman's second season (over equally new rival to the south, Lime Bay); and the jersey of a player who tragically drowned in a drunk-boating accident.

Bachman was a hulk of a man whose slight stoop and hunched-forward shoulders shortened his six-foot-six frame. He wore a mop of tousled sandy-brown hair and wire-rimmed glasses. He walked with the nonchalant, loping strides common to beefy big men who carry a lot of weight and need to be careful they don't bump into smaller people who aren't in their line of sight. He resembled a cowboy in a Ford F-series pickup commercial heaving massive bales of hay from the truck bed before hopping out to wrestle a steer, or a brute pulling an airplane in the World's Strongest Man competition.

Bachman grew up in the western Nebraska town of Scottsbluff and played nose tackle at Nebraska's Kearney State College. Bachman indeed was a rancher's son and played football mostly because his high school barely had enough boys to field a team, and, well, he was the biggest of them all. He continued on at Kearney because football money was his only prayer for attending college.

He graduated with a degree in business and did what many budding businesspeople from Kearney did—went straight to work in sales for ConAgra Foods in Omaha. Bachman was the rep for ConAgra's Chef Boyardee and Van Camp's Pork & Beans lines and spent two years traveling a vast heartland territory of Nebraska, Iowa, Kansas, and Missouri in a God-awful wood-paneled 1974 Chevrolet Caprice station wagon whose only saving grace was its boat-like dimensions, which allowed it to carry pallet loads of shrink-wrapped twenty-four-can boxes of Beefaroni and Pork & Beans.

Bachman hated visiting the Hy-Vees, IGAs, Schnucks, and Piggly Wigglys groceries and Kwik Shop convenience stores trying to secure more prominent shelf placement. Not even the addition of Manwich

THREE YARDS AND A PLATE OF MULLET

Sloppy Joe Sauce to his product line could ameliorate the detachment he felt while working deals with middle-aged, balding store managers wearing cheap retail vests, Old Spice cologne, and name tags emblazoned with sayings like "Save Bucks, Shop Schnucks."

Out of boredom during motel overnights, Bachman would tune into any high school or college football game he could find. He found himself analyzing the defensive formations and predicting what play the offense would run and whether the defense was set up in best position to stop it. He started charting games off the TV, literally recording every play, the defensive alignment, the offensive play, and the result. Soon he discovered he could predict offensive tendencies and whether the play would be successful. In a Super 8 Motel in Dodge City, Kansas, one night, sitting on a stack of Manwich he had to deliver to seventeen supermarkets the next day, charting the Friday Night Prep Showdown out of Wichita, it dawned on Bachman that maybe he did have a calling beyond canned food hucksterism: he had a mind for the strategy of football. As a player, he had relied on brute strength and mass to engulf anyone with the pigskin and had paid little attention to schemes. But after two years of this mind-numbing corporate slog, living out of the Caprice rig and one-night-stand motels, he was all about the Xs and Os.

The next day, at a pay phone outside Gene's Heartland Foods in Dodge City, Bachman called his old high school coach to check for any coaching openings in his boyhood area. It happened the coach knew of the pending retirement of a head man in Box Butte County. When Bachman contacted Hemingford High School, the principal was elated to find that a four-year college player was interested in coaching at his tiny school. Heck, his current coach, Berl "Bronco" Devilbiss, had never even finished high school but had climbed the local Pop Warner ranks while working as an Anheuser-Busch distributor.

At the conclusion of his interview, the principal offered Bachman an apprenticeship as an assistant under Devilbiss for one season on the contingency that if all went well, he would be hired as the head man when

BUILDING A BETTER MOUSE TRAP

Devilbiss retired. Because Box Butte County was so sparsely populated—twelve thousand residents over one thousand square miles—as were surrounding counties, not to mention the lack of tax base to pay for equipment, support personnel, and other basics, the only football possible was seven-on-seven. Hemingford had seventy boys in grades seven through twelve from which to choose.

The principal offered a $1,000 stipend and $500 per semester for teaching a General Equivalency Diploma (GED) course. Desperate to get out from under the crushing avalanche of Chef Boyardee Spaghetti & Meatballs, Coach Bachman took the deal and quit ConAgra. He got a job as a ranch hand, working early mornings, coached football in the afternoons, and taught the GED course at night while earning his teacher's certification.

Bachman captured three straight Western Nebraska Seven Shooter championships at Hemingford with a radical, razzle-dazzle offensive system featuring end-arounds, Statue of Liberty, and other ball fakes, and multiple-lateral plays. It was the epitome of sandlot football, missing only a few trees or parked cars on the field as landmarks for diagramming plays. In 1982, Coach Bachman got a call from former colleague Devilbiss, who, in retirement, had traded his Anheuser beer truck for a modular home in Drabenville's Tranquility Waves Villa but still couldn't let go of football. He became a volunteer coach in the local Pop Warner football league, where he met Principal Warner Brix, a fellow coach who was preparing to open the new Great Bay High. When Brix mentioned his search for a young hotshot coach, Devilbiss became his recruiter.

"I reckon yous heard of Nebraska football," he asked Brix, knowing the reference to the mighty Cornhuskers would resonate. "Well, what if I tol' yous I could git yous a reigning three-time Nebraska state champeen coach, r'aught 'ere in Drabenville?"

"I'm interested, Berl. How do I get in touch with him?"

"You jus' leave that to me, and you'll git'cher man. Now, what's it worth to yous?"

"Well, Berl, the board of ed offers five hundred dollars for referrals that lead to full-time hires. And I suppose I could dig up a few hundred more somewhere in our booster fund. That is, if this guy, what's his name…?"

"Bachman, Ballin' Butch Bachman."

"If we hire Ballin' Butch, you'll get yours, Berl."

❖ ❖ ❖

By summer 1982, Coach Bachman was in Drabenville as Great Bay's football coach, stocking the new program with blocking sleds, weight-lifting equipment, goalposts, pads, and uniforms, meeting with the newly formed Loggerhead Booster Club president, and sending all boys redistricted to attend Great Bay a letter to introduce himself and encourage them to try out, with recommended summer training routines.

In my interview with Coach Bachman in the Loggerhead lounge, he told me he was a distant cousin of Canadian Randy Bachman, rockin' lead guitarist of Bachman-Turner Overdrive. I never confirmed that connection, but Coach Bachman demonstrated his familial devotion by blasting BTO tunes from a huge boom box perched on his concrete-block shoulder every day at practice during warm-ups and water breaks—"You Ain't Seen Nothing Yet" before intense, mano a mano survivor drills; "Takin' Care of Business" as his exhausted players, helmets in hand, headed to the locker room; and "Let It Ride" anytime he needed to fire up his troops.

Confident that he had masterminded a dynasty at Nebraska's Hemingford, Coach Bachman installed his bedazzling seven-on-seven offense, which he called "the Mouse Trap" after the odd-contraption board game, or "Mouse" for short, adding a few more moving parts to the chicanery for eleven on eleven. He neglected to consider that the additional four players on each side cause exponentially more chaos and congestion on the field, and that his players didn't have the skills set to pull off intricately choreographed plays while controlling a figurative hot potato. His first season in 1982 was disastrous, an embarrassing bagel, 0–11, in which the team scored six points per game and the same number of turnovers and was led in scoring by a defensive lineman. That season earned Coach Bachman the nickname "The McKay of Great Bay," after John McKay, a four-time national championship winner at the University of Southern California who lost his first twenty-six NFL games as coach of the woeful expansion team, the Tampa Bay Bucs, in 1976/77.

His players loved playing the Mouse offense, knowing that on any given play, three or more players might handle the ball. It was much more fun than the three-yards-and-a-cloud-of-dust-and-pile-of-arms-and-legs style of play that many conservative coaches afraid of losing their jobs employed. But Bachman was smart enough to know he wouldn't be around to run the Mouse if he suffered another winless season, so he modified it into "the Rabbit." The Rabbit featured less risk in ball transactions but more sleight of hand—like a magician pulling a rabbit out of a hat. It depended on the quarterback's ability to fake hand-offs, end-arounds, and passes and hide the ball, so defenders never knew in what direction to go, and by the time they figured it out, they were out of position. And he had just the quarterback to pull it off—a bleached-blond, spiky-haired, pierced-eared, rubbery-bodied skate rat named Dylan "Rowdy" Rawley, who ordinarily would have shunned football as too organized and conventional for individual expression but was captivated by Coach Bachman's eccentric system that emphasized flair and creativity over brute power and disciplined toil.

Rowdy had a Pop Warner background, and the same talents that made him a competitive skateboarder allowed him to shine in the Rabbit—balance, flexibility, and fearlessness. When Rowdy led seven-on-seven drills, Bachman would blast "Rebel Yell"—"She want more… More, more, more, more, MORE!"—because of Rowdy's resemblance to Billy Idol and his rebellious nature. But Rowdy conformed to the structure and togetherness of football enough to become a serious offensive threat and a good teammate and even a leader—not surprising, since he had always led his 'boarder buddies on skating adventures in empty neighborhood swimming pools and on midnight rampages through parking garages.

Growing up in western Nebraska, Bachman was equidistant from the Denver Broncos and Kansas City Chiefs. That meant he also saw the division rival Oakland Raiders four times a year, and that's the team he identified with, the Silver and Black, rebels, renegades, misfits, and larger-than-life characters, the eye-patched pirate on the helmet, the loony fans.

That's the identity he wanted to give his defense, and he found a few characters that fit the mold. Nose tackle Dwight Dumar shaved his head to a sweat-glistened shine and played with an intimidating snarl, which reminded Bachman of Otis Sistrunk, the Raider whose extraterrestrial-looking, steaming bald head and service in the US Marines (abbreviated in the Raiders' program as US Mars) led a TV commentator to announce his college as the University of Mars. Dwight became known as "Otis." Petey Pritchard was a pesky little defensive back with quick feet and a fast motor, the kind of hyperactive kid who couldn't keep his hands to himself. He was always grabbing someone, throwing someone down in gym class, and putting someone in a headlock just for fun. Those annoying habits translated well to the football field, where he would bump and grab and obstruct receivers in ways referees rarely noticed, like Raiders' shutdown cornerback Lester "the Molester" Hayes, known for smearing stickum all over his uniform and hands so he could stick to receivers. It sounded unseemly when Bachman would call out, "Yo, Molester, play bump-and-run," so he G-rated it to Little Mo. And then there was linebacker Dougy Peacock, a gangly six foot five, 180 pounds—the perfect build for Bachman to tag him with the alias "The Mad Stork" after the Raiders' eccentric beanpole Ted Hendricks.

Bachman progressed from winless in 1982 to five wins in 1985, when he spotted an Asian kid on the soccer team who took all the goal kicks, sending each ball past midfield. "If we could get that kid on our team," he told his assistant, French Lytle, "we could do some real damage on kick-offs and field goals. Lord knows, we need the points." He set out to recruit Stanley Chung to football, convincing him that his chances of earning a college scholarship as a football kicker were far greater than as a soccer player. The idea appealed to Chung's parents, part of a new wave of Asian immigrants coming to the area, who ran the Dynasty Cleaners and tried to assimilate by renaming their three boys with the bedrock American but obsolete names Stanley, Norman, and Milton.

The catch song was a no-brainer for Bachman. When the field goal team lined up for practice kicks, Bachman had the CD ready: "Everybody Have Fun Tonight!" by Wang Chung. Stanley Chung had range out to forty-five yards, a significant advantage over other teams whose mostly pathetic kickers were only capable of thirty yards or less.

Bachman liked to make practices fun and get some whoopin' and hollerin' going. Of all the schools, Great Bay's practices were worth the most laughs. If a receiver dropped two balls, a call for "TAU! TAU! TAU!" (Time for Asses Up) reverberated, practice stopped, and players gathered to watch quarterbacks rifle tight spirals from ten yards at the receiver with the dropsies, who bent over for punishment, making his skyward ass the bull's-eye.

Another hilarious, purposeful, but politically incorrect drill was HAM—Hammer a Mannequin. Bachman took discarded mannequins from a closed Dillard's department store, taped foam cushioning around them, and outfitted them with sexy gowns, gloves, shoulder-strap purses, and stylish hats, turning the mannequins into comely tackling dummies. When the defender beat the blocker, he would make a beeline to the ball-carrying beauty and practice textbook tackling technique, head up, shoulders lowered, arms wrapped around the waist, legs churning, driving through the body. When the drill was performed well, the mannequin would be lifted and deposited onto the pole vaulters' cushion, its hat, purse, and gloves flying, its legs tilting skyward, and its dress billowing to expose frilly underwear or frumpy bloomers, enticing hoots and hollers.

THREE YARDS AND A PLATE OF MULLET

In my first meeting with Bachman, I got the sense that he enjoyed winning, but not at all costs, and didn't take all this magnified attention on pimply faced adolescents' performance on the gridiron too seriously.

"I've talked to coaches here, and it seems to me this is an absolutely cutthroat business," I told Bachman. "If you go easy, you'll be eaten alive and out of a job. But you seem kind of laid-back. How do you reconcile your nature with the fierce competition?"

"If it ain't fun, it ain't worth doin'," Bachman responded, dropping a metal ball onto the Mouse Trap and watching the chain reaction begin. "Hell yeah, I'd love to win a state championship, but you know what the odds are of that with East Grove in our division and all the other great 4A programs from Miami to Pensacola? Not great. We'll shoot for that, but we'll have a blast along the way. These kids will have enough time for drudgery when they ain't kids no more. Don't browbeat the kid out of them now, for Chrissakes, like some other coaches I've seen around here.

"Hey, *it's a game, man, for fuuuun*. Football ain't work. It's like my cousin Randy Bachman sang in 'Takin' Care of Business,'" he said, drumming the desk as he belted out a few lines. "It's the work that we avoid / And we're all self-employed / We love to work at nothing all day…"

Bachman chuckled at the thought. "Way to go, Randy."

Two down, two to go. If the next two coaches were anything like Magnusson and Bachman, I was in for entertaining days.

The Palmertown Six

I headed north from Drabenville, over the Blue Fin River Bridge to DeVaca City, named after Álvar Núñez Cabeza de Vaca (in Spanish, "head of the cow"), a sixteenth-century Spanish explorer who led an expedition to colonize the Gulf Coast of what the Spanish called *La Florida*. There, I found my first hint that my job would extend beyond merely covering football.

In many ways, the bridge linked separate worlds, except for the Promenade along the waterfront, with its opulent riverside mansions with verandas, gazebos, and three-tiered decks—in essence an extension of wealthier Drabenville communities like River Overlook. A kid from the Promenade wouldn't be caught dead joining the proletariat at DeVaca City High School, not when his parents could afford one of the private schools in Drabenville or the granddaddy of Catholic prep schools further south in New Palm City, Cardinal Saint John the Pius, which had a powerhouse sports program known to turn out Division I athletes.

DeVaca City (or "the D.C.," as locals called it) was an American throwback town where the old adage rang true: a railroad ran through it, and you knew when you were on the wrong side of the tracks. The right side was known as Old DeVaca City, a working-class, mostly white neighborhood of tidy, modest homes shaded by hulking loblolly pines on arrow-straight, pancake-flat streets and avenues laid out in an unimaginative A-B-C/First-Second-Third grid. It had the traditional Main Street with mom-and-pop diners competing with a McDonald's and a Burger King; drug, convenience, and variety stores; antique and furniture dealers; and clothing shops that were all beginning to lose out to the burgeoning corporate megastores like Walmart that were popping up off the interstate, and more upscale outlets at Drabenville's new Pelican's Triangle Mall. As a claim to fame, the D.C. was the proud birthplace of Voracious Vinnie's All-You-Can-Eat Pizza & Pasta, a franchise spreading like wildfire across Florida.

Just to the wrong side of the tracks was the Roma Rojo Tomatoes Company processing plant and distribution center, which received overflowing boxcars of ripe and green tomatoes from farms to the north. Conveyor belts carried the fruit to be crushed, diced, stewed, peeled, and pureed, mostly by the local African-American workforce and Central American migrant workers who divided their time between the farms and the plant.

Around Roma Rojo and outside the DeVaca City limits on the edges of tomato and fruit groves to the north were clusters of military-style barracks that housed tomato plant processing hands and Central American migrant farm workers. The kids were first-generation US school students, and their parents worked side jobs in addition to their regular hard labor to ensure that their kids would have a chance to graduate high school and take their best shot at the American dream, *el sueno Americano*. So not only did the DeVaca Conquistadors football team have the Tyrones, Javons, and D'Quans, but also the Joaquins, Pedros, and Miguels.

A wrong-side migration trickle started in the 1960s and became a small wave by the 1970s, mixing black families into the historically alabaster Old DeVaca City. These new migrants were from an adjacent yet for all practical purposes faraway and foreign land. Many of the new residents of Old DeVaca City featured the stabilizing force of a male at home. Fathers were typically AWOL on the wrong side, which I toured before meeting DeVaca City High School coach Ricky Huckerbee.

One large community there, Palmertown, was straight out of the Deep South's *Mississippi Burning*—a string of ramshackle neighborhoods of small homes with peeling paint, sagging gutters, and front yard dogs on chains, dotted with community churches, cemeteries, and street corner businesses. But I came to learn that, like the civil rights protestors, the families in these neighborhoods were strong of spirit and bonded in church, at school, in the picking fields, on the factory floors, and at the beauty salons and roadside barbecues. Single moms held Palmertown together. The men drifted in and out of unemployment lines, church pews, liquor stores, and their kids' lives, but there was always a solid corps to coach youth football and baseball and to appear as stalwarts for birthdays, Christmases, Saturday night fish fries, and July 4 parades.

For more than a decade, since the closing of the Palmertown Primary and High School—formerly the Palmertown Colored School—Palmertown students had comprised a pillar of DeVaca City High School. Early on during the melding of races and ethnicities on the DeVaca football team, there were fights, expulsions, and public skepticism, perhaps unmerited and stoked by racial tensions, over whether white offensive linemen were blocking full-out for a black running back, or whether DeVaca's first-ever Hispanic quarterback intentionally avoided looking over the middle for a white tight end.

Coach Ralph LaGarde, DeVaca's old-school coach for twenty years, had lost his job because he and his all-white staff couldn't relate to the different cultures on the team and couldn't blend the "diversity" into one unit where all players had each other's backs and created a harmonious locker room of brothers. Without the brotherly love and with a lack of football experience and knowledge among some players—many of the best Hispanic athletes switched from soccer in tenth grade after realizing nobody cared about the real futbol in their new football-mad homeland—it was a recipe for disaster for LaGarde, and his record for his last three years reflected that, 9–24.

When a young Ricky Huckerbee was hired, he immediately integrated his staff by hiring a successful Palmertown Pop Warner coach and recruiting a former Augustana College teammate of Mexican heritage as assistants. To build rapport and communicate better with his Hispanic players, Huckerbee took a crash course in Spanish and became proficient enough to speak hackneyed Spanglish to them: *"Bu-nos tar-days May-gwel,"* he would greet his quarterback, Miguel Lecha, on the practice field. *"Cwo-mos ay-stas u-stid? Vamanos, mi amigo!"*

I quickly discovered that Palmertown's progressive assimilation into DeVaca City High had been largely undone two years earlier, ostensibly for the altruistic purpose of all-county integration. But there were rumblings throughout DeVaca City that football actually may have been the countervailing force behind the Dolphin County Board of Education's 1984 redistricting decision.

Palmertown was divided into north and south by the major thoroughfare running through DeVaca City, Judge Higginbotham Boulevard. North and South Palmertown had separate youth football teams that competed against each other and other area teams. For years, South Palmertown youth dominated their brethren to the north—and often they were playing against half-brothers, God-brothers, and cousins—practically owning the annual Turkey Bowl game and the Red Ripe Tomato Cup prize sponsored by Roma Rojo Tomatoes from Pee Wees to Midgets up through Ponies and Broncos. Palmertown residents speculated that the reason for the south's dominance may have been natural selection—generation upon generation of superior genetics migrating south, closer to the Blue Fin River and Drabenville—or simply better coaching, club organization, and community support, or a combination of the two.

The precise reason didn't matter to Coach Bamford, Dolphin High, and its boosters. What did matter was that South Palmertown was a hotbed of talent that, redirected through redistricting, could solidify Dolphin High as a perennial state championship contender—or at least that's what I heard from conspiracy theorists throughout DeVaca City. And from what I was learning, their suspicions may not have been so Lee Harvey Oswald–esque.

DeVaca High lost several top players in Dolphin County when South Palmertown was redistricted. These students took the bus over the Blue

THE PALMERTOWN SIX

Fin River to Dolphin High starting in the 1984/85 school year. That first talented group became known as the Palmertown Six and included offensive dynamos Sammy Sammons, Nate "Flea" Hilliard, and Dexter Cartwright, who spearheaded Dolphin High's state championship in 1985. DeVaca City coach Ricky Huckerbee was convinced that it was a football conspiracy engineered by the Dolphin High power elites, and it pissed him off to no end.

OKEECHOBEE UNDERDOG

Johnny Littleman told me that Huckerbee was an acquired taste and not to take anything he said too personally, as he had a big mouth but a bigger heart. I found out what Johnny meant upon introduction.

"For Chrissakes, why does that dang *Dinqy* always har some dadgum green Yankee who don't know jackshit about Flurda hahschool fuhbah? Guess yer big shot editors think us Crackers cain't write. Nothin' personal," Huckerbee said, spitting brown, tobacco-saturated liquid between his upper and lower teeth into a Florida District 3A Athletic Association coffee mug, which I soon found was permanently superglued to his left hand as his personal spittoon.

"You and me might as well git on with knowin' each other. I'm a friend of the media, cuz we don't git bupkus in pub with Dolphin and East Grove cleaning clocks over the bridge and hoggin' the ink. And I'm dang quotable, you'll find that out right quick. Besides, you look like you *might* know yer ass from yer elba; you'll figger it out."

Huckerbee was short and wiry, with sinewy muscles, and walked with a big bounce in his step, spending an extra split second on the balls of his feet, maybe to feel on the rise for a little longer than everybody else.

He wore ratty, faded T-shirts with permanent pit sweat stains, Augustana College gym shorts, Puma cleats, and ball caps with tattered bills, broken in after years of slapping them against his thigh and slamming them into the dirt when his players made frustrating mistakes. The DeVaca City administration tried for years to get Huckerbee to wear the school's official coaching gear, or at least more presentable clothing, but Huckerbee argued that it just wasn't him. The administration gave up trying to change him, as long as he wore official gear on game nights, his kids kept graduating, and the team kept winning.

Huckerbee maintained a year-round, fried-chicken-golden-brown tan and sported sun-bleached, unkempt, hat-head hair suggesting semiannual visits to the barber. He displayed a *Hee Haw*–style grin that showed a mouthful of yellowing and brown-specked Chiclets from years of chomping Red Man chaw.

Huckerbee was a Cracker—a self-avowed native Floridian redneck—and proud of it. In fact, he constantly used the word *Cracker* to describe people, places, and culture, as in "Okeechobee ain't no more Cracker than DeVaca City," and "I did my Cracker duty over the weekend—watched NASCAR and went fishin'."

Once he got to know me, he ribbed me mercilessly about my aversion to auto racing: "Hey, Yank, I'm gonna tell O-Dog we need more De Leon Raceway coverage and assign yer ass out there. Who knows, maybe you can pick up the Ponce Princess for a date," he joked, ending his mockery with a "HooooWHEEEEE!"

He peppered his speech with NASCAR-type invectives like dadgum, goshdang, frickin', doggone, dangnab, and horsepucky, censoring his natural instinct to drop an F-bomb that could land him in trouble. When he got really frustrated with his team in practice, he would let loose with, "MARSHMALLOWS! You got to be kidding me!" or "What the FUDGESICLES, guys?" He was quick to anger, and these expressions would be accompanied by his face rapidly morphing from fried-chicken brown to red-wine burgundy.

He was abrasive, on the verge of shocking, but once I got to know Huckerbee and realized it was just his style, I saw him as loyal, fair, and passionate about his kids and the game.

At five nine, 160 pounds, Huckerbee burned with a Napoleonic complex from coaching against Dolphin and Mirabella counties' Goliaths of the profession at larger schools. That Napoleonic complex also explains how he made the journey from dogged quarterback at Florida's backwater, Class 1A Okeechobee High School to fourth-string walk-on at Seminole Community College, where he set a state community college record for rushing for a quarterback. He was Doug Flutie before Doug Flutie.

Still, no Division I colleges were interested in a five-nine quarterback, but Division III Augustana in Rockford, Illinois, offered the chance to back up starter Ken Anderson, who went on to play sixteen NFL seasons with the Cincinnati Bengals and played his helter-skelter, high-motor style as a senior.

The Conquistadors reflected Huckerbee's scrappy, Napoleonic nature. As the smallest school in Dolphin County, the only Class 3A among three 4A and 5As, it came down to a pure numbers game as far as size and talent went. Dolphin High had 1,300 boys to draw from. Statistically, Dolphin had a three times greater chance to land the six-foot-plus, 200-pound-plus kid than DeVaca did, drawing from a student body of 425 boys. What DeVaca lacked in height and girth, it made up for with heart and spirit, infused through Huckerbee's embrace of the underdog role.

Success for some Palmertown residents meant leaving Palmertown—which had the associated by-product of avoiding redistricting—for Old DeVaca City across the tracks, which promised more possibility of upward mobility. DeVaca City's two best players made that move—running back / linebacker Charles Heyward, and diminutive, speedy wide receiver / cornerback Demetrius "Squiggs" Parker. Charles Heyward (no one called him Charlie or Chuck or Chuckie because if he did, he would quickly be corrected with a stern glare: "My name is Charles. Is that clear?") appeared chiseled from granite. At five eleven, 195 pounds, he was a somewhat undersized but an explosive and cerebral player and the unquestioned, no-nonsense leader of the Conquistadors. To boot, Charles also carried a 3.85 GPA and was the spitting image of Raj from the *What's Happening!!* TV comedy, looking sharp in the school's halls with black-framed glasses and plaid button-down shirts, pressed pants, and dress shoes.

There was no college prototype, six-foot-three, rifled-armed pocket passer to be found in DeVaca City. So Huckerbee held an open tryout for his signal caller and looked for a prospect in his own image. He liked what he saw in the raw, five-foot-nine, elusive, speed burner Miguel Lecha, who also had the best fastball on the baseball team. Combined with even smaller Parker, the two formed a duo that was hard to find among the opposing big bodies and even harder to catch.

At the end of my first meeting with Huckerbee, he sized me up, and with his usual candor, told me what he hoped to get from our relationship during the upcoming season. "Mr. Yankelovich, you 'n' me 'er different. I come from the gator swamps and sugar cane fields of Okeechobee County, where even those slack-jawed yokels from Appalachia would be considered Renaissance men. I reckon yer more comfortable in those ol' N'wingland places with the town squares and church steeples and ivy-covered colleges. Hell, our town square in Okeechobee was Wrong Way Ray's Junk and Guns Emporium. Yer like NPR-AM and ahm like K-ASS-FM. But you'll see I git along with all kinds 'a people; I got to with all the different cultures and kids and parents on this team. I read you like a straight-up gah and ah'll be straight up with you. We'll be jus' faahn if we trade respect for respect. I can tell you respect the little guy, and that's me...That's us. That's DeVaca Conquistadors fuhball."

I felt good about Huckerbee. He was the only coach I could see eye to eye with—literally. He was right, I had an affinity for the underdog.

But now it was time to meet the Big Dog, Jimbo Bamford and his revived Dolphin machine. I had saved the best for last, Jimbo Bamford and the revered Fightin' Dorsals, and it made me a little queasy. If I didn't get along with this outfit, I'd likely be run out of town. Would it be possible to coddle the Dolphin program to stay in good favor while retaining journalistic integrity? My intuition told me Dolphin—and Coach Bamford—would be a rocky relationship, with hard feelings still simmering from the Palmertown Six outcome.

Dolphin Scion

Jimbo Bamford was such a good college player, he became one of three attendees at an open tryout to earn an invitation to training camp with Don Shula's Miami Dolphins. Bamford earned playing time in the Dolphins' exhibition season opener, protecting third-string quarterback Jim Del Gaizo. But even in the 1970s, the trend was toward ever-bigger offensive linemen. Bamford had dropped to 240 pounds after two-a-days in the sweltering Florida summer heat. He was cut after the second exhibition game, which earned him an extra $150 for his drive home.

Bamford got certified as a personal trainer and worked as a fitness club trainer while continuing his own training in hopes that an injury-plagued NFL team might give him a midseason call based on a good word from Shula. During the fall, he checked the NFL waiver wires and injury reports daily to identify teams that could use his services. He had heard countless stories of bums from the street *a la* Rocky Balboa—substitute teachers, delivery drivers, bartenders—who had gotten a call out of the blue from a team in dire circumstances, and who not only made a roster for a partial season but went on to have respectable NFL careers. Herb Mul-Key, who played only one year in college, not only made George Allen's Washington Redskins after attending an open tryout in 1971, but played in a Super Bowl and made the Pro Bowl as a kick returner. Kicker Tim Mazzetti tried out for five NFL teams before working as a bartender at Smokey Joe's for fifty dollars a night near his alma mater Penn, until signing with the Atlanta Falcons six games into the 1978 season and making four game-winning field goals. Hell, even Johnny Unitas was cut by the Steelers as a rookie and worked construction while moonlighting for a semipro team for six dollars per game before latching on the next season with the Baltimore Colts.

But the call never came. He grew complacent about his fitness trainer job, where his prime market was sixty-plus—blue-haired ladies with time to kill and men with flab roles and hunched-over walks—a clientele that made him cringe in disgust and sent him home every day depressed that his exhilarating dream of a football life had crumbled so quickly and absolutely.

So he quit and made the inevitable plunge—joining the family development business started by his grandfather Barnaby "Buzz" Bamford and expanded to new heights under his father, Jed Bamford. What had started as a run-of-the-mill bulldozer and backhoe earth-moving company had grown into one of the premier waterfront land development and home-building outfits on the Gulf Coast, a business that really took off when Jed Bamford partnered with Augustus "Gus" Papadopoulos in the early 1960s. Bamford's crew supplied the grunt labor and handled the unglamorous aspects of creating dream retirement homes and condos overlooking the turquoise-blue waters and dazzling, multihued sunsets of the Gulf's beaches—digging sewer and water lines, clearing and grading earth, laying asphalt, pouring concrete. Papadopoulos Diversified Properties Management (PDPM Inc.) handled the government planning, zoning, and application approval process, architecture, amenities, landscaping design, and home construction, and provided the charm, sizzle, and business connections to buttress the marketing and sales teams.

Jed Bamford made a small fortune, especially by sleepy Drabenville standards, in the 1960s and '70s, as Interstate 95 was extended from Jacksonville to Miami and the proliferation of air conditioning spurred a gold rush-like pilgrimage from the Northeast and the Midwest to the promised land of eternal youth, eighteen holes year round, and 4:00 p.m. all-you-can-eats. Jimbo's older brother Jackson had already joined Jed straight out of college, learning the business as a paving and excavating laborer working alongside seven-dollar-an-hour El Salvadoran immigrants, then as a crew foreman with a refuge in the air-conditioned job-site trailers, before ascending in five years to the executive suite of the corporate office of Bamford & Sons Gulfcoast Development Services Inc. as vice-president.

In the boardroom, there was a chair reserved for young Jimbo as well after he served his apprenticeship. Jimbo had done labor for the company on summer breaks during college and tolerated it—if only for building his strength by carrying bundles of pipe and hundred-pound bags of concrete mix and keeping his weight down by burning thousands of calories daily—so that when he reported to preseason practice at Troy State, he was buff, calloused, tireless, and mentally hardened toward hard work, whether backbreaking labor or pulling on a power sweep. Jimbo Bamford took a quick look at his other employment prospects, but the market for recreational sports management majors was not good, unless he wanted to organize leagues for the beer-swilling, angry, and regretful adult softball player who swears he could have been somebody if only he had gotten a break and now lives vicariously through his own younger self by flopping belly first into second on what should be a stand-up triple and arguing balls and strikes with a twenty-dollar-a-game home-plate ump. That was no job for a winner like Jimbo. So he became crew foreman with Bamford & Sons and, like his brother Jackson, was poised to climb to the management level after three years of running preconstruction operations. The promise of *really* big money as a company executive was not far off if he proved that he had the management skills to squeeze every drop of profit out of the business, and he knew he did. Jimbo was nothing if not confident. He *was* a winner, and his experience in football translated well to the development and construction business: preparation, attention to detail, work ethic, focus, teamwork, endurance, competitor analysis, setting and reaching goals, responding to adversity—it was all the same, only now he'd be dealing with work flow charts, budgets, and workers instead of playbooks, scouting reports, and players.

On the verge of his big move up the ladder, Jimbo started feeling uneasy, like a Parisian street mime getting squeezed inside the imaginary box. He worried that the rest of his life was being gift wrapped and was about to be sealed with a pretty bow, only now he didn't want the present, and as he let it stew longer, he realized that he never had wanted it. Jimbo felt pressure from his dad and Jackson, and even from the ghost of Buzz Bamford, who launched the family on the path to prominence when Dolphin County was a sleepy backwater. If he wasn't going to be one of the sons reflected on the "Bamford & Sons" marquee, who would he be?

Scapegoat

Bamford knew he liked sports. Outsmarting opponents. Out-working and out-hustling. Imposing his will. Feeling superior. Intimidating. Dominating. Winning. Looking at the clock. Seeing a number next to his team that was greater than the other team's. The finality and decisiveness of it all gave him a rush that nothing in business did. Business was infinite, always juggling multiple projects in various stages of development, all the while scoping for new ventures. The completion of one project only meant that PDPM would take the reins and Bamford & Sons would transfer equipment to another plot to move new earth—hardly the motivation for an end zone spike or high-five celebration.

So he called his old college coach DeLand "Bubba" Burnell, the head man at Northwest Florida University, to see if there were any openings for assistants. Burnell offered Bamford a volunteer assistant job coaching special teams and helping with the offensive line and wrangled Jimbo a paid job as coordinator of Intramural Sports and Outdoor Adventures. Bamford reasoned that he'd have money in the bank, in the millions, no matter what he did with his life, as long as Bamford & Sons and PDPM didn't implode in a feud or get sucked down a vortex of greed, and Dolphin County retained its growing reputation as the Nirvana for the newly retired. And if he rose through the ranks to a college head coaching position as he expected, he would be pulling a six-figure salary anyway. He told Jed and Jackson that he'd be leaving the family business to chart his own path.

Sure enough, just two years after Bamford arrived at NWFU, family patriarch Buzz Bamford passed away, leaving Jimbo a multimillion-dollar inheritance. Money wasn't Bamford's passion or driving motivation—he didn't need or want to lead a luxurious, cushy life. In fact, with the football lineman's mentality in his blood, he loved the grind, the struggle, the good fight, digging deep when you think nothing's left inside and finding a spare tank. That's what drove him. To Jimbo, money in the bank symbolized the freedom to pursue his chosen lifestyle. And now, he was set for life, whatever path he chose.

Bamford loved the coaching job. He had no regrets about giving up his corner office and blue blazer at Bamford & Sons. His seat would always be there, but now he saw his future. Within four years, he had joined the paid football staff and worked his way up to offensive coordinator as NWFU became a Division I-AA powerhouse, making deep runs in the I-AA National Championship Play-offs each year against the likes of Southern Illinois, Georgia Southern, and Western Kentucky on the strength of a devastating running game he devised. For two straight years, NWFU led all colleges, Division I and I-AA, in rushing, and NWFU sent a string of offensive linemen and running backs to the NFL. A buzz started growing around Bamford as the next hot coach who would do for a moribund program what Howard Schnellenberger was accomplishing at the University of Miami. ESPN featured Bamford in analyses of potential next hires for major college programs that had just fired a coach.

Burnell sent Bamford to Hattiesburg, Mississippi, two days before High School National Signing Day to make sure NWFU locked up Marquiche DuBose, one of the state's top running back prospects who had verbally committed to the NWFU Pelicans but was quoted in the local papers as giving mixed signals. Burnell called Bamford into his office.

"Jimbo, the vultures are circling," Burnell told him. "I hear recruiters from Jackson State, Southern Miss and Nicholls State have been in the area chatting up DuBose's high school coaches and dropping by his church and barber shop and whatnot. Buncha bastards.

"Jimbo, we got to keep DuBose under wraps for the next two days. This boy ain't the most sophisticated book in the library. No tellin' what might influence him to change his mind. Get 'im outta town until it's time to sign the papers. You know, witness protection-like."

So Bamford trekked across Florida's Redneck Riviera to Hattiesburg to keep the wolves at bay. He met with DuBose and enticed him to take a two-night trip to the Gulf beach town of Gulfport—bringing all of his homework, of course—under the guise of getting some intensive, high-quality tutoring (to lend the trip legitimacy) so he would maintain a 2.5 or better GPA and remain eligible for freshman college ball. It was all on the up-and-up, Bamford assured the future star and his mom. Turned out the "tutor" was Bamford's old pal from Troy State who was working security on a riverboat casino and whose only experience in tutoring was teaching casino floor managers how to spot cheating gamblers.

Bamford was exceedingly careful, even convincing DuBose's mom to pay twenty-four dollars for round-trip bus fare, so he could avoid the impropriety of driving DuBose, and thirty dollars for tutoring, even though it was a hardship for the beauty-salon stylist. Bamford satisfied Ms. DuBose that the small investment would pay off big with her son's full college scholarship at a premier Southern university with an up-and-coming football program.

Bamford booked the room at the Holiday Inn Gulf Shores in his name, met DuBose at the Gulfport Greyhound station, and walked with him the two miles to the hotel overlooking a sugar-white Gulf beach, where he had parked, again with the thought that if he offered no physical assistance or tangible financial remuneration, NWFU would come out of the escapade clean should any NCAA investigators come snooping with their ridiculous rulebook.

Bamford didn't know the NCAA recruiting rules inside and out. He just abided by a few basic principles—no exchanges of money or property, no enticements of material gain, no gifts to relatives, no direct communications too early in an athlete's scholastic career—and that had always been enough to avoid the NCAA Fuzz's magnifying glass, or so he believed. It was just as likely that the NCAA didn't give a shit about a second-rate, AA school in the Redneck Riviera, despite how Burnell and Bamford oversold its modest virtues.

So Bamford secreted DuBose into the hotel room under his name and told him to make himself scarce during the day on the beach or at the arcade on the boardwalk. DuBose gladly complied, changing thirty of the forty-two dollars in spending money he'd brought into coins for arcade games, with the leftover twelve dollars allocated to four McDonald's meals to complement the Holiday Inn's continental breakfast. Scarce, except for the one hour each day during which DuBose was to meet with the riverboat gambler at the library for "tutoring," which consisted of statistics, economics, psychology, and criminology as they related to gambling.

Bamford, meanwhile, camped out in his NWFU van in the Holiday Inn parking lot and made side recruiting visits during the day before a nightly rendezvous with DuBose. On the last night, he pulled DuBose aside and asked him to keep the trip between the two of them, explaining that he didn't want other recruits to feel slighted.

"Sure, coach, I know where you at. We cool," DuBose assured him.

"Then I'll see ya at Signing Day tomorrow."

"I be there. Wouldn't miss it for nothin'!"

❖ ❖ ❖

The next day, DuBose took the Greyhound back to Hattiesburg and arrived at the South Hattiesburg High School gym, where other highly touted local recruits had gathered for the press conference with local media to announce their decisions. The students were lined up along a long table, with every three players sharing one microphone, college ball caps turned upside down in front of them, the school names to be revealed atop their heads when they made their dramatic announcements.

It came DuBose's turn, and he primed the audience with a long, moving lead-in about being the youngest of five brothers, one already dead and another in prison, and how his single mother swore that she would not only shield him from the PCP and crack that doomed her older sons, but that he would be the first DuBose to attend college, so help her God, and how she worked two and three jobs, cleaning rooms at the Super 8 Motel on weekends and waitressing at Red Lobster in addition to her beauty salon gig, so she could buy his Pop Warner uniforms and spiffy clothes for school, because, as she said, if you gonna do good, you gotta look good, and that she was right, that he did good, well, good enough to stay eligible, unlike many of his middle-school buddies, and made grades and SAT scores good enough to be sitting here today, thanks to Mama, and no thanks to Paps, who he last saw in prison when he was eleven, and he thinks now may be pimping and dealing in Mobile, except thanks for showing him the route he didn't want to travel and for the athletic ability that Paps showed as a state-champion 100- and 220-meter sprinter and All-County wide receiver back in his day before the crack strangled his brain and he got arrested and expelled from school with a scholarship in sight, and how just recently he was able to get away from all the pressure and phone calls and recruiting visits to his apartment and clear his head while taking in some peaceful Gulf scenery where he'd never been, even though it's only fifty miles away in Gulfport, thanks to Coach Bamford, and that was all he needed to decide:

"I'm gonna be a Pelican, y'all!" DuBose announced to the sportswriters and sports anchors, who had put down their pens and notebooks in mid-monologue. DuBose grabbed the bill of the Pelicans cap and flipped it in the air, catching it on his head, pulling it tight around his ears. "I'm taking my one-man highlight reel to NWFU, baby," he said, pointing to the front of his NWFU-emblazoned cap. "We be unstoppable. All glory to God!"

Bamford had his man. The junket was worth it. But he cringed when he heard DuBose mention his name. Maybe he hadn't been clear enough that their escapade was an all-in-the-family deal, not for media consumption. Ah, hell, Bamford thought, everyone cheats a little around the edges, and nobody is worse off for it. What difference did it make if DuBose went to NWFU or MSU or SMU or FSU—it was a free ride any way you cut it, a chance to make something of himself and make his mama proud, if not in the NFL, then in life. He knew that any recruiter at National Signing Day was standing on a bed of dirt ten times deeper than his own, and they'd be wise to keep their mouths shut lest someone come 'a diggin'. Besides, no recruiters were paying attention to a teenager's overinflated blather unless it was their own guy, then all the superlatives qualified as nothing less than gospel. No, he was confident that the mention of his name had dissipated into the ether.

So Bamford almost choked on his buttered maple grits at the Hattiesburg Waffle House the next morning before hitting Interstate 10 back to NWFU when he opened the *Delta Valley Beacon* sports section and read this:

> *DuBose said he was undecided between Southern Mississippi, Nicholls State, and Northwest Florida University until the day before National Signing, when he met with NWFU offensive coordinator Jimbo Bamford in Gulfport. "Coach Bamford and me, we tight. Coach says I can be the featured back right away. SMU and Nicholls are more like, 'Wait your turn, rook.' Well, now is my turn at NWFU. NWFU really cares about their recruits. I learned a lot from those guys in Gulfport."*
>
> *Asked what he was doing in Gulfport, DuBose responded, "Just learning about life, man, nothing about football, just life."*

If Bamford hadn't already tossed his grits, he was ready to shit some scrapple bricks. DuBose's quotes were a little cryptic, but there was his name again, in print this time, associated with something a star recruit was doing fifty miles from his hometown.

Bamford went on to spring practice and the fall season, coaching the offensive line and calling plays. As the 9–2 Pelicans were preparing for another run at the Division I-AA championship, Burnell called Bamford into his office for what Bamford thought was a strategy session for attacking the Delaware Blue Hens.

"Jimbo, have a seat," Burnell began. "NCAA Enforcement has been here asking questions about DuBose. Seems someone forwarded an article about his trip to Gulfport way back when. Now, I'm pretty sure we didn't break any rules, but they're digging through every receipt and phone call and goddamned fart and had DuBose create a timeline around Signing Day. They're crawling up my ass, Jimbo, and they're about to bring the hammer down."

"I swear I was careful as hell, Bubba," Bamford protested. "No money, no rides, no promises, no gifts for mama. What the hell, he paid for his own Big Macs. That little blowhard just started running his mouth. I warned him not to. Some SMU bastard must have picked up on it and tried to nail us cuz they couldn't get him."

"Jimbo, I know you're straight up. But we've seen some outrageous recruiting scandals in college football going on right under these clowns' noses, making them look like they're part of the conspiracy. Hell, these booster clubs might as well park a Brinks armored delivery truck with a "Self-Serve" sign outside their recruits' homes for all the efforts they make to hide it. The NCAA ain't lettin' nothin' go now, won't even let a recruit use a university porta-potty. All of a sudden, the rulebook is their Holy Bible, and those clowns are snooping around like a bunch of Jesus Christs, Holier Than Thou.

"Here's the bottom line, Jimbo. They need a goat. It's like some ancient fuckin' sacrificial ritual of the Tutu tribe. We let you go, we get a one-year probation from the I-AA play-offs and a $100,000 fine, and we sweep it under the rug. Never happened. We keep you, and they're gonna ram-dick us with a two-year prohibition on football scholarships and a $500,000 fine. You know what that means, Jimbo? Fuckin' scrawny astrophysics majors and the boy cheerleaders and all the stoners from the Theta Chi House thinking they can nab their fifteen minutes of fame as a walk-on playing against Florida State. I can't do that, Jimbo. I ain't coachin' a team of never-was, never-will-bes. It would ruin us for years, and the president won't tolerate that. Putrid college football doesn't fly in Florida, Jimbo. It don't pay the bills for the research labs, libraries, luxury dorms, and the president's goddamned mansion. Got no option, Jimbo. Sorry."

Bamford knew there *was* another option. Burnell could be the captain who goes down with the ship and fire his own ass. The old ball coach's time was up anyway. Keep dreaming, he told himself. His fate was sealed.

Bamford knew no other college would touch him with the stench of a recruiting violation shrouding him like the cloud over Charlie Brown's friend, Pig-Pen. His short road to a head college job just became a major reconstruction project with potholes and orange barrels and Jersey barriers and detour signs to navigate. He would have to take the route less traveled. Bamford was devastated. He was just playing the game the way everyone played it—to win, by gaining advantage through hard work and passion and outsmarting opponents around the margins. But he'd seen coaches go straight from the high school ranks after dominating tenures to college head jobs—just look at Gerry Faust, who won four mythical national high school championships according to coaches' polls and media ballots at Cincinnati's Moeller High before jumping to vaunted Notre Dame in 1981.

Bamford knew that as in politics, people in sports have short memories and love a redemption story. He was determined to be included in whirlwind time in Faust's elite group—once the DuBose fiasco became a distant memory to college presidents and athletic directors hungry for a winner. His college experience would bolster his resume. And he knew just the pit stop to make it happen.

The Prodigal Son Returns

Dolphin High School had been a powerhouse in Bamford's playing days in the late 1960s, winning back-to-back state championships. By the late 1970s, Dolphin started the slippery slide toward mediocrity that all dominating champions eventually suffer, as complacency began its insidious erosion and several elite private schools and the new Great Bay siphoned off talent.

Worst of all, legendary coach Fred Zipf—Coach Z, the Z-Man, the Big Zipfer, mastermind of the Zipf Code offense and the Zipf-Loc defense, winner of six state championships since he arrived in 1956—was now in his midsixties and suffering from dementia, though no one dared to say it publicly, and his team was experiencing an inexorable decline along with him that reached blasphemous proportions in 1982, a 3–8 catastrophe.

It got so bad that Coach Z couldn't remember his players' names, fell asleep during team meetings led by his assistants, and wandered aimlessly on the sidelines during games, quizzically scanning the stands, pointing and waving at random as much as he watched the game.

Bamford had followed his alma mater's woebegone season from afar through his connections with the Fightin' Fins Alumni Boosters Club. Bamford's connection went from passing interest to keen focus after Burnell dropped the ax on him. He called Fightin' Fins president Landers Pembroke, the father of his teammate on the 1969 championship team.

"Mr. Pembroke, I know Coach Z is still there, and I've got all the respect in the world, but if you're looking for a change, I'm interested.

Me and Coach Burnell had different philosophies, so we parted ways. I'm ready to run my own show, and there would be nothing sweeter than returning Dolphin to prominence."

"Damn glad you called, Jimbo. I heard about some problems up there at NWFU. Wha's 'is name…DuPree? DeBone? We know you here, Jimbo, your character. You come from good stock, the best. You could get your ship right here, prove you're the best in Florida, and have plenty of time to give college another shot. Hey, we're meeting with Principal Bosley next week to see how we can graciously move the old warhorse to the football glue factory and start a new era of pride in the Fin. Bringing Mrs. Z and everything. She's pleading with him to step down with some dignity still intact. Mind if we drop your name?"

"Yeah, do that, and let me know the reaction."

"You got it, Jimbo."

❖ ❖ ❖

Two weeks later, Coach Zipf held a news conference to announce his retirement, Mrs. Z by his side, saying in a halting three-paragraph ode to Dolphin football that he gave the kids all he had, Dolphin was the best place to coach in the country, he enjoyed every moment of the twenty-eight-year ride, and now it was time to spend more time with his family. Mrs. Z held his arm and helped him shuffle away from the podium without taking any questions. Principal Bosley took the podium and swatted away the first and most obvious question: who will replace the legend?

"We're conducting a nationwide search for a coach who will bring Dolphin football back to where it should be, where our parents and the whole community expect us to be, and where Coach Zipf had us for so many years. We're looking for someone who can not only lead boys into becoming fine young men but who can be a pillar of Dolphin County."

Of course, it was a lie—sort of. Principal Bosley had interviewed Bamford before Coach Zipf's announcement and offered him a contract a day later to be football coach and athletic director. They agreed not to announce it for a month out of respect for Coach Zipf, so it would not look as though he'd been forced out callously.

With his hard-driving, no-nonsense style, Bamford brought Dolphin back to the State 5A play-offs, a first-round loss his first year in 1983, and to the semifinals in 1984. But it wasn't until 1985 when the infusion of new talent—not from Drabenville but from over the Blue Fin River Bridge in Palmertown, the Palmertown Six, because of redistricting—that Dolphin got over the hump and reclaimed its rightful place as king of Florida high school football. Detractors complained that Dolphin had reascended to the mountaintop—or in Florida's case, more like the drawbridge apex—with gate-crashers leading the ascent.

But if anyone perceived something amiss about the sudden appearance of play-making talent in Dolphin blue and gold, especially knowing about Bamford's scandalous dismissal from NWFU, nobody dared come forward publicly with his suspicion for fear of committing sacrilege against Dolphin's version of Britain's Royal Family. No, following up on a suspicion and a whiff of impropriety would fall to me, the unwitting and naïve sports reporter new to this steamy foreign land and oblivious to its tribal customs and ruling order.

Bamford was unconcerned with the way he won the 1985 championship. His only concern was doing it again in 1986, proving it was no fluke, and serving notice to the NCAA Division I universe that he was young, hungry, and a winner who could bring millions to a university's coffers. Bamford was convinced that back-to-back Florida 5A championships would stamp him a hot commodity and confer upon him redemption and a big-time college job, and he wasn't going to let anything or anyone stand in his way—least of all a liberal, Yankee, elitist, punk-ass, slightly built, neophyte sports reporter who had never brawled in the line-of-scrimmage trenches and didn't know jack shit about the intricacies of this cunning chess match on grass between helmeted warriors.

It was just that *I didn't know that*. Old Littleman didn't give me that Bamford attaché case during our tour. So I would have to find out the hard way, and in so doing, learn an age-old lesson writ large by the likes of Woodward and Bernstein that even a snot-nosed, spindly, barely pubescent reporter could rival entrenched, mighty, all-but-deified majesty through the power of the pen, and maybe even bring the big kahuna down.

Three Yards and a Plate of Mullet

I met Coach Bamford on an oppressive July day, after taking the wrong road in the Turdmobile, not knowing that Eleventh Street West dead-ends before Ferdinand Boulevard, so I had to reroute, which wouldn't have been a big deal, except for the broken air conditioner, which made me drive with all four windows cranked all the way down, which was like having four hair dryers turned on high blow-drying, only it was blow-wetting, and my increased stress about being late and missing the interview made me sweat even more, so that by the time I pulled into the sandy lot alongside the Dolphin High athletic complex, my elitist, gold, Ralph Lauren Polo shirt (worn purposely to subconsciously ingratiate myself with Coach Bamford by donning a school color) was plastered with sweat to the frying, brown vinyl seat, and I felt sweat droplets plunging from my underarms and splashing on my rib cage, forcing me to find a hallway alcove inside the building and sit Zen-like for ten minutes to allow the AC to slow my perspiration rate and to regain my composure.

Coach Bamford was in his office, which belied Dolphin High School's elite image. It featured old-school, reel-to-reel film projectors and a wall screen, bureaucratic metal file cabinets, a hand-me-down plaid couch, and Dolphin football memorabilia and tchotchkes decorating the walls and shelves. In the athletic wing's corridor outside the office was the football display case, filled with trophies, plaques, newspaper clippings, and retired jerseys, including Jimbo Bamford's 77. One obvious detail of his office was the high standard for organization—everything was neat and in its place. Discipline in all aspects of the program, Coach Bamford believed, translated to on-the-field performance, whether you're talking about the codified arrangement of pages in the offensive playbook or arriving on time to team meetings, a lesson he had internalized in his short time with Coach Shula.

"You the guy from the *Dinqy*?" Bamford barked as I entered the office.

"Yes, I'm Jake Yankelovich. Good to meet you, Coach Bamford," I said as I approached the coach and extended my hand.

Coach Bamford didn't get up or look up from the film projected on the wall and continued scribbling notes.

"Take a seat," he ordered, motioning to the couch. He remained silent for what seemed like an eternity, eyes glued to the images on the wall. I could almost see the football gears grinding inside Bamford's tunnel-vision dome (If we pull-block the A gap on a counter trey to the tailback and lock up our strong-side tight end on the outside LB in the C gap, we'll spring it against the two-deep…). I didn't know whether to begin or wait until he indicated he was ready to talk.

"Wha'd you say your name was," Bamford finally said, the projector still whirring and flickering.

"Uh, Jake, Jake Yankelovich," I responded, admittedly intimidated but also a little irked by the lack of attention. I had a job to do too.

"You caught me at a bad time, Yankerman," Bamford announced, finally swiveling in his chair to face me. "I've got fifteen minutes for you."

Now I started sweating again. I had an hour's worth of questions planned to get through a rundown of his team, an analysis of rivalries, and goals for the season. Now I had to pare it to the bare bones on the fly.

"When we talked on the phone, we booked an hour," I protested feebly.

THREE YARDS AND A PLATE OF MULLET

"Schedule changed. You got to do your homework, son. Didn't Littleman give you articles from the last few years to read? Probably not; guy's a lazy slob. That's not my job. I don't got time to tell you things you should already know if you're a reporter worth your salt. We're wasting time. Thirteen minutes. Shoot."

I asked the most basic, cursory questions to make sure I'd have enough material for the Football Preview Guide, even if not insightful, about offensive and defensive leaders, newcomers, team identity, and style of play.

"What's your offensive philosophy?" I asked, a giant softball.

"Hobie, come on in here a minute," Coach Bamford called to the neighboring office. Offensive coordinator Hobie Schlorf popped his head in the doorway.

"Hobie, what kind of offense we gonna run?" Coach Bamford asked his assistant, leaning back in his chair and clasping his hands behind his head, a sly grin forming as if he knew exactly what was coming next.

"Three yards and a plate of mullet, all night long, Coach," Schlorf responded.

"Next question," Bamford said.

"Coach, can you explain the three yards and the mullet? I don't understand," I said nervously, knowing that if I wrote something so cryptic for the Football Guide, preps editor Skip Blintzer would have a field day asking me questions to which I wouldn't have the foggiest answer. "I know a lot about football, but maybe that's a Florida expression I haven't—"

Coach Bamford stopped reclining and leaned forward across his desk, a deadly serious look on his face. "You've heard of 'three yards and a cloud of dust,' haven't ya?"

"Yes, like the old Lombardi Green Bay Packers."

"Exactly. That's who we are. Power. Smashmouth. Ground and pound. Rush and crush. Break your will, then stomp on it, baby. No excuses and no mercy. That's Dolphin football. And when we're done with the W, we go to the best damn fish fry in town and have ourselves a heaping plate of mullet to celebrate," Bamford said, with Schlorf nodding approvingly in the doorway. "Of course, we're pretty good throwing the ball, too, so if you sell out for the run, we'll burn you through the air until the cows come home."

Time was running short, and I needed Bamford to tell me how he would define success for the season, an answer I already knew, but I needed the quote.

"Dolphin's standard of excellence has always been the state championship, and this year's no different," Bamford said with conviction, his animation increasing after his mullet reference. "We got the pedigree, we got the horses, and we got the moxie, but that's all talk until you prove it on the field. We will; I guarantee that."

Beautiful. A preseason throwdown for Dolphin rivals throughout the region.

I had a minute left. Might as well ask the one question that most intrigued me, based on what little information I *had* gotten from Littleman.

"Coach, several of the leaders you named are from Palmertown. Do you think your team would have won the championship last year and would you have the same chance this year without them?"

"That's a ridiculous question," Coach Bamford bellowed, his face growing red and his voice even more animated, but not in an enthralling way. "That has nothing to do with this team or football, period. I've never been asked such an asinine question. You don't know anything about Dolphin County football, do you? Did someone tell you to ask that question? Littleman? Or are you just an idiot? I know it wasn't Blintzer; he ain't that dumb. God have mercy, Jesus, Mary, and Joseph. I thought I'd heard everything from reporters, but nothing's beneath you guys. You're all the same.

"Yankelson, if this is how you're gonna conduct yourself, we're going to have a rough season, you and me," Bamford said, shaking his head, flicking on the projector, and announcing emphatically over the whir, "Interview's over."

So was my introductory tour of Dolphin County football. Next was the GridFest Jubilee, the real deal. Let the fish fries begin.

GridFest Jubilee: The Smackdown

August 28. Drabenville's Mardi Gras, Cinco de Mayo, and All Saints Day rolled into one. Time for GridFest Jubilee, a Drabenville tradition since the 1960s when there were only four area high schools. Now there were eight in Dolphin and Mirabella counties, and they all convened two weeks after two-a-day practices started, along with their raucous, color-coordinated fans, at Dolphin High's Jed Bamford Field at Roop Stadium, where each school had a section cordoned off for its supporters. So in one-eighth pie slices of seats, you had blue and gold for Dolphin, teal and salmon for Great Bay, red and black for DeVaca, and so forth, making the stadium look like a peacock or a kaleidoscope with psychedelic colors and designs. Fans had their choice of culinary delights from the boiled peanuts cart, the barbecue beef trailer, the smoked-mullet grill, and the corn dog shack.

For football purists, the event was a two-fer—each team played two quarters of football total against two opponents to be determined by a draw out of a fish bowl performed by the 1986 tiara- and gown-bedecked Ponce Princess from the De Leon Raceway, which had bought its way into the hub of the event in a brilliant marketing ploy. The football addicts got eight quarters instead of the usual four to dissect, meaning that the Drabenville bars would be open until 4:00 a.m.—two hours later than usual, as per the GridFest Jubilee Liquor Exception Ordinance passed in 1984 by the Drabenville City Council, which realized that a

GRIDFEST JUBILEE: THE SMACKDOWN

2:00 a.m. closing on GridFest didn't allow the loyalists enough time to debate the strengths and weaknesses of the eight teams and make their season prognostications, especially considering that many fans didn't even make it to the bars until midnight after attending GridFest Mullet Mania in the old fishing village of Balboa Shores, four miles due west of Roop Stadium and billed as the biggest and best damn fish fry on the East Coast, with enough mullet, grouper, snapper, wahoo, snook, and king mackerel to feed an entire crew on a naval aircraft carrier.

Competition in the stands and on the sidelines was nearly as fierce at that on the field. Fans of one team would stand up and hurl clever chants with pointed fingers at rival fans ("Dolphin wears the 5A crown! / East Grove will be going DOWN!"). Cheerleaders, dance troupes, and flag drill teams tried to one-up each other with more flip-in-the-air hang time for diminutive cheerleaders and funkier dance routines in skimpy costumes that skimmed the edge of the school dress code.

The event took on the aura of a community religious revival when clergy from Drabenville, DeVaca City, and New Palm City led the stadium's gridiron congregation in a recital of the Lord's Prayer, a benediction directing God to watch over the players and their families throughout the evening and during the season, and a passionate rendition of "God Bless America" to launch the night's featured event.

❖ ❖ ❖

It was also the first time I met competing reporters from the rival *Drabenville Times-Democrat*, known as the *T-D* (I wondered whether the acronym was coincidentally or purposely related to football); the region's news and sports radio station, WFIN-AM 980, the Fin, which station execs claimed was unrelated to Dolphin High's Fightin' Dorsal Fin mascot (I wondered about that too); and even the freelance sportswriters from my own paper who would be spending every Friday night until Christmas immersed in football, as I would be. After getting to know this motley cast of characters, I knew I would be entertained even if a game was a snoozer.

THREE YARDS AND A PLATE OF MULLET

My *Dinqy* freelancer partner was Mitch Mahotie, the quintessential utility infielder—he did it all, from state play-off football games to girls' volleyball matches, wherever the *Dinqy* would send him for thirty dollars per story and no benefits, and he loved it all. A Long Island, New York, native, Mahotie had a cheesy mustache, a mop of dark hair, greasy skin with residual acne, hangdog eyes, and a wardrobe that came directly from the Goodwill racks, with clownish Hush Puppy and Desert shoes that looked three sizes too big. Mahotie often bragged about winning election to the Dolphin County Mosquito Control Board, claiming how he protected "thousands upon thousands of fine Dolphin citizens from suffering and certain death by the scourge of West Nile virus" and how "larviciding and adulticiding is an incredible power rush."

Mahotie was a big talker and spoke in clichés, such as "let's get down to brass tacks" and "grasping at straws" and "barking up the wrong tree." But his motormouth served him well. He had a knack for finding out shit and getting people to talk to him and breaking stories, and he was a good-enough writer to make him an effective and cheap pinch-hit reporter. Mahotie talked so much that he had the habit of talking to himself, to the point where you didn't know if he was addressing you or just amusing himself with his own banter.

Mahotie once gave me a ride to my car after a game, which is how I knew of his affinity for fast food, as I had to clear the floorboard and the front seat of his AMC Matador of hamburger and fried chicken bags, condiment packets and wrappers, and Styrofoam containers.

The thing that entertained me most about Mahotie was when, without warning, he broke into his *Gong Show*–like song and dance performance of the 1985 Chicago Bears Shufflin' Crew's one-hit wonder, the "Super Bowl Shuffle," the amateurish rap video of the dominating team made famous by Walter "Sweetness" Payton, Jim McMahon, William "the Fridge" Perry, Mike Singletary, and others who rapped a verse. Mahotie had all the players' parts memorized, and as he sang the chorus, he laid down the most ridiculous soft-shoe tap dance with bigfoot-sized Hush

GRIDFEST JUBILEE: THE SMACKDOWN

Puppies floppin' that I'd ever seen. ("We are the Bears Shufflin' Crew (flop-flop) / Shufflin' on down, doin' it for you (flop-flop, flop-flop).")

At GridFest, Mahotie was working the sidelines, grabbing interviews with coaches and star players as they left the field after their quarter of action. Mahotie was my sidekick, but our act paled in comparison to the puppeteer of the *Drabenville T-D*'s sports operation, high school preps director and sportswriter Tab Reindollar, who was watching the action closely from the press box as he coordinated the actions of his four sideline reporters and press box gopher marionettes.

As slovenly as Mahotie appeared, Reindollar was just as meticulous. He wore pleated pants and bright Polo and madras shirts, and tasseled loafers and outdoorsy Bass shoes, which made him look more like an activities director on a cruise ship than an ink-stained wretch in the newspaper's toy department. He stored a pencil behind his ear, always at the ready, and notebooks in the inside pockets of his stylish sport jackets, the kind you'd see members of Duran Duran or the Human League wearing with rolled up sleeves on *Friday Night Videos*. Tab was tall, six two, and looked erudite with dark-framed glasses, and he walked erect with a purposeful air of confidence. He was the unquestioned leader of the *T-D*'s sports staff, constantly feeding information and tips and ideas to his top henchmen, Ernie McCorkle and Donny Monday.

Reindollar was a Southern gentleman—he was competitive as hell and always working, but you'd never know he wanted to beat you to a pulp by how pleasant he was in person. In that way, he was the silent assassin. I had many a sleepless night wondering what scoop would turn up the next morning in the *T-D* under Reindollar's byline, and indigestion-inducing afternoons chasing down the next-day bread crumbs of his stories.

While the sight of Reindollar at any event or the mention of his name by someone I was interviewing put the fear of God in me, his preps beat reporter and high school sports columnist Ernie McCorkle didn't scare me at all. McCorkle was roly-poly, a Mr. Potato Head look-alike, with tight Jheri curls, wire-rimmed glasses, bushy eyebrows and mustache, and a high-pitched laugh that belied his rotund physique. In his columns,

THREE YARDS AND A PLATE OF MULLET

McCorkle constantly made references to his hometown of Youngstown, Ohio, where he also went to college at Youngstown State and worked as the assistant sports information director during the era of longtime Eagles quarterback Ron Jaworski, "The Polish Rifle," whom he always found a way to work into his column, as in, "DeVaca's Miguel Lecha reminds me of a young Ron Jaworski with his arm strength," or "Great Bay's Dylan Rawley has a natural instinct for making the right decision, making the Loggerheads a factor this year, just like the Polish Rifle's smarts turned around the hapless Eagles." He often reflected nostalgically on his hometown roots, saying he sometimes missed the grit and grime and Polish delis, Victorian mansions, and bygone industrial might of Youngstown but had no regrets about leaving it for the sunshine and blue waters of Drabenville.

Finally, there was Donny Monday, the part-time columnist who seemed to have free rein to write his "Monday Morning Quarterback" column about whatever he wanted and was an unabashed homer for Dolphin High, where both he and his two sons were alums. I guessed that his column space might have been a quid pro quo for bargain deals for the *T-D* at Drabenville's Bob Beemus Ford, where Monday was sales manager and director of used-car acquisition. Monday was a foul-mouthed chain smoker, never without a pack of Marlboros in his shirt pocket, with a raspy voice and relentless smoker's hack. Monday had that typical Florida look of an aging male who ingested nicotine for breakfast and spent too much time unprotected in the sun and in the pool. His skin was dry and wrinkly and edging toward the color of rotting carrot, and he wore his wispy and brittle hair in a full-stretch comb-over, attempting to hide looming baldness. Monday was also opinionated and entertaining as hell, the type of guy who had no filter, who would say aloud what others might think but were too polite or respectful to say. His ongoing verbal jousting with the local sports radio personality, Walter Kornbaum, was always a hoot for everyone in the press box.

Walter Kornbaum, the sports voice of WFIN-AM 980, host of the Whalebait Wally Show, was rotund, large, and in charge. If McCorkle was

GRIDFEST JUBILEE: THE SMACKDOWN

plump, Whalebait was downright corpulent, a wobbling sumo wrestler. When Wally sat in a chair, he didn't just perch on it, he enveloped it. You couldn't miss his presence physically, but just in case you did, he always announced it loudly whenever he walked into a press box—or any room, for that matter—with his "Anchors aweigh, whalers!" greeting. He had his own lingo for his talk show, opening with: "I'm Whalebait Wally here to talk local sports, and I'm looking for some chum. Steve in Bougainvillea Estates, you're my first chum tonight. Go ahead and blow." His callers were cetaceans, the order of marine mammals including whales. He labeled his callers who had the most bombastic takes "Orca"; those who were feeble were "Planks," as in plankton; frequent callers were "Humpbacks"; and those who liked to argue were "Squidaholics," because, as Wally said, they were addicted to being devoured by the highest order of Cetacea, Whalebait himself.

He was from New Jersey and had that New York wit, acerbity, and sensibility. New Jerseyites and New Yorkers can break one of two ways: they can walk by a stranger being assaulted in the street and go on their merry way, not blinking an eye; or they can be that stranger's sudden guardian angel. I saw Wally as the latter. He had a huge soft spot once you got past his blowhard exterior; he was always sponsoring radiothons for needy kids and library programs and cancer patients and hospice organizations—the comfort-for-the-dying homes, in particular, having crushing budget demands in this retirement mecca—drawing on his connections with local sports celebrities to raise money and visibility. He was even known to cry on air.

I had to do battle against the *T-D* in its home territory with a much smaller staff, usually just me and freelancer Mahotie, and whatever assistance Blintzer—who, of course, took the cushier, noncompetitive Mirabella County preps coverage for himself—could provide from afar. But at least I had a stringer who could back us up when we were stretched thin or contribute to stories, Bert Halumka. If Jimbo Bamford was the poster child for the bully who shoved scrawny middle-schoolers into lockers, Halumka served in the same role for the victim. Halumka had an extreme overbite that made him appear to be a slack-jawed, borderline mentally retarded hillbilly from *Deliverance*'s Aintry backwoods (Mountain Man: "Now, let's you just drop them pants." Bobby/Ned Beatty: "Drop?" Mountain Man: "Just take 'em right off...I bet you can squeal like a pig." Bobby/Poor Ned: "Weeeeeeeee!"). This unfortunate genetic characteristic, which Halumka's parents obviously didn't have the orthodontia money to fix, combined with his Coke-bottle glasses, the kind for the nearly blind, belied Bert's intelligence, enthusiasm, and get-after-it nature. Those who took him for a fool quickly were proved wrong.

Halumka had wavy black hair and long sideburns, mutton chops at least a decade out of style, but I'm not sure if he wore them that way out of preference or just didn't know how to shave them. Halumka's quirk was giving himself continual hits of Binaca Blast, as if breath as sweet as mint leaves would make up for his genetic homeliness. Halumka's primary job was assistant manager at the Southern Smorg All-You-Can-Eat, where he purposely worked the lunch shift on Fridays and Saturdays so he'd be available to cover evening high school football and basketball games. Halumka grew up in Drabenville and graduated from East Grove—one of the trailer-trash white—and was a high school football junkie with steel-trap recollection of each school's football history, their current rosters, previous year's players' stats, and head-to-head results of each team's eleven-game schedules dating back five years. Halumka's football knowledge was invaluable to me, and I was glad to have him on my side. But ask Bert to name one player on the Tampa Bay Bucs, and he couldn't do it; he was that provincial.

❖ ❖ ❖

Halumka was my gopher, undermanned against Reindollar's *T-D* harem, gathering color along the sidelines and quotes from the two opening-act Dolphin County teams, Great Bay and DeVaca, while I focused on the headliners, East Grove and Dolphin.

GRIDFEST JUBILEE: THE SMACKDOWN

As fate would have it, for the second round of quarters, the Ponce Princess drew East Grove and Dolphin out of the glove compartment—substituting for a fishbowl—of a new Bob Beemus Ford Bronco, setting up a pairing for the final quarter that would make the rest of the GridFest's matchups seem superfluous. East Grove versus Dolphin, the top of the marquee, the title fight, what everyone came to see, a preview of the Thanksgiving Draben Bowl, Dolphin County's Super Bowl. You had to wonder whether De Leon Raceway, Bob Beemus Ford, and the Fightin' Dorsals' boosters club had conspired to rig the Bronco's glove compartment so East Grove and Dolphin would be the only cards left, so the fans would get the show they wanted.

I took copious notes on all the Dolphin County teams. Yes, DeVaca quarterback Miguel Lecha had a gun and Great Bay quarterback Rowdy Rawley had a reckless flair; Great Bay's offense was an anomaly compared with the seven other basic vanilla variations for its trickery and high-risk ball handling; and DeVaca's defense reflected Coach Huckerbee, undersized, fiery, and scrappy as hell. But my main focus was East Grove and Dolphin, based on Blintzer's marching orders, so I channeled my observational and analytical energies into the last quarter.

At the night's outset, I instructed the *Dingy*'s top sports photographer, Henry Bendbough, who would be my sidekick on Friday night games, to save his best work for the East Grove versus Dolphin quarter, and to make sure he got a money shot of coaches Bamford and Magnusson greeting each other at midfield after the quarter; I was sure we could use that shot in countless features and advance stories leading up to the Draben Bowl.

Bendbough resembled Shaggy from *Scooby Doo*. He earned the moniker Bend-Over, which was really a tribute in his line of work, because he excitedly accepted any assignment the editors threw his way, mornings, nights, weekends, days off, and holidays—4-H fairs and ground breakings—it didn't matter, even if it meant whatever plans he had would be screwed. He chugged two sixty-seven-ounce bottles of Mountain Dew daily, saying it kept his energy up. He was tall and rail thin, about six four,

160 pounds, including all his dangling camera gear. He was only twenty-six, but looked about forty with his scruffy beard, receding hairline, and long, flyaway hair, which trailed him in an L-shape as he scurried after his subjects in a forward-bent run-walk with long, loping strides like a cigar-chomping, stooped Groucho Marx, cameras and bags and lenses swinging from his bony shoulders and slapping off his back and around his hips. Bendbough always talked about his post-late-night-assignment escapades with a woman he called "Wicked Juanita," who was seemingly ethereal, like Blintzer's mystery wife.

I once hung out with Bend-Over after a game at his tiny studio apartment in a one-story strip complex that could have doubled as a one-night-stand fleabag motel, and had to dance around his four darting cats, which leaped from windowsills to the frayed couch to their scratching posts. The apartment was jammed with camera and darkroom equipment, and framed photos—including a few presumably of Wicked Juanita, always clad in black—on the floor and stacked on chairs, and photography and vintage-car magazines and artwork. I was worried that one day I would read an obituary of Bend-Over, with the cause of death listed as "buried by hoard in apartment." Since we kept the same hours at the same events, Bend-Over and I became semiregular late-night drinking and chick-scoping buddies at the Pirate's Ransom Lounge at the Drabenville Holiday Inn Waterfront, where I finally did meet the vampiresque Wicked Juanita, a knock-off of Herman Munster's ghoulish wife, Lily.

As Dolphin and East Grove took the field for the GridFest grand finale, the teams' fans on opposite sides of the stadium kicked off the battle before the kickoff.

"Dolphin is king in town / East Grove is goin' down!" blue-and-gold-clad Dolphin students and parents stood and chanted.

With more funk and swagger, the orange and brown Calusa Warriors' side retorted: "East Grove's got the Jenkins boys / C'mon Warriors, let's make some noise!"

The fans battled to a draw, but on the field, it was no contest. Led by the Palmertown Six, Dolphin rolled to a 20–0 lead behind two long runs by Sammons and Hilliard and a signature Fightin' Dorsals ground-and-pound drive.

After East Grove failed to convert a fourth down on Dolphin's forty-two with thirty-three seconds left, fans started heading for the gates to get a head start for the Balboa Shores fish fry. The Dolphin offense returned for what presumably would be the final dive play before players from all eight teams joined hands and ringed the field—a tradition called the Ring of Fire and formed to the sounds of the iconic Johnny Cash tune, "I went down, down, down, and the flames went higher"—for another tradition, the post-GridFest prayer led by the ecumenical gathering of clergy.

But when Sammons pulled the ball out of the fullback's gut, dropped three steps, and set to throw, fans stopped descending the stands and paused before exiting the gates to see what was unfolding.

Sammons pump-faked left to Hilliard to freeze the defensive backs, and then unleashed a tight-spiral bomb to a streaking Dexter Cartwright, another Palmertown Sixer, down the right sideline. Cartwright caught it in stride at the East Grove twenty-five, ten yards beyond any defender. He high-stepped into the end zone, holding the ball aloft and nodding his head tauntingly, until his teammates arrived to mob him.

As soon as I saw Sammons make the fake, I bolted the press box to round up my motley crew on the sidelines.

"Gentlemen, we're going to have an iconic moment after the final whistle, and we need to capture it. Bend-Over, focus on the coaches' faces as they meet. Snap the shit out of 'em; there's gonna be sparks flyin'!

"Bert, go ahead on the field right after the whistle and try to hear what Bamford and Magnusson say to each other. Then stick with Magnusson and get his reaction, and I'll tail Bamford."

I sent Bert on the field because I didn't want to get tagged by overzealous Dolphin security manager Lerch Lessard, whose overinflated sense of duty made him believe he was Dirty Harry, and reported to Paddy for leaving the sidelines too early and interfering with end-of-game traditions. Bert was more expendable, looked more the part for prison, and would do a better job of playing dumb.

As Bamford and Magnusson headed to midfield to greet, players and coaches from all eight teams formed a ring around the field and held hands for the traditional post-GridFest prayer.

Following my advice, Halumka and Bend-Over sneaked inside the ring and onto the playing field as the melee of bodies stumbled toward forming the connection. The two offbeat stragglers weren't noticed by Lessard and managed to get within lassoing distance of the two coaches. An adroit Bend-Over had skillfully changed to his longest of four lenses while moving his way through the scrum.

Bamford stuck out his meaty hand at midfield but Magnusson didn't take it. From what I already knew of Magnusson's integrity and character, his refusal could be interpreted only as an extraordinary symbol of protest. Through the ring of players, I noticed Halumka scribbling notes furtively and saw both coaches become animated, jawing and gesturing. Bend-Over had staked out his territory and had his eye glued to the viewfinder, no doubt snapping furiously in his photographer's crouch, circling the two combatants like a matador sizing up a bull.

Fortunately for me, the *T-D*'s McCorkle was his lackadaisical self and waiting by the locker room for coaches. I saw Mahotie flip-floppin' around the Ring of Fire looking for key players to interview. What shocked me was that the astute Reindollar was nowhere to be found, apparently oblivious. He must have been in the bathroom, gabbing with the blowhard Monday, compiling stats or writing his story, when Dolphin eschewed the unwritten law of sportsmanship and chose to rub East Grove's nose in dog shit with the last-second trick to run up the score in a blowout. The *Dinqy* would have the exclusive on this explosive encounter, and my motley crew did not disappoint.

Once the Ring of Fire broke and the players swarmed midfield, the two coaches, each tugged by assistants, separated without a handshake and stomped off.

Seeing the two passionate adversaries quarreling face-to-face and vying head-to-head for supremacy in the game depicted in terms of war—bombs, blitzes, flankers, suicide squads, gunners, interceptions, Raiders, Patriots—I couldn't help but think of the movie I had just seen, *Platoon*,

GRIDFEST JUBILEE: THE SMACKDOWN

and Charlie Sheen's line about his unit's warring leaders of two factions, Sergeant Elias and Sergeant Barnes, as the military helicopter whisked him away from the hell of Vietnam: "The war is over for me now, but it will always be there, the rest of my days. As I'm sure Elias will be, fighting with Barnes…for possession of my soul." Elias as Magnusson, soulful and compassionate and affable, who was fragged in the jungle by compatriot/nemesis Barnes as Bamford, ruthless and menacing and hard-bitten and emotionally void. Magnusson, running out of the dense jungle after Bamford fragged him, chased by a legion of Viet Cong, as Bamford watched remorselessly from the airborne helicopter. Of course, I empathized with Elias, but damn if that Barnes wasn't one badass MF'er.

The Saturday *Dinqy*, which outsold even the Sunday edition during high school football season, featured a huge headline, "GRIDFEST SMACKDOWN," and a monster color front-page, tight-shot Bend-Over photo of a red-faced, brow-knitted Magnusson pointing a finger near Bamford's grill, with Bamford looking a cross between dumbfounded and bemused. You could see the lines in their faces, sweat on their necks, the flare in Magnusson's nostrils—superb work by Bend-Over, who celebrated with me and night prowler Wicked Juanita at 2:00 a.m. at the Pirate's Ransom Lounge with three Red Stripes in rapid succession. The caption read:

> *East Grove coach Gunnar Magnusson shows displeasure with Dolphin coach Jimbo Bamford, refusing midfield handshake after finishing on short end of 27–0 GridFest Jubilee thumping.*

I jacked this lede out of the park; so said Paddy and even Chenault, who merely tolerated the testosterone-overloaded sports scene:

> *More than 300 football players from eight Citrus Coast high schools grappled in Friday night's twenty-eighth Annual GridFest Jubilee, but the Main Event turned out to be more WWF than NFL: coaches from powerhouses East Grove and Dolphin squaring off at center ring over*

the perception that Dolphin humiliated its crosstown rival by running up the score.

And Halumka's quotes from the midfield meeting of the minds made for compelling dialogue to amplify the lede:

"That was bush league, Jimbo, and you know it," Magnusson charged, pointing his finger at the Dolphin coach. "We teach our kids to respect themselves and our opponents. I don't know what you're teaching yours, the value of humiliation?"

"We play to win. We play to score, period. That's football," Bamford retorted. "If you don't like it, play some defense...Or drop down to 3A with DeVaca."

"We're not going to forget this; we're going to remind you right here on this field. See you in November," Magnusson shot back.

"We'll be waiting," Bamford said. "You didn't even see half of what we got tonight, and you're complaining that we should go easy. Better tell your boys to buckle their chin straps up tight for the Draben Bowl because we don't go easy on anybody."

The *Dinqy*'s GridFest showdown coverage was the talk of the Citrus Coast's sports community for the next week, even preempting the usual tripe about the latest NASCAR standings during my routine Wednesday night visit with Crash and his crew at the Float Inn.

If the regular season proved to be anything like GridFest, I was likely to be on a constant adrenaline-fueled high—along with Mountain Dew–stoked Bend-Over and Binaca Blast–injected Halumka and flip-floppin' Mahotie. Unfortunately, though, adrenaline highs are typically followed by empty-tank lows, and I intuited that I would likely be visiting that pole as well.

The Yarmulke Yeti

As I was writing the "County Players of the Week" column early in the football season, I got a call from the do-it-all headmaster and athletic director of the new Father Ignacio Our Savior Episcopal School, Biff Scully. Biff was a founder of Father Ignacio, the first private school in Dolphin County that had an athletic program, and an endless promoter along the lines of boxing's Don King and baseball's Bill Veeck. He was always calling me to tout the county's next great athlete, who could (supposedly) dunk as a seventh grader, or a gimmick like starting the first fencing team on the Gulf Coast.

"Yank, I got a great story for you," Biff began.

Oh, shit, I thought. How can I get rid of this loquacious schmoozer quickly without seeming rude and losing a good contact so I can meet my deadline and get to Dolphin's practice in time to gather quotes for tomorrow's story? I liked Biff's enthusiasm, but whenever he called, I needed a half hour, at a minimum.

"We've got a new English teacher and basketball coach, Shlomo Grubner, played Division I. He's going to be trying out for the Citrus Coast Sea Nettles, the new Continental Basketball Association team. We've got the tryouts right here in Father Gill Gym; you should come down and cover it."

I wasn't sure if Biff was running a publicity stunt or if this could be the real deal, a combo high school English teacher by day, semipro basketball player by night.

"Where did...what was his name again?"
"Grubner, Shlomo Grubner, from New York."
"Where did Grubner play his college ball?"
"Villanova."
"Wow, that's impressive. Let me talk to him."
"You got it. I'll have him call you tomorrow after school."

❖ ❖ ❖

The next day, as Biff promised, Grubner was on the line.
"Mr. Scully said you wanted to interview me."
"Yeah. I'm gonna be covering the Sea Nettles. I hadn't really planned on writing about them until preseason camp, but since you're trying out, that could make a good feature. Mr. Scully said you played at Villanova—were you a reserve on the '85 championship team?" I asked, probing to get some compelling inside stories from a benchwarmer about the low-seeded Rollie Massimino-coached team that famously toppled the heavily favored, Patrick Ewing-led Georgetown Hoyas.
"Villanova? I once played against Ed Pinckney in AAU, but no, he got that wrong. It's Villa Janis, Villa Janis College. It's Division III. I started at center my junior and senior years."
I should have known. Biff, the hyperbole machine, was at it again.
"Villa Janis? Isn't that an all-girls school?"
"It was till the 1970s. It's real liberal artsy-fartsy. Merry Lynn Stripes went there; you know, the actress? You probably know that. Everyone thinks all the students are like Merry Lynn Stripes. Most of the guys *are* like Merry Lynn Stripes."
"Why'd you go *there* for basketball?"
"I didn't. I went there to get laid. But I found out there were a lot of lesbos, and a lot of the others were granola girls with hairy armpits and tank tops and Birkenstocks, and I wasn't into that. So I thought I'd have a

big advantage with a 75–25 split, but it turned out to be more like 51–49, if you didn't count the lesbos and granolas."

I tried to muffle my laughter, but I couldn't contain it. I was cracking up. I had to ask Grubner in a choking voice to hold on for a minute while I put him on hold so I could finish laughing and wipe the tears from my eyes.

"OK, I'm back. So…"

"Haven't you ever done it with a granola?" Grubner interrupted. "They're usually switch hitters, so you can't count on any relationship lasting too long. Eventually, they want someone sensitive they can talk to and don't care about the salami, so they find a Striper on campus. But it's not bad if you can get used to the hairy armpits and leg stubble. You have to ask them to use deodorant."

I cracked up again and I heard Grubner starting to laugh. Where was this guy's filter? This guy was a real character. I composed myself and got back to business, though I was tempted to pursue whether he had had any lesbo escapades at Villa Janis just for kicks.

"So, Villa Janis College. Who do you guys play?"

"We play some other gay schools like Sarah Lawrence and Skidmore and some geeks like Rochester Institute of Technology. But in my senior year I went up against the Dutch Boy in the Paint two times and held my own. One time I dominated him. It was one of my best games."

"Who's Dutch Boy in the Paint?"

"Rik Smits, the Dunkin' Dutchman from the Netherlands. He goes to Marist College—they're right across the river from Villa Janis in Poughkeepsie. He's huge, seven four. He'll be a first-round NBA pick. But I could play him; that's how I know I have a chance for the Sea Nettles.

"My best game was against Fredonia State. I was in the zone. I had five dunks and six blocked shots. I hardly remember any of it; I smoked two doobies before the game."

"Doobies?"

"You know, joints. Mary J. It helped me relax. Unfortunately, it also killed my motivation. I probably could have gotten a Division I scholarship instead of going to a chick school if I wasn't a stoner in high school."

"So where'd you get a name like Shlomo? The only other Shlomo I've heard of is Shlomo Glickstein, the Israeli tennis player."

"My grandparents were hayseeds from Lithuania—"

"Lithuanian rednecks?"

"No, Hasids. Hasidic Jews."

"Oh."

"My dad is Shmuel, and my brothers are Shmikel and Zev. We were part of the Brooklyn Hasid community, but my dad became Americanized and we moved to Yonkers and kinda left our heritage behind. I was glad to stop wearing the black clothes and hat—I was so tall it made me stand out even more. But I still wore my yarmulke during games. I was known as the Yarmulke Yeti in high school."

"What's a Yeti?"

"You know, the abominable snowman of the Himalayas. Sasquatch... bigfoot. Haven't you heard of bigfoot? He starred in a *Six Million Dollar Man* episode."

"All right, we'll cover that later. We're getting off track. How will I know who you are at the tryout?"

"Just look for the dorky Jewish-looking guy with curly dark hair and a big nose. I'm the stereotype. Can't imagine there'll be another one."

"Shouldn't be too hard—not many of you trying to play pro ball on a team other than Maccabi. See you Friday in Father Gill."

❖ ❖ ❖

THE YARMULKE YETI

When I arrived at Father Gill, I picked out Grubner immediately. He was one of only five white guys and a couple of Hispanics from South Florida schools among the twenty or so candidates. They were divided up at four baskets with Grubner joining the centers working on low-post moves. He was a load, six nine, 260 pounds, according to the tryout roster the Sea Nettles PR guy handed me.

During a break, I introduced myself.

"You must be Shlomo."

"How'd you know?"

THREE YARDS AND A PLATE OF MULLET

"Curly hair, big nose. The other white guys are pure goyim."

We shared a laugh at the silly religious slur.

I could tell Shlomo liked to laugh, even at his own expense. Some big guys are intimidating and menacing; others are goofy and self-deprecating and become conspicuous targets for good-natured ribbing. I knew that Shlomo was the latter.

"Hey, where are you living?" I asked.

"I'm in the Camelot Cay Apartments over on Seventy-Fifth Ave and Tierra Hacienda. Hey, I need a roommate. Scully doesn't pay shit for rookie teachers. Where are you?"

"I'm at Whispering Willow, over by the Float Inn Bar—you know, the place with the palm trees and hammock and neon wine glass on the roof. Going month to month. You're closer to the beach, right?"

"Yeah, it's a straight shot down Hacienda, only four miles. It's right next to Albertson's and Bennigan's. Hey, you lookin'?"

"Yeah, the Willow is kind of a pit. Lots of drifters, boozers, and sluts."

"I hear ya. The Cay ain't no Camelot either. More like the Garden of Eden with all the frogs and little lizards running around. But we've got a lot of characters living there and some hot chicks, maybe cuz it's close to the beach. You should check it out."

"I will, I will."

❖ ❖ ❖

I watched as Shlomo returned to the court for skills tests. Amazingly, he outperformed all centers in drills requiring fast-twitch jumping and touching the backboard for thirty seconds and making hook shots with alternating hands off post feeds for a minute. Shlomo kinda looked like he belonged.

The real test would be the scrimmage, where Shlomo would go up against former midmajor college players from places like South Alabama and College of Charleston, some of whom had tryouts with NBA teams or prior CBA experience.

Shlomo was a sub for the Red team in a twenty-minute, no-time-stoppage scrimmage. With seven minutes left and Red's starting center running on fumes, the Sea Nettles' assistant coach eyed his roster sheet and looked down the bench.

"Janis!" he commanded, giving Shlomo the come-'ere hand signal. Shlomo bounded to the coach's side, towering over him as the coach extended his arm to put a hand on Shlomo's shoulder.

"Go in for Stukes; he's gassed. You better show you're in better shape. This ain't pussy ball—there's some hungry dudes out there scrapping for a living.

"Hold your ground on D. Axelrod's got a big butt, and he'll use it to clear you out. And use your hook shot just like in the drill."

With that, the coach gave Shlomo a push on the butt on a dead ball break to propel him onto the court. Shlomo sprang like a deer, nearly running Stukes over as he gave him the heave-ho back to the bench. He took his spot in the lane on defense, taking little hops and waving his arms as Yellow's point guard brought the ball over half court. I could nearly see the adrenaline pumping through his veins. He was twitching like one of those jittery, sweaty, guilty-as-sin executives chain-smoking and feigning innocence during a gotcha interview by *60 Minutes*'s Mike Wallace. I knew Shlomo would have to do something aggressive quickly to release some nervous energy and stop acting like a heroin addict in withdrawal, and he did.

Axelrod caught an entry pass in the post, back to the basket. Shlomo bodied up to him, expecting to fend off a butt thrust. Instead, a surprisingly nimble Axelrod spun, pinned Shlomo with his left arm, and opened a straight path to the hole. Knowing he was beat, Shlomo made a quick recovery and reached out to try to slap the ball from Axelrod's hands from behind. But Axelrod already had the ball above his head, rising for a dunk. Shlomo caught his shoulder, causing Axelrod to fall backward awkwardly on his back, his head snapping back and hitting the floor.

Axelrod writhed for a moment with Shlomo standing over him, offering him a hand up. Axelrod knocked Shlomo's hand away and bounced to his feet, scowling and reddening, and got face-to-face with Shlomo.

"What the fuck, Janis!" Axelrod barked, spittle spraying in Shlomo's grill, and he gave Shlomo a chest bump and a push. "Just cuz you don't got a prayer, don't fuck up *my* chances by being a goon!" and he rifled the ball at Shlomo's chest.

Initially apologetic, Shlomo summoned his inner chutzpah and instantly grew some nads. "Back off, a-hole," Shlomo responded, and the two began to tussle, Sumo-style.

"Let 'em go, let 'em go," head coach Storm Musselchamp said to his assistants. "We need to ratchet up the intensity. Let's see who can respond."

The assistants held their players back and let Shlomo and Axelrod go mano a mano.

The two combatants pushed apart from each other. Both squared up to be ready for a punch, but it looked like neither wanted a real fight. At that point, players from each team surrounded their teammate like a scrum and started moving them away from the fracas. That way, the scrappers could save face by still looking like they wouldn't back down, if only their teammates weren't obstructing them, and nobody would be embarrassed by getting his ass kicked.

Shlomo and Axelrod did some gesturing and woofing, acting like they were trying to break free to defend their manhood, but I could tell it was all for show for the coaches.

Red and Yellow took a time-out to cool down and regroup.

"We're going to go right to Janis, see what he's made of," Red's coach told his team. "You ready, V?"

"Bring it," Shlomo replied, breaking the huddle. Shlomo met Axelrod at the foul line, where he was setting up for two shots. He shook Axelrod's hand and patted him on the back, then took his rebounding position on the lane, a look of intensity in his eyes. Axelrod clanked his second shot. Yellow's Melvin "Popeye" Boykin, a bald and burly rebounding monster from Middle Tennessee State, made a quick move into the lane and sealed off challengers with a wide stance and splayed elbows, putting himself in perfect position to grab the carom for a follow-up dunk.

Beaten to a spot again, Shlomo wasn't going to let bad positioning ruin his next chance to impress the coaches. He soared from behind Boykin and reached one giant hand over Boykin's head. He snared the ball with his right hand and, in a swooping motion, brought it to meet his left above his head, making a clapping sound that reverberated throughout the gym as ball hit hand. Stunned that he had grabbed air, Boykin went to the flop to try to draw a foul call. He got off the floor, palms raised, with the sourpuss you-got-to-be-kidding look on his face. His pleading fell flat. The ref was gone.

Shlomo snapped an outlet pass to the point guard on the right wing near midcourt. The guard took the ball to the middle, as Shlomo bounded like a gazelle to fill the lane on the right. The guard penetrated inside the foul line, drawing two defenders, and made a no-look shovel pass to Shlomo barreling in from the right foul-line elbow. Shlomo caught it in stride, elevated off his left foot, and with wide, psychopathic eyes and mouth agape in a preroar, he threw down a thunderous, one-hand slam over Axelrod's outstretched arms, cruising through a semicircle under the basket, and headed back downcourt, collecting high fives from teammates along the way. Players on the sidelines from both teams rose out of their seats, waved their towels, and trash-talked Yellow with the glee that only an in-your-face throwdown can provide.

"Who the hell is that guy?" one Red player asked.

"Shlomo something," came the reply.

"Shlomo?...Shlo-MO...Shlo-MO...Shlo...MO!"

Others joined in the chant, and it got louder as players stomped the floor on "mo" for emphasis.

SHLOOOO-MO! (stomp)...SHLOOOO-MO! (stomp)...

"Hey, settle!" the coach yelled. "This is a tryout, not a freak show. Concentrate! Know...your...job!"

Shlomo couldn't repress a grin as he took his position on defense.

On another offensive possession, his team looking for him to continue his duel with Axelrod, Shlomo received an entry pass in the lane, backed his defender down, and went for a sweeping hook shot. It didn't have the feathery touch he showed in the drill—the truly gifted players can translate their practice techniques to the pressures of game conditions—but he still banked it in hard off the backboard.

The coup de grace came on the next sequence. Shlomo came out of nowhere to block a layup attempt off the backboard and went tumbling out of bounds. He arrived late at the offensive end as a trailer and caught a pass beyond the top of the key. Standing alone and finding no open cutters, he hoisted a high-arching three-pointer that hit nothing but net, inspiring the towel wavers again.

Unfortunately, after an exhilarating four minutes of action, Shlomo was spent and had nowhere to go but down. As the scrimmage wound down, he committed two turnovers on errant passes, missed a baby hook, air-balled an ill-advised jumper from the baseline, and got beat for two scores on defense. Still, he had a respectable stat line for seven minutes: 3–5 FGs, 7 PTS, 3 REB, 2 BLCK.

❖ ❖ ❖

The tryout lasted one more day, but Shlomo's genie had mostly escaped from the bottle. His concentration wavered. He said he got preoccupied with getting laid by another rookie teacher the night before because he felt so pumped up about his performance that it messed with his karma, that and some recreational spliff. He still had his highlights—like sinking sixteen foul shots in a row in a shooting drill and finger-rolling a reverse double-clutch layup off a pick-and-roll in the scrimmage—but he was outplayed by Axelrod, who had more consistent fundamentals and skilled footwork, and couldn't get a more resolute Stukes off the floor for more playing time.

At the end of practice, as the players were changing, Coach Musselchamp had an assistant post the names of five players who would be invited to the Sea Nettles' preseason camp on the Father Gill main entrance door. Axelrod was there; Shlomo wasn't. I hung around the door waiting to talk to Shlomo to get his final reactions for my feature, but Coach Musselchamp pulled him aside first.

"Shlomo, you did some good things out there…when your head wasn't in the clouds," Musselchamp told him. "Axelrod told me he'd much rather go up against Stukes than you. Take that as a compliment. Stay in shape. You never know in the CBA. It's a revolving door with all the NBA call-ups, injuries, and drug suspensions. Sometimes players quit midseason 'cause they have to make a *real living*. Hell, I may quit midseason if I can't hack another January bus trip to Sioux City," Musselchamp said, chuckling.

"Let us know if you change your phone number. You miss your call, we move on. Be ready."

I caught up with Shlomo on the way to the parking lot to put the finishing touches in my notebook: "From Shakespeare to Sea Nettles: Yarmulke Yeti Chases a Dream."

"Shlomo, sorry you didn't make the cut, but seems like you impressed Musselchamp."

"I'm supposed to be a teacher and a coach; that's Elijah's calling for me. I proved I could ball with these studs, and that's good enough for me. Who knows, if I had something other than Villa Janis on my basketball resume, maybe I would have been top five. They see Villa Janis and think I can't compete. Go ask Rik Smits. But I have no regrets. No regrets."

Great stuff. I pushed Shlomo a little harder about the Elijah crap and his "no regrets" statement. I had the sense there was a battle going on inside Shlomo between his old-world Hasid obligations and his modern-world desires. I wanted more honest reflection.

"What happened with your intensity today? You think if you improved your intensity and consistency, you'd be right there?"

"Don't put this in the paper. Didn't we talk about this on the phone? I can only keep up my intensity for short bursts. Weed mellows me out. Just say it this way: I had a couple of letdowns that cost me. When you want to play at the highest level, you can't have any mental lapses because everyone is hungry for your spot. They'll eat your lunch and steal your lunch box."

A superb final quote. I had a great feature, the kind the editors like: "Local Boy Makes [Almost] Good."

I headed for the Turdmobile, eager to start writing while the details were fresh in my mind.

"Hey, Jake, ya doin' anything tonight? I'm goin' to Benny's for dinner and watch the Mets game. You can meet Leatherman."

"Where's Benny's?"

"Bennigan's, right next to the Camelot."

"Leatherman?"

"Louie the Leatherman, my buddy from Camelot."

I could highlight my notes and type up some key observations and do the writing tomorrow. My social life needed a jolt. "Sure, meet you at seven."

It was the start of a new social "club" with many names—Club Camelot, No Fishing Off Bridges, Sloppy Seconds, Le Château—with me and Shlomo at the center and a host of oddballs, eccentrics, bons vivants, sluts, and other characters rotating around its orbit.

It was the time of my life.

CRASHED

I HAD BEEN at the Whispering Willow Apartments only two months, but knowing the area better, I had already started thinking about moving up the next rung of Drabenville Society—or at least closer to the beach. I was month-to-month and living a Spartan life—much closer to halfway house than *Animal House*. I hadn't had time, or the interest, to furnish or decorate, so I became an adherent of minimalism. I slept on a mattress on the beige-carpeted floor, under the interrogation-room glare of a Kmart floor lamp. For clothes, I used the same little wooden dresser with the red drawers and blue handles that my dad painted when I was five because it fit in the Turdmobile. The yellowing walls were bare. My one concession to domestication was a Saturday spree when I rented a van, scanned the Yellow Pages under "Furniture Used," hunted down a wooden kitchen table and two folding chairs, a Grandma's plastic-encased sofa, and a TV stand. The kitchen table doubled as my desk and office. My freezer was stocked with Benihana and Old El Paso frozen dinners from the adjacent Kash & Karry. It was pathetic.

I had scouted the Willow for potential dates and had a stunning success initially when I met an elementary school music teacher in the laundry room, Valerie Darling. I hung out with Val at the Jacuzzi-sized Willow swimming pool on Sundays and at her apartment on weeknights, bringing over pizza and cheap wine and listening to her plan music lessons on her piano. Things started getting hot when, after a bottle of wine one night, we hopped the fence to the Willow pool. The wine had worked its magic, and soon our bathing suits were off as we practiced underwater wrestling.

We made out on the chaise lounge chair, but our legs and arms kept getting stuck in the straps, and twice we tipped the chair over, sending us sprawling and laughing onto the concrete deck, so we decided to adjourn to her apartment.

I spent the night, enjoying the comfort and regality of a real, elevated bed almost as much as Val's warm body. I thought this would be great, a hot girlfriend just across the complex's trampled burnt-brown lawn, behind the industrial-size Dumpsters. It might even be enough to convince me to stay at the Willow. But often when I called her after filing my daily story around 7:30 p.m., she would demure, saying she had too much lesson planning to do or was too tired. On the nights she was available during that two-week stretch, I couldn't get enough, but Val was hard to read. Finally, one night I dropped by unannounced with Chinese takeout and a six-pack of Tsing Tao beer—what I thought would surely be seen as a romantic gesture that would sway her to put aside music lessons and just wing it with the kiddies the next day. Hand out harmonicas or tambourines or something. I knocked on the door and was shocked when it opened to see Crash, the roughneck I met on my first day in town at the Float Inn, wearing only a bathrobe.

"Dude, I know you—you're the new guy who was lost and stopped by the bar for advice," Crash said, raising his hand for a high five. I obliged reluctantly. "I haven't seen ya at the Floaty lately. Come on by for Thursday night NASCAR shots; it's two-for-one Checkered Flag Night, dude."

"What are you doing here, Crash?"

"I live here, downstairs in 2B, man. I told ya the Willow was a cool place to live, 'member? You *were* kinda buzzed that night."

"No, I mean *here*," I repeated, this time gesturing toward Val's piano, as if Crash might suddenly realize that such a symbol of cultural arts represented a society with which he was not naturally associated.

"Me and Vally are kinda on-again-off-again; like I tell her, '2B or not 2B, that is the question.' Tonight she chose 3D. Get it? I never knew Shakespeare would come in handy for something," he said, his scraggly goatee framing a smug grin.

Just then, Val wandered out of the bedroom wearing nothing but a long T-shirt. Her hair was mussed, and she was surprised to see me.

"Jake, did you say you were coming by?"

"No, I thought I would surprise you with Chinese."

"That was nice of you, but I'm kind of busy tonight."

"Busy doing what?"

Like a Ping-Pong spectator, Crash looked back and forth at Val and me with his goofy grin, clueless about our undercover, sordid little ménage à trois. I felt as though a grapefruit had just dropped to the pit of my stomach.

"I got you Moo Goo Gai Pan and Emperor's Delight because I know you like that, and those little chickens-on-a-stick. Does Crash know what kind of Chinese food you like?" I asked, about to blow a gasket.

"Huh?" interjected Crash, still not catching on. "Whatever, dude, Vally and me usually get Bojangles takeout or eat at the Floaty, but I'll do Chinky tonight. I'm kinda hungry, if you know what I mean, Bud," and he gave me a wink.

I did, and I should have left, but out of a perverse need for masochism, I went in to join Val and Crash for a "Chinky" dinner, after they put on some clothes. Crash guzzled three of my Tsing Taos in fifteen minutes, and, true to his word, devoured most of the Moo Goo without compunction. I sat in silence, barely touching the food, twirling a chicken satay stick between my fingers.

When Crash burped and got up, announcing, "I gotta use the crapper," I finally turned to Val, and words came spilling out erratically: "What the hell are you doing with that…I thought we might…you know…I mean, the night at the pool, the lounge chair…and how you said you really enjoyed…we…You seemed to…We were having really good…I really liked… What do you see in him?"

"It's not *serious*. We're just friends. I didn't know you were so…*serious*. I'm really glad you came over. You're so nice. Can't we be just friends? I'm not into being *serious*. I just want to have fun. Know what I mean?"

Blow me! Dicked over by the Cyndi Lauper line. That pink-haired tramp should have called her song "Girls Just Want to be Whores."

No longer feeling generous, I bagged up the last Tsing Tao, half a carton of Emperor's Delight, the few remaining crispy wonton sticks in the cellophane bag, and *all* the fortune cookies, and got up to leave.

Crash reemerged from the bathroom, hiked up his zipper, and belched.

"Dude, Vally and me are gonna cap off the night at the Floaty. Wanna join us?"

"Thanks, Crash, but I'm having a bad reaction to the monosodium glutamate. I better take it easy tonight."

"Whatever, dude. You better go easy on those designer drugs and stick to the tried and true weed and 'ludes, man. I'm a little worried about you."

"Yeah, Crash. I'm gonna go cold turkey on the glutamate and try to kick ass on the withdrawal. You and Vally have a good time."

I walked out of Val's apartment, trying to figure out the magnetism of Crash, coming up blank, and wondering if my night at the bottom of the Willow pool with Val was really just a vivid wet dream. When I dragged my sad ass back to my sadder apartment, I made a call right away.

"Shlomo, it's Jake from the *Dinqy*. You still looking for a roommate?"

Walrus Love in Camelot

IT WASN'T HARD to make the move from the Whispering Willow to Camelot Cay. Shlomo got permission from Biff Scully to borrow the Father Ignacio van for the weekend, and we loaded up my few pathetic vestiges of an adult life and made the three-mile trip west on Tierra Hacienda like the Jeffersons—"We're movin' on up / to the West Side / to the lizard-infested apartments / near the tide."

I immediately became familiar with Shlomo's odd collection of neighbors. Next door was the Camelot Queen, an aging, platinum-blond, Marilyn

Monroe wannabe, who strutted around the Cay with an ever-present cigarette, in bikinis and nightgowns, showing off her fake boobs and calling everyone "dahling" and "sweetheart."

Across the hall was Louie the Leatherman, aka Samsonite, who had skin as taut as an alligator suitcase from a life as a Florida landscaper. Above us were our contemporaries, early twenty-something wild things, Stephanie and Rosie, who together, like Thelma and Louise, had escaped the misnamed town of Hope, Indiana, and a probable existence of alcoholism, young motherhood, domestic violence, and low-wage, dead-end employment. What advantages Shlomo and I maintained on the socioeconomic side of the equation, these girls more than made up for with joie de vivre, which made us good company for hanging out. They enjoyed our wit and humor, and we relished their anything-goes attitudes and potential for sluttiness, a welcomed relief from the artsy, intellectual feminista granolas and butch jocks to whom we were accustomed in college.

However, I was a little afraid of Rosie. I sensed a streak of raunchiness in her that went several degrees beyond the bounds of mere sluttiness. I could see Rosie as a dominatrix with whips and chains, snarling and lording over a guy on all fours, yanking him by a neck collar and commanding him to beg for mercy. I'm all for sluttiness, but when it carries the threat of whipping, then I prefer nuns. So Shlomo and I gravitated more toward Sweet Stephanie than Raunchy Rosie.

On the third floor of our unit, two flights above us, were Crackhead Carl and Jackie Blue and their little boy, Tank. Unfortunately, Crackhead Carl and Jackie Blue were the classic case of a couple who married too young, probably at shotgun. The pressures of marriage, fatherhood, and a low-wage, blue-collar job at FloRite Corporation plagued Carl, who turned to booze and bargain-basement crack cocaine, which induced his violent outbursts. We heard screaming matches and stuff smashing against walls, and we became chummy with the cops assigned to Crackhead Carl watch.

On the uplifting side, Camelot Cay was blessed to have Washboard Wayne as its musician-in-residence. When we heard Washboard Wayne rattling the washboard in the evening out in the courtyard, Shlomo, Stephanie,

Rosie, and I would rush to put on hard-soled shoes and join Washboard. We'd deposit a five-spot in his cup, and then commence the most God-awful, talentless tap-dancing routine that somehow synched with Washboard's frenzied rhythms. Washboard would hang the washboard over his neck and play it with a spoon, a screwdriver, a ruler, or any other common household implement. He would mix in the cowbell, the triangle, a block of wood, and anything else he could hang from his neck or belt. After a few Washboard hoedowns, Leatherman and Camelot Queen partnered and joined in, and Jackie Blue and Tank started coming for a joyous respite from Crackhead Carl. Some neighbors began complaining about the racket, and Camelot management told Washboard to cease and desist, but he didn't—his revenue stream had been increasing. Soon, Washboard was attracting crowds of thirty or forty, even old-timer square dancers, and all the Camelot Cay regulars knew where to be Wednesdays at 8:00 p.m. Camelot management stopped harassing Washboard once it realized the free entertainment was an attraction rather than a nuisance. Shlomo became Washboard's honored accompanist, becoming accomplished at drumming on the metal garbage can on loan from Camelot maintenance man Trash Can Bob.

Soon after I moved to Camelot, a new business reporter started at the *Dinqy*, Dieter Klingenmeier, a fellow Colgate University grad by way of Milwaukee. I thought Dieter would get along well with Shlomo, so I arranged a get-together at the Jib & Jibe, a restaurant and bar on a spit of land overlooking Isla Balboa Bay, a half mile from the Tio Fernandez Bridge leading to the paradise of Conquista Island. We hit it off, and when we found out that Dieter was living in a motel, we recommended Camelot. Soon we had a new neighbor, and a new social organization, the No Fishing Off Bridges Club.

❖ ❖ ❖

For a week after his tryout, Shlomo had experienced pain in his elbow from a fall. He was diagnosed with a hairline fracture and put in a full-length arm cast to immobilize his arm.

"That'll put a damper on your sex life," I joked with the partially mummified Yeti.

"No, it actually won't," Shlomo shot back. "There's a history teacher at school, Debbie Bazarko from Pawtucket, Rhode Island. She's got the hots for me."

"How do you know?"

"You know the limerick about Pawtucket, right?"

"No."

"There once was a girl from Pawtucket; if it had a pulse, she'd fuck it; she—"

"Seriously."

"She's always hanging on me in the teachers' lounge, putting her hand on my good arm and nudging me when she makes a joke. She's always calling me Big Guy and Cloud Buster and other goofy names and giving me her woodchuck grin. I can just tell. I can have her any time I want."

"Bullshit," I said. "You're awkward as a giraffe under the best of conditions, and now you look like a math teacher perpetually trying to demonstrate a right angle with your square-ruler appendage. Even if…what's her name?"

"Deborah…Debbie…Big Deb…Bazarko."

"Even if Big Deb doesn't mind being clubbed in the head in the sack by plaster of paris, you're too mummified to maneuver. She ain't gonna want any part of that, if she's more than shit for brains."

"Then she's shit for brains. Let's put some money on it. I'm going to meet Big Deb and another teacher Saturday night at the Jib & Jibe. It can be a double date, except the other teacher, Melanie, is tall, about six feet. What are you, five five?"

"Fuck you. Five nine. Six feet and a half inch with my elevator shoes."

"You've got elevator shoes?" Shlomo started laughing hysterically.

"Yeah, they've got extra padding, but you can't tell, not like Elton John and his clumsy stilettos."

Tears of laughter. I was kidding, but I goaded him on.

"What's so funny? I like to be tall, but I don't feel like wearing stilts and a red nose and joining the fuckin' circus! Tall people don't understand."

"I get it, the Napoleon complex," Shlomo said, finally regaining his composure. "What kind are they?"

"Blue suede, high-top Sahara Deserts."

He cracked up again. "Wear your Saharas and I'll tell Melanie to wear flats. Do you have bell bottoms to go with them?"

"Fuck the elevator shoes. Let's get back to the bet."

"I'll bet you a hundred dollars I get laid Saturday night."

"How will I know?"

"I'll steal her panties. I'll just tell her they got lost in my shit pile of clothes and books and papers."

"How will I know they're Big Deb's?"

"You can sniff 'em. They'll be fresh."

"Oh, you mean like Sniff 'n' the Tears. Right."

"Yeah, 'Driver's Seat.' That's what that song's about. Fingering in the front seat. 'Jenny is sweet'…That's code."

"Stop! No it's not…maybe…I don't care. You're on. Produce the panties, and I'll do Sniff 'n' the Tears for a hundred bucks."

❖ ❖ ❖

We met Big Deb and Melanie at the Jib & Jibe.

Despite Shlomo's insistence that I wear my Sahara Desert elevator shoes to boost my confidence with Melanie, I didn't because I didn't have a pair. But I didn't tell Shlomo that because he got such a kick out of the idea. I just said they were chic in the '70s but out of style in the '80s.

Big Deb was about five eight and big-boned. She was pear shaped, with broad shoulders, back, and torso, and wide hips balanced on disproportionately skinny legs. She talked a lot about her days as a competitive swimmer, which might have explained her bulky build, but I think it was more genetics. Shlomo was right; when she smiled, she did resemble a woodchuck with choppers that looked like they could gnaw through a thin tree and puffy cheeks that appeared to be full of nuts.

I saw what Shlomo was talking about: she was draped all over him, nudging him, squeezing his shoulder, wrapping her arm around his back, and annoyingly making up nicknames for him, such as Mr. Studly and Timber. She had some talent for imitating cartoon characters like Barney Rubble, Porky Pig, and Astro, the Jetsons' dog, but I could see how this offbeat trait could grate on a person.

Melanie and I did not hit it off. She was too tall and, as tall girls often are, awkward in social settings. Elevator shoes wouldn't have helped; I want soft and cuddly, not going one-on-one to eleven, winner's take. She seemed just as blasé about me, focusing more on maneuvering her fries through ketchup than on looking at me.

But Shlomo and Big Deb were another story. Now Shlomo was reciprocating, pawing his one good mitt all over her. I began to worry about my hundred dollars; that was about one-third of my weekly take-home pay on the verge of being pimped away.

After two rounds of tequila shots with lemon chasers and our horrid karaoke performance of the Pet Shop Boys' "West End Girls," we left the Jib & Jibe in our separate boys' and girls' cars.

Shlomo, driving his Saab from his usual reclining, backseat position, one-armed like Captain Hook, against doctors' orders, turned off Tierra Hacienda on Seventy-Eighth Avenue before reaching Camelot Cay, following Big Deb's sporty, red Pontiac Fiero.

"Where are you going?"

"I'm following Big Deb to drop off Mel's Diner. Then Big Deb's gonna follow me to Camelot."

"When did you make that plan?"

"When you and Mel's Diner went to the bar for the tequila shots and me and Big Deb were making out in the booth. You better get to Barnett Bank in the morning. I'm tellin' ya, she's cake."

"We'll see; she may change her mind when she gets concussed by the peg arm."

WALRUS LOVE IN CAMELOT

The spiffy Fiero trailed us back to Camelot. Louie the Leatherman was hanging out in the courtyard enjoying a Marlboro and a Schlitz as we walked by, with Big Deb attached to the Yeti's torso as if she were his Siamese twin.

Leatherman gave Shlomo an approving nod and a thumbs-up as the enormous Siamese couple approached our door. Shlomo replied to the gesture with a triumphant fist pump, far enough behind Big Deb's gaze that she didn't notice. I imagine the communication hasn't changed much since the Cavemanistoa Era, when club bumps were probably the universal signal. Trailing behind, I felt repulsed. I gave Leatherman the gag sign; he laughed so hard that beer foamed from his mouth.

The Siamese made a beeline for the den of pending iniquity and shut the door. I retreated to my adjacent room, put Van Halen's "Runnin' with the Devil" on my Sony Walkman headphones and cranked it up to nine to try to avoid hearing the inevitable groaning and moaning, amplified by the Siamese's considerable bulk, through the paper-thin walls. The image of walruses (walrii?) making love popped into my mind, and I turned Van Halen up to ten.

❖ ❖ ❖

I was eating my Lucky Charms when the walrii emerged from the Den of Iniquity, Shlomo still in his coffee- and Temp Tee cream cheese-stained bathrobe. Shlomo kissed Big Deb at the door, and she gave him her squirrel-storing-up-nuts-for-the-winter smile, a love punch to the shoulder, and a schmaltzy good-bye salute: "See you in the teachers' lounge, if you know what I mean, Big Guy."

As soon as Big Deb exited, Shlomo pulled a pair of purple panties from his bathrobe pocket and stretched and twirled them like a magician who wraps balloons into cats for kids. I almost choked on a green clover.

"Bank's open until noon," Shlomo announced.

"I need more proof," I demanded.

"Sniff 'n' the Tears," Shlomo offered and stretched the panties wide over my bowl of Charms, "if you don't mind the smell of cumquat juice with your cereal."

I launched my spoon like a catapult in a reflexive body-lurch that caused my bowl to upend and spill pink and green milk all over my lap. Shlomo turned the panties inside out and dangled them in front of my face.

"OK, OK, all right…'Jenny is sweet…The news is blue…' whatever. I'll pay. Just put that purple petri rag back in your robe!"

Thus began a short-lived, simultaneously torrid and horrid romance between the Walrii. Little did I know then that I'd eventually become an accomplice in this unseemly mud bath.

Everybody Stan Chung Tonight

Great Bay had never beaten Dolphin in its short history, 0–4, having been outscored 162–64, but in the last two years under Bachman, the team had become more competitive, playing Dolphin tight into the fourth quarter in 1985, even holding a 24–21 lead, until two late turnovers doomed them, 34–24.

The game was at Great Bay's Loggerhead Stadium, and there was a party atmosphere in anticipation of a big night. The fans really believed for the first time that their finesse and razzle-dazzle outfit had a chance against the steamroller known as the Fightin' Dorsals.

The other heavy hitters in Dolphin County's sports media also identified Great Bay–Dolphin as the game of the week. Reporter Tab Reindollar and columnist/Dolphin homer Donny Monday from the *T-D* and Whalebait Wally of WFIN-AM were in the press box by the time I arrived, debating whether Great Bay had any chance against the state powerhouse.

"No way in hell Great Bay comes within three touchdowns," Monday asserted in a raspy voice, pausing to take a long drag on a Marlboro and cough. "Some things never change, and this is one of them. Great Bay is dog meat tonight."

"I dunno, Donny. I think you're wrong about that," retorted the glib Whalebait, who filled any room he was in as well as the airwaves with nonstop chatter. "Bachman finally has the right kids to run his system.

THREE YARDS AND A PLATE OF MULLET

I'll bet one hundred dollars if you take Dolphin and lay eighteen points. Whadya say, homer?"

This made Donny a little nervous. He liked to talk a big game, but he was afraid to back up the bluster.

"You cocksucker, Wally," he growled, took a drag on his Marlboro, and blew a ring cloud. "You don't bet on high school kids. That's like pimping your daughter as a whore."

Whalebait let Monday's comment hang for a few seconds, as if contemplating the validity of its righteousness.

"Pussy!" Whalebait bellowed.

Tab Reindollar, who was typing pregame material on his computer and neatly arranging his roster sheets and newspaper clippings while trying to stay out of the tête-à-tête, broke out in laughter, as did the camera crew on the ledge above us.

"Scumbags," Monday retorted as the camera crew tried to stifle guffaws. "Talk to me after the game, Wally. Oh, but you won't be able to. You'll be eating shit pie," he cackled, blowing smoke in Wally's direction as the whole press box cracked up.

❖ ❖ ❖

Dolphin jumped on top early, taking a 13–0 first-quarter lead on a sixty-yard Sammy Sammons run and a long, grinding drive featuring the relentless running game of Hilliard and fullback Tommy "Mondo" Mondello. Dolphin needed only one pass on the seventy-five-yard drive, capped by Mondo's power plunge from two yards out.

In the second quarter, Great Bay crowded the line to stop the run behind Otis and the Mad Stork, and the defense stiffened, holding Dolphin to a short field goal attempt that was shanked. That was one area where Great Bay had a clear advantage. High school kickers were notoriously unreliable; many flat-out sucked. Dolphin's Cal Stimson was in that category. Bamford cringed when he had to call on him. But he knew he might need Stimson late in the season when games were tight in the play-offs.

EVERYBODY STAN CHUNG TONIGHT

Meanwhile, Great Bay quarterback Rowdy Rawley led his team on two drives that stalled in Dolphin territory, prompting Coach Bachman to call on his weapon, kicker Stanley Chung, who connected on field goals of thirty-six and forty yards for a 13–6 half-time deficit.

Coach Bamford was irate at half time, I learned from a source. "We need to punch them in the mouth, and we're prancing like ballerinas. We're gonna storm out of this locker room and pancake these finesse pansies like Aunt Jemima's business," he commanded his players.

And they did. With Mondo busting up the middle and Sammons and Hilliard using their speed on the option to turn corners, Dolphin marched to the end zone and a 19–6 lead after Stimson botched his second extra point of the game, causing Coach Bamford to throw down his headset in disgust.

In the press box, Monday slapped the writer's ledge and whooped and pivoted toward Whalebait. "Whadya say that bet was for, Wally?" he asked, dripping with snark and eyebrows forming rainbows on his wrinkled forehead. "I was gonna take your bet and double you up; only reason I didn't is I'm such a nice guy. I know you have trouble finding clothes at the Big and Bigger Shop, and I don't want to see your ass naked, so keep your money, cocksucker!" Again, the press box choked back tears of laughter—the Whalebait and Monday show entertained as much as the game did.

After a long kickoff return and a double reverse got Great Bay to Dolphin's twenty-five, Stanley Chung trotted out for an even longer, forty-two-yard field goal attempt. For the third time of the night, the PA announcer cranked up Wang Chung's "Everybody Have Fun Tonight." The fans stood and went wild, shaking their hands in the air and singing in unison, "Everybody have fun tonight! Everybody Stan Chung tonight!"

Chung split the uprights on the forty-two-yarder, with a few yards to spare. The speakers blared and the fans shouted and pointed toward Stanley, shouting, "Everybody STAN CHUNG TONIGHT!" as the special teams headed for the sidelines.

Great Bay loaded up the box again and forced Dolphin to pass, at which Sammons excelled at short range but struggled with distance. So Great

THREE YARDS AND A PLATE OF MULLET

Bay's secondary crowded Dolphin receivers at the line and had success breaking up quick slants and outs, while the linebackers' pursuit limited gains on screens. The teams headed into the fourth quarter with Dolphin leading 19–9.

Dolphin got the ball with eight minutes left. I could see Bamford and offensive coordinator Hobie Schlorf embroiled in an animated discussion. From backup quarterback Connor Crane, who huddles with the coaches along with Sammons during breaks, I learned about the exchange:

"Fuck the pass, Hobie. Three yards and a plate of mullet, all night long, baby, and goodnight Irene," Bamford asserted.

"But Jimbo, they got eight in the box—it's too jammed. We got to spread it out before we go back to pounding."

"As I said, fuck the pass. Pound!"

"OK, OK."

And so Dolphin pounded, in a smashmouth display, with Hilliard and Mondo running off tackle and Sammons keeping on sweeps, the bigger Dolphin linemen blowing a weary Great Bay line off the ball, moving from their own eighteen to the Great Bay twelve and chewing nearly six minutes off the clock. Great Bay called time-out.

I heard from Otis later what Bachman told them:

"Guys, no way in hell Dolphin puts the ball in the air. Ain't got the guts or the imagination. So we're crowding all eleven near the line and stormin' the backfield like a bunch of wild banshees. Pin your ears back, boys. We got to take it from them."

The rest and the thought of an all-out Banshee Blitz energized the Great Bay defense. They lined up looking like they were poised for the starting gun of a hundred-meter sprint. Dolphin ran an option play, with Sammons faking the inside dive to Mondo, and then wheeling left. Two steps into his run, Sammons was hit square by the Mad Stork. The ball popped into the air. Petey Pritchard, who was racing to the edge to cover the option pitch, snatched the ball on the run and scampered eighty-two yards for a score. Great Bay lined up for two points and used a Bachman rabbit special—a fake jump pass, hidden ball hand-off—to convert and cut the deficit to 19–17 with under two minutes left.

I could see the bravado drain from the Dolphin sideline. It was replaced with fear—fear of losing to a team that not long ago was the laughingstock of Dolphin County football, the team Monday once described in print as "an embarrassment to the pigskin god."

On the other side, I could sense the adrenaline soaring for Great Bay, now one big play away from an upset for the ages.

After a deep Chung kickoff, Dolphin took over at its own nineteen with a minute and thirty-five seconds left. Great Bay loaded nine on the line and dared Dolphin to pass. Bamford would have none of it. Two running plays into a pile netted only three yards before a time-out with fifty-two seconds left.

Punter Rill Shur was warming up on the sideline, practicing air punts. The coaches were afraid to use him—Rill wasn't known as Shur Shank-a-lot for nothing. He was almost as putrid as kicker Cal "Wide Right" Stimson was, but Dolphin usually didn't need to depend on either of them much after rolling up big leads. Tonight, they did.

❖ ❖ ❖

In the press box, old Monday was chain-smoking Marlboros, and the muscle between his eyes constricted, forming a *V* on his forehead, the stress inducing a clenched-jaw frown. "We're gonna hold on, just one more big play," Monday muttered to no one in particular, staring out the open press box window intently at the lonely ball and the zebra hovering over it at the twenty-two. "Let's beat these…" and his voice trailed off.

At the microphone, Whalebait was having a conniption, no doubt raising Monday's blood pressure to a boil. "Don't go anywhere, Dolphin Nation. Don't turn out the lights; the party is not over! Great Bay is the fly that won't leave the horse's tail alone, and now the horse is spooked. If Jimbo doesn't come up with something special, we could be in for a wild

THREE YARDS AND A PLATE OF MULLET

ride. Can Great Bay pull off the upset of the year, if not the decade? We'll be right back, Whalers, to find out."

"Blow me, Wally," Monday barked after Whalebait went to a commercial break. "Why are you getting the Loggerheads' hopes up like that? You're worse than the Grinch."

On the field, Schlorf argued with Bamford about the third-and-long call. "We can't afford to get another run stuffed and go to Shank-a-lot, Jimbo. He's a nervous wreck. He'll give them field position, and they got a helluva kicker. We can bust Cartwright free on a skinny post off a fake with nothing but green grass and fried mullet in front of him."

Bamford weighed the variables, and there were many. Sometimes a football coach had to be like a computer, receiving and scanning many inputs, such as time, distance, geographic coordinates, weather, human behavior, past performance, probabilities, and competitive intelligence to determine one output based on predicted outcome. This was one of those situations. Bamford preferred smashmouth, especially at the high school level, where unpredictability and imprecision meant more could go wrong than right on a pass. But he wasn't averse to airing it out. His NWFU team's ability to throw the ball, commanding respect from defenses, was a huge factor in making the Pelicans' running game so prolific.

The output ticker spit out.

"Call the post to Cartwright. Time to execute, boys."

Sammons faked the plunge hand-off to Mondo, causing the Great Bay line to converge and drawing Little Mo Pritchard forward from his defensive backfield position. By the time Pritchard could react, Cartwright had blown by him, angling for the midfield emblem. Sammons revealed the ball as he set himself and stepped forward to launch. On the sideline, Bamford saw the play developing. Clipboard in hand, he started taking fox-trot-like steps in front of the bench, covering ten yards, mirroring Cartwright's progress as if he was vicariously willing the play forward toward the opposite end zone.

Just as Sammons released the ball, the Mad Stork hit him from the blindside, causing the ball to wobble like a wounded quail. Little Mo turned around, located the misguided projectile, and stopped trying to catch Cartwright, who was ten yards past him. Little Mo became a center fielder, camping out under the duck and catching it in his breadbasket. Cartwright had circled back to the ball but only got there in time to wrestle Little Mo to the ground at the Dolphin forty-five with forty-one seconds left. Bamford threw his clipboard down in disgust and maniacally ran around in search of Schlorf, his jaw a-flappin'.

The Great Bay sideline erupted, and one of Bachman's favorites blasted from the speakers: "You Ain't Seen Nothin' Yet" by BTO.

"Here's somethin', here's somethin' you're never gonna forget, baby, y' know, y'know, y' know, you just ain't seen nothin' yet!"

"Fuck'n A! Unbelievable," Monday croaked. "What a stupid-ass call."

"You better double up on your hypertension medication tonight, Donny-boy," Whalebait cracked during a thirty-second commercial break. The rest of the press box was too keyed up by the prospect of an enormous and landscape-changing upset even to laugh.

Rawley dropped back to pass but was forced to scramble, making it to the Dolphin thirty-eight and requiring Great Bay to call its final time-out with thirty seconds remaining. On the next play, Dolphin left the middle of the field open, taking away the sideline patterns that could kill the clock. Rawley took it, hitting his receiver on a quick slant to the twenty-six. Great Bay scrambled to get back in formation as the clock wound down. Rawley took the snap and threw the ball away to stop the clock at 0:05. Time for one more play.

Wang Chung started up on the loudspeakers. In trotted Stanley Chung for the potential game winner, with Rawley staying in as his holder. Dolphin overpacked the middle, planning to bum-rush Chung for a block.

What Dolphin didn't recognize in the rapid-fire exchange of chess pieces was that Great Bay's second-string quarterback, Marty Bilger, was lined up on the far left of Great Bay's blocking formation, unaccounted for. Wang Chung faded, and the crowd hushed. Rowdy snatched the snap cleanly and placed the ball down for Chung. Chung approached, planted his left foot aside the ball, cocked his right leg behind him, lowered his

THREE YARDS AND A PLATE OF MULLET

head, and made a powerful, sweeping arc motion with his leg. Just before he made contact, Rowdy scooped up the ball and wheeled to his left behind Chung. Stunned Dolphin players all flowed to their right, now totally out of the scheme and discipline and read responsibility that had been drilled into them since August 15. They were reacting on the fly.

Before Dolphin could corral Rowdy, he pitched to quarterback Bilger, who was circling in the other direction toward empty space. The defense shifted and started to pursue, but Great Bay held its blocks. Suddenly, Bilger stopped on a dime and hurled the ball back across the field, where he had started from, to a forgotten and lonely Stanley Chung, standing as if waiting for a bus on the fifteen-yard line. The ball seemed to hang in the air for an eternity as Stanley braced to receive it. Dolphin coaches frantically pointed at the wide-open Loggerhead, and Dolphin defenders changed direction again in desperation.

"I don't fuckin' believe it," Monday muttered, his cigarette falling from his mouth. "No fuckin' way."

Stanley smothered the ball into his belly, paused for a split second to make sure he actually possessed the golden egg, and then took off for the goal line. Luckily for Great Bay, Stanley had developed speed as a soccer player. Two Dolphin defenders caught up to Stanley at the three-yard line. They jumped on his back and hit him from the side, but Stanley's momentum propelled him forward into the end zone before the three players tumbled in a heap of arms and legs. Stanley rose from the wreckage, the ball held over his head. Two referees, still catching up to the play, looked at each other, nodded, and threw their arms over their heads in the touchdown signal. The Great Bay sideline went berserk and stormed the field, swinging their helmets in joy, and dog-piling Stanley until he was nowhere to be seen. "Everybody have fun tonight...Everybody Stan Chung tonight!" reverberated through Loggerhead Stadium.

"I don't believe it! I don't believe it! Twenty-three to nineteen, Great Bay! Somebody, please, wake the whale!" Whalebait practically screamed into the mic. "Dolphin goes DOWN! Dolphin goes DOWN! Whalers, you've just heard Dolphin County history being made. I thought I'd seen it all with the Steelers' Immaculate Reception. We've just witnessed the Immaculate DE-ception!"

Whalebait gobbled one deep breath and continued: "Ho-ly Man-a-tee! Stanley Chung, run for mayor of Loggertown right now, my friend! They pulled it off! They pulled it off! Don't go anywhere, Whalers, we'll have your postgame interviews right here. You won't want to miss the explanations the 'Baiter is gonna get from the coaches, believe me!"

When Whalebait finished his rant and took off his headphones, sweat pouring off his forehead, he turned and looked for Monday, but Monday had slipped out of the press box quickly and quietly, certainly to avoid the humiliation of a Whalebait gloatfest. Nobody ever said that in small-town Florida high school football, all "journalists" had to maintain a public semblance of impartiality.

Alert Great Bay coaches came onto the field to corral their delirious players and herd them back to the bench, realizing that the extra point conversion was necessary to make the game official, wanting to avoid a forfeit in case fans crashed the field too early—or maybe Dolphin even had its hands in the referees' pockets. Nothing was for sure until the final whistle blew.

Stanley nailed the conversion kick, and the refs blew their whistles and waved their arms in a crossing motion to signal "game over." With that, the stands emptied. Students and adults hopped the fence circling the track as if the generation gap had disappeared—grandparents as giddy as acne-pocked teens—and mobbed the Great Bay players, who were hugging each other and hollering declarations of bravado the way only teenage boys can do on the cusp of the prime of their lives.

❖ ❖ ❖

Later in the locker room, I asked Coach Bachman about his bold decision to go for a touchdown rather than the seemingly higher-percentage play of a field goal, down by two, to win the game, especially given Chung's leg strength and range.

"I would have gone for the field goal, but during our last time-out, Stanley and I had a very detailed conversation going over hypothetical situations," Bachman told me.

"Stanley's a brilliant kid. He analyzed the wind pattern and the trajectory he would need at different distances. Now, I've seen Stanley bomb field goals in practice from forty-five yards with three yards to spare. This would have been a forty-three-yarder, but Stanley calculated that with the steady headwind we faced in the fourth quarter—between fifteen and twenty miles per hour, gusting to twenty-five—his range was reduced to forty yards. And to try to stretch it to forty-three, he would have to use a low trajectory, and with Dolphin fully expecting a field goal attempt, they'd be selling out to block a low kick.

"When Stanley figures something out, you don't question it, you go with it. Do I claim to be smarter than him, just because I'm a football coach from down on the farm?

"No. So I called one of our Rabbit plays, the Numba Nine Chung Pow Special, and it worked. A thing of beauty. Sometimes it helps to be lucky. But usually, it helps even more just to be smart."

With that, Coach Bachman broke into a shit-eating grin, clasped his hands behind his head, leaned back in his chair, and looked up at the ceiling in disbelief, like a new father who had just glimpsed his son for the first time. All he needed was a stogie...and to imagine a red-faced Bamford berating his team in the visitors' locker room and a roomful of obnoxious Fightin' Fins alumni at the next boosters club meeting gnashing their teeth in embarrassment.

"It's a long way from Box Butte, Nebraska, baby, a loooong way," Bachman said, lost in his own thoughts. "Sweet. Sweet."

Praise Palmertown

The Saturday after Great Bay's big upset, I was assigned weekend mop-up. That meant covering something lame, like an amateur golf tournament, preliminary Figure Eight heats at De Leon Raceway, or, believe it or not, a seniors' shuffleboard tournament, and then working the desk or the slot at night, which meant taking calls from high school coaches and writing briefs about their cross-country or volleyball results, assembling summaries of the local golf clubs' weekly foursomes, scrambles, and best-ball events, checking on the tournament exploits of the studs at the Sergio Bonatelli Tennis Academy, adding local angles to AP wire stories, and compiling "agate"—all the box scores, statistical information, standings, listings, and schedules in small font size that makes the sports page something you scour over breakfast.

That Saturday, I was assigned to cover the dedication of the Praise Palmertown Athletic & Education Complex, a combination football-soccer field, baseball diamond, and tennis and basketball courts, built on fallow farmland owned by Bible Praise Deliverance Southern Baptist Church that used to be part of a beef cattle operation. The project also included the conversion of a church annex into a desperately needed, subsidized preschool, day care, and after-school center that would allow parents to work extra hours to provide a better life for their kids.

The dedication included local dignitaries from DeVaca City and Palmertown, including DeVaca City's mayor; Coach Huckerbee; football stars from yesteryear's Palmertown Colored School; a current Tampa Bay Buc from Palmertown; Bible Praise Deliverance reverend Josiah

Mayweather Jr.; and Clarence "Boots" Walker, the Dolphin County school board member representing DeVaca City. Reverend Mayweather, after praising God who made all things possible and the Lord Jesus Our Savior for doing our heavy lifting, explained that Bible Praise Deliverance had received $200,000 from five anonymous contributors. All he knew was that three came from employees at Roma Rojo Tomatoes and two from DeVaca Prime Realty, the city's leading home seller whose founder and president, Tony Finizio, appeared on folksy local TV commercials proclaiming, "Your house is my job. If your house isn't happy with me, fire me." Bible Praise Deliverance was able to scrape together another $75,000 from its building-improvement fund to make the project a reality.

I wrote a colorful, metaphorical lede that I knew Paddy would like because all of the editors were under orders from Chenault to make the ledes flowery and sensational no matter how dry the story. "Overwrought" was not part of Chenault's vocabulary:

> *Where once cornstalks grew high and verdant soybeans stretched as far as the eye could see, Palmertown dignitaries and coaches are envisioning the cultivation of another type of crop: stellar student-athletes who sprout at the newly dedicated Praise Palmertown Athletic & Education Complex.*

Big Papa's Pipeline

The next Saturday, I followed my typical post-game-night routine, waking up feeling an alcohol-free hangover at 9:30 a.m., going for a four-mile run along River Overlook Drive, hitting Denny's for the grand-slam breakfast, and stopping by Sunshine State Bank & Trust to deposit my paycheck. From my regular visits since August, I had gotten to know the Saturday morning teller through small talk while she processed my paycheck. I always made one or two additional transactions, moving some money from checking to savings, or opening a pathetic certificate of deposit, so I could flirt longer.

A good share of Dolphin County's female population was comprised of jailbait, trailer trash, desperate divorcees, overtanned prunes, alcoholics, and the nearly dead. For sure, there were lots of knockouts in Florida, but the Citrus Coast was not the place they flocked, not with more happening locales for nightlife and professional opportunities, such as Miami, Orlando, and Tampa. I learned that the teller's name was Julie Jansen, that she was a DeVaca High and Dolphin Community College graduate who had lived her whole life in DeVaca City, and that she was trying to work her way up to be a loan officer, which required a bachelor's degree, which required her to take evening classes at Kissimmee State. She was a cute blonde with dancing blue eyes and a killer, aerobics-toned body—at least the part I could see through the teller window. As Julie jumped through hoops processing an utterly meaningless shell-game series of transactions so I could buy more time, I struck up a conversation. "So you went to DeVaca?"

"Yeah, class of '84. It got me here...not very far, I guess. Did I tell you I started at Kissimmee State?"

"Yeah, what are you taking?"

"Accounting and macroeconomics. BOOORRRRINNNG," she said with a singsong voice, punctuated with a cute giggle that made me want to blow my wad. Atlanta Rhythm Section's "So Into You" popped into my head, intensifying my lust. "Now I stand here helplessly, hoping you get into me...Me into you, you into me, me into you!"

"JJ—can I call you JJ?"

"Sure, my girlfriends do...and my boyfriend."

Blow me! Always happens. Such a sweetie and then she utters the dreaded b-word. I plumbed for confidence and Etch-A-Sketched my mind, turning disappointment into purpose—wresting this fair damsel from the clutches of a boyfriend who was surely a dim-witted, beer-swilling redneck and a life of chasing after a brood of incorrigible ragamuffins and waiting in food-stamp lines while her unemployed, live-in boyfriend invested the welfare cash in G-strings at the Furr 'n Purr Lounge nudie bar and monster tires for his pickup.

"JJ, did you know Coach Huckerbee?"

"Yeah, I had him for gym. He was great. We used to bug him about when he was ever going to beat Dolphin. That really got him riled up. Sometimes he'd go off on a tirade about Dolphin and call them a bunch of marshmallows or something. Cracked us up. For the rest of the day, we'd call each other 'marshmallow.'"

"Yeah, I can tell there's no love lost between him and Coach Bamford."

I guess JJ let her banker's guard down because then she told me something that piqued my interest as a journalist, not just as a sex-deprived, horny dog.

"Funny that you mention Coach Bamford. Every so often, I've handled a big check from him to Gus Papadopoulos's company. You've heard of Papadopoulos Diversified Property Management, right? It's huge in Dolphin County, and Gus is head of the school board and everything. Anyway, ordinarily, I wouldn't think anything of it because I know their families are business partners. But those transactions are always written on the account of Bamford & Sons, the business. These checks come from a James Bamford trust account. It just seems a little odd. Oh well, I don't know why I went into all of that. Just thought you might be interested as a sportswriter and all."

That did sound curious, and it started the journalistic wheels grinding. I made a mental note to jot this down in my ideas file when I was back in the office and look into it when I had time.

"Yeah, the Bamfords are the big cheese around here, that's for sure."

Big Cheese? God, that sounded stupid. Now she'll think I'm a dork. Better exit gracefully.

"Good talking to you, Julie. Catch you next time."

It was an official date…at the teller's window. I thought about asking her out, but I couldn't stand the thought of being rejected out of her loyalty to Mr. Fuzzy Dice. It would ruin the weekly flirting.

A Bribe Blinds the Eyes of the Wise

I got a call the next week from Boots Walker saying he wanted to meet. I had met Boots at the sports complex dedication, where he told the audience how, if he had been involved with a facility like Praise Palmertown Athletic & Education Complex, he might have avoided a lot of the missteps of his youth. He had thanked the Lord for the five blessed souls who made large contributions, saying he never knew of a formal plan to grow a youth center in abandoned soybean fields and that the Lord moved in mysterious ways. Boots would have a small office in the after-school center, where he would provide free counseling to youth, funded by Dolphin County Mental Health Services.

I asked Boots if he had already found a heartwarming feature story about a family at the complex. He said the story he wanted to discuss in person did involve the complex. I met Boots in his office at the complex and was surprised to see the Reverend Mayweather with him.

"Thanks for coming on short notice. Please have a seat," Boots said.

"No problem. I was in DeVaca City anyway to talk to Coach Huckerbee and the players at practice for an advance on Friday's game."

"I really appreciate the *Daily Inquirer* covering the Praise Palmertown Complex dedication," Boots said, gesturing to a framed copy of the article on his wall. Then he fell silent and looked down at his hands on the table for a long moment.

"Jake, I called you here 'cause somethin' ain't right."

A BRIBE BLINDS THE EYES OF THE WISE

"Did I make a mistake in the story? I wasn't aware. I'm sorry. Just let me know what it is and—"

"No, no, no. The story's great. Palmertown's been talking about it all week. We never get attention like that, at least not for somethin' positive. Usually just drug busts and shootings.

"I mean somethin' ain't right *with me*. I ain't right with God, and He's been tellin' me. I'm not sleeping, and I'm feeling anxious. And I'm noticing bad things happening. Are you a God-fearin' man?"

I fumbled for a response. "I believe in *a* God, but I've never really thought He's targeting me to settle a score. So I guess no, not really."

"Well, I am," Boots said. "I've seen too much in my life to think anything other than God is in control and God knows all and God speaks to you clearly if you will only tune in. In the three weeks we've been open, we've had one kid break his arm on the football field, and another suffered a concussion when he was hit by a pitch. We've had an outbreak of flu in the preschool, and the after-school program had an electrical fire that could have killed someone. You can say these are all just coincidences. Bad luck. Things happen. But I get a different sense in my bones.

"You see, here's what I want to tell you. The Praise Palmertown Complex is a great thing. It puts our community on the map. Come back to observe us in action one day and you'll see the pride, the love. But it's eating me up inside that Palmertown's treasure is tainted." Then Boots bowed his head, closed his eyes, and recited a verse from the Bible: "'You shall not pervert justice. You shall not show partiality, and you shall not accept a bribe, for a bribe blinds the eyes of the wise and subverts the cause of the righteous.' That's Deuteronomy verses sixteen to nineteen."

Huh? I had no clue what Boots was talking about. Boots looked at me for a reaction, which wasn't forthcoming. Then the reverend chimed in to fill in the gaps, recognizing that Boots was struggling in an awkward attempt to cleanse his soul. The Reverend Mayweather had redirected Boots from trouble before and shown him the way to a better life.

❖ ❖ ❖

Clarence "Boots" Walker was a wayward Palmertown youth in the early 1960s, often chased down by truant officers until he graduated to bigger juvenile offenses, such as shoplifting, destruction of property, and burglary. He was sixteen and going nowhere except the Dolphin Juvenile Corrections Center when he met the Reverend Mayweather of Palmertown's Bible Praise Deliverance at a Dolphin County juvenile offenders program, a last chance to break a hardening shell before indoctrination into the thug life was likely irreversible.

The Reverend Mayweather took a special interest in Clarence. Although Clarence's mother didn't worship at his church, he knew her from his volunteer work at the Palmertown Rec Center, a dilapidated facility where Yolanda Walker had taken Clarence and his two younger brothers while she worked on the belt at Roma Rojo Tomatoes and as a nursing assistant, wiping asses and slopping up drool for DeVaca Convalescent. Clarence's father was in and out of jail for petty street crimes and drug violations. He provided occasional court-ordered financial support when he could resume work on a cemetery grounds crew, and he professed to Yolanda that raising kids was strictly a woman's work, so he came around only when he wanted sex. In Clarence, Cornelius Joseph Walker's rotting apple didn't fall far from the infested tree.

The Reverend Mayweather, realizing that Clarence had an anchor in Yolanda and just needed a strong male role model and tough love to change his ways, made the boy his project. He taught Clarence about the Bible, subtly at first, and what it truly meant to be an authentic man. Initially, Clarence fought him with his street-life bravado, but the reverend could tell there was a smart and curious soul underneath trying to break through the armor Clarence wore to shield himself for a tough life to come. The reverend picked out films from the library about Europe and the South Pacific and watched them with Clarence after Bible study, opening the eyes of a boy who had never been beyond DeVaca City. He promised Clarence that if he stayed in school and joined the JROTC, he would help him to see those places. Clarence had no idea how, but it lit his imagination's fuse.

A BRIBE BLINDS THE EYES OF THE WISE

That summer of 1963, the Reverend Mayweather accompanied Clarence on two trips that changed his future. The first was a trip upstate to the state prison in Suwannee to visit Clarence's father, who went by Corny or CJ, whom he hadn't seen in two years. The reverend had laid the groundwork with a prison phone call appealing to Corny's pride by telling him that he had a smart and capable boy who could accomplish great things in life and be a role model for his younger brothers if he would accept Jesus Christ as his savior and develop a personal relationship with God.

Corny wasn't much for the religious hogwash—his God was an unforgiving, punishing God, and he believed Jesus would reject shouldering his sins as too heavy—but he did like the idea that someone who came from his DNA was handpicked by a man of the cloth for his potential. Perhaps, he thought, participating in his son's turnaround, even in his current shackled and thus limited capacity, could be the key to his own salvation.

Corny told Clarence that his deepest regret, despite his outward indifference, was his abject failure as a father and provider. He had numbed that feeling for years with booze and drugs and women and gambling, but as much as he tried to bury it, it burned a hole through the core of his soul. Corny told Clarence that he had the ability to make up for the sins of his father and make them both proud, and that he would be rooting for him, even praying. Clarence didn't know what to make of his dad's sudden interest, but he knew right then that he didn't want to end up a sorry, hopeless case like him, and if it took a father-son role reversal to model an honorable life, so be it.

For the other trip, just before school started, the reverend took Clarence and other teenagers on a twenty-hour bus ride to Martin Luther King's March on Washington for jobs and equality. Clarence was moved by Dr. King's command of the English language and oratorical power and the way he gave hope and strength and energy to so many men not much older than he was. Clarence was only just beginning to understand his people's struggle for liberty, but the empowerment and grace he experienced was visceral.

Clarence joined the JROTC at Palmertown Primary and High School, joined the school's football team as an offensive lineman, though he wasn't very good, and began applying himself in the classroom and getting mostly *A*s and *B*s. With his newfound discipline, he enlisted in the US Army upon graduation and shoved out for Fort Bragg for basic training. He rose through the ranks from private to staff sergeant, serving two tours of duty in Vietnam, leading a gunnery squad. After Vietnam, he was stationed at Wiesbaden Army Airfield in Germany, living out the images of the film he saw in the Reverend Mayweather's office. When he came back stateside, he trained grunts at Fort Campbell and took advantage of the G.I. Bill to earn a degree in social work.

After eighteen years of stellar service, Clarence retired from the military and returned to Palmertown to mentor youth as a counselor. In 1984, he was elected as the first African American on the Dolphin County school board. You could tell the discipline Clarence retained from the army by the impeccable way he dressed, his regimented walking cadence, his clear and forceful voice, his direct gaze, and the military-style boots he always wore. He became known throughout the community for those boots, which symbolized his transformation from hellion youth to community pillar, hence the nickname "Boots" Walker.

❖ ❖ ❖

"Clarence and I had a long discussion about the funding for the Praise Palmertown Complex," the Reverend Mayweather told me, "and I have to preface what I'm going to say by letting you know that in my role as clergy, our discussion was private and confidential, between me, Clarence, and the Lord. You got that?"

"Well, yeah, but I'm not sure what it means for me."

"It means Clarence gave me permission to explain certain things, but it is—how do you reporters refer to it—off the table?"

"Off the record."

"Right, off the record. This situation involves a number of people, good people, with reputations to protect and families to honor, and Clarence doesn't feel it's his calling to make it right for them. That's for them and their gods. Clarence feels he only answers to One, his God. You understand?"

"I think so." If the reverend got any more cryptic, I was about to experience the mystery of speaking in tongues.

"So what Clarence feels compelled to let you know is that the money used to build the Praise Palmertown Complex was ill-gotten. By that, I mean it was illegitimate and impure by the Bible's standards. As Clarence said, tainted. Now this falls into a big gray area of ethics, and we prayed to the Lord Our God to help us see the light. You know what I mean?"

"I'm following," I said, bracing for a convoluted Sunday morning sermon with a zinger to tie it all together in the end. As I waited, I mulled how my semibackwater sportswriter job brought me to a lesson on religious ethics from two disciples of Martin Luther King's March on Washington.

"Listen up in here. You know the question about whether it's ethically wrong for a man who has no land and no money and lost his job and can't feed his starving family to steal food from a place of abundance? Well, Palmertown ain't got nothing; Drabenville has abundance. There was a transactional opportunity to acquire something of sustenance for Palmertown's youth who are starving—some of them literally, others for attention and love and guidance and opportunity. What Clarence is saying is that he had a role in making that happen. In a nutshell, Clarence may have run afoul of man's law in his financial transactions—we don't know, not for me to say if all of Clarence's dealings were on the up and up—but did he break God's law by helping to bless children who were born into deprivation, children who deserve a break in this world, no matter how it comes? That's not for you or me to judge. That's between Clarence and the Almighty."

"Why are you telling me all this?" I asked. "What do you want me to do?"

Boots rejoined the conversation, feeling better now that the reverend had explained the delicate situation the way only a man of the cloth could.

"I don't want to deceive, but at the same time, the code of the street from my youth and the honor code from the military, they're from different worlds but they're both in my blood, and they dictate that I don't give people up—you know, snitch, rat them out, in street talk. That's on their conscience. Do what you have to do to investigate. I feel right. I leave it in God's hands—and yours."

Boots had gone to his pastor in confidence. Why wasn't he taking this to a lawyer if he felt compelled to bring it to the light of day outside the church's walls?

"But why me, Boots?"

"You were chosen, weren't you? You were there. You were called, and you will be led."

❖ ❖ ❖

By the time I returned to see JJ at Sunshine State Bank with my next paycheck, I had pieces of what was starting to look like a financial puzzle that appeared to have links connecting Drabenville and DeVaca City, the Dolphin County school board, Dolphin County's most powerful developers, and maybe even—nah, couldn't be. Then I thought back to my investigative journalism class at Colgate: never assume. Let the facts tell the story. Never assume you know the truth and never assume the truth is being told to you; never assume you know what someone meant if you don't know; never assume you are right; never assume the unlikely is not possible. It seemed unlikely that Coach Bamford could be involved in something shady, maybe illegal, right here where he was king. But was it possible? His past college scandal, despite his claims of scapegoating, said it was.

A BRIBE BLINDS THE EYES OF THE WISE

I began to think that JJ would be more valuable to me as a bank insider than as a longshot girlfriend. If I lost at that all-or-nothing romantic pursuit, she'd probably clam up and try to avoid me. If I kept harmless flirtation alive, she could be a good source of information. At least those were my assumptions.

Monsieur: The Bon Vivant

I took what I had gathered from JJ at the bank and Boots Walker—that some big checks had been deposited by a Nikolas Karras in the account of Pondcypress III LLC from a James Bamford trust account, and that something shady had gone down in the financing of the Praise Palmertown Athletic & Education Complex—to the *Dinqy*'s best investigative reporter, Jean-Paul Boneau.

An everyman's bon vivant who could discuss French Renaissance art as adroitly as prohibition-era Chicago mob figures, Boneau was an indefatigable and unstoppable courts and crime reporter, and he knew how to follow a trail. Known to friends simply as Monsieur for his French-Canadian roots, he used his unassuming, disheveled appearance to his advantage. He was no Harvard man out to prove how smart he was during a cup of coffee in the bush league on his way up to the *Wall Street Journal*. Boneau was from the street—Flanagan Street in the union-heavy, blue-collar East Side of Chicago—not Wall Street. He had a bush of unkempt, long, macaroni-twirl hair, bulging eyes, a crooked nose, and a potbelly, which he covered with untucked shirts from his collection of Hawaiian and Panamanian button-downs. He lived in a bottom-floor apartment known as The Hovel in a Conquista Island bungalow on the beach. He held court on his patio with a beautiful view of the Gulf sunset on Saturday nights, regaling his friends from the *Dinqy* with stories of his journalistic findings of brazen crooks, dim-witted thieves, scammers, frauds, adulterers, greedy bastards, and lowlifes from Dolphin County's high society and mean streets alike.

MONSIEUR: THE BON VIVANT

He would often down too many Pabst Blue Ribbons and slur his words, making his stories funnier until he passed out on his couch.

I recounted my visit with Boots Walker and the Palmertown complex dedication made possible by $200,000 in anonymous donations from DeVaca City businesses, and Boots's discomfort with the source of the funds. From his previous digging into preferential treatment granted by Dolphin County government to Papadopoulos Diversified Property Management on development projects that lacked the requisite environmental impact studies and zoning reclassification hearings, Monsieur immediately recognized Karras as the son-in-law of Gus Papadopoulos, who married into the business (Monsieur even knew Gus's daughter, Eugenia, from Gus's divorce documents) and was working his way up from sales associate. From there, the connection was easy for Monsieur. Pondcypress III LLC was the subsidiary formed by PDPM to construct, market, and sell luxury condos in the Esperanza Preciosa Condominium complex on the bay side of Conquista Island, and a mixed-use, tourist-attraction Main Street promenade to revitalize the 1940s-era Conquista Village. Monsieur drew the line from Karras to Papadopoulos, or Big Papa, who was also chairman of the Dolphin County Board of Education.

Then the link to Boots Walker became obvious to Monsieur, who knew all the politicos in the quad-county Citrus Coast region, from those in the U.S. Congress to the register of wills: Boots was the board of education representative from East DeVaca City, the Palmertown area.

"Jake, I smell armadillo shit going on here, man, and my nose for corruption is never wrong. Look how big it is," Monsieur told me. "I'm hunting other scoundrels at the moment, so I want you to do some digging and bring me some dirt. We can co-byline this bad boy, but we'll need to do a lot of corroborating and fact-checking. I know something's there. You've just tossed the first shovel of weeds off the grave, and if I know my shit, there's gonna be a pile of dead bodies inside."

"Monsieur, I'm just the sports reporter; I don't know anything about court records and real estate transactions and ethics statements and financial disclosures and shit. That's your bailiwick."

THREE YARDS AND A PLATE OF MULLET

"Welcome to Investigative Journalism 101, Jake. This'll be good for your career. You won't want to cover sweaty, dumb jocks forever, dude. Do what I do, man, bust some nuts and take no prisoners. It's a blast. Maybe that's not you—I have to remember not everyone is from the East Side of Chicago. Hang around me enough and some of that Polish sausage will rub off on you. Sorry, that sounded a little disgusting. I didn't mean it in a sexual way or nothin'. You know what I mean—Mike Ditka's scowl and Mike Royko's kickass *Chicago Sun-Times* columns and shit. I'll take you to the Dolphin County Courthouse and show you how to look up anything that's been filed and everything coming before a judge, and I'll introduce you to the clerks. You have to know how to sweet-talk the clerks. They can open the gates to the kingdom and save you time."

❖ ❖ ❖

I was too eager to wait to fit into Monsieur's busy schedule, so I went to the courthouse solo. It was the first time I had ever entered a courthouse. Dolphin County's was a Byzantine labyrinth of file rooms, law libraries, industrial-sized cabinets filled with coded folders, huge logbooks with handwritten entries, microfiche machines, and the beginnings of a computerized network.

I didn't know where to start, so I followed Monsieur's advice and dropped his name with a clerk. "I work with Jean-Paul Boneau at the *Daily Inquirer*. He says the prosecutors and judges and defendants give this place its drama, but it would all grind to a halt without y'all."

"That J-P, he knows his way around here…and with the ladies," the clerk said, laughing. "How can I help you, hon?"

I asked if she recalled any cases involving Pondcypress III LLC as a plaintiff or defendant over the last four years.

"Let me see…a lot of cases involve LLCs. It doesn't ring a bell. Do you know the parent company?"

"Yeah, I'm pretty sure it's Papadopoulos Diversified Property Management."

"Oh, that's a biggie. Big Papa probably has a whole room here filled with legal filings from real estate purchases and zoning battles and contract disputes."

The clerk entered data into her computer, made a printout, and then retrieved four big logbooks from the file room.

"I cross-referenced PDPM and Pondcypress from 1983 to 1986 but didn't find a match. But I found more than fifty filings where PDPM was a plaintiff or defendant for breach of contract, workers' comp, equal employment, negligence, sexual harassment, personal injury, you name it. We just started logging cases electronically, and we're still backtracking, but we don't have the data fields set up to capture all the information. Those tech guys play with wires and keyboards and little doohickeys all day, and they still can't get it right!

"Anyway, these books, they're much more thorough. Sometimes they'll list a DBA. They go in chronological order from the date entered by the clerk of the court."

"DBA?"

"I forgot. I'm used to dealing with J-P. He knows this place better than I do. 'Doing Business As.' That's how Pondcypress may be listed."

"Thanks, that's a big help, Ms...."

"Sugar, sweetie."

"What?"

"Florence Sugar, hon."

I lugged the four logbooks to a table and commenced my Evelyn Wood speed-reading strategy, using my hand to lead my eyes in a winding wave down each page, searching for a keyword. Maybe that stupid Evelyn class my dad foisted upon me for SAT prep wasn't worthless after all.

It took two hours to scan the entries in the first two books, and I didn't find Pondcypress, but lots of PDPM, like Sugar said. If I didn't find Pondcypress, I would have to start pulling each PDPM case one at a time to search for clues. How does Monsieur have the patience for this shit? My lazy alter ego would rather write who won and lost and why and call it a day, but my ego knew that would keep me at the bottom rung of the journalism ladder.

Then, gold! February 13, 1984, CV0294-83, here comes Plaintiff, the International Union of Bricklayers and Affiliated Craftworkers, Local 182 v. Defendants, Augustus K. Papadopoulos and Papadopoulos Diversified Property Management, D/B/A Pondcypress III LLC.

There were twenty-eight pages of legal mumbo jumbo, loaded with "henceforths" and "hereinafters" and "affidavits" and "fiduciaries" and a long, numbered sequence of events. It boiled down to this: PDPM gave the bricklayers and other tradesmen working on the Esperanza Preciosa condo and Conquista Village revitalization projects—masons, plasterers, tile layers, mosaic workers, sandblasters, and caulkers—paychecks that bounced like Goodyears over the fence at a Daytona 500 crash. Then, after the Bricklayers Local 182 union management met with PDPM executives to work out the issue civilly, and the PDPM honchos expressed surprise that the paychecks weren't valid and assured the union bosses that it was most likely an administrative error on the part of the company's banking institution due to the recent establishment of new LLC accounts and closure of certain other PDPM accounts, and that PDPM's accounting department would look into the situation and rectify it promptly and include 2.75 percent interest in the next biweekly paycheck to make up for workers' compound interest losses, the same "oversight," as PDPM called it, occurred again two weeks later.

At that point, the Bricklayers Local threatened to take its members off the job if the "oversight" wasn't remediated within forty-eight hours, with the caveat that such a drastic action was not the union's preference because their members had families and needed every paycheck they could earn in a fair-weather industry with unavoidable unemployment gaps to pay for their housing and groceries and gas, noting that the members were committed to, and counting on, these PDPM contracts for the long term, and they needed PDPM to show the same commitment. The Bricklayers' threatened job action resulted in an emergency meeting a day later with the PDPM C-suite, directors of the HR and accounting departments, and a vice-president from Sunshine State Bank & Trust. On the Bricklayers' side, the union flew in the lead counsel and negotiator from Washington to join the Southeast Regional Bricklayers Chapter president, and had representatives from each of the Local 182 trades attend as a show of unity and force. The PDPM side negotiated to give the company one more pay period to work out the problem. The bank vice-president explained the regulatory complexities that must be followed to restructure PDPM's accounts and credit lines, apologizing for the mix-ups and promising to straighten them out.

Two weeks later, no paychecks were issued. The Bricklayers gave PDPM a last chance for a meeting but were stonewalled. The lawsuit ensued for breach of contract for $160,238.25 plus legal fees.

The case never made it to trial, however, and the condo/revitalization project, which had an ambitious three-year timetable, proceeded. I assumed that the two sides worked out a deal. And now I was stuck. Was this a dead end or a bread crumb in the trail that led to a scandal? Did this have any connection to Boots Walker? Or was it just an obscure business dispute buried in the bowels of Dolphin's legal pad? I needed Monsieur to point me down the rabbit hole.

Entering the Lion's Den

"C'mon, Jake, put it together. What's the common thread?" Monsieur pressed me when I visited him at the Hovel for guidance the night of my courthouse initiation. He offered me a choice of Pinot Noir or Pabst Blue Ribbon with stone wheat crackers and Brie. I took the Pabst Blue Ribbon.

"Boots and Gus are both on the school board. But I can't figure out Pondcypress…"

"Slow down, rookie. A quick scoop may make you look good to the assholes in the corporate fortress, but it's the four *M*s that're the real journalism: methodically making minutiae into meaning. A gonzo journalism professor at Northwestern gave me that advice, and I still follow it."

"I like it, Jean-Paul."

"No shit. Hey, man, you're a detective, not a sniper. Get out your print-duster and go to work. We'll connect the dots after you do your due diligence, as my lawyer buddies say. Now what are you gonna do next, Woodward?"

With my neglectful lack of training from the sports junkies in the *Dinqy*'s proverbial toy department, I wasn't used to analyzing stories so deeply. They were all basically slam dunks, or in legal terms, prima facie, obvious and revelatory at first sight. But now I challenged myself to think more like Monsieur than like Skip Blintzer.

"I've got to start researching all the other school board members and see if I can find any connections, Monsieur."

ENTERING THE LION'S DEN

"Or even just anything out of the ordinary. Remember, you don't know exactly what you're looking for yet. That's how detectives trip themselves up, when they've already climbed and rapelled the denouement before they've finished the opening chapter. Anything can be a clue. I'd love to help you more, but I'm up to my ass in alligators with this FloRite Corporation embezzlement case.

"One thing you gotta do is set the context, build the frame that the big bad wolf is gonna blow down right on top of these cocksuckers. So what was happening in the early 1980s?"

"Fuck if I know, Jean-Paul. I was staggering from the Beta Theta Pi fraternity party trying to make it up Cardiac Hill to my Sellman Dorm bathroom before I puked and hoping against hope I'd get lucky with anything other than a double-bagger…OK, even a double-bagger."

"C'mon, Jake, it was almost yesterday. Reagan and his country club Neanderthals plunged us into a big recession, oil went through the roof, and housing sales were about as slow as me running the hundred meters. The housing boom of the '70s went bust real quick here by 1982, and I'll bet that bunghole, Big Papa, didn't read the tea leaves and overbuilt on blind speculation—just let the good times roll, the greedy bastard. Now the cock has come home to roost—he can't sell the properties and he can't pay his workers.

"Now swash down that swill and clear your palette with some crackers and oysters from my fridge and savor some Pinot. It's exquisite, imported from Quebec. You got to get cultured, man. Don't worry, rook, I'll school ya."

If Monsieur believed something was amiss, I knew I wouldn't be wasting my time.

❖ ❖ ❖

Monday morning I was back at Sugar's courthouse desk, practicing my sweet talk as Monsieur instructed.

"It was great to see Roll Tide Roll over LSU," I told her, knowing from Monsieur's tip that Sugar was from Alabama and a huge Crimson Tide fan. "I love any team known for having a legendary coach named Bear with a houndstooth-check hat."

Sugar laughed. "Now just imagine the Bear and Broadway Joe Namath teaming up. Of course, that was before he was Broadway Joe. He was just a blue-collar boy from Beaver Dam, Pennsylvania, or someplace like that. I still love him in that Noxzema commercial with Farrah Fawcett."

And then she chirped the Noxzema jingle: "Let Noxzema cream your face…so the razor…won't!

Ahhh, the '60s…'70s…whenever. I was young like Broadway Joe…like you…yeah," she said dreamily. "You didn't come here to hear all this stuff. What can I do for you?"

"I love that slow-motion image of Namath from behind, wagging his number one finger in the air as he jogs off the field through a crowd after the Jets beat the Colts in Super Bowl III," I said, building on the connection. "Sad to say, I was so young I mostly remember Broadway Joe as a broken-down washout with the Rams who starred in Grade D *Chattanooga Choo Choo* with that *Little House on the Prairie* girl, Melissa Sue Anderson."

Sugar frowned. Oops, blew the schmooze. Not as smooth as Monsieur yet.

"OK, let's get down to business."

I gave Sugar a list of six names to research—all the Dolphin County school board members who had been serving with Big Papa since 1983. The computerized records went back only to 1985, so I had Sugar help me look up the names in indexes, logbooks, registries, plats, deeds, and other paper records.

I found a nugget. The school board member representing the Great Bay district, Shelley Jochnowitz, purchased a condo in 1984 on Solo Calcetino Key, the more upscale barrier island south of Conquista Island, for $149,900. She paid for it outright, no bank lien. That seemed odd. I did some digging. Had she sold her house and bought the condo with the proceeds? No record of that, and current election records confirmed she was still at her longtime address in the Great Bay district.

I had Monsieur help me with more investigation through public records, his bulging Rolodex of contacts, and old-fashioned, shoe-leather, door-to-door reporting. It turned out that Jochnowitz's mother had moved to the condo from Iron Mountain, Michigan. We identified Jochnowitz's current job, sales associate at Sunny Daze Treatments and Blinds, and determined that her annual income was between $18,000 and $32,500 for the top-commission associate—hardly enough to plunk down full price for a luxury condo on affluent Solo Calcetino Key. Monsieur had me check out the wills and estates unit, but my search turned up no evidence that some wealthy relative of Jochnowitz had croaked and left her a booty.

Next, I searched Lenzell Langston from East Drabenville and hit the jackpot. Langston was the owner of Lounging Lizard Liquors in East Drabenville, which had been fined several times by the Dolphin County Liquor Board for selling booze to minors and closed in 1983 under Chapter 11 bankruptcy protection, allowing him time to stave off creditors and reorganize his finances. Now, not only was the once-vacant storefront reopened for business, but it was renovated inside and out from seedy to shiny and expanded to include a cigar and hookah section. And that's not all. Since 1984, Langston had opened Got Jack Pay Day Loans & Check Cashing in the empty space next to Lounging Lizard, charging interest rates that amounted to more than 300 percent annually and taking 5.95 percent off the top from welfare recipients looking to leverage their monthly dole into immediate gratification and blue-collar workers too suspicious of banks to open a checking account. Langston also bought a Popeye's Louisiana Chicken franchise that replaced a long-departed Bob's Big Boy on the Flume's East Drabenville commercial strip. I did some research and found that Popeye's up-front investment costs, including franchise fees, were north of $150,000. From bankruptcy to owner of three businesses in two years' time—quite a spectacular turnaround, especially for a denizen of poorly resourced and undercapitalized East Drab.

❖ ❖ ❖

I took my documentation to Monsieur. He rifled through the papers and came to his conclusion within a minute.

"Somebody paid these fuckers off, plain as the mole on my left butt cheek."

That triggered the Bible verse Boots Walker had quoted to me. I flipped through my notebook to find it.

"Jean-Paul, listen to this, from my interview with Boots…Clarence Walker, the school board member from Palmertown. He called me to his office after the dedication of the Praise Palmertown Athletic & Education Complex to get something off his chest, but I didn't know what the hell he was talking about."

I found the verse and recited it for Monsieur: "You shall not pervert justice. You shall not show partiality, and you shall not accept a bribe, for a bribe blinds the eyes of the wise and subverts the cause of the righteous."

"Boots handed it to you on a silver platter. He just buried it in all that Jesus Our Lord and Savior crap," Monsieur said. "He gave you the turkey. We just gotta dress it with gravy and stuffing and chitlins and then pull the fuckin' gizzards out of that sucker. You're doing a good job on the gravy, and when I go for the gizzard, I never miss.

"So let's do a shot of tequila with a lemon-and-clam chaser to get really lucid, then give me the whole rundown."

I licked my hand between my thumb and forefinger, Monsieur poured some coarse salt on the sticky spot, I lapped up the salt, and in synchronicity with Monsieur, on his command of "grease the gullet," I poured back a big-ass shot of Cuervo Gold, sucked the pulp out of a lemon wedge, and slurped a clam off the half shell. Now I was ready.

ENTERING THE LION'S DEN

"Augustus Papadopoulos, aka Gus, aka Big Papa, founder and president of Papadopoulos Diversified Property Management, falls on hard times in the aftermath of the Reagan recession of '82 as the spigot closes on trickle-down economics and stiffs his workers on the Esperanza Preciosa Condo and Conquista Village revitalization projects. The Bricklayers Union files suit, claiming Big Papa dicked them over after promising to make good on wages. The suit is settled before trial, and we have no explanation for how it is resolved.

"Within two years of the lawsuit, Big Papa's school board colleagues become wheelers and dealers way above their stations in life. Shelley Jochnowitz, the blind saleswoman—er, the chick who sells window treatments—buys an upscale condo on Solo Calcetino Key outright for her mother, without selling her primary residence. Lenzell Langston goes bankrupt, and in an amazing reversal of fortune, transforms himself into the Michael Milken of East Drab's fast-cash, hard-liquor, fried-food, industrial-complex economy.

"In the meantime, hometown boy-made-good Clarence "Boots" Walker has a crisis of conscience with his own personal Jesus after basking in the greatest new development in Palmertown in a generation. Those three, plus Big Papa, comprise a majority of the seven-member school board."

As I recounted the facts and connections into a narrative, the conclusion became as clear as a Mitch Mahotie size-fifteen Hush Puppies shoeprint in the mud. Coach Bamford was funneling money derived from the Bamford & Sons empire to Big Papa so he wouldn't go belly up on the potentially lucrative Esperanza Preciosa venture, with the quid pro quo that Big Papa get three school-board members to join him in what would be a highly controversial vote to redistrict South Palmertown to Dolphin High under the social engineering guise of "increasing diversity" and "closing the achievement gap" but with the real purpose of sending the best football players in Dolphin County—including several in every grade whom the Mel Kipers of the world would label athletic "freaks"—to help rebuild the Dolphin Fightin'

THREE YARDS AND A PLATE OF MULLET

Dorsal Fins' dynasty. Money under the table was the worm he used to reel in the hungry fish.

"Keep workin' it, Jake, your due diligence," Monsieur said. "You gotta crawl under rocks until you know more than all of these bastards all together. Then we'll pump their concentric circles of friends and acquaintances for any more intel we can get before we track down these friggin' perps and nail 'em with the ultimate questions of truth, justice, and the American way. It'll be all Mike Wallace-esque and shit, I guarantee you, dude. You've stumbled into a hornet's nest, but with the fuckin' yokels around here, I'd call it more like a lion's den. Are you up for it, Jake?"

"Yeah, I think so, J-P. But I really like Boots…"

"It ain't personal. It's just your job. The cops and the DAs don't think everyone they arrest and prosecute is a scumbag. Hell, they grew up playing Little League with some of them. But it's their job. If the whole law enforcement system pursued justice based on likability quotient—and believe me, there's too much of that already—we might as well flush the whole American jurisprudence, *E pluribus unum*, habeas corpus, and all that crap down the terlet and go back to King Henry presiding over beheadings in the village square and the Romans cheering on the lions—and I don't mean Detroit—mauling their opponents in the Roman Colosseum.

"You're the good guy, man. The truth will never lead you wrong. The truth will set you free and shit. Now, you ready?"

"Yeah, Monsieur. Let's do it."

❖ ❖ ❖

My next step was to research the *Dinqy*'s archives for stories about the 1984 school redistricting decision. It was clear that Palmertown and DeVaca City residents opposed the move because it would cause divisions in the proud and tight-knit Palmertown community and weaken DeVaca High. Old-guard Drabenvillians didn't like it either, ostensibly because they felt that Dolphin High was already at capacity and shipping Palmertown students in would mean carving a chunk of current students out to go to

ENTERING THE LION'S DEN

Great Bay, and no Dolphin parents wanted their kids to leave the county's premier and storied educational institution for an unproven start-up. Another reason was only inferred—that the addition of poor blacks would ignite rumors, however ridiculous, exaggerated, and unfounded, but spread from clique to clique and through Publix grocery, golf clubs, and fish fries, that Dolphin High was starting down the slippery slope toward transformation into a ghetto school, and of the harm to property values and the sanctified way of life. But Big Papa, as the school board's leader, argued that Dolphin High was bigger than that, that diversity should not only be embraced but actively pursued, and that Dolphin High and South Palmertown kids would be better for it. Big Papa was hailed by a small cadre of activists as the most progressive school-board leader Dolphin County had ever seen—though perhaps had never wanted.

Great Bay parents opposed the redistricting because the rapid development in their district was projected to put their school at capacity within three years and 10 percent over capacity within six years. The Dolphin High transfer would push that figure closer to 15 percent, and everyone knew that meant the dreaded boxcar portable classrooms and sardine-can hallways bursting like a New York subway train at rush hour.

East Grove had the opposite problem. Its enrollment had been declining for years as more houses were abandoned or foreclosed upon, and more families moved out for jobs elsewhere. If South Palmertown were to be redistricted anywhere, it should be to East Grove, the Calusa Warriors alumni argued. Of course, the Warriors knew just as well as the Dorsals' boosters did the athletic gifts that such a transfer would bestow on their school.

Despite the prevalence of opposition at public hearings, Chairman Papadopoulos, Walker, Jochnowitz, and Langston voted for the proposal, which passed 4–3. Letters to the editor decried the decision as "rigged" and an "inside job." The *Dinqy*'s editorial board hailed the move as a "long-overdue advancement toward diversity and opportunity that awakened the Dolphin County Board of Education from a Rip Van Winkle slumber through years of civil rights progress," while the more conservative *T-D* proffered a veiled racist and stereotypical warning that "redrawing boundary lines is the easy part; ensuring the new Palmertown students can adapt to Dolphin High's rigorous standards and expectations is a challenge that will require additional resources. We hope the Dolphin school board has considered this consequence but thus far see no evidence."

❖ ❖ ❖

My next move was to visit JJ at Sunshine State Bank & Trust. I got her to get a cover for her teller window so we could go to one of the partitioned cubicles, as though I was applying for a loan, so we'd have more time and privacy. Taking a page from Monsieur's book and building on my experience with Flo Sugar at the courthouse, I struck up a conversation with JJ about Kissimmee State, having researched it beforehand.

"K State's rolling in the dough with Tropicana's seventy-five-million-dollar building fund and Disney's matching endowment," I told JJ. "In a few years, it's gonna be the university of choice in Florida anywhere outside of Gainesville and Tallahassee. It must be construction city."

JJ giggled. "Yeah, it's like the students have to wear hard hats to class because of all the construction zones. You should see the new library and science and technology buildings going up, super modern. I might even do my studying in the library when it's open—if they put in some comfortable couches...with pillows." She giggled again.

"I'm gonna get my finance degree, you know," she said, getting serious. "I'm not gonna be a teller forever. Ya know, most girls from DeVaca High become hair stylists or nannies or drop out of Dolphin Community with a loaf in the oven. I've got bigger dreams. After I move up at this bank and learn more about investing, I'm going to be a wealth management adviser."

I could swear JJ was trying to impress me, and I was flattered. Did she want to dump her loser boyfriend and pull the ol' Yank after all? Mr. Horny beckoned, and I had to exercise self-control to conduct the business at hand.

"Hey, JJ, remember you mentioned that you handled some unusual checks from a Bamford trust account to a Papadopoulos business?"

"Yeah. Does that mean something important?"

The way her eyes widened, her head tilted, and her voice rose at the end of the question, as if she was a kindergartner watching gorillas humping at the zoo ("Mommy, what's *THAT*?"), made me want to blow my wad again.

"Could be. I'm just lookin' into something, you know, investigative journalism." I thought a hint of intrigue would draw her in, knowing the tedium of her job and her desire to break loose.

"Could you help me?"

"Whadya need?"

"I want to know if it's been a regular occurrence to have checks deposited into a Papadopoulos account from James Bamford's trust account going back to 1983. Can you trace that through your database?"

"You know I'm not supposed to research anything like that without the branch manager's authorization."

She looked troubled. My spirits plummeted.

"But he's at a training this week. And I don't think anyone will ask. Or notice. Or care. I shouldn't tell you this, but this bank is really lax, like slacker city. All the manager cares about is making his tee time at three. The assistant manager takes two-and-a-half-hour 'business lunches'"—JJ paused and added air quotes for emphasis, then continued—"and then closes her office door behind the trail of alcohol she leaves in the lobby for the last hour of the day. Even if they found out I did this, they wouldn't give a shit. They wouldn't have a clue. I'm bored. Let's do it."

It was the most excited I had ever seen JJ at her job.

"Don't worry, this is strictly confidential. I won't blow your cover," I promised. "Just to be safe, I'll start going to other branches to do my business so there's no obvious link. So I may have to see you after hours, if you know what I mean."

God, that was slick, like Sam fleecing Diane from *Cheers*. And goddamn if it didn't work.

THREE YARDS AND A PLATE OF MULLET

JJ giggled and gave me a coy smile. She punched some information into the system, and then went to a back room and closed the door. She reemerged with a sheath of perforated printout papers.

"Holy shit, you were right. Almost like clockwork, every three months since March 1983, a check from Bamford Trust to PDPM. Are you ready for this?"

"Shoot."

"One million, eight hundred seventy-five thousand dollars. What do you think that's all about?"

"I'm pretty sure it's a quid pro quo, but I can't tell you exactly what for. Got to investigate." I had JJ make me a copy; she kept another locked in a file.

"What are you gonna do now?" she asked.

"I'm gonna crawl under some rocks."

"What?"

"My mentor, the Bon Vivant...I'm entering the lion's den...Never mind. I'm gonna try to break this story open, get some people to crack.

"Ya think I can get you to crack, maybe this Saturday night, since I'm gonna have to avoid banking hours?"

JJ looked down, smiled, and blushed. I think the charm assault was working. "Well, we'll sEEE-eee," she replied in a singsong voice and slid me her phone number on a deposit slip.

I left fired up to track down some lions and rendezvous with the person who, I hoped, would be my new tiger.

Rattling a Bunny's Cage

I spent the week rattling cages in between football coverage—school board members, the East Drabenville civic leaders, the Bricklayers Union's new president, Popeye's national headquarters, the owner of Sunny Daze Treatments and Blinds, Voracious Vinnie himself, and South Palmertown Little League coaches—searching for clues that would lead me to a Bamford bribe, while being so obtuse and, frankly, mildly though justifiably dishonest in my explanation of my journalistic purpose and my line of questioning that they didn't know what the hell I was after. People were just glad for the attention and the possibility of getting their names in the paper, especially those with business interests, who viewed any newspaper interview as free advertising.

Through research in the *Dinqy*'s archives, I pegged an at-large school board member, Bunny Heavener, who had pulled her learning-disabled son out of Dolphin County public schools to homeschool him when such a plan was still considered the exclusive domain of fruitcakes, aging hippies, and cultists, as the most outspoken critic of department of education proposals and school-board insider horse trading. That disdain for funny business had prompted her to run for a seat in the first place, to ensure that regular parents' views were heard and considered with equal weight as those of the superintendent and the school-board heavies.

I asked Bunny for an interview under the guise of writing a story about a school board member's proposal to move ninth grade back to middle school to relieve overcrowding in high schools and reduce the maturity and developmental gap among high schoolers, which was leading to an epidemic of bullying. How would this proposal, I wanted to know, affect high school sports?

"What about the athletes who develop their skills and have real coaching on freshman teams? There's no equivalent in middle school; in fact, there's no budget for interscholastic sports. Has the board discussed the impact on high school athletic programs?" I asked.

"Yes, that's one of the arguments against the change, and I agree with that, but not for the same reasons that you or all the coaches would think," she responded. "For me, academics is the top priority, and all the research shows that kids involved in sports get better grades and have a higher graduation rate. That's one of my concerns with homeschooling Noah. He loves sports, but he's got a learning disability, and the school system won't let him participate because he's homeschooled. But he wasn't getting the support he needed and was failing at Dolphin High because he couldn't do the work, so he would be ineligible anyway. I'm worried that he'll lose motivation with academics without the inspiration of being on a team."

I saw an opening. "So do you think the redistricting of the Palmertown kids to Dolphin was good for their athletics and academics?"

"It was good for the elite athletes, but on the whole, no," she replied. "Do you know how competitive and cutthroat it is at Dolphin for everything? The majority of Palmertown kids who would have lots of opportunity and attention at DeVaca are lost at sea at Dolphin. You know Coach Huck and how much he cares about every player. Well, *all* the teachers and coaches are like that at DeVaca. It's special. They're not getting that same kind of attention at Dolphin. It's more like a factory."

"So you voted against the redistricting, right?"

"Yeah, but the pressure was intense. Gus was vote counting and wasn't sure if he had four, so he put the heat on me and Clarence Walker. It was really ridiculous. He said he could arrange for my son to go to the best private school in Florida for kids with learning disabilities, but he needed my vote to make it happen."

Now we were getting somewhere.

"Did he say how he would make it happen?"

"Just that he had connections and not to worry about the details."
"What did you think of that offer?"
"If I didn't know better, I'd think it might be a bribe…"
I made sure to capture that quote word for word.
"But Gus is such a highly regarded pillar of the community and well-respected school leader, I just thought he was really trying to help me out, like with all his philanthropic activities, and that he really felt this decision was important."
"So how did you respond?"
"I asked him how much the school would cost, and he said twenty thousand a year with boarding. I said there was no way I could afford that, and he said what if money wasn't the issue."
"Did you ask what he meant when he said money wasn't the issue?"
"He just said he had a close relationship with the headmaster; they were old friends, and not to worry about it, this is what friends do for each other."
"So why didn't you go for it?"
Bunny was one of those women who loves to talk and to hear herself talk and to talk first and think later. But suddenly she grew cautious. Furrowing her brow and lowering her voice, she asked, "Is this, what do you say, on deep record?"
"You mean 'on deep background' or 'off the record'?"
"Whatever. Are you going to write about this and quote me?"
"I don't know yet. But I never said we were off the record. You should know that, as a public official."
I braced for Bunny to yell at me and call me a scheming, underhanded, low-life scum bucket like all the other reporters, but the vitriol never materialized. "I was tempted, but I also couldn't stand the thought of Noah being so far away. And I always thought there was something sleazy about it. I know this kind of stuff happens in politics all the time. I couldn't really tell if it was a bribe or just one of those political favors—you know, an inside deal—that's just what's supposed to happen in politics. So finally, I said no. I've got ethics, you know."

"Then what happened?"

"He moved on to Clarence. But Clarence was going to be a tougher sell. He loved his Palmertown kids and didn't want to weaken DeVaca City High. But obviously, it worked.

"Hey, Jake, if you find something really shady, like, you know, wrongdoing, come back to me. I always had a bad feeling about this, and it's been weighing on my conscience. I didn't run for school board to be part of the status quo; I ran to challenge the status quo. I got to speak out to be true to myself when something violates the public's trust."

"I will, I will."

Tomato Vines

With Bunny's story in my pocket, I figured it was time to round up Boots's posse and zero in on the biggest domino of them all. I knew Boots had a more powerful moral compass and a heavier conscience than other school board members who likely were involved. If Boots would crack, Bunny would provide a second confirmation, and the whole sordid scheme would tumble down like a wobbly cheerleaders' pyramid girding to support a thunder thighs.

I started with the Roma Rojo Tomatoes Company, where the bulk of the money for the Praise Palmertown Complex purportedly came from anonymously. I met with the union leaders of the Tomato Pickers and Packers and the Conveyor and Canning Amalgamated, but neither knew of any donors within their organizations. It would be unusual for any rank-and-file union member to contribute a significant sum of money, but I thought they might have made a good cover for funneling money.

I knew that a lot of Roma Rojo employees—support staff and middle-manager types—gathered at a park by the Blue Fin River for lunch, so I dropped in one day, ostensibly to gather color for Friday's big rivalry game between DeVaca and Mirabella Dunes High. During all of my conversations, I mentioned how great it was that Roma Rojo made construction of the Praise Palmertown Complex possible. Employees just agreed, saying Roma Rojo workers were civic-minded people devoted to improving the community.

I nearly left before deciding to chat up one more table. That's when my break came. I dropped my usual line about the generous Roma Rojo donations, and a floor manager named LeRoy Pitts immediately offered that he never knew his supervisor, line production manager Jerome "Romey" Salters, had saved so much money that he could make such a large donation, but then again, Salters was single and had worked at Roma Rojo for twenty-five years. I asked how he knew Salters had made one of the donations.

"Everyone knows, at least on my floor; Romey brags about it all the time, how one day they're going to name a baseball diamond after him and dedicate a college scholarship fund in his name, how Boots had told him that. The other two guys are jealous because they didn't get the same promises."

"Who are the other two guys?"

"Norris Colbert, over in canning, and Jahidi Brown, from quality control. We was all friends growin' up back at the old Palmertown Colored School, played ball together. They're right over there."

LeRoy motioned to a table in the shade in a grove of palms, where four men were bantering and cracking on each other like one had just one-upped another with a cruder yo-mama joke. By now, I realized that even though I was sure that Boots had sworn his old buddies to secrecy, they were just itching to let the world know that they had cabbage, that they were philanthropists, pillars of their community, and if the *Dinqy* only realized that, they would be invited to the Annual Quad County Rotary Club Charity Gala and get their names mentioned in the Sunday society section by "Out and About" columnist Penelope Southwick. And photos of them wearing rented fuchsia or neon-green tuxedos would be published adjacent to photos of the Quad's other debonair, well-dressed, and even better-heeled, transplanted society elites.

I sat at the end of the table, waiting for the initial awkwardness of the intrusion to subside. The temptation to tell a yo-mama joke flashed through my mind, but I resisted the pull of a Tourette's moment and zapped it.

I introduced myself, and the guys perked up right away.

"Did any of you guys read the story in the *Dinqy* about the dedication of the Praise Palmertown Athletic & Education Complex?"

Heads nodded in unison. "Ain't no one in Palmertown hasn't seen it," Norris offered.

"Well, I covered that, and I think it would be great to follow up with a story on who made this great facility possible, you know, the anonymous donors. Could be a great human-interest feature if the donors came forward. Romey sent me over here; said you guys may know something."

"Who want to know?" asked Jahidi.

"Who want to know? Everyone want to know," I answered. "I want to know. Right now, it's a mystery. Everyone want to solve a mystery. Don'tcha hear the talk around town?"

"Hell yea-yah," said Norris. "It on the street, man, you know it," he said, laughed, and leaned forward to give a high five to his buddy.

"You put the donors in the paper?" Jahidi asked.

"Yeah, if my editor likes the story, and I don't see why he wouldn't. And the managing editor, she's a Southern belle, right off the plantation; she loves the heartwarming shit; she'll eat it up. If I was a betting man—and I am—I'd go all in on front page, man!"

I sounded so convincing—it wasn't hard because it was true—that I fooled myself into becoming as excited as the brothas at the prospect.

God, the power of the pen *was* mythical. I could feel the fellas' resistance crumbling, like a chocolate-doughnut binger's on the sixth day of a cabbage soup diet.

Norris and Jahidi did some telepathic communicating with each other, opening eyes wider, furrowing brows, nodding heads, and then Norris ended the pregnant pause by turning to face me.

"Me and Jahidi, we was tryin' to keep it a secret, but you know what they say about secrets: the skeleton's got to come out of the closet, or the secret will take you to the grave, or some shit like that. All I know is secrets eat you up inside."

He had me hanging, waiting for the money shot.

"Go a'haid No-No, ain't no big thang," Jahidi encouraged.

"OK. We—me and J-man—we been saving for a long time because we always wanted to make our community better, give back," Norris said. "When we found out about Bible Praise Palmertown's plan for a community complex, that was like two ships passing in the night—y' know, fate and all that shit.

"So, a'ight, yeah, we each ponied up a donation. Boots gave us the idea, said we'd be blessed by giving back. If it come from Boots, it must be true. We didn't want no credit or nothin'. It ain't about us, man. We wanted to help Boots out and give back to the kids. They was us twenty-five years ago. Times change, and we want them to have better than we did. We had to scratch and claw for a damn biscuit, word. We got a few cuz to come up with some cash, too.

"I guess it's OK for people to know now, since it's all built and everything. Boots was kind of funny about that, keeping it a secret. I don't always understand my man Boots, the military really change him, got all up in his head and shit. I don't ask Boots questions. I'm just like, 'Yes sir, Boots.' And that's what we did."

"So when we gonna be in the *Dinqy*? You gonna send your photo man?"

I had what I needed from my new Roma Rojo contacts—plausible if circumstantial evidence of a money-funneling connection between Boots and the no longer "anonymous" donors from Roma Rojo Tomatoes to the Praise Palmertown Athletic and Education Complex. The dirty money stream would still have to be proved, and I certainly didn't want to hang these Roma Rojo guys out to dry. I liked them. But these were not the type of guys that struck me as foresightful, save-for-a-rainy-day philanthropists. They appeared more like marionettes in the grand puppeteer's scheme. If all this chicanery did unfold into a criminal investigation, I was hoping that Norris and Jahidi would get good immunity deals to roll over as law enforcement followed the money trail up the pyramid. But as Monsieur emphasized, I was just doing my job, seeking the truth, which is virtuous unto itself—the granite foundation of American jurisprudence and all that stuff Monsieur fed me. I hoped it was true because I felt myself getting in deep the more I pursued the story, which made me feel like a real journalist but also a potential target for hatred and vengeance, should things turn out bad for the people I would expose for perverting the public's trust.

I was sure Norris and Jahidi were not familiar with bribery and kickback laws, though I was certain—as Mitch Mahotie would say, "dollars to doughnuts"—they got their own piece of cake for participating in the convoluted ruse. It was doubtful they ever heard of the corrupt Jersey boys of Abscam fame, whose bribery kickback schemes brought down powerful members of Congress.

Hell, maybe they weren't even guilty of anything, but somebody was. They were the pawns that had to be captured to open the way for attacking the king. Producing a stalemate out of this quagmire wasn't going to get me shit from the O-Dog, much less from the higher-pedigreed Chenault and Wellington. This was my Bobby Fischer moment, and Bamford was my foil, my Boris Spassky, the chess grand master. Hopefully, I wouldn't end up a paranoid recluse like Bobby did after he vanquished his Cold War rival in the 1972 match of the century.

❖ ❖ ❖

My opportune meeting with Norris and Jahidi came just two days before Dolphin took on Clear Vista in the Friday night game of the week. Word must have traveled fast from the Roma Rojo plant to the Praise Palmertown Complex, through Palmertown to the Palmertown Six, and ultimately—or so I believed but would have a heck of a time proving—straight to the Dolphin High football coaches' lair. I could imagine no other logical explanation for my postgame bungle in the jungle in the middle of Ninth Avenue West with a couple of blue-and-gold-clad, helmeted roughnecks, five blocks from Dolphin High's Jed Bamford Field at Roop Stadium. Thanks to shotgun-toting Good Samaritan Norville Haggard, I escaped the Ninth Avenue Beatdown with only minor injuries and a lesson in intimidation, Southern-style, which paled in comparison to my motivation to see this thing through.

It would have been a hell of a lot easier just to drop it, pretend I didn't know anything, write about the games, prop up the high school star athletes who may be enjoying the pinnacles of their lives, fawn over the football coaches who rivaled Gainesville High School's own spindly Tom Petty as Florida pop-culture gods, and give some precious ink to the cross-country runners and volleyball spikers and soccer strikers who worked hard but were overlooked. But I like a challenge. No, I live for a challenge. If it's not a challenge, it's boring. And if it's boring, I might as well go back to an urban street corner and sell more Kabir leather-and-lace wear.

The thing I fear most is a boring life. I fear that more than I fear two Neanderthals trying to pummel me into tomorrow to make me afraid to do my job. With the warning blow delivered, I was ready for *anything*. I hoped Boots Walker could say the same about our upcoming visit.

Gotcha

Dieter Klingenmeier worked on Wall Street for a commodities and securities firm for three years after Colgate University. But Dieter sought a creative and independent career path, rather than climbing a preordained ladder and kowtowing to the unwritten rules and self-aggrandized masters of the street. He loved the business world but abhorred being a small cog in a big firm that didn't register as a blip on the world's exchanges. He wanted to spread his genius around, be a jack-of-all-trades, seamlessly swing from expounding on business institutions, mergers and acquisitions, futures, hedge funds, derivatives, REITS, and the titans of industry who undergirded capitalism to investment gurus, venture capitalists, real estate moguls, entrepreneurs, inventors, tech wizards, and even labor leaders and consumer advocates, because they were all part of the tapestry. He'd also met his share of schemers, shysters, fast-talkers, and con artists on Wall Street and was equally fascinated and repulsed by their greed and megalomania. He studied what made them tick, how they built rapport and reconciled their dichotomous natures, how they sucked trusting people into their orbits and maintained the gravitational pull until it was too late for their victims to achieve escape velocity.

What better way to be part of all the constellations in this infinite universe, Dieter came to realize, than to be a top-notch business reporter, ideally an investigative journalist, and he believed that one day in the not-too-distant future, he would return to "The Street"—the revered *Wall Street Journal*—to ply his chosen trade, uncover massive wrongdoings and secretive blockbuster deals, and, in general, crack some heads.

Without a byline to his name, he enrolled in the prestigious Columbia University School of Journalism to learn the craft and build up some clips.

To Dieter's chagrin and to the considerable detriment of his over-inflated ego, none of the big boys of the fourth estate wanted a green journalist with J-school incubated, sponsored, and contrived clips. Most didn't even respond to his overly ambitious application packages stuffed with his articles from *Columbia Business Review* and his internship on the business desk of Long Island's *Nassau County Citizen*, which was considered bush league by the likes of *The New York Times*, *The Washington Post*, the *Chicago Tribune*, the *Los Angeles Times*, *The Baltimore Sun*, and all the other arrogant, ivory tower media outlets to which Dieter aspired and that condescendingly prefer to shit on J-school graduates as people not naturally talented enough to write their way onto the big stage so instead must buy overpriced and useless "educations" that give them the necessary connections and let them avoid paying their dues.

Even Dieter's hometown *Milwaukee Journal-Sentinel*, one of the few third- or fourth-tier newspapers that deigned him worthy enough to respond to, had no allegiance to the local boy and advised him to do what all the others did: go make your amateurish mistakes and get your hackneyed prose out of your system at a small-town fish-wrapper and call us back in three years when you have something legitimate to show, and then maybe we'll consider you for the most godforsaken beat nobody else wants—maybe agriculture or retail.

So Dieter set his sights lower and focused on building his portfolio. He sent applications all over Florida, with its numerous newly sprouting metro areas and culture of accepting transplants. He landed at the *Dinqy* covering Dolphin County business, and, in short order, was a regular in our Camelot Cay living room, after he settled in his own Camelot apartment. Before there ever was a Kramer bursting through an apartment door uninvited to visit good-natured neighbor Jerry, there was Dieter.

❖ ❖ ❖

GOTCHA

Dieter was an adherent of gonzo journalism and idolized its pioneer and poster child, Hunter S. Thompson, who wrote in the first-person narrative style, his adventures as much the story as the story was, without claims of objectivity. If he didn't have the chance to go gonzo, which was rare at typically staid newspapers, all he talked about was getting a good scoop or engaging in "gotcha journalism, D-man style."

"C'mon, Jake, you gotta have 'gotcha' in your balls if you're going to be a good journalist. You gotta have a scoop. You just gotta slam 'em," Dieter would tell me when I expressed reticence about approaching Boots again or going toe-to-toe with heavyweight champeen Bamford.

No doubt, Dieter was a Pied Piper of Monsieur, a natural for the role of the Bon Vivant's prodigal son. That made Dieter the Disciple the perfect addition to my undercover I-Team, along with Monsieur, to advance the story. I wasn't going to let Skip Blintzer or Paddy know what I had until I knew I had the goods and Bamford and Big Papa dead to rights, because I pegged both Skip and Paddy as the ultimate homers—*Dinqy* lifers who wanted to sail through a blissful life of golf and fishing and boating and tennis and seafood feasts—a step up from fish fries—and margaritas on the pier overlooking the most gorgeous pink- and yellow- and orange-hued sunsets imaginable in a place that was absolute paradise compared with the decrepit industrial wastelands from which they had escaped. And who could blame them? But I knew that they would be leery of rocking the boat and biting the hand that fed them, especially Skip, who was more reliant on a cordial relationship and good feelings with all the region's high schools. I knew broaching this developing scandal with him would throw him into a stuttering tizzy. I could hear it already: "Hu-Hu-How can you be s-s-so sh-sure about your s-s-sss-sources? You better-better be able…able to back…back this up. This is bu-bu-big. I want solid…solid pru-pru-prooofffff. If you're wrong, J-J-Jake, we're f-fu-fu-fucked."

❖ ❖ ❖

I had no problem sharing a "contributing writer" byline or even a co-byline with Dieter. If this burgeoning scandal came to light, it would play out in the paper over a long time and multiple stories that would, as Chiefs coach Hank Stram said in Super Bowl IV, "matriculate the ball down the field"—in this case, ball meaning scandal—with twists and turns that couldn't be predicted. I welcomed Dieter's smarts and tenacity and gotcha inclinations and business instincts and didn't feel the need to hog the glory. In fact, I knew Dieter's reporting would solidify the stories and provide more valuable sources of confirmation and documentation. There would be enough kudos to go around.

I told Dieter not to discuss the story with his editor until we gathered more background, so Dieter did investigative work on his own time. But he also found ways to integrate the shoe-leather reporting into his daily assignments. He convinced his editor to do a regular Sunday "Our Homes" feature on the Finizio Realtors agency in DeVaca City, where the two other anonymous donations for the Praise Palmertown Complex came from. Dieter talked up insiders at the Quad County Association of Realtors' monthly meeting and infiltrated Finizio Realtors to get color for his feature story. In so doing, he deftly zeroed in on the anonymous donors, and, true to form, we were able to draw a straight line from the pair to long-standing relationships with Boots Walker. I had Dieter painstakingly document all his conversations and paper records on business and personal relationships and transactions and make multiple copies—one for the office, one for each of us, and one for the You-Store Mini-Storage locker I rented. After my Friday night slugfest on Ninth Avenue, I felt I couldn't be too safe with my evidence.

Next, I convinced Dieter to do a feature story on Lenzell Langston, the hard-liquor, quick-cash, fast-food mogul of East Drabenville, which Dieter sold to his editor as perfect for the "Movers and Shakers" column—the business editor told Dieter what a great idea it was to feature a businessman from "that side of town" where circulation was weaker—and told Dieter to press Langston hard on how he bounced back so fast from bankruptcy to owner of a mini-Slumdog empire.

GOTCHA

Meanwhile, it was time for me to pay another visit to Boots Walker, and likely the Reverend Mayweather, with my growing stockpile of information. This wouldn't be easy; I had to keep Monsieur's mantra in mind: I was doing my job. I would let the chips fall where they may, including possibly in the halls of American jurisprudence. Still, I dreaded making the call. I suddenly felt the unsettling power of holding the future of several lives in my hands.

The Chosen

As I dialed Boots's number, I tried to will my enzymes to dissipate the huge peach pit lodged in my gut.

"Hi, Boots, it's Jake Yankelovich from the *Daily Inquirer*."

"I thought you might call."

"Remember the last time we met, you said something about how I was chosen to be the envoy simply because I was at the Praise Palmertown Complex dedication?"

"Yes. I don't believe in coincidences."

"Well, I feel like I know what you mean. That's why I'd like to talk to you again."

I waited a few seconds to see if Boots would hang up or express a change of heart. He may have violated the law and probably ethics, but I still felt that I was dealing with a man of extraordinary integrity, who nevertheless was fallible and might have made an error in judgment.

"I'll be at DeVaca's practice on Thursday. Do you have any time around six?" I suggested.

"Come to my office," Boots replied. "I'll have Reverend Mayweather here."

I didn't know how to end it. It felt like I had just scheduled an interrogation or a day of reckoning.

"Lookin' forward to seeing you again, Boots," I said with a mix of sincerity and dread.

❖ ❖ ❖

Boots was waiting for me behind his desk at the Praise Palmertown Complex, the reverend on the couch. I was tired and sweaty from two hours at DeVaca's practice. The three Jolt Colas I had consumed were kicking in, and the pep talk I gave myself before entering the complex had further energized me—and kept me from turning around and walking away. I was psyched about the developing story and doing a good job and proving myself as a journalist and not just a game narrator, but despite Monsieur's take-no-prisoners reassurances, I was uneasy with potentially holding someone's future in my hands. And this would be the moment of truth—likely one of many.

"Have a seat," the reverend said, motioning to the section of couch next to him. I expected a sermon ("Lord, we are gathered here today..."), but there was silence.

The reverend and Boots avoided my gaze and looked at each other, but I strangely felt eyes upon me anyway—God? Really? Do certain clergy really have such a direct connection to the great Yahweh in the sky? I brushed my existential thoughts aside, switched into Monsieur mode, and got down to business.

"Hi Boots...Clarence. Good to see you again. You may know why I'm here."

"I'm thinking I do. Word gets around town."

I started feeling a wave of Jackie Gleason from *The Honeymooners* coming over me, with an urge to break out in Ralph Kramden's trademark "Hummina-hummina-hummina-hummina," the nervous, tongue-tied patter he resorted to when he was stumped for words. Again, I summoned the image of Monsieur—unkempt, frizzy hair, potbelly, Hawaiian shirt, clam in one hand, Pinot in the other—and refocused while stifling a grin. I took a deep breath, ready to dive into the deep end.

"Boots, I want to be straight with you. Since our last meeting, I've been doing research, and I have strong reason to believe that money was channeled inappropriately from the top level of the Dolphin County school board in exchange for favors, and the trail leads through you, Boots. I think I know now what you meant before with that

Deuteronomy verse about not accepting a bribe. You can convince me I'm wrong."

Boots glanced at the reverend, who nodded.

"D'you got your notebook ready?" Boots asked.

I hadn't gotten it out. I hadn't wanted to be so official—I'd just wanted to connect. But now I pulled it out.

Boots got up and exchanged whispers with the reverend while I waited uncomfortably. "God doesn't give anything to a man he can't handle," the reverend said, a hand on Boots's shoulder. Boots paced, his eyes on the Conquistador-red carpet, and then faced me.

"I did it for the kids and their parents, for their glory, not mine," Boots said. "A bribe? A blessing? Call it what you want. Both. It was there for the taking, and I took it. And I'd do it again, a thousand times, from here to kingdom come."

"Amen to that, my brother," Reverend Mayweather amplified.

"I can sleep just fine at night," Boots continued. "Have you seen the hope? Seen the joy? The pride? I have, every glorious day. I've searched my soul, and I'm right with God, and I'm ready. So Jake, what do you want to know?"

For the next hour, Boots opened up, on the record, with my microcassette tape recorder running. He described the transactions that led to the departure of the Palmertown Six from their home base, the erection of the new crown jewel of Palmertown, his role in the multifaceted deal, and, breaking from his antisnitch street code, the roles of other players involved—the desperation of Big Papa; the behind-the-curtains manipulations of the great and powerful Oz of Drabenville, Jimbo Bamford; the barely concealed avarice of East Drabenville's Lenzell Langston; the naïveté of the publicity hounds at Roma Rojo; and the opportunism of the window-blinds saleswoman.

What a carnival it turned out to be, Boots admitted. He said that he should have been more clued into the dark side of people, the ugly sideshow of life, being in social work. Even the military had its fair share of wack jobs. Still, he said, his vision of hope and the irrepressible feeling of God's hand guiding him down this simultaneously treacherous and life-affirming path—after all, money was man's creation and bribery was man's law, not God's—compelled him to act.

When we were done, I had confirmation. It was a big one, but still only one, and not enough. There's a reason why an endless parade of witnesses and mounds of evidence are presented at any well-prepared trial. As in journalism, one source cannot be relied upon as the be-all and end-all, open-and-shut grand finale. There was more work to do to make Boots's inside story into an ironclad front-page story.

With Dieter added to the ad hoc I-Team and Monsieur serving as the guru/Renaissance man, I was becoming confident that this blockbuster was going to come to fruition. It was gaining an aura of inevitability, like the famous Ronald Reagan verbal throwdown aimed at the Soviet Union leader about the East-West Berlin border that soon came true: "Mr. Gorbachev, tear down this wall!"

But it's never easy to take down the kingpin. Just look at Pablo Escobar, the Colombian billionaire godfather of international cocaine trafficking. He survived for nearly two decades as the high-profile mastermind of the Medellin Cartel and such intense assassination plots that he was memorialized in a book called *Killing Pablo.*

Bamford was Dolphin County's Escobar, only, instead of cocaine, he dealt in influence and stature and prestige and, yes, big money—Dolphin Fightin' Dorsal Fins football put Dolphin County on the national radar and brought millions into the county's economy. I knew that Bamford, like Escobar, wouldn't let his grip on his stock-in-trade cartel slip easily. Also like Escobar, whose cartel ordered a successful hit on Colombian soccer player Andrés Escobar after he scored an own-side goal for the United States that sank an all-time great Colombia futbol team's fortunes in the World Cup and cost millions in bets, Bamford was not above whacking a couple of players for the greater good, as I discovered during DeVaca-Dolphin week. The plot was thickening.

Eaten for Lunch

It was my worst nightmare. Forget Black Friday shopping mobs or the Black Monday stock market crash. This was Terrible Tuesday. I followed my usual routine, rolling off my floor-bound mattress, stumbling to the front door to retrieve my *Drabenville Times-Democrat*, taking a deep breath to settle my nerves, and then rifling to the sports page to see if Tab Reindollar or Ernie McCorkle or Donny Monday or any *T-D* minor-league sports staffer had a story that I should have had. It was great to have Mahotie and Halumka to help me, but they didn't break jack shit, they just took orders and executed. I felt like a one-man band; Mahotie and Halumka were like third graders just starting on the viola with hopes that maybe one day they'd advance to the violin. Reindollar, by comparison, was conducting a symphony orchestra that at times could overwhelm me with its wall of constant sound.

My body temperature must have risen five degrees, and I could feel the sweat forming on my forehead and in my pits—it didn't help that it was ninety degrees at 9:30 a.m. in October—when, before I could even get to Sports, the front-page above-the-fold headline screamed at me:

DOLPHIN FIGHTIN' DORSALS SUSPEND TWO STAR PLAYERS, OFFENSIVE COORDINATOR
Coach Jimbo Bamford Cites 'Detrimental Conduct'

Our air conditioner had been broken for two weeks, and Camelot maintenance man Trash Can Bob hadn't gotten around to fixing it, so we had fans blowing in each room, but it was still like living in the boiler room of the *Titanic*—Shlomo's pat line every night was, "Look at me, I'm sweating!"—so as I sat at the table reading the story, I could see my sweat running down my arms and dripping onto the paper. As my anxiety built and my mind began racing, I had an ethereal vision of a trademark scene from *Dennis the Menace*—Mr. Wilson, nerves frayed by Dennis's mischief, calling out in anguish: "Martha, my nerve medicine!" Crackhead Carl was probably well stocked upstairs, but I resisted the temptation.

Monday had been a big day at Dolphin practice. Being the one-man band in the *Dinqy*'s Dolphin County bureau—Mahotie and Halumka's flat-fee, per-article compensation provided little incentive to engage in the daily grind of legwork—I had chosen to visit undefeated East Grove's practice and then race back to the office to write my "Players of the Week" and "News and Notes" columns and begin calling Friday night's opposing coaches. I was sure that Reindollar sent a *T-D* reporter to every team's practice every day, while he seemed to stay almost exclusively with Dolphin High, because the *T-D* would always come up with tidbits that made me wonder how the hell *they* got them when I was busting my ass running around to practices, sometimes two a day, and calling the other coaches I didn't visit to check in as afternoons gave way to evenings.

Quarterback Sammy Sammons and running back Nate "Flea" Hilliard, who doubled as a cornerback, had been suspended indefinitely for "conduct detrimental to the team" pending further investigation. They were two of the Palmertown Six, pure athletes, and the tandem that made the Dolphin offense go. Both were Division I prospects. The *T-D* said that Hobie Schlorf had been suspended from the coaching staff for an unspecified reason, but not from the high school, where he was a well-regarded social studies teacher who had pioneered courses in ethics, Greek philosophy, religion and spirituality, and other uncommon electives that distinguished Dolphin High as enlightened, progressive, and elite—not just by football standards, but as the Harvard of the Quad Counties.

Before I finished reading the jump, I heard preps editor Skip Blintzer rattling around my brain.

"J-J-Juhh-Jake. Did you see the *T-D* tu-tu-today? Did ya know 'bout that? We gotta-gotta…gotta get it! You just gotta cuh-cuh-call around…call around. We gotta have what the *T-D* has ta-ma…ta-ma…tomorrow. No. Need more. More. Just cuh-call around."

I'd usually go into the bureau office around noon because my workday would extend well into evening with afternoon football practices, phone calls to coaches, covering second-tier high school sports such as cross-country and volleyball, and writing the features I was always working on the side—the latest eight-year-old grunting robotic phenom at the Sergio Bonatelli Tennis Academy, the sailing instructor crewing on an America's Cup yacht, the eighty-eight-year-old unbeatable men's rec league softball pitcher, the rabid cyclist competing in the Race Across America, the ministock champion at the De Leon Raceway who lost an eye and a leg in an accident, and any other athletic oddity or absurdity featuring normal people doing extraordinary things.

But this day was like one of the four questions at Passover seder:

Question: "On all other days, I go to work at noon, but why on this day do I go at nine thirty without even eating my Quisp cereal or showering?"

Answer: Because Reindollar just ate me for lunch, and Blintzer's going to be in my head for real any minute on the home phone, and the O-Dog is probably right this minute trying to explain to Wellington and Chenault why the *Dinqy* had nothing on the biggest sports story of the year—check that, the biggest story of the year, period, out of the Drabenville bureau—and while looming over them in his oafish way, attempting to placate the hell out of them by promising what a great story we'll have tomorrow that will undoubtedly be way out ahead of the *T-D*, with no compunction about putting my neck on the line because he's going to make damn sure he backs up his word by scaring the bejeezus out of my rookie, not-off-probation-period ass. So this was a day I reported early. I decided I'd hold off on contacting Bamford until I gathered as much intelligence from those involved or others with knowledge of the situation that I could find, knowing that Bamford would stonewall if I was clueless, and maybe give me bupkis even if I knew everything.

I started by rereading Reindollar and McCorkle's *Times-Democrat* story. It had the facts and the look ahead to what the suspensions would mean for the lineup and coaching responsibilities for Friday night's annual Rivalry Week game with the DeVaca City Conquistadors, and a bland statement from Coach Bamford:

> *Sammy Sammons and Nate Hilliard have been suspended for conduct detrimental to the team. The suspensions are a coach's decision, and it will be a coach's decision for reinstatement. Offensive coordinator Hobart Schlorf has been suspended from his coaching duties, which will be reassigned. These decisions are backed by the Dolphin High School administration. Dolphin High and its football team are committed to the highest standards of integrity. We are disappointed that we had to take these disciplinary actions. We will move forward and focus our attention on DeVaca City.*

The *T-D* story noted that Sammons and Hilliard were not at practice and could not be reached for comment. Schlorf also was not at practice, but the *T-D* reported that Schlorf said he would explore appealing his suspension and that it resulted from a "misunderstanding," but he wouldn't elaborate.

❖ ❖ ❖

Clearly, there was more second-day information to come out, many leaks in the dike to find, and that was my mission until the 12:30 a.m. final deadline.

I started with my contacts in the Fightin' Dorsals' booster club, thinking word may have traveled there through the grapevine. It would be up to me to separate rumor from fact.

I had formed friendly relationships with several boosters at the fish fries—I knew there was another good reason for going besides all-you-can-eat mullet and hush puppies. Whenever I met anyone involved in the

Dolphin County sports scene, I obtained his or her phone number for my growing Rolodex and gave out my card. This time, the source-development work—more Journalism 101—paid off.

My first two contacts had no insights. I hit BINGO on the third, treasurer Mitzi Retzlaff, Dolphin High '68, a contemporary of Bamford's who had a son on the junior varsity team. Should have known a woman would know more than the two men I tried first.

Mitzi told me about a big Dolphin High party Saturday night at a minimansion on River Overlook Drive that was broken up by the police. Apparently, a complaint about sexual harassment had ensnared Sammons and Hilliard. As soon as I hung up, I bolted through the newsroom to find Monsieur. Predictably, he was out of the office, humping his cops and courts beat, or nursing a wicked hangover in the Hovel. I paged him. He was already at the police station on his morning rounds when he called my extension.

"Jakey, what's up? You got some news?"

"Yeah, Monsieur, I do."

"You got something on Bamford or Gus or one of the other cretins you're chasing?"

"Sorta. I dunno. It involves Bamford indirectly, but I don't know if it's connected to the whole school board thing," I said. "Monsieur, can you check with your sources there and see if you can find a police report about a rowdy party on River Overlook on Saturday night?"

"Jakey, that's almost always piss-ant stuff—disturbing the peace, destruction of property, urinating in public, lewd and lascivious behavior. What are you sniffin'?"

"I heard some Palmertown players were at the party, and now two of them are suspended. You saw the *T-D* this morning, right? Well, predictably, Blintzer's got his sphincter in an uproar, and Paddy will have my ass in a sling if I don't at least keep pace with the *T-D*."

"Well, get your ass down here, and we'll open a can of whoop-ass on Reindollar and company."

"There in fifteen. See ya."

By the time I arrived at the station, Monsieur was already talking to the public information officer, scanning a log of run-of-the-mill Saturday-night police reports. There were three from River Overlook Drive: a stolen boat trailer, domestic abuse, and disturbing the peace. We asked to see the disturbance report and found deep within a long description of bottle smashing, loud music, public nudity, and general debauchery an allegation made at 10:45 p.m. by two seventeen-year-old females of nonconsensual groping by two males. The complainants were not identified by name, as potential victims of a sexual assault. But the alleged perpetrators were, and there they were—Sammons and Hilliard, in a permanent record in the police files. The report noted that the girls had declined to press charges.

It was not surprising that neither Monsieur nor the *T-D*'s cops reporter had zeroed in on this item on Sunday or Monday. It didn't scream out for attention, as the typical police blotter material does—shootings, armed robberies, fatal accidents, explosions, rapes, drug busts, prostitution stings, and the like.

You'd have to know exactly what you were looking for to find it, and those who knew about it did a great job keeping it hush-hush and laying low for two days, but now this was set to blow like a gas leak meeting a match. And journalistically speaking, it was a powder keg. It had all the elements of race, class, sex, celebrity—yes, high school football stars are as famous as anyone was in Dolphin County—and as-yet unsubstantiated, volatile allegations. Futures were at stake. Reputations were on the line. Integrity was in question. It was going to be hard, as Kansans and Mitch Mahotie would say, to separate the wheat from the chaff. The two things I knew I couldn't do were allude to the allegations, since there were no official charges and I couldn't see dragging the Palmertown boys into the mud any deeper than they already were, or identify victims of alleged sexual crimes.

With this find, I may have been ahead of the *T-D*. I knew Reindollar, McCorkle, and crew would be rattling cages and shaking trees in all corners of Dolphin County on Tuesday and were likely to hit the bull's-eye at some point, but my early luck may have given me a running head start.

I left a message for Dolphin High English teacher Billy Lackenback, the young cross-country coach from Indiana whom I had befriended because we were close in age and I was a road-race runner and the only sports reporter in the Quad Counties who gave two shits about this exercise in pain tolerance, dubbed by the "real athletes" as the sport for "anyone who can't make a real team." I knew Lackenback had Sammons and Hilliard in his class, and I wanted to see what kind of character reference he could offer.

"I don't know anything about why they were suspended," Lackenback told me. "All I can say is that they're good kids, quiet, respectful, hard workers. They're the kind of kids you'd want on your team. Talk about being down, these guys were shadows of themselves today. I don't know what happened, but as a coach myself who knows how important sports are to a kid's sense of self, it's a real shame, a cryin' doggone shame."

Lackenback's assessment confirmed my opinion: Sammons and Hilliard were not troublemakers; they had good characters. Could they have been caught in the wrong place at the wrong time, being wrongheadedly impulsive, as emotionally immature teenagers are prone to be? Certainly. But I was far from ready to stamp them GUILTY. It was time to get the story from them.

LIES

I DID AS Skip Blintzer advised and just cu-cu-called around...Called around. There were several Sammonses and Hilliards in the DeVaca City phone book, probably mostly relatives. It was the middle of the day, but people answered the phone. I hit the right Sammons on the second try and Hilliard on the third. I knew the boys wouldn't be home yet, but I wanted to nail down their correct numbers for later and leave messages in case they'd call back.

Later, when school was out, I ditched the phone altogether. I recalled from my relational psychology class at Colgate that establishing rapport, active listening, reflecting understanding, and showing empathy were the keys to open communications. I knew I couldn't accomplish that on the phone, so I headed to Palmertown.

I had already built rapport with Sammons from my preseason, postgame, and midweek interviews with him, but we rarely deviated from football. Still, I knew enough to know that he was academically curious and spiritual—not a one-dimensional jock. I didn't know Hilliard as well, though he impressed me as being good-natured.

Sammons answered the door. "I thought you might be comin' 'round," he said and invited me in.

His home was a modest one-floor box, like most in Palmertown, and clean. Several pictures of Sammy in stages of his youth and high school football career were displayed on end tables around the living room, as was a picture of his brother in cap and gown, diploma in hand. A Holy Bible sat on the coffee table, along with a photo book, *Great Men and*

Achievements in Black History. A family photo on the wall showed the two boys, separated by a younger sister, ringed around Mom seated below, but no Dad.

"Sammy, first I just want to let you know I'm sorry about what's happened. This has got to be tough for you."

I paused to watch Sammy's reaction. Sammy put his head in his hands and looked down. "Yeah, tough," he mumbled.

"Look, Sammy, I have a feeling there's more to this story than the facts I know so far. I really need your side, or I'm afraid I'll do you a disservice. You may not understand, but it's my job, and there *will* be a story in tomorrow's paper, one way or another. Do you feel like you can talk?"

"Coach said I shouldn't talk to the media, that I'm better off staying quiet."

"What do you think?"

"It's unfair."

"What's unfair?"

"Everything. The whole thing."

"What got you in trouble?"

"Just being there. Is that a crime?"

"Of course not. Can you tell me what happened, why you got suspended?"

"Coach said I can't."

"Can't or shouldn't?"

"What does it matter?"

"Coach Bamford can't prohibit you from talking to the media. You have a right to free speech. Nobody can take that from you."

"Shouldn't."

"I'd like to hear your story. What do you want to do?"

Sammy was no stranger to media interviews; he had been doing them since he was eleven, in the Bronco League, and Donny Monday glorified him continually in his column as a "Dolphin Dandy" or "the DeVaca Dynamo" or "Super Sammy Sammons."

"I just want to play football," Sammy said.

My pager beeped. It was Monsieur. I asked Sammy if I could use his phone.

"Monsieur, what do you got?"

"You ready for this, Jake? It's a whole new ball game. The two Dolphin chicks have pressed charges—sexual assault. They just raised the stakes. What do you got goin'?"

"I'm here with Sammons right now, at his house. Monsieur, something doesn't seem right. Sammy's a good kid, quiet and respectful and smart. I can't see him doing something he knows could ruin his future. I know hormones can make these kids do stupid things, but my intuition says not Sammy. I think it could be a setup."

"What's the kid have to say?"

"Nothing so far, except it's unfair. He's under a Bamford gag order."

"See if you can get him to talk before the lawyers get involved and muzzle him."

"Will do, Monsieur."

I returned from the kitchen to the living room to find Sammy fidgeting with the framed photo of himself in his Bronco twelve-and-under uniform.

"Sammy, I have to apologize again for being the bearer of bad news. That was our police reporter, at the station. He just found out the girls pressed charges against you for sexual assault."

Sammy put his elbows back on his knees and smothered his face in his hands.

"This may all come out in court someday, if it gets that far. But this is your chance to state your case to the football world, coaches, teachers, Palmertown, everyone, if you think you've gotten a raw deal. You won't have to wait for your day in court. You'll have your day in the paper tomorrow, and you'll either have a voice or you won't."

Wow, I was only five years older than Sammy was, and I felt like I was holding together a nimbus cloud, desperately trying to prevent a burst and avoid a deluge. I couldn't imagine what he was feeling at the center of this storm.

"Total bullshit, Mr. Yankelovich. Excuse my language," Sammons said, dropping his head and pounding a fist on the table. I thought he might start bawling, but he did the opposite. He raised his head and met my eyes with the determined, self-assured, calm-under-pressure look of a leader. He looked as if he had just called the last play of a game in a do-or-die situation, knowing that success or failure depended squarely on him.

"OK, let's rephrase that in a way that can be printed in the paper," I encouraged.

"Completely untrue. Lies. I did nothing wrong, and I'll stand behind that with my hand on the Bible, until the day I die."

Strong quote, good stuff. That'll be high up in the story, I thought.

Then Sammy told me his story. He was invited to the party with other players, including his Palmertown teammates. He decided to go because it had always been a struggle to assimilate into the Dolphin High culture, and he wanted to feel more comfortable socializing with different crowds away from football. He knew he'd be facing those situations in college and for the rest of his life, so he might as well learn now.

A girl he didn't know enthusiastically recruited him and Flea to the game room. Two smallish girls were riding on the shoulders of two husky boys, playing chicken between two couches, like in a pool, where combatants try to knock each other off shoulders into the water. The boys had worn out and Sammy and Flea were to replace them. It seemed that all four had been drinking, and Sammy and Flea wanted no part of that. The four prodded and cajoled Sammy and Flea to join in the way that drunken people make everything seem so fun and carefree. What the heck, Sammy thought, maybe this is just what white kids did at their parties; maybe this is what we do to fit in. Sammy and Flea sat on a couch as the two girls climbed aboard and strapped their legs over the boys' shoulders. The husky boys left the room. The girls were grappling with each other and screeching and giggling as Sammy and Flea stumbled, trying to maintain their balance. The boys were having fun and lightening up. Then the girls got overly aggressive. The girl on

Flea's shoulders ripped the shirt of Sammy's girl, tearing the buttons off. The girls' moods changed. They started yelling angrily and pounding the boys on their backs and heads. It shocked and scared the boys; they didn't know what to do.

"Get off!"

"Let me go!"

"Stop! Stop!"

"You're hurting me!"

And then, in chorus, with the shrill inflection of a *Nightmare on Elm Street* slasher victim: "Somebody help me! Help!"

As several teens rushed to the room to see what was happening, Sammy staggered and dumped the girl unceremoniously on the pool table. Her bra was exposed, giving the unfortunate appearance of a situation that wasn't what it seemed.

Flea, meanwhile, tumbled his girl onto a couch, lost his balance, and sprawled on top of her, which looked just as incriminating.

Within fifteen minutes, to Sammy's growing disbelief and dismay, the cops arrived—Sammy didn't know why they were called—and questioned Sammy and Flea and the girls in separate rooms. Word traveled fast, and his life had been hell ever since. And now, the girls with whom Sammy and Flea had been good-naturedly clowning, girls they didn't even know, had done the unimaginable by leveling sexual assault charges.

"Mr. Yankelovich, do you believe me?" Sammy asked earnestly when he finished telling his story.

"Yeah, Sammy, I have no reason not to," I replied. I was trying to stay objective but couldn't help feeling emotionally involved. Was I prejudiced and given to believe a wealthier white girl's claims over a poorer black boy's defense? Whatever my unintended biases, as a journalist it was my job to focus on the facts and documentation and give equal weight and a fair opportunity for comment.

"Anything else you want to add, Sammy? I got to go find Flea."

"Yeah. I will be vindicated. And I'll be back on the field leading Dolphin to the 5A championship. People who really know Sammy Sammons know that this ain't what I'm all about."

❖ ❖ ❖

I found Flea at home. These were guys who loved the structure and predictability of football practices and didn't know what to do with themselves without it. Where else would they be?

Flea was known for his speed and elusiveness, but he wasn't that small anymore. He was listed at five ten, 175 pounds. He'd earned the nickname in Pee Wee ball, when he *was* the tiniest and no one could catch him. He was legendary for getting lost in a pile of bodies and emerging upright, his little legs churning frenetically, on the back end.

Flea was a prodigious talent. He ran a 4.45 forty and had a thirty-eight-inch vertical leap. He was often compared to the Dallas Cowboys' Tony Dorsett for his take-it-to-the-house abilities. He was more boisterous than Sammy was and more prone to showboating—known to high-step like a marching band member for the last ten yards to the end zone on a breakaway run—but he was respectful of authority, hard-working, disciplined, and polite. Besides his speed, another trademark of Flea's was his hair. Now he was experimenting with the newfangled high-top fade, which added two inches to his height. In the 1985 team picture, he sported a huge Afro that added four inches. It became dreads later in the season and shrank him.

Flea was also more lighthearted and jovial than the more intense Sammy, and probably more naïve, so he initially didn't seem as distraught as Sammy did. He seemed unaware that he was ensnared in a situation that begged for a lawyer, but he knew his future could be on the line. He expressed no reluctance in talking to me about his ordeal—likely he had no one to advise him about the pros and cons of talking to a reporter, or anyone else, for that matter.

I reviewed with Flea the story that Sammy had told me, and he corroborated Sammy's version.

"It was nothing more than innocent playing around," Flea said. "It was the girls' idea; we just went along."

If Sammy and Flea were young, naïve, and in over their heads, Coach Schlorf certainly wasn't. If there was more to this strange and seemingly demoralizing twist in the Dolphin's championship aspirations and the football—and life!—prospects of its star players, Schlorf would be the most likely to know.

Is It Safe?

I HAD OFTEN called Hobie Schlorf at home in the evenings to find out more about his offensive players and system, game analyses, and scouting reports of defenses for upcoming games, since at practice, I often had time only to talk to several players and Coach Bamford. I quoted Hobie only occasionally, but he always gave me insight on what to look for on the field and the Fightin' Dorsals' offensive strategy. Our conversations usually were split between football and Aristotle or Sartre or Locke or Milton or Nietzsche, since Hobie loved intellectual discussions about the philosophers and I had taken philosophy courses at Colgate. It would be typical to transition easily from the intricacies of a motion offense to Friedrich Nietzsche's "will to power," the innate human ambition and drive for achievement and high position that was perfectly manifested in Bamford, or John Locke's "theory of mind," or "tabula rasa"—we are all blank slates until our experiences and senses imprint our brains with complex knowledge, which, in a weird way, can explain our understanding of football with all its imprinted sounds and visual images and symbols and idiosyncratic languages and kinesiologic experiences.

I reached Hobie, and he was willing to talk, but only off the record and not on the phone. Too impersonal, he said. I offered to meet him at Bennie's, er, Bennigan's, where Shlomo and I had practically reserved bar stools for the baseball play-offs, Shlomo for the Mets and me for the Red Sox.

We passed the Pac-Man game adjacent to the bar, which Shlomo and I played to determine who would treat for the night, and took a table in the back, ordering nachos and Old Milwaukees.

Hobie was a rare New Englander on the Citrus Coast—in fact, Big Deb Bazarko was the only other one I'd met. I could see him as a college professor, in tasseled loafers, tweed jacket, and wire-rimmed glasses, and he'd mentioned before that he'd actually considered that occupation but didn't want to get trapped in the political bullshit, tenure-or-bust, publish-or-perish world of academia. He loved working with kids and teaching and coaching football to build character in young men, and like many coaches in the region, he had gravitated to the Citrus Coast as Richard Dreyfuss had to Wyoming's Devil's Tower monolithic mountain in *Close Encounters of the Third Kind*.

"Jake, the only reason I'm here talking to you is the opposite of what you would think," Hobie opened.

"What do you mean?"

"You're new. You don't seem to have set ideas or allegiances. The *T-D*'s guys have been around forever, and they're just rookies compared to their Mesozoic-era editors, and that paper's so deep up coach's ass, I just don't think it's worth my while to talk to them about this; they'll believe what they want to believe. I'd get crushed, labeled a malcontent or disloyal or a flake. 'Poor Hobie, full of sour grapes. What a schmuck.' I don't think the *T-D*'s top brass will want any part of digging into this too deeply, even if the sportswriters would, and that's an open question. But I think you may be open-minded enough and the *Dinqy* may be removed enough from Dolphin County that you'll give it a fair look."

Hobie was right about me. Sure, I needed access to Coach Bamford and the Dolphin High program, but I was personally more interested in breaking big stories and doing kick-ass journalism than I was in sucking up to Bamford, which did make me a polar opposite to, say, Johnny Littleman or the *T-D*'s Ernie McCorkle, who were more concerned about preserving their cushy lives. And I perceived that the *Dinqy*'s top editors, Chenault and Wellington, were more interested in establishing the *Dinqy* as a highly respected journalistic powerhouse that could compete with Florida's premier investigative news source, the *St. Petersburg Times*, and being recognized by the ivory-tower elites of the business as a bastion of intellectual prowess in the South, than they were in kowtowing to something as gauche and trivial as a high school football program.

After all, the *Dinqy* had a solid monopoly in upscale Mirabella County and was merely trying to expand into Dolphin County and raid the *T-D*'s subscription base and, more importantly, its advertisers. In contrast, the *T-D*'s survival depended on maintaining an unbreakable hometown bond with its more hardscrabble base. But obviously, Hobie didn't know Skip Blintzer well. While the snooty Chenault and Wellington may have been oblivious to the nuances—and indeed, to the outsized influence on readership and revenue—of high school football coverage, preps editor Blintzer's worth and effectiveness would be evaluated by the O-Dog based on the success of Dolphin County sports coverage and the *Dinqy*'s ability to penetrate the incestuous attachments between Dolphin County sports fans and their hometown rag. The deeper this story went, the more Blintzer would stammer, knowing it was likely to turn off a large portion of the audience he wanted to capture. He feared that Dolphin County readers would see the *Dinqy* as the arrogant, carpetbagger newspaper from the south running roughshod over the peasantry to the north to prove its superiority, damn community traditions and history and values and everything held sacred in Dolphin, primarily football. Blintzer wasn't averse to chasing a great story; it was just the competing goals that gave him indigestion.

"This is strictly off the record," Hobie said, swiping his hand for emphasis. "My job's in jeopardy as it is—not just as a coach, but as a teacher. Anyone who thinks Principal Bosley's the top dog at Dolphin doesn't know shit about the power of Jimbo Bamford and family. Do I have your word you will keep this safe?"

I had an immediate flash to a favorite movie thriller, *Marathon Man*, where Nazi war criminal dentist Szell (Laurence Olivier) tortures Babe (Dustin Hoffman) for information that he doesn't have. Szell's thugs strap

IS IT SAFE?

Babe to a chair, and Szell inflicts pain in ways that only a dentist can, seeking assurance that all is "safe."

Szell: "Is it safe?"
Szell: "Is it safe?"
Babe: "Are you talking to me?"
Szell: "Is it safe?"
Babe: "Is what safe?"
Szell: "Is it safe?"
Babe: "I don't know what you mean. I can't tell you if something is safe or not unless I know specifically what you're talking about."
Szell: "Is it safe?"
Babe: "Tell me what the 'it' refers to."
Szell: "Is it safe?"
Babe (*Attitude: What the fuck is this OCD line of questioning, Szell?*): "Yes, it's safe. It's very safe. So safe you wouldn't believe it."
Szell: "Is it safe?"
Babe (*Attitude: This guy's a Nazi fruitcake*): "No, it's not safe. It's very dangerous. Be careful."

I assured Hobie that our conversation was safe, very safe. He took me at my word, and I unclenched my jaw.

"This may sound bizarre, but I have a strong suspicion that Sammy and Nate were set up to take a fall," Hobie told me. "As the season's gone on, Jimbo's been talking more and more about how the Palmertown players are overrated, that they get all the credit for the team he's molded. We win, it's the superior talent of the Palmertown boys. We lose, like at Great Bay, and it's bad coaching.

"You were at the Clear Vista game, right?" he asked.

"Yeah, talked to Sammy afterward. He wasn't happy," I said, pretty sure that Hobie wasn't one of the helmeted guys who'd popped me in the street after the game.

"Exactly. Jimbo put a straitjacket on my play calling and Sammy's natural talents by dumbing down our offense. It was so simple it was like we were back at the first week of training camp. We should have blown out

Clear Vista. Instead, we squeaked out a win and looked hardly mediocre doing it. I argued with him to take off the shackles, take some risks, and let our boys shine, do what they do best, but he wouldn't have it. How many carries did Flea have that game? Six? And Mondo? Twenty-two. Three yards and a plate of mullet, all night long. I think that's just a cover to diminish the star of Sammy and Nate and our other Palmertown guys and put the focus squarely back on Jimbo."

"So what happened between you and Coach Bamford that put you on the skids?" I asked.

"I confronted him and argued against suspending Sammy and Nate when there weren't even any charges. I talked to the guys, and they said they did nothing wrong. I told Jimbo I had faith in my players, and I wouldn't call the DeVaca game without my guys in the lineup, and he suspended me.

"Of course, once the girls pressed charges, there was no choice. Rumors have been flying, and I have a good idea who the girls are. Their parents are big hoo-hahs in the boosters club. I'd be willing to bet someone put them up to this, and they were gullible enough to accept—why I don't know—some twisted loyalties."

"It seems pretty farfetched, Hobie. Really?"

"You may think you know Coach Bamford, but you don't. As a football coach, I love the guy. He's a winner, and he demands the best of everyone around him. He's a great football mind and a motivator, though maybe more through fear than respect. Our guys would run through a brick wall for him.

"But as a person, he can be unbelievably ruthless to get what he wants. How do you think the Bamford family got to where they are? What he wants is to be known as the best high school coach in Florida, or even the country. He wants a major college job. If he wins another state championship with All-American players, it was the players. If he wins without two All-Americans, it was coaching—three yards and a plate of mullet. Pretty or ugly doesn't matter to Coach. He's from the Al Davis school: 'Just win, baby.'

"Manipulating a scheme to get Sammy and Nate kicked off the team?" he added. "Sounds outlandish, but I wouldn't put it past him. I know how his mind works. He proved he could win with them, and he needed them for the first championship. What could make him look more brilliant as a coach and motivator than repeating without them?"

I wasn't totally buying Hobie's theory of underhandedness, but in my short time knowing Bamford, I couldn't dismiss it, either. We finished our beers and mopped up the guacamole. Game 2 of the Red Sox–Mets World Series was coming on, but I couldn't claim my reserved bar stool next to Shlomo; I had to call Coach Bamford and write a story.

I asked Hobie what he could say on the record.

"I'm appealing my suspension. And don't judge too soon. Wait for the facts to come out, the full story. I know Sammy and Nate, who they are. I had a conversation with them about this incident, and I stand behind them. I'd stake my job on that."

❖ ❖ ❖

I left Bennigan's for my office, but didn't have the nerve or confidence yet to call Coach Bamford, so drove right past the *Dingy* Drabenville bureau and down Hernandez Ave. to Conquista Island and The Hovel to discuss with Monsieur what I learned from Hobie. Sure enough, Monsieur was home, nursing a glass of cabernet sauvignon and watching a PBS documentary on 15th century Incan Empire monumental architecture.

"Whadya got Jake?"

"Monsieur, I just had an off-the-record interview with Hobie Schlorf, the Dolphin coach who got suspended. I don't know if I buy what he's selling. I wanted to get your opinion, 'cause this will blow your mind."

"It takes a lot to blow my mind, rookie. Give it up."

"Hobie thinks Coach Bamford might have orchestrated this whole ugly mess to get Sammons and Hilliard in trouble and suspended from the team. He thinks Bamford might have masterminded a conspiracy involving loyal boosters and a couple of gullible girls eager to please. High school girls? Really? All so he could try to win a state championship *without his star players*, the same ones he might have cheated for and stolen in the first place?"

"Hubris, my friend. Hubris conquers all. It knows no bounds, and Bamford could be a hubris case study. Would Bamford pull something like that to make himself look good, to make him look like a principled coach with an ironclad sense of ethics, who would do the right thing no matter how high the stakes, who can win no matter what? Fuck yeah.

"I've covered multi-millionaires who have killed their wives for an extra two hundred fifty thou in life insurance and the freedom to doink a pretty young thang. I've seen so-called investment geniuses con whole nursing homes and their families into forking over their life savings on guaranteed get-rich-quick schemes built on a house of cards. Are they sorry? Only when they get caught. Jake, you just haven't been around long enough to understand the true warped and diabolical nature of the human psyche. I gotta warn ya, you're in the wrong business to remain an innocent rube.

"Bamford using a few kids to elevate himself, embellish his cred, and get what he wants?" Monsieur continued his lecture. "As I said, fuck yeah! I can see it 20-20.

"Now go grab my *pâté de foie gras* out of the fridge and some crackers. This Incan cyclopean polygonal masonry, *now that will blow your mind*."

Don't Be a Hero

I FINALLY GOT to the deserted bureau office at nine thirty after an exhausting day. I pumped myself up to call Coach Bamford as if I was entering the stadium for the final lap of an Olympic marathon. "Coach, Jake Yankelovich from the *Daily Inquirer*."

"What's it about," Bamford responded.

"The suspension, I'm writing a—"

"Did you get my statement from Dolphin County Athletics?"

"Yeah, but I had—"

"That's my statement. What don't you understand?"

"Sammy and Nate deny the allegations—"

"They're suspended. We're moving on. We've got DeVaca City Friday night."

"Coach, just give me two minutes. It's really important that I get your responses."

"I'll give you an hour. My answers aren't going to change."

"What about Hobie Schlorf? Why—"

"Suspended. Indefinitely."

"Why?"

"Read the statement."

"Who's going to replace Sammy?"

"Connor Crane. He's a highly rated prospect, got a great arm, he lit it up on junior varsity. Just needs more big game experience. Now he'll get it."

"How do you think the team will handle the controversy?"

"What controversy? We made decisions. We're moving on."

"Will you consider reinstatements?"

"Read. The. Statement."

I didn't feel I could press Coach Bamford further without triggering a Mount Vesuvius. I kept Hobie's conspiracy theory, validated as plausible by Monsieur, under my cap for the time being to protect my source. Time for the open-ended softball wrap-up question. Surprisingly, it did get Bamford talking.

"Is there anything I didn't ask about that you'd want to add?"

"It's an unfortunate situation. Our team has strict rules, and our players have to abide by them, no exceptions. I don't care whether it's the starting quarterback or third-string guard. Everyone will be held accountable, coaches too. We're preparing to play the rest of the season without Sammy and Nate. It's a loss, but I know how we'll react—like state champions."

"Thanks, Coach, I know it's late and been a tough couple days, so 'preciate it."

"Yankowitz, one more thing. Off the record," Coach Bamford said, stopping me from hanging up. "Just want you to know. For your own good. Be careful. Don't try to be a hero. You're not from around here, and you don't understand our community, our culture. You'll be just fine if you stick with covering the games. That's what people want to know. They don't care *how* we become state champions, just that we *are* state champions. Are you gettin' me?"

"Yeah, I think I know what you mean, Coach. See ya at practice."

Yeah, I knew what he meant. The condensed version: "Don't fuck with me or you'll be sorry." I already got that message on the street with a body blow and head gash after the Clear Vista game.

Despite the barely concealed intimidation, I was growing to enjoy my dealings with Coach Bamford. He made my job a challenge in an exciting and unpredictable way. I was always nervous about talking to him, but I also realized that some stress was good, even necessary, to think sharper, perform better, persevere longer. He was also a fascinating character study, a narcissist with a twist of obsessive-compulsive. I think he was developing a grudging respect for me, as much as a narcissist could allow, as a legitimate threat to be reckoned with, just like the East Grove offense. As much as he'd hate to admit it, he needed me to spread the word of the Fightin' Dorsals' greatness beyond the parochial borders of the *T-D*'s circulation. We were bound together—Coach Bamford needed me for the publicity I could provide to a larger metropolitan region and, by extension, to sports reporters statewide; and I needed him for the high-profile story and program only Coach Bamford could provide in comparatively backwater Drabenville that ultimately could punch my ticket to major college and pro sports locker rooms.

It was unlikely we both could win, which lent a winner-take-all aura to our relationship.

❖ ❖ ❖

The next day's *Dinqy* lived up to the billing the O-Dog gave me in his meeting with Chenault and Wellington to save all our asses. The *T-D* had the basic information on charges and Sammons and Hilliard denying the allegations. But the *T-D* didn't have anything colorful and hard-hitting from its interview with Sammons, and nothing about Schlorf appealing or teachers vouching for the boys' character, or even a live quote from Bamford instead of the canned statement he kept pressing on me, despite having two writers listed as contributing to Reindollar and McCorkle's report, whereas I had none. The slothful McCorkle must have come down with narcolepsy, as usual. I claimed victory in round two with this lede:

> *The two suspended Dolphin High School football players from Palmertown vehemently denied charges of sexual assault filed by the Dolphin County state's attorney yesterday, the team's star quarterback,*

Sammy Sammons, calling the accusations "lies" and vowing he would be "vindicated" and play again this season.

While Dolphin offensive coordinator Hobart Schlorf, who was also suspended for an unspecified reason, indicated he would appeal and staked his job on Sammons's and backfield mate Nate Hilliard's innocence, Dolphin coach Jimbo Bamford acknowledged his defending state championship team is preparing to play the rest of the season "like state champions" without its two star Palmertown players and the offensive play-caller.

The second-day lede may have angered women's rights groups with its slant in support of the players, but what the hell, I was a sportswriter, and this was a sports story as much as a crime story. Besides, I was oblivious to the budding political-correctness movement and women's sensitivities. I buried the details of the police report below the implications for Dolphin football, and apparently, Chenault and Wellington were fine with that. Misplaced priorities? Dolphin County didn't look at it that way, and the *Dinqy*'s top brass was smart enough to realize it.

The story got Mitch Mahotie as excited as a towel salesman in a Turkish bathhouse. He called and regaled me with a cliché-ridden recitation of my work:

"If you want my two cents, you really got down to brass tacks, Jake. That quote from Hobie is going to open up a can of worms for Bamford, but I'll bet you dollars to doughnuts he's right. This is a sticky wicket, but we've got to follow this story six ways to Sunday, you know, the whole ball of wax. If you need me to help, I'll be on this story like white on rice."

I told Mahotie I was digging, but "the devil is in the details," and then felt like gagging when I realized I was talking just like he did.

"Let's see if Dolphin lives up to Bamford's bravado against DeVaca on Friday," I said.

"The proof is in the pudding," Mahotie said. "I wouldn't miss that game for all the tea in China."

Just Couldn't Make It

It's not only sports that bring me back to my teenage years. It's calling a girl and asking for a date—and the feeling is anything but wistful and nostalgic. It brings back memories of butterflies in the stomach, hours or even days of procrastination and inertia, tongue-tied rehearsals, and dread of a rejection.

These symptoms had diminished only moderately by the time I moved on from Val Darling's incomprehensible decision to dally with Crash and took a chance on the adorable JJ at the bank, who gave me signals that made me optimistic. Uncharacteristically, I dialed her number the first time I picked up the phone and didn't hang up before it rang. JJ agreed to a date at the tropical-themed, open-air bar-restaurant Svelte Boy Sven's on Conquista Island, featuring steel-drum-reggae happy hours on the beach as the sun gets swallowed up by the Gulf, producing the kind of amazing, hazy pastel combinations of pink, peach, maize, and rose that people frame and hang in their beach houses to create the Margaritaville atmosphere.

I showed up to meet her wearing my best beach outfit—white pants, Docksiders boat shoes, no socks, and a silky, sapphire-blue shirt splashed with garish hot-pink, green, and silver geometric shapes and featuring a top button barely midway up my chest. I got it at a surf shop. It was my favorite Florida look—the closest I could get to Tubbs and Crockett on *Miami Vice*—but not as good as Shlomo's full clam-digger, all-white beach leisure suit with pants elongating halfway down his calves and a cottony, loose-fitting, cascading-neckline shirt, the kind associated with African safari adventurers and Jamaican conch fisherman.

I arrived first and ordered a strawberry daiquiri, which fit the mood of the locale and my prediction of the kind of drink JJ would order. I also thought that the daiquiri, along with my gaudy shirt and prep-school shoes, might mark me as a metrosexual, the kind of urbane male overly attuned to his appearance and inclined toward indulging in pastimes and tastes normally associated with refined women. I figured the "boyfriend" JJ had mentioned was a real man's man—a goateed, beer-swiller with work boots and a pickup truck, who would be appalled at drinking a frothy, pink alcoholic beverage—so if she was looking for something different, that could be me.

I finished my drink and looked at my watch—twenty minutes late, maybe she's one of those chronically tardy girls, taking too long to beautify. It would be worth the wait if she was as hot as I thought she was. I had a flashback to the scene in *Fast Times at Ridgemont High* in which an aggravated teacher, Mr. Hand, scolds the barefoot surfer dude, Spicoli:

Mr. Hand: "What's the reason for your truancy?"

Spicoli: "Just couldn't make it on time."

Mr. Hand: "You couldn't, or you wouldn't?"

I ordered another drink and downed it. Now she was forty-five minutes late. I scanned the bar and the deck by the beach for single women—I had a good buzz going, why waste it? After an hour, I got up my nerve to call JJ. "JJ, I'm here at Svelte Boy Sven's on Conquista. Calypso Irie Mama Seed is playing. It's great; it's paradise. We were supposed to meet at 6:30 p.m. and watch the sunset at 7:57 p.m. Can you make it by then?"

"Didn't you get my message?"

"What message? Where?"

"At your office."

"I was off today. What was it?"

"Ohhh. Saaaaaw-reeeeee," JJ said in her singsong voice. This time it wasn't cute. "Something came up, and I just can't make it."

My good-times buzz was turning to angry-drunk buzz.

Then she added, "I kinda have a boyfriend, and I told him I was going to meet a friend tonight, but he didn't think that would be a good idea and he wanted to be with me, sooooooo…" Another giggle.

It was endearing at the bank, but now I wanted to throw a bottle against the wall.

"Sooooo…" I countered. "Should we try another time?" I cringed as I waited for an annoying response.

"Wehhh-elllll…Can't we just be friends at the bank? Like a really good teller-customer relationship?"

"I'm not going to your branch anymore, remember, cuz you got me that information about Bamford, and I didn't want to get you in trouble?"

"Oh yeah, I forgot. With Drake around and everything…"

"Drake, your boyfriend?"

"Yeah, well, kinda, on-again-off-again. You know. He likes me. He always wants to be with me…when he's not out drinking and playing pool with his buddies. But he's so possessive! He gets so mad when I go out with my friends."

"Good luck with that, JJ. You know where to reach me when Drake lets you. Maybe I'll pop into the bank sometime. You were a big help. I really thought we might hit it off. Keep the Dolphin Domestic Violence Center number handy."

Sloppy Seconds

Meanwhile, Shlomo was growing weary of his interscholastic relationship with teacher Big Deb Bazarko, who was practically setting up house with him at our Camelot Cay apartment. She was constantly pawing Shlomo, melting into his sequoia-like physique with hugs, sitting on his lap, and giving him her woodchuck grin as she peppered him with affectionate nicknames like Big Guy, Studly Dudley, and Tower Power. Shlomo dropped hints that his interest was waning, but Big Deb didn't pick up any, or chose to ignore them.

One night, after Big Deb, who was an excellent cook, made Shlomo a nice dinner in our kitchen and set a candlelight table with a bottle of wine, she grabbed his hand on the table and said, "Couldn't you see us being married and having special dinners like this all the time, Big Guy? This feels so right."

Shlomo nodded and stuffed a big piece of grouper fish and a whole red potato in his mouth. I saw him start to sweat, his eyes avoiding Big Deb's to stare at the grouper, his hand twitching in a subconscious effort to release Big Deb's.

The next night, Big Deb came over early with ingredients to cook Shlomo another gourmet dinner and crème brûlée for dessert. Early in their courtship, a period that lasted all of three days, Shlomo had shown Big Deb where we hid a spare key to the apartment. His regret was growing by the day, as Big Deb made liberal use of it. She probably topped Trash Can Bob of maintenance in frequency of entering a Camelot Cay apartment by a nontenant.

Shlomo was in his favorite recliner after a satiating dinner and bottle of Riesling, schoolbooks and students' papers scattered around him, watching his beloved New York Mets play the Houston Astros in the baseball play-offs. Big Deb sat in his lap and wrapped her arms around his neck as if he was going to get up and carry her across the threshold. Shlomo tried to adjust his head to see the Mets' batter, but now Big Deb was playing a game with him, purposely blocking his view.

"Can't we watch in your room? It might be a little more...*exciting*," Big Deb said in a bedroom voice, with a woodchuck grin, a squeeze on the shoulder, and a wink.

But Shlomo wasn't getting his ass out of his favorite La-Z-Boy recliner in the bottom of the third to do anything except fetch another Pabst Blue Ribbon, especially not to watch on a fuzzy-screened small tube when he had his new Sony big-screen in the living room.

When Darryl Strawberry blasted a home run and Shlomo missed it, he finally snapped.

"Deborah, have you heard that new song, 'We Don't Have to Take Our Clothes Off to Have a Good Time?'" Shlomo asked, referring to the catchy, schmaltzy dance hit by Jermaine Stewart that was playing around the clock on MTV.

"Yeah, we danced to it at the Pirate's Ransom. Don't you remember when you tripped over that really short girl, Studly Dudley?"

"That song has a really good message," Shlomo persisted. "You know that line, 'Come on, baby, won't you show some class, why you want to move so fast.'"

It finally dawned on Big Deb. Shlomo was choosing baseball and beer over sex...with her. She got out of his lap and grew silent. Shlomo looked at me and made the universal, palms up, what-the-hell-just-happened gesture with a shit-eating grin. He stayed planted, while for the next twenty minutes Big Deb downed the rest of the Riesling, cleared the table, put away food, and washed dishes, sniffling loudly to send her own message, and left without saying good-bye. She slammed the door with such force that it shook the building.

A minute later, Louie the Leatherman knocked.
"Everything OK?"
"Yeah, Leatherman," Shlomo responded, eyes still glued to the game. "Just a little fight. Big Deb and me just don't like the same song."

❖ ❖ ❖

Apparently, Big Deb was willing to give Shlomo another chance, or maybe she was desperate, because later that weekend, we went to Svelte Boy Sven's with Melanie. We had a few drinks and loosened up, and on a group dare, each picked a karaoke song to perform. I picked AC/DC's "Back in Black" so I could shriek instead of sing.

Big Deb chose Rupert Holmes's "Escape (The Piña Colada Song)." I grew uncomfortable when I noticed her eyes and corny gestures were aimed at me. I nearly swallowed the maraschino cherry in my daiquiri when she pointed at me and motioned like she wanted me to join her when she sang this line: "If you like making love at midnight in the dunes on the cape, / Then I'm the love that you've looked for, write to me and escape."

Back at the table, Big Deb rubbed up against me and massaged my leg. The woodchuck grin was plastered on her chubby-cheeked face. She did her Astro imitation from *The Jetsons*, which she apparently believed was a turn-on, and came up with new endearing names for me: Write Stuff and Sir Yank-a-lot. By now, I knew where this night was heading if I would deign to be a willing participant. I didn't know if Big Deb was in revenge mode, had misgivings about walrus love and wanted to try a lither species, or actually liked me. I did know that after one more drink, it wouldn't have mattered.

While Shlomo ordered his third plate of Buffalo wings, Big Deb and I strolled out back to the beach and sat on the sand, listening to waves lap the shore. My mind was racing: Should I let something happen? Should I make a move? Would I regret it in the morning? Would I regret it in five minutes? Then Big Deb leaned in for a kiss. The alcohol won out. I dove in head first, rolling around in the sand with Astro.

THREE YARDS AND A PLATE OF MULLET

When we returned to Camelot Cay, Melanie left, but Big Deb came in. She never left. Shlomo, being enormous and having to lug his vastness around all day, fell asleep as heavily as a hibernating bear every night, usually on the floor. The alcohol served as an accelerant, knocking him out within five minutes, and he had no idea that Big Deb was still in his lair.

Big Deb stealthily departed my bedroom in the morning and tried to sneak out the door, but Shlomo was already up making his English muffin with Temp Tee cream cheese.

"Deb, I didn't know you were here."

"Got to go, Big Guy."

Oh shit, I thought. Busted. I didn't know if Shlomo still wanted a relationship with Big Deb. I felt guilty and embarrassed when I emerged from my room. Shlomo quickly absolved my guilt.

"You had sloppy seconds, huh?"

"What's that?"

"You had some fun with the buttered bun," Shlomo elaborated, now laughing.

"I don't like to think of it that way, but I guess you could say that."

"It *is* that way, it's sloppy seconds," Shlomo repeated, doing a full recline in the La-Z-Boy and laughing uncontrollably at the ceiling.

"It wasn't that sloppy."

"Jake, look up the definition of sloppy seconds. You just met it, congratulations, be proud, it all counts."

"OK, whatever, sloppy seconds. I've been in a drought, and the bank teller blew me off. Big Deb was looking pretty good last night, wasn't she?"

"You had sloppy seconds last night," is all Shlomo could muster in response to my fishing expedition for endorsement. "Sloppy seconds!"

Over Before It Started

Big Deb and I hit it off pretty well over the next couple of weeks. I usually went for petite, but it wasn't too hard to adjust to a woman a bit rounder and heftier to cuddle. She had a strong libido—the drought had given way to a flood. The relationship also came with excellent fringe benefits—frequent culinary delights, clothing gifts, laundry services, grocery shopping, errands I would have skipped, favors, thoughtful acts of kindness, and overall attentiveness that the most doting mother couldn't match for a mama's boy.

Meanwhile, Shlomo was having some regrets. He had been suffering a cold streak since Big Deb helped him win the bet with me. On a Saturday morning, we went to the IHOP where our neighbor, Sweet Stephanie, worked as a server. Shlomo and Steph had developed a unique relationship where they could talk freely about anything, including sex and relationships, but no matter how much Shlomo wanted to get in her pants, Steph wouldn't let it happen because she knew it would ruin the friendship.

While Steph waited on us, Shlomo unloaded his laments.

"Steph, I'm not gettin' any, and I need to take my mind off school and basketball. Where are all the girls in their twenties around here? I'm going to have to look for single mothers already. Hey, what are *you* doing tonight, Steph?" Shlomo asked, knowing the solicitation would be met with the usual playful indignation.

"Shlomo, I tol' ya, all your gittin' from me is pancakes…and maybe some grits, if you're good. Hey, but you may be in luck. I was just talking to Virginia in the kitchen, and she was saying she's horny as all hell. I bet I could set you up. Do you want me to?"

"Is she tall?"

"I don't know, Shlomo, five something. Yeah, taller than me. Nobody's tall compared to you, you giraffe."

"Is she hot?"

"Yeah, when she goes out. You might not think so in an IHOP uniform."

"Does she like a pearl necklace?"

"Shlomo, I can't ask her that. Stop! Do you want me to or not? I'm trying to help ya, ya big André the Giant!"

"Yeah, I'm up for it."

Steph returned with our pancakes. "It's all set. Virginia's working a double shift. She's going to get herself ready in the bathroom here. Come back at ten fifteen tonight to pick her up. You better leave me a big tip for the service, Shlomo."

"I'll give you a big bonus if it's a pearl necklace."

"Shut up! You're horrible!" Steph said, laughing.

❖ ❖ ❖

My embarrassment about sloppy seconds was dissipating the more time I spent with Big Deb and the more I enjoyed her company and her broad array of services, bedroom and otherwise. She seemed to have gotten over Shlomo's insensitive dumping in favor of the Mets and was spending a lot of time at our apartment. However, I still wasn't completely sure that she wasn't just trying to make Shlomo jealous and reunite for a walrus romp.

Big Deb and I were hanging out in the apartment Saturday night watching *Spenser: For Hire* when Shlomo came home trailed by a tall woman with bleached-blond hair, wearing high heels, tight jeans, hoop earrings, a black leather jacket, and lots of makeup. Big Deb puffed out her cheeks, put on her grumpy face, and stared at the TV. I tried to keep my eyes from bulging. I felt Big Deb hit me in the ribs. Wow, I thought, a little skanky, but for one night, Steph really did Shlomo up right!

Shlomo, carrying a bag from Liquor Haven, quickly ushered Virginia into his bedroom with the bare minimum of pleasantries, as if Virginia was in the witness protection program.

An hour later, while we were watching *Saturday Night Live*, Virginia reemerged barefoot, disheveled, and carrying her high heels and jacket under her purse. She offered a perfunctory "Nice to meet you" to me and Big Deb before leaving.

The next morning, I grilled Shlomo about his by-the-hour encounter with the IHOP Short-stop.

"Shlomo, we're not running a brothel here, and I'm not a pimp counting time. The Short-stop could have stayed more than an hour. You at least could have made it to the end of *Saturday Night Live*. Was her rate too high?"

"I really liked her. She had a nice body, big tits. I had just gone too long."

"What do you mean?"

"Too pent up. Bad for your prostate."

"So?"

"So...it was over before it started."

"Couldn't you spend some time pleasing her and then run it back in the morning? Seems like a lost opportunity. You're gonna owe Sweet Steph an apology."

"I tried to keep myself awake so I could do something for her. She wanted me to keep saying her name, it makes her hot, but then she got mad because she said I kept calling her 'Vagina' instead of Virginia. I didn't realize it, but I was pretty sleepy. Maybe my subconscious took over. It ruined the mood."

"So she wouldn't stay longer?"

"No, she was going to stay for the night."

"Well, what happened?"

"I asked her how she felt about a pearl necklace. She didn't know what it was, so I explained it. Then she told me I was too self-centered and she wasn't horny anymore and she got dressed."

"Maybe you should hold off on the pearl necklace until the second date; you don't want to spoil her with that gift too soon. You going to see her again?"

"I don't know. I'll just have to keep eating at IHOP and leave big tips."

Born Free

Soon after we connected with Dieter Klingenmeier, he moved to his own apartment at Camelot Cay and became a regular uninvited but welcome visitor at our pad. We were all Northerners from elitist universities, out of our element, like Mork from Ork arriving in Boulder in his egg spaceship, and embarking on unpredictable career paths, adapting to an unfamiliar but intriguing land with its own customs and rhythms and ambiance and yin and yang—tropical paradise and suburban blight, retirement haven and revivalist mecca, cosmopolitan and redneck.

Every night between eight and nine o'clock, Dieter would walk across the Cay quad by the frog-infested pool, carrying an empty yogurt container as his drinking cup, enter our patio door, holler, "You have any *B*s"—beers—head straight to the refrigerator for a Pabst, and take his spot on the couch to join us for the baseball play-offs or Monday Night Football.

We called our Drabenville-transplant group No Fishing Off Bridges and sought out Florida adventures together.

There was the trip inland to Iroquikka River State Park, where, while exploring the one-stoplight Iroquikka City, we stumbled upon Four Rings Animal Circus Farm, a training site for traveling circus animals. A sign on the road out of town announced the circus operation and advised, "Warning: Dangerous Animals. Visitors and Trespassers Prohibited. Violators Enter at Their Own Risk and Will Be Prosecuted." We turned down the long dirt driveway anyway. Trailers were strewn across the property, interspersed with barrack-like structures, cages, and big metal rings,

THREE YARDS AND A PLATE OF MULLET

surrounded by a ten-foot fence. We stood outside the fence for a while, looking for any lions or tigers roaming the grounds or animal trainers with whips and chairs. "Let's check it out," Shlomo suggested.

We climbed the fence. Shlomo, as usual, tried to make himself inconspicuous by looking as if he belonged there as a staff member, checking the fence, stacking some bales of hay, and picking up a rake and moving dirt around a ring. Dieter and I stayed closer to the fence while Shlomo roamed, joking that Shlomo would dwarf and scare away any bear he encountered and that he'd better be careful not to get caught by the circus farm owner or he'd wind up a caged main attraction in Four Rings as Sasquatch, along with Bearded Lady and Lobster Boy.

Shlomo became emboldened and started checking out the back end of the trailers, which had ramps to the ground. Apparently, they were closed or empty—except one. As Shlomo wandered into one trailer to examine the animals' digs, Dieter and I spotted Leo the Lion meandering down his trailer's ramp behind the trailer Shlomo was exploring. Holy fuckin' *Born Free*! It wasn't surprising that Leo emerged, given Shlomo's similarity to sub-Saharan mammals. Terror gripped us. If Leo had a bubble-thought image above his head when he saw Shlomo, I'm sure it would have been the sides of beef in the meat locker that Paulie provided to boxer Rocky for pummeling.

"Shlomo, a lion!" Dieter yelled.

"No there's not, there's nothing here. Real funny."

"Shlomo, a fuckin' lion behind you, get the fuck outta there!" I screamed more vehemently as I leaped halfway up the fence, Dieter right behind.

Shlomo came out of the trailer and looked. By now, Leo, with his big bushy mane and regal face, was on the ground and ambling in Shlomo's direction. I dropped the ten feet on the other side of the fence and looked back to see Shlomo rumbling toward the fence like a Thoroughbred in the home stretch of the Kentucky Derby, panic plastered on his face and eyes bulging. Just as Shlomo jumped and clung onto the fence like Spiderman on steroids, Leo let out a thunderous roar and started galloping toward us. Dieter and I were beneath Shlomo when he dove over the top, flipping back-first and knocking us to the ground just seconds before Leo reached the fence and started pacing its perimeter, casting us cautionary, my-lunch-is-late glances intensified by guttural growls.

"Go home!" Shlomo yelled at Leo, lunging at him like an attacker.

Leo looked at him, expressionless, and growled, showing his gaping mouth and huge fangs.

"Shlomo, you wuss. He's not your neighborhood stray dog," Dieter said, and we laughed hysterically as we headed back to the car at the image of Shlomo flopping over the fence like Dick Fosbury, Olympian innovator of the high jump back flop, and then turning lion tamer.

Dieter went operatic and belted out a line: "Born free, as free as the wind blows!"

Shlomo was still in fight-or-flight mode and too scared to find the humor.

Typical Tourists

Leo was not the only wild animal we tussled with that day. We continued on from Iroquikka City to Iroquikka River State Park, known as Gator Gateway for the large population of alligators that inhabit its swamps, marshes, and rivers. From a bridge overpass, we observed a river infested with alligators, with kayakers paddling over and around them undeterred.

We hiked through pineland and found a spot on the river shore where several alligators were resting motionless. Shlomo wanted a picture with the gators in the background. He came within ten yards, and they didn't move. He pushed the boundary more, cutting the distance in half. Still no movement.

"I think I can get a little closer. They're lazy, or used to people," Shlomo declared. He took two more big steps toward the gators, and just as he was about to turn around, a gator launched itself five feet in the air and knocked Shlomo backward into the water. None of us knew that alligators could propel themselves five feet off the surface with their tails. Shlomo had no choice but to become an alligator wrestler just long enough to repel the gator, which, luckily, appeared more interested in defending turf than in aggression, and clamber up the riverbank.

"Did you get the shot?" Shlomo gasped.

"Yeah, Shlomo, I did continuous shutter. You're gonna want to frame one of those babies," I said, keeping an eye on the retreating gator.

"Good. I have to prove I wrestled an alligator. Now let's get the hell out of this safari while I'm still alive. I miss my recliner."

❖ ❖ ❖

Then there was the time Tropical Storm Esmerelda was approaching the Gulf Coast, and we decided to rent a small catamaran sailboat for an adventure on the Gulf high seas. We pulled it into the Gulf and hopped onto the platform. As we reached a quarter mile out on our Hobie Cat, winds were whipping at thirty to fifty miles an hour and waves were tossing us relentlessly. We all clutched the pole holding the main sail as wind caught the sails flush, sending us airborne and hurtling through waves. We had no control, and even if we had known what we were doing, we would have been out of control anyway. We hung on to our ride as long as we could, like John Travolta's Bud Davis clinging to the mechanical bull in *Urban Cowboy*, as we blew far out to sea.

The catamaran finally hit a wave just right and went vertical, throwing us off and capsizing. We were stupid Northerners—you don't sail small crafts preceding a tropical storm. We'd ignored the rental shop's warning and signed the disclaimers. But we did one smart thing—we wore life jackets.

We tried mightily to right the catamaran, but the sails were too heavy underwater and we had no leverage. So we sprawled out over the parallel hulls to keep ourselves afloat, debating whose stupid idea this was, busting on Shlomo for capsizing us because of his excessive ballast, unaware that our lives were in jeopardy. We let the waves take us for half an hour before a Florida Department of Natural Resources patrol boat arrived.

The deckhands threw us lines to pull us to the boat's ladder, where we climbed on board, exhausted and shivering, and attached a tow to the Hobie Cat.

"Are you guys idiots?" the captain accosted us. "Are you out of your minds? Did you know it's illegal to be out on a boat like this today? Didn't you listen to the weather report?"

"Yeah, we did. We thought it would make a great day for sailing," Dieter responded. "I guess we underestimated a tropical storm."

"I'm from New York," Shlomo offered up as an excuse for senselessness.

"It didn't seem so bad on shore, just a little breezy. I thought we could handle it," I said.

"Do you guys have any sailing experience?" the captain asked.

We shook our heads no.

"Typical tourists. Don't know when you're risking your lives."

"No, we live here; we're Floridians now," Shlomo objected.

"I don't give a rat's ass if you live here now—unless you were born here, you're a tourist when you come onto my waters. And now you're a lawbreaker. I'm going to have to arrest you for unlawful sailing during a state weather emergency. You not only risked your lives being out here, you put my crew members' lives at risk, dumbasses. And that jackass who rented to you should have his license suspended, too."

"Aye-aye, Captain," Shlomo barked. He pressed his legs together, stood erect, and gave a dramatic salute. I didn't know whether Shlomo was mocking him or trying to show proper respect. Either way, the captain didn't take kindly to it.

"You better shut the fuck up, Jack and the Beanstalk, or I'll add disorderly conduct on the high seas to your rap," the captain told Shlomo. Then he pointed a meaty hand at Dieter and me. "That goes for you two homos also; you're in enough trouble already. Keep your mouths shut until we come ashore."

Wow, a foul-mouthed comedian captain. I guess anything goes in international waters.

We docked in Mirabella County, about twenty-five miles south of where we shoved off on Conquista Island. We were taken by Department of Natural Resources deputies to the police booking station, and spent a night in county jail in orange jumpsuits with DUI, simple assault, disorderly conduct, and public drunkenness violators. Having been charged with such mundane illegal acts, our cellmates were intrigued by our story of treason on the high seas, and we told it repeatedly, with more and more grandiose embellishment, adding a ride atop a school of dolphins and a daring bucket rescue by helicopter, before we were released in the morning with $500 fines.

Sneekey the Manatee

We had heard so much about the manatee—there's even a county on Florida's Gulf Coast named after the lovable, docile sea cow, also known as floating speed bumps by callous motor boaters who carve them up and threaten to drive them into extinction—we decided to visit one at the Drabenville Sloane Marine Aquarium. We approached the admission window and saw the marquee announcing fifteen dollars for general admission and twenty dollars including the fifteen-minute film, *Manatee: Peaceful Giant of the Shallow*. As I reached for my wallet, I heard an unusual sound behind me.

"BU-BU-BU-bu-bu-bu-bb-bb-b-b…"

"What the hell is that?"

Again: "BU-BU-BU-bu-bu-bu-bb-bb-b-b…"

"Shlomo, is that you? What's that noise?"

"That's the radioactive bagel."

"The what?"

"You know, the Jew-dar."

"Judo? You're practicing karate?"

"No. Don't you know? Jewish radar. The Hebe-horn."

"I don't get it."

"Whenever I'm about to pay too much, I start to sweat, and the bagel goes off in my head. You know, BU-BU-BU-bu-bu-bu-bb-bb-b-b…It's automatic. It's a common Jewish affliction, but it's also helped us survive and prosper—you know, control all the banks and media and Hollywood."

Shlomo motioned for me to step out of line before I forked over a couple hours' worth of paycheck. "Let's go around to the side. I saw a door to the theater there. You got to go through the side to get in free," he said as he excused himself from the line and loped toward the theater.

The manatee film was finishing its fifteen-minute loop, and several aquarium patrons were leaving via the exterior door. Shlomo dutifully held the door open for the departing patrons and wished them "good day" as if he were the doorman at an exclusive Park Avenue apartment in New York. "Follow my lead," he said. As the last patron left, he casually entered with Dieter and me trailing and continued loping along, feigning all-encompassing interest in anything that caught his eye—an aquarium guide he found on a seat, a photo on the wall, a velvet rope—any distraction that would make him seemingly oblivious to anything else around him.

I followed Shlomo's lead by meticulously inspecting a seat cushion, as if investigating for DNA. Eventually a Sloane employee cleaning and preparing the theater for the next showing addressed the elephant in the room: "Can I help you?"

Shlomo continued intently reading the educational display on the wall about the manatee's diet and gestation cycle, completely enraptured.

"Can. I. Help. You?" the usher asked again, this time in the loud, slow, meticulously enunciated cadence typically used with eighty-year-old tourists. The usher approached Shlomo. Just as she did, Shlomo loped obliviously toward a statue of a giant loggerhead turtle on the opposite side of the theater.

Visibly frustrated, and probably paid six dollars an hour with no financial incentive to enforce any rules, the usher gave up chasing the rogue giraffe, finished her duties, and left the theater, not even bothering to question Dieter and me, still curiously examining the architecture of the theater seats, and with our more humanlike size, much less conspicuous than the Sasquatch was.

We hunkered down in our seats as paying customers began filing through the proper entry door and handing tickets to the usher. After the film, we sauntered into the main exhibit hall, right by the elderly security guy working a cushy retirement job, alongside the suckers who paid full price. Shlomo's side-door, intensely curious-demeanor ruse had worked.

"I like to do things for free," Shlomo repeated as we visited each exhibit room and aquarium tank.

Sneekey the Manatee's tank was a sad and dirty circular, blue pool, like the oversized bathtubs that people who can't afford in-ground swimming pools put in their backyards and euphemistically call "above-ground" pools. Sneekey weighed 1,200 pounds and was forty years old and had lived most of his life in the oversized bathtub at Sloane Marine. He was used to people watching him but apparently had encountered few as enormous and affectionate as Shlomo was.

"Oh, Sneekey, you're so beautiful. You're so large and gray and gorgeous. I love you, Sneekey," Shlomo kept repeating in his best bedroom voice. It seemed to have an effect on Sneekey, who elevated himself above the water to the top of the tank to get closer to Shlomo to…see?…smell?…hear? Who knows, but to get a better sense of a fellow gargantuan mammal speaking the language of love.

I wouldn't have believed it if I hadn't actually seen it, but it was clear that Sneekey was returning Shlomo's affection by nuzzling up to him and coming out of the water to visit Shlomo frequently while ignoring the loud and obnoxious kids screaming for his attention. "Oh, Sneekey, blow me some lovin' out of your pretty blowholes, you big boy, you. I've missed you so much!" Shlomo prattled on to Sneekey's growing delight.

This love-at-first-sight encounter lasted thirty minutes until Dieter and I pried Shlomo away from the tank.

"I have to go, but I will return. We will see each other again, Sneekey. I love you; don't forget that," Shlomo said as we left, in a scene as maudlin as Rhett Butler leaving Scarlett O'Hara in *Gone with the Wind*. Before we left Sloane, Cheap Bagelman Shlomo plunked down $195 for a lifetime membership in the Save the Manatee Club.

❖ ❖ ❖

Shlomo was so enamored with Sneekey that we took another adventure to Silver Moon River, an inlet to the Gulf fed by warmwater springs where manatees congregate by the hundreds when temperatures get colder. At Silver Moon, we could commune up close and personal with manatees on a Swim with the Manatees snorkeling outing. Before we could board the charter boat in our wetsuits—of course, none fit Shlomo, so he went unzipped—we were required to watch a Florida Department of Natural Resources video advising us of the dos and don'ts when in the water with manatees.

Once in the water, Shlomo promptly broke all the rules, riding on manatees' backs, chasing them, talking to them, holding onto their tails. Our host, pontoon boat Captain Scooter, issued Shlomo two stern warnings that his manatee adventure privileges were in jeopardy. When Captain Scooter saw Shlomo walking—another no-no, the video cautioned us to swim flat on the surface—in the most shallow water next to river grass, stumbling and tripping as he most certainly stepped on resting manatees—he apparently had seen enough. Within minutes, a Florida Department of Natural Resources boat was in the cove, the police ordering Shlomo aboard. Shlomo was issued a citation for disturbing manatees on guided recreational tour, which came with a $250 fine.

"These DNR police are hard-asses. This is my second bust," Shlomo announced once back aboard the pontoon.

"Only with idiots," Captain Scooter replied, "and we get more than we can handle down here. You ain't the first dumb-ass to think he's one with the manatee."

"I really am, Captain Scooter," Shlomo protested. "You ever heard of Sneekey the Manatee? I talked to him and—"

"If I were you, big man, I'd shut up for the rest of the trip," Captain Scooter interrupted, "or DNR will haul you out to the ruins on Turquoise Key where they keep the most incorrigible lawbreakers overnight."

Le Château: Living It Up

Since Shlomo, Dieter, and I were spending so much time together seeking Florida adventures and hanging out in our apartment and watching quirky shows like *Max Headroom* and *Pee-wee's Playhouse*, we decided to pool our resources and live the dream as beach bums. To make the dream work financially, we needed one more roommate and a Realtor to find us a bargain-basement rental on Conquista Island.

I called the *Dinqy*'s new sports columnist, Stevie Spoonhauer, a three-sport high school athlete in Michigan and a shooting guard at Saginaw Valley State University, who arrived from Michigan's *Ypsilanti Courier*

THREE YARDS AND A PLATE OF MULLET

newspaper. We met Spooner at the Jib & Jibe and convinced him to join us on Conquista. An island Realtor found us a cheap, neglected bungalow that couldn't have been any closer to the Gulf.

It was in the town of Duffy Beach on a street paralleling the beach, three blocks from Monsieur's hovel. Down the street was a trailer on a barren beachside lot fronted by a pickup truck carrying a pop-up camper, the homestead and workshop of Chainsaw Chet, a local-legend chainsaw artist, who may have lived in either abode. Chainsaw did his carving work on three huge tree stumps on his property, which was strewn with metal signs and massive wood carvings of bears, moose, and other animals and protected by two old dogs who wandered the grounds.

Our backyard was crushed shell and sand and one palm tree, beyond which was a seawall that dropped to a wide Gulf beach. We could watch the Gulf sunsets from the roof of our screened-in porch. If someone had told me nine months earlier as I trudged up Cardiac Hill to class through eighteen inches of snow in my Timberland boots and parka, my wet hair frozen, that by the time another arctic Upstate New York winter rolled around, I'd be running in shorts and a T-shirt and walking out my back door for a dip in the Gulf, I would have said that would be paradise.

LE CHÂTEAU: LIVING IT UP

It was no Taj Mahal, but it was our Le Château. The one-floor bungalow was horribly outdated, verging on dilapidated, but it had four bedrooms, working appliances, hot water, and electricity. One thing we discovered quickly was that our air-conditioner-less bungalow, with its rotting wood and moist atmosphere, was a natural refuge for the palmetto bug, Florida's ubiquitous cockroach. When we came home at night, we'd arm ourselves with a broom, because as soon as the lights went on, we'd face a legion of the panicked, crusty, brown critters.

We had memorable nights soon after we moved in. The first was Game 6 of the World Series between the Red Sox and the Mets. Shlomo was on the phone with his New York buddies during the bottom of the tenth, lamenting a season that fell just short, when the Mets, down two runs and down to their last strike, launched their miracle comeback, culminating with Mookie Wilson's grounder to first that rolled through Bill Buckner's legs. Shlomo was so excited to see Ray Knight score the winning run that he yanked the cord from the wall and threw the phone through our front window.

Later, we christened Le Château with a Halloween Party. Word spread throughout the *Dinqy*, the *T-D*, Camelot Cay, and Father Ignacio School, attracting more than a hundred people to our humble abode. It happened to be a once-in-a-blue-moon night when the lunar alignment exerted an enormous pull on the Gulf tide. As the party progressed, the Gulf lapped the seawall and spilled into our backyard. Soon we had hammered attendees in vampire and gorilla and Pee-wee Herman outfits dancing in two feet of foamy Gulf water, which by midnight rose even more and began pouring into our patio, three steps down from our main living level. We turned the patio into a water-wrestling ring and had twenty-five costumed people grappling and splashing like some odd theatrical cult orgy. The rising tide receded one foot short of flowing into the house. We woke up the next morning to a dozen guests in borrowed clothes splayed across our couches and recliners, plastic cups and beer cans floating in our patio and yard, and a few more partiers tapping the keg up the ladder on our patio roof.

LE CHÂTEAU: LIVING IT UP

We spent our Saturday mornings playing spirited two-on-two basketball for bragging rights at the local elementary school playground—Spooner's superior ball handling and shooting versus Shlomo's inside prowess, with Dieter's rebounding and my offensive skills often neutralizing each other—and our Saturday evening happy hours at Barnacle Beau's Tiki Bar on the Beach and the Ram Shackle on Duffy's Pier, a World War II-era, old Florida fisherman's bar-restaurant hut built on a pier a hundred yards into the Gulf, the location making the beer and steamed shrimp taste that much better.

We frequently dropped in at the Hovel unannounced, and Monsieur was always an impromptu host par excellence, offering us shellfish and wine du jour and entertaining us with a preposterous crime or justice story with perfectly inserted profanity.

We were four singles grabbing a foothold on the first rung of the career ladder, in a place none of us dreamed we'd be, wondering how we got there, experiencing a shared journey with no real plan. There were moments on our patio or at the Ram Shackle when Shlomo and I would turn to each and ask the same question: "Are we living it up?"

The answer, always, was yes.

The Cannon and a Big Blast

I was heading into the November home stretch of the high school football regular season, the annual drive for the post-season playoffs. To Mitch Mahotie's chagrin, Blintzer assigned him to cover the next East Grove game, because East Grove was undefeated, and a blossoming story in its own right, and Mahotie was a better writer and interviewer than was Bert Halumka, who was assigned to contribute to my game, Dolphin–DeVaca. It would be a night Bert would remember—or maybe not.

Dolphin, being the larger and more affluent school, had virtually owned DeVaca during the Fred Zipf era. Still, it was an intracounty rivalry with a long history that stirred community pride and attracted big crowds and commerce—each school held its own fish fry after the game. Dolphin's fish fry also served as the Annual Dolphin County Mullet Toss Championship, which is like an egg toss competition, where pitch-and-catch partners keep moving farther apart until the egg breaks, except with slippery fish from the Mugilidae family as the preciously preserved possession.

DeVaca City added its own twist to the rivalry festivities with its annual Corndog Cook-off Culinary Championship, featuring a cornucopia of hot dog recipes. So the neighborly feud wasn't about to end even though DeVaca rarely won, except in the early '80s when the Conquistadors stole two in a row after the fiery Coach Huckerbee took over from the archaic Coach LaGarde and showed no respect for the legendary but sputtering

Zipf Code offense and Zipf-Loc defense. Nor did Huckerbee show any mercy for the Zipf legend itself as it slowly succumbed to Alzheimer's, until prodigal son Bamford returned and halted such foolishness.

The game usually was no gimme for Dolphin, however, despite the 5A/3A disparity. Bamford may have scarfed a bevy of blue-chippers away from DeVaca City, but the Conquistadors still had a stockpile of talent and speed at the skill positions, thanks partly to the influx of Latin American futbol converts like quarterback Miguel Lecha, and a rich football tradition that boasted three state championships since the 1960s.

Jed Bamford Field at Roop Stadium was packed to the rafters in red-and-black and blue-and-gold sections. Whalebait Wally, already sweat-stained and spritzing about the calamitous week and its impact on the game, was at the controls in the press box when I arrived. The *T-D*'s Donny Monday stood behind him grimacing, a cigarette between his twitching fingers.

"All you chummers who love Fightin' Dorsals football know it's been a tense and sad week for Coach Bamford's crew," Wally opened. "Harpooners, you may not know Sammy Sammons and Nate Hilliard personally, but I've interviewed them many times. Great kids. Bright futures. I love these boys. It just makes me sick, what they're going through, sick as a landlubber caught in a perfect storm. Let's hope it's not true, Whalers, and they're exonerated. And let's not forget the girls. We talk football on Whalebait Wally, but some things—not many—are more important, and if it's true, my heart goes out to them. There will be no winners. I don't know about you, Clam Diggers, but I'm devastated.

"And this could be devastating to Dolphin's season and their reputation, Trawlers, so buck up and get ready for that. But if any coach can weather the storm, it's Jimbo Bamford. We'll see if Coach Bamford and untested Connor "the Cannon" Crane can right the ship against Coach Huckerbee's Conquistadors and All-Universe Charles "Na-Na-Na-Hey-Hey-Hey-Good-bye" Heyward. A fifty-four-year rivalry between

THE CANNON AND A BIG BLAST

the two oldest schools in the county—it doesn't get any better, Crabbers. Fasten your jibs for kickoff coming up next."

"Jesus H. Fuckin' Christ Almighty, Wally, do you have to be so fuckin' maudlin," Monday griped as soon as Whalebait went to commercial. Other media members looked at each other and, as usual, couldn't stifle chuckles. "If you knew *anything* about football, you'd know Crane is *better* than Sammons. You should be praising those whores, Wally."

The press box cracked up—at least, the guys did—though we all knew that Monday was wrong and depraved. The lone woman, a TV production assistant, muttered, "Disgusting pigs," and walked out.

"Yeah, Donny, you're a pig...and a man-whore," said the young, handsome TV play-by-play guy, in an effort to goad Monday.

"Thank you for the compliment, asswipe. Now go back to pulling your pud," Monday shot back and blew smoke at him.

"Hey, shut up, all you assholes, Jeannie's coming back; she's probably been crying in the bathroom. I don't want to get fired for insensitivity or sexual harassment or whatever," said Play-by-Play.

"Quit your worrying, fruitcake. Have I ever been fired?" Monday asked, palms held out, shoulders shrugged, an upside down Bozo smile plastered on his craggy face. If Donny wasn't a car salesman / sports columnist, he would work as a Goodfella.

"You need sensitivity training, Donny," Play-by-Play advised.

"Sensitivity my ass, Beefcake," Donny barked. "Grow a pair, numnut. That goes for your estrogenic assistant too."

"Donny, I've got a heart," Whalebait interjected, providing the last word before returning to air. "I know your heart, and I've got three words, and I quote: Stink! Stank! Stunk!" he bellowed in his best Mr. Grinch impression to howls of laughter, even from Jeannie. His switchboard light came on.

"Good evening, Whalers, coming to you live from Jed Bamford Field…"

❖ ❖ ❖

— 240 —

Bert Halumka was roving the Dolphin sideline, reporting on the team's response to the Cannon.

DeVaca got the ball first. Their strategy became clear immediately. They challenged Flea Hilliard's replacement at cornerback with speedy Demetrius "Squiggs" Parker, mixing short passes to elusive receivers with a heavy dose of brick-body Heyward's running. The plan worked on the Conqs' first drive. Parker, split wide, beat the second-string corner on a five-yard out pattern. But where Flea likely would have forced Parker out of bounds, Parker was able to turn up the field against the less-agile replacement for a forty-two-yard touchdown.

On Dolphin's first possession, Crane fumbled a hand-off to Mondo, recovered by Heyward on Dolphin's thirty-five. On the Conquistadors' first play, Lecha handed to Heyward, who plunged toward the line. But instead of plowing for yardage, he turned and pitched back to Lecha, who launched a strike to an uncovered Parker for a quick 14–0 DeVaca lead. Huckerbee went high-stepping down his sideline, hugging assistants and yelling, "The Bummerooski! The Bummerooski! HooooWheeee!" Cryptic, but I knew exactly what he meant.

From my time watching DeVaca practices, I knew that Huckerbee was infatuated with Bum Phillips (What would *you* call yourself if your real name was Oail?), the NFL Houston Oilers coach known for his buzz cut and glasses, eight-gallon cowboy hats, alligator boots, and Texas twang—and his powder-blue winning teams led by steamroller Earl Campbell.

"Ah cain't believe a gah can make it to the big time goin' bah the name 'Bum.' Ah don't know if Owl or Oil or O'Whale or whatever the hell his real name is, is any better, but Bum? Ya gotta be kiddin' me!" Huckerbee told me during my first interview with him and his assistant in August, laughing and slapping his leg with his dirty Florida State cap. "Ah mean, I knew a gah named Fart who hung around the streets in Okeechobee, but Fart really was a bum. Bum ain't no bum!"

Huckerbee cracked himself up with his Bum rant. I think he just liked hearing himself say the name. "The only thing I can see good about Bum bein' called Bum is if yer team sucked and the fans yelled, 'Yer a bum!'

you wouldn't take it as insult if *everybody* called you Bum. Bum! Git outta here!"

He took it so far as to appropriate the What Would Jesus Do mantra and substituted *Bum* for *Jesus*, so when he would consult with his coaching staff about dealing with a problem player or stopping a high-powered opposing offense, he'd ask, WWBD? And the staffers would shake their heads, cover their eyes with their hands, and try to stifle their guffaws. "C'mon gahs, ya know what ah mean," Huckerbee would bark, holding back a laugh himself. "Think like a Bum!" and they'd all crack up.

Apparently, Huckerbee had seen the NFL Films episode featuring coaches mic'ed up and saying ridiculous things. In one scene, Bum turns around after watching a play, and seemingly out of desperation—like what other choice could he possibly make?—instructs his staff, "Let's run the Bummerooski."

So Huckerbee installed the "Bummerooski," which was code for whenever the team wanted a trick play like a fake punt. "Let's run the Bummerooski!" he'd yell near the end of practice as the team ran through its library of trick plays coded as Bummerooski One, Bummerooski Two and so forth. "I love the Bummerooski!"

After DeVaca City's successful Bummerooski, I could see Bamford trying to calm down a jittery Crane on the sideline, as the red-and-black fans' cacophony drowned out the stunned Fightin' Dorsals' supporters.

Dolphin had run the ball five straight times on its opening possession, but its ground game was plodding without Sammons and Hilliard—Mondo was a good power runner but less effective without the breakaway threats—and played to DeVaca's strength, its speed. I was wondering whether Bamford would deviate from his "three yards and a plate of mullet" script and let the Cannon do what he did best and air it out.

Connor Crane was a golden boy blue-chipper. Tall, clean-cut, and blond, he set passing records on junior varsity and moved up to varsity as a sophomore. But Schlorf favored the faster and more athletic Sammons, one year ahead of the Cannon, for his multiple-threat capabilities at the high school level while acknowledging that the Cannon may make a better college passer. Schlorf was rewarded for that decision when Sammons led the team to the 1985 state championship. Schlorf saw no reason to jump off the Sammons bandwagon while the team attempted to repeat, so the Cannon, now a junior, assumed the backup role again.

Connor was a quiet and sensitive kid, the kind who displayed superior talent at seven, but didn't let his natural abilities mushroom into a sense of superiority and privilege over his peers. He was also a kid whose dad recognized his talent and pushed him relentlessly to develop it, like tennis dads I'd observed who were hypercritical of their progeny and sought devotion and perfection as if their own self-worth depended on it. Connor had dutifully gone along with his dad's pugilistic program, the individual training sessions with self-anointed quarterback gurus, summer camps under the tutelage of NFL quarterbacks and college coaches, boot-camp-style early morning conditioning drills, and weekend afternoons practicing five- and seven-step drops and pirouettes and bootlegs, throwing at targets with Dad castigating him for every misstep. It was hard to tell through all that practice and dedication whether Connor considered his talents a gift or a burden. Instead of growing more confident as he matured and his six-two, 195-pound body developed to complement his skill, he seemed to become more withdrawn and unsure, often asking coaches questions about plays in practice when everyone knew he knew the answer or seeking a critique of the minutiae of his mechanics like the ultimate perfectionist, even though the coaches instructed him not to overthink and to let his natural talent and instincts take over.

I had heard of Connor's prodigious talent and made sure to talk to him several times, not to quote him, but just to get to know him, anticipating that he would burst on the scene whenever he got his chance, and here it was. He struck me as reserved and humble, perhaps too much so for someone who had greatness within his grasp, albeit in a game with only loose parallels to real life, but greatness nonetheless.

I once asked Connor whether he had ever considered transferring so he could get playing time sooner. He said he was interested in attending Cardinal St. John the Pius for its character education as much as for football, but his father didn't approve because Cardinal played in a much smaller, private-school league, lacked the resources that came with taxpayer-backed Dolphin High, and didn't have the opportunity to compete for the biggest prize in the land—the 5A championship—and all the recognition and potential big-name college scholarships that came with it.

High School Football Prospects Monthly had Crane rated above Sammons in its list of the top one hundred quarterbacks nationally despite the JV-only sample size, taking into account scouting reports and measurements and potential and projections that Sammons could be converted to running back in college.

I couldn't help but wonder whether Connor's big chance to climb the college recruiters' rankings had come about as a result of another intriguing conspiracy, this one involving Coach Bamford, an overbearing Dad Crane, high-stature Fightin' Dorsals' boosters, and—who knows—maybe even Donny Monday.

The weight of expectations and fear of disappointment appeared to be crashing down on the Cannon on his big opportunity finally to make Dad proud. It seemed Bamford might have underestimated the fragility of Connor's ego and the deterioration of his confidence while spending a year and a half on the bench witnessing Sammons's successful run.

❖ ❖ ❖

Bamford wasn't one to panic or second-guess himself, but he wasn't stupid either. He knew he had to get Crane—and his offense—going, and that without his two primary speedsters, the Fightin' Dorsals' "three yards and a plate of mullet" game might not be enough to win. Besides, he had to adapt to the new complexion of his team and look beyond this game; if Dolphin was going to repeat, it would ride the Cannon's arm now.

It was as if I was in Bamford's head. I had spent so much time and psychic energy researching him, talking to others about him, interviewing him, and observing him that I was now thinking like he did. On

Dolphin's next possession, Bamford—who was calling plays—dialed up a first-down bomb, so uncharacteristic that it fooled the DeVaca defense, which bit on the fake to Mondo. Dexter Cartwright was streaking uncovered down the right sideline. The Cannon strode forward and let it fly. He threw a frozen rope instead of an arching touch pass, overthrowing Cartwright by ten yards. The next play was an eight-yard out pattern, and Crane was wild high, the ball sailing over bystanders on the Dolphin sidelines.

"He just needs to settle down, just settle down. C'mon, boy," Monday commentated to himself. "Time to turn this dunghill into a rose garden, champ."

DeVaca called a time-out, and WFIN-AM went to a Finizio Realty commercial.

"Your boy's lookin' a little rattled," Wally announced to Monday. "Sammons's arm isn't as strong, but he would have made those plays."

"Maybe they got him on that goddamn Ritalin or some shit," Monday replied. "Don't get your gonads in an uproar, Wally. He'll be fine. He's got Dolphin superstar written all over him."

"Whalers, if you've just anchored ahoy, Dolphin and the Cannon have had a shaky start, very shaky. They've been Conq'd, down fourteen-zippo, third and ten at their own thirty."

Dolphin came to the line in a newly installed shotgun formation. Crane took the snap and wheeled to face the right sideline, where Cartwright had taken three driving upfield strides and then come back two for a wide receiver screen. Cartwright should have been open, what with his speed and the third-and-long situation dictating that DeVaca defenders would give him a cushion to keep the play in front of them. But Squiggs Parker jumped the route into the Cannon's throwing lane, as if he was in Dolphin's huddle. The Cannon was so locked in on Cartwright that he threw the screen anyway. I could hear the Dolphin fans gasp even before the Cannon released the ball, as they collectively experienced an Amazing Kreskin moment and foresaw the future unfolding. Squiggs intercepted the ill-advised pass in stride and waltzed

THE CANNON AND A BIG BLAST

to the end zone for a 21–0 DeVaca lead, as Coach Huckerbee slapped his assistants' backs.

Play-by-Play guy, prone to hyperbole, took his cue. "Holy cow heads, Cabeza de Vaca fans! Pass the smelling salts…please! I can't believe what I'm seeing. DeVaca City should open an IHOP because they're pancaking Dolphin! Jimbo Bamford is going to see Squiggles interrupting his sweet dreams tonight, folks, twenty-one–zero Conqs!"

"Chummers, it hasn't been the Cannon's night so far," Wally offered. "If he doesn't reload fast, it's going to be a long one."

I asked Huckerbee about the play after the game. He called a time-out to tell his cornerbacks, "Time to steal their lunch money and send them home cryin'. I knew ol' Jimbo would try to pick up Crane's confidence by calling an easy completion, so I had my corners sell out on the short route, and it was there for the taking like free corned-beef samples at DeVaca Deli and Donut."

The *T-D*'s Reindollar, the consummate pro, was placid as ever, scanning the field and meticulously recording each play in his notebook.

But Monday, ever the homer, was exasperated. "Fuckin' A, this is Choke City, baby. All this just to have this overhyped schmuck lay an egg. A fuckin' Grade A, jumbo egg," Donny muttered.

I had had passing thoughts about Monday being involved in this tangled Dolphin conspiracy, but now his comment had me seriously considering it. I was tempted to ask Monday what "all this" meant but didn't want to incur his wrath or smell his dismissive smoke cloud. Besides, he *was* from Brooklyn, and it wasn't out of the realm of possibility that he had Goodfella connections—or even that it was Monday who'd ordered me kneecapped on Ninth Avenue.

Mahotie would declare that things were "going to hell in a handbasket" for Dolphin. Then it went from "bad to worse," in Mahotie-speak.

After two runs, Bamford tried to get Crane untracked again. Crane double-clutched and, in his hesitation, lost synch with the alarm clock all good quarterbacks have in their heads. As he cocked his arm again to throw, Heyward thumped him from his blind side and jarred the ball loose. A DeVaca lineman recovered and rumbled for a score. Astonishingly, Dolphin retreated to the half-time locker room trailing 28–0.

❖ ❖ ❖

As Dolphin players trotted to their sideline for the second half, an exasperated fan leaned over the railing and yelled, "Wake up! We got another half to play. Y'all are embarrassing me, shameful for y'all to be wearing a Dolphin's uniform. Let's go, wake 'em up or you should turn 'em in!"

Ugly as it was, it may have sparked Cartwright. He took the kickoff, found a gap up the middle, and then broke toward the sideline, setting up a footrace with the last two DeVaca defenders, who were taking pursuit angles to cut him off. The three players collided at full speed near midfield and went careening out of bounds. Players and coaches on Dolphin's sideline parted to avoid getting bowled over, but the field-pass people behind them couldn't see and had no time to react. A cameraman was knocked backward by the force and lost his camera; another bystander was buried. The two DeVaca players untangled, got up, and jogged back toward their bench on the other side of the field. Cartwright stayed to help up the sprawled bystander, but he wasn't getting up. Cartwright motioned for help. Athletic trainers ran to the spot, and Dolphin coaches moved their players back. The trainers kneeled down with the bystander, and sent a student assistant toward the entry gate to summon paramedics. Two paramedics, carrying medical bags, trotted to the scene and dropped to one knee. Bend-Over, using his photographer's instincts, circled the periphery, snapping away.

I thought it must be a student assistant or some Dolphin High special invitee who was down. But after seeing Bend-Over, I recalled that Halumka was posted on the Dolphin sideline, and scanned for him, but couldn't locate him. Then I saw Bend-Over, no longer with his eye glued to the viewfinder, waving frantically at the press box. Here was a guy accustomed to staying cool and focused on recording images during all kinds of mayhem—car crashes, fires, hurricanes, angry court defendants

THE CANNON AND A BIG BLAST

trying to punch his lights out—and now, uncharacteristically, he wasn't even trying to do his job. I caught Bend-Over's attention from the press box and gestured with both hands raised as if to say, What's up?

Bend-Over gestured back by holding his hands up to his own eyeglasses and forming circles with his thumbs and fingers. Bifocals! It was Halumka.

I scurried out of the press box and rushed to the sideline, just in time to see the paramedics roll Halumka onto a stretcher and wheel him toward the ambulance. I asked one paramedic for information as they hurried by. "Possible concussion." I caught a glimpse of Bert. His arms were above his head, as if frozen in place. His glasses were shattered. He looked unconscious. When I got back to the press box, I phoned the sports desk and told a copy editor what had happened and to get in touch with Bert's parents.

Without Bert, I decided to spend the rest of the game roving the sidelines. It was there that I witnessed the reincarnation of the Cannon. I don't know if the Cannon felt he had nothing more to lose, or if seeing Bert legitimately down and out may have allowed him to ease up on himself and relax, but the Cannon returned to the field a different person. He started confidently directing traffic and hitting his passes in rhythm, just as he practiced with his dad at the park. No more hesitation or double-clutching; no more adrenaline-stoked throws requiring a Werner Ladders salesperson to complete. Finally, here was the guy *High School Football Prospects Monthly* pegged as a top one hundred quarterback before he'd ever thrown a varsity pass.

The Cannon led three straight touchdown drives, throwing for two and running for one, pulling Dolphin to 28–21.

Huckerbee's unabashed joy from the first half was turning acerbic as the game tightened.

"Hell-a-pee-na peppers, boys! What are ya doin' out there!" he cried to his defense as the Cannon turned a third-and-twenty into an over-the-top forty-yard touchdown pass, bringing Dolphin to within one score with six minutes to go.

At that point, Huckerbee turned to the indomitable Heyward on the ground, mixed with short passes by Miguel Lecha, to put the game away. They moved it fifty-five yards and killed five minutes, reaching a third-and-three on Dolphin's fifteen. Lecha faked a dive up the middle to Heyward and then rolled right, where Squiggs Parker was running parallel to him and wide open for an easy first down, if not a touchdown. But Lecha overthrew him, and the pass was intercepted.

"Funyuns!" Huckerbee exploded. "Awww, Funyuns Mee-gwell!"

Off came the tattered ball cap, smashed to the ground. Then he went stomping around looking for assistant coaches, the team manager, the ten-year-old volunteer ball boys—anyone to vent at. "Goll dang it, DOUBLE MARSHMALLOWS, Conqs!" he wailed to nobody in particular.

Pacing back to gather his defense, he recomposed. "Awwright, D, let's stop these cornflakes and get back over the river with a dubya."

The Cannon connected on three straight passes to move the ball to DeVaca's forty-eight with twenty-one seconds left. He hurled his next pass sixty yards in the air into Cartwright's outstretched arms to bring the Fightin' Dorsals to one point down, 28–27, the crowd going crazy. Now Coach Bamford had a decision: go for the win with a two-point conversion or play for overtime with an extra point. He sent out the kicking team.

Huckerbee sent his two best athletes, Heyward and Squiggs, to play special teams for the first time. Dolphin double-teamed Heyward's burst up the middle, but that left Squiggs unaccounted for on the edge. The erratic Cal "Wide Right" Stimson was three for three on the night but never saw the darting Squiggs, who laid out in a full dive and smothered the kick.

DeVaca fans jumped and hugged in rhythm with the players, rattling the stands, as Huckerbee congratulated the special teamers. When the final gun sounded, Huckerbee calmly sought out Bamford for a handshake, and then strode toward the locker room, bouncing high on the balls of his feet, drawing out the cadence of each step as if to wring every ounce of joy from the walk, sweat-stained hat held aloft, sun-bleached hair plastered to his head. As he neared the locker room, I heard an unmistakable

THE CANNON AND A BIG BLAST

Huckerbeeism fill the air: Goobers and Raisinets, DeVaca City, Goobers and Raisinets! Whooooooo!"

After I finished filing my story, I headed to Dolphin Memorial Hospital to check on Halumka. In the emergency room, I encountered a man and a woman who looked familiar, though I had never met them. They were all protruding teeth, thick glasses, flapping ears, and stubbly sideburns, even the woman. The opening riff of *Deliverance*'s "Dueling Banjos" reverberated in my head, and I couldn't help but think about squealin' Bobby and twitchy bowhunter Ed, mentally traumatized for life, trying to get the hell out of Aintry before the local lawmen found one of their third cousins arrowed to death along the Cahulawassee River.

> Sheriff Bullard: Don't ever do nothin' like this again. Don't come back up here.
>
> Squealin' Bobby (with a tortured smile): You don't have to worry about that Sheriff.
>
> Twitchy Bowhunter Ed (with feigned earnestness): I hope Deputy Queen finds his brother-in-law.
>
> Sheriff Bullard: Oh...he'll come in drunk, probably.

"Are you the Halumkas?" I asked, stating the obvious.

I cringed, expecting a response that would conjure the image of Aintry's toothless mountain man and his sodomite sidekick.

"Why, yes, son. To whom do I owe this honor?" replied Mr. Halumka, dignified as could be.

"I'm Jake Yankelovich from the *Citrus Coast Daily Inquirer*. I was working the game with Bert tonight when he got pancaked...umm, got his clock cleaned...I mean knocked over. Sorry, I've gotten used to the Drabenville football lingo. How is he?"

"That's quite all right. Bless your heart for coming here at such a late hour and caring so much about our Bertie," said Mrs. Halumka. "He has a concussion, and he was out cold for a while, but now he's awake and talking, thank the Lord, and all he can talk about is the game and the deadline and getting his information to Jake for the bulldog edition—what's that, a dog show?—and who won and something about the Cannon? That made me worried when he kept mentioning the Cannon, how did the Cannon work out, was the Cannon good, did the Cannon reload. I thought he was hallucinating that he was a Confederate soldier in the Civil War or some cuckoo thing like that. Do you know what he was talking about, Mr. Yankelovich?"

I felt terrible. The Halumkas were the epitome of Southern grace and hospitality, yet all I could associate the Halumka clan with was coarseness and bestiality. I saw Bert in a whole new light and tried to banish my Appalachian stereotype, the way Bobby and Ed tried to bury the memory of the Aintry sodomite corpse on the riverbank.

"Bert's not cuckoo, Mrs. Halumka. And call me Jake. A little obsessed—in a good way—but not cuckoo. In fact, the Cannon talk is a positive sign. The Cannon is Connor Crane, Dolphin's new quarterback, and the bulldog edition is the early edition of the *Dinqy*. I'm amazed he's thinking so clearly after the shot he took. He may not have any sense of time right now, but he remembers exactly what he was doing."

"Bert loves working with you, son," Mr. Halumka told me. "He's always talking about you and how much he's learning about reporting and writing from you. Mrs. Halumka and I have always preferred music and the arts and literature, but Bert loves his football. It's all he wants to do. He wants to be a full-time high school sportswriter and quit the Southern Smorg as soon as he can get his opportunity, and I can see you're helping to make his dream come true, son."

I felt even worse and humbled. I had virtually dismissed Bert as a slack-jawed yokel, now come to learn he had looked up to me, depended on me to help him achieve his goal, even though I was nearly ten years his junior. I was glad to have met the Halumkas.

"Mr. and Mrs. Halumka, call me Sunday, or have Bert call if he can and let me know how he's doing," I said, scrawling my number on a page from my Sparco Reporter's Notebook. "We've got a lot of plans to make for the end of the season. It's gonna be an exciting finish, and I know Bert will want to be part of it."

"Bless your heart, Jake," said Mrs. Halumka, placing a hand on my shoulder. "We sure will. I am so glad we made your acquaintance, even in these most unfortunate of circumstances for Bert. We are praying Bert will be all right, and you will be in our prayers as well."

It was 2:30 a.m., too late for Bert to receive visitors, so I left, stopping at Waffle House for a Belgian waffle and to pick up the *Dinqy* bulldog edition.

I read over the quote I got from Coach Bamford, who made no apologies.

> *We play the percentages, and the percentages told me we'd make the extra point and win in overtime,"* he said. *"There are no moral victories, but Connor Crane became a man tonight. The Man. That's going to help us reach our ultimate goal. We have no margin left; our season's on the line every game from here on out.*

Bamford was right. A third loss could eliminate Dolphin from the playoffs. It struck me that Bamford may have been referring to himself walking the tightrope as much as to his team.

Vindication

On the Monday morning before Thanksgiving, Monsieur called me at home from the courthouse and told me to get there for a big announcement.

"These cocksuckers in the State attorney's office are so tight-lipped they have to burp through their asses, but I'm hearing rumors it's about the Sammons and Hilliard case," he told me.

When I arrived, microphones were arranged on the top step of the courthouse, and reporters were stationed below—just in case the ink-stained wretches like Monsieur and the blathering TV airheads didn't know their place in the hierarchy.

The police chief joined the State attorney. The State attorney thanked the media for convening on short notice. Then he transitioned to the substance of the presser, reading from a prepared statement.

"After depositions and several rounds of interrogation, two seventeen-year-old girls, both seniors at a Dolphin County high school who shall remain unidentified, have recanted their stories in the cases of Dolphin High School seniors Samuel T. Sammons and Nathaniel D. Hilliard, who had been charged with sexual assault in connection with an incident that occurred in the 10500 block of River Overlook Drive in Drabenville on the night of October 20. All charges against Mr. Sammons and Mr. Hilliard have been dropped.

"The State attorney's office is now investigating the two subjects who originally filed charges in this case for filing a false police report. We cannot reveal the details of the case at this time, as our investigation is ongoing. Please refer your questions to the State's attorney's public information office. I will have nothing more to say on this matter at this time."

The police chief took center stage and said, "Our detectives have conducted thorough police work on this matter and have interviewed many witnesses in addition to the complainants. The truth is not always easy to find but sometimes can be determined with the right amount of persistence, skepticism, logic, and common sense. That is what happened in this case, and because of that, two innocent young men will go free instead of facing juvenile detention or jail. This is an example of police work at its best, and I want to thank my officers. I will take questions."

A female TV reporter asked the chief whether he was concerned that the girls felt pressured to change their story and that the department was about to let two dangerous sexual offenders loose.

"Not in the least," the chief answered. "Sexual assaults did not happen; the evidence supports that conclusion. The girls admitted their stories were not true. They were not coerced or intimidated by our detectives. In fact, our detectives had every reason to believe them until the details of their story started changing and detectives noticed the dissonance between the seriousness of the situation and, quite frankly, the girls' nonchalant reactions, like it was amusing. That gave us reasonable doubt to continue questioning. Next question..."

"What about your investigation of the girls? What can you tell us about that?" asked a radio reporter.

"We don't know their motivation. They each have hired attorneys, and they aren't talking. We'll keep workin' it," the chief responded.

It was guaranteed front-page news for Tuesday's *Dinqy*, and I'd co-byline with Monsieur by contributing the sports angle. I attended Dolphin's practice, where Coach Bamford confirmed that Sammons and Hilliard had been reinstated and were dressed for practice.

Dolphin had won its last two games heading into the Draben Bowl, with the Cannon looking more impressive in each. I asked Bamford whether Sammons would get his starting job back and whether Hilliard would get some carries that had been going to Mondo.

"We're going to ride the hot hand," Bamford said. "We'll use Sammy in spot situations to give us a different look, a change of pace. Nate may help us with his speed in the passing game, but Mondo's been totin' the mail like a mule bustin' out of a glue factory, and we're sticking with that."

I knew I should have avoided it, but I couldn't help dropping some bait for Bamford, just to see if he would bite in an unguarded moment.

"I really feel for Sammy and Nate," I told the Coach. "How do you think they get caught up in something like that? Almost seems like they got set up, you know?"

"Wrong place at the wrong time, that's all," Bamford said. "As far as Dolphin football is concerned, it's over, and we're moving on. If you got any sense, you will too. You're a half-ass sports reporter, I'd have to bet you'd make a piss poor police reporter."

I had to drop it. Dolphin was in its stretch run to defend its state championship, and I needed Bamford, conspiracy or not.

Sammy and Nate said they were just happy to try to put the incident behind them and focus on football and making the play-offs.

"Sure, I want to be the starter, and I'll battle for the job," Sammy told me. "We're winning, and I'm just glad to be out here. I'm vindicated, just like I said I would be. I'm going to show everyone what I'm all about. I'll help any way I can."

I admired Sammy even more for his selfless attitude when he had been given a raw deal that may have dashed his opportunity for a major college scholarship. I gave him credit for his smarts and maturity—he had every reason to quit the team, but he realized that would have hurt him more in the long run.

Hobie Schlorf was another story. Coach Bamford did not bring him back, and Hobie was convinced it was because he was a Sammons supporter, and Bamford needed to prove he could win with homegrown players like Crane after notching one championship due largely to the Palmertown pipeline.

I wondered if there was any connection between Bamford and the party girls, and if so, how many degrees of separation there might be, and whether the girls would admit it if there was a conspiracy involving Bamford or anyone else connected with Dolphin football. If there had been a conspiracy, I didn't think they would be able to stay silent for long, since pampered suburban teenage girls would not have the resilience to hold out under tenacious police questioning. But then again, money had probably bought them good legal representation that would get them off quietly under a back room deal, any incriminating details staying buried.

For now, Bamford was not a suspect, just a coach with the biggest game of the season coming up against crosstown rival East Grove in the Draben Bowl, the grudge match from the GridFest Jubilee skirmish. I doubted East Grove would have a short memory for the disrespect shown by Dolphin. That was confirmed later that day when I crossed the Wallatatchie River Bridge to observe East Grove's practice and talk to Coach Magnusson and caught the marquee outside Lenzell Langston's East Drabenville Popeye's: "Ragin' Cajun Wings, 12 for $4.99. Run Up The Score We'll BLOW OFF YOUR DOOR. Go Warriors Beat Fins!"

Draben Bowl: The Warrior Whack

I stopped by Mudville Mike's for the traditional Mudville Munch on the Wednesday night before the Thanksgiving Day Draben Bowl, the winner of which would keep the Golden Manatee trophy in its display case for a year. Dolphin High boosters, alumni, and fans packed the place for an unconventional feast of alligator tenders, crawdads, stone crab legs, Tupelo honey wings, hearts of palm Pilgrim's Slaw, maple-glazed fried plantains, and Mudville Mike mullet sliders.

Celebrants raised their mugs and joined in the annual Thanksgiving Eve fight song:

> The Draben Bowl is ours to win
> Before we feast on tur-duck-en
> We'll whack East Grove on the chin
> With a mighty Dorsal Fin! Fin! Fin!

Then they chugged their beers, slammed mugs on the tables, and did "the Fin"—arms outstretched, hands touching to form a triangle like a fin above their heads, and bobbing and weaving like a dolphin surfacing and submerging amid the waves. It was all rather foolish, but fun and infectious nonetheless. It got me excited for the next day's game and festivities. Mitzi Retzlaff, a Dolphin High booster, was there, and I asked her what the hell a "turducken" was.

"It's a chicken stuffed into a duck stuffed into a turkey," she said. "That's common around here. You wouldn't believe what we stuff into a turkey. We've had tur-gator, tur-dillo, tur-rabbit, tur-balls, you name it. It all works inside a deep-fried turkey smothered with bread crumbs."

Mitzi told me with a mix of horror and humor about the time in '75 when a group of tailgaters in the Dolphin parking lot dropped a frozen turkey into a vat of hot oil and blew up their VW van. Luckily, the tailgaters came away with only second-degree burns because of the quick reaction of firefighters on site. Back then, tailgating was a free-for-all, she told me, but now Dolphin Public Safety restricts turkey cooking to designated chef stations and uses the event to warn all attendees about the dangers of frozen turkeys.

❖ ❖ ❖

The next morning, I arrived for the noon kickoff at 10:30 a.m. and the deep-fryer turkey stations were already humming with signs identifying the crossbreeds, such as "Tur-Daddy" (crawdad-stuffed) and "Tur-Crappie." Whole elementary schools from each side of Drabenville came dressed as pilgrims and prairie girls and Daniel Boones and Davy Crocketts and Betsy Rosses, but I'm sure they had a hard time imagining the threadbare frontiersmen foraging in barren fields for scraps of edible crops as the unforgiving New England winter closed in. The overheated kids were marching in suffocating garb across the asphalt in eighty-five-degree heat.

It is little known that the tomahawk chop made famous by Florida State Seminoles fans and later adopted by the Atlanta Braves baseball team during their championship runs—a repetitive chopping motion that fans make with their arms in rhythm with a repetitive, howling Indian war chant—actually started with the East Grove High Calusa Warriors in 1984. In the two years since, it had spread widely throughout the East Drabenville community and was rehearsed not only at sporting events but also at community celebrations like July 4 parades. The East Drabs took pride in this expression of identity, but it grated on the rest of Dolphin County and others who encountered a partisan East Grove crowd. Coach Magnusson had tried to tone down the display of pride but only a bit, because without that pride, many East Grove families had little. Once the chant got going, it was only a matter of time before it built to a deafening crescendo that would overwhelm the coaches' pleas to maintain a certain level of decorum. The chanting drowned out all bullhorn admonitions. The Warrior Whack was here to stay.

As team captains walked to midfield for the coin flip, it started: "Ooooooooohhh-oh-oh-whoa-whoa...Whoooooooaaa-wo-wo-oooh-oh." The chant drowned out the Dorsal Fins' trademark pregame song, Jimmy Buffett's "Fins," even over the loudspeaker. "You got FINS to the left, FINS to the right," Dolphin fans yelled at the chorus, emphasizing "fins" and gesturing to Dolphin sections on each side. Then, pointing at the opposing fans, they finished off the chorus: "And you're the only bait in town!"

Dolphin fans were noticeably disturbed that their spirit had been disrupted by an obnoxious chant—just another ancillary part of the rivalry, I thought. But I would find later that the agitation ran deep.

As for the game, Dolphin was on a roll and picked up pretty much where they had left off nearly three months earlier when they humiliated East Grove for a quarter in the GridFest, leading to the angry handshake exchange between Magnusson and Bamford. DeVaca City had caught Dolphin at just the right time, during its transition at quarterback and running back and offensive coordinator, when things were in chaos and the players lost focus. But after two straight wins and adjustment to a new style with the Cannon, and with the play-offs in sight, the mojo had returned. The Warriors had only one loss and had already earned a play-off berth, which may have taken some edge off their performance, no matter how much they hated Dolphin and how much Magnusson's crew drove home the haves versus have-nots rallying cry. The Warriors had several major talents, but they weren't as deep as the Dorsal Fins, and it showed. Behind another spectacular performance by the Cannon, Dolphin carried a 37–12 lead into the fourth quarter.

With five minutes and thirty seconds left to play, East Grove scored to cut the lead to eighteen, and its fans revved up the Warrior Whack, the volume of which far exceeded the celebration of a score or the yearn for an unlikely comeback. The decibel level grew as Dolphin took possession. Dolphin fans began their own chant, yelling "Scoreboard! Scoreboard!" and pointing at "Dolphin 37 East Grove 19" in lights. I wouldn't call it lighthearted fun; it was more like taunting by each side. And then it happened. I saw turkey legs flying from a Dolphin section to an adjacent East Grove section. East Grove fans reacted, uprooting to move toward the Dolphin section. The football stands took on the property of Newton's third law of physics: one action producing an equal and opposite reaction. Dolphin fans stood and countered, creating a confrontation. I could tell that heated words were exchanged, and then arms began flailing and bodies tumbling.

It quickly turned into a full-blown rumble in the stands, with engagement multiplying while many tried to get out of the way. People were falling and getting trampled, clothes were getting ripped, and punches were being thrown. The Dolphin sidelines watched in seeming disbelief, but the East Grove coaching staff followed Magnusson's lead, hopping the fence to separate the feuding factions. A big group of East Grove players followed them, despite one coach trying to keep the players together on the field, out of harm's way. The East Grove coaches succeeded in breaking apart the primary combatants and formed a wall along with their players as truce makers until the police on site—who were probably slumbering in their cars—arrived to enforce order. East Grove coaches paid a price for their bravery—Zach Polansky's nose was bloodied, and Hank Gamble's eye was swollen shut, and each required attention from paramedics.

Several fans were hauled away by police, order was restored, and play resumed after twenty minutes. The game ended uneventfully, Dolphin winning 37–25, to secure a play-off berth. Sammons played sparingly at running back; Flea assumed a role as a third-down back, as Mondo continued serving as the workhorse in the backfield; and the offense maintained its evolution to a spread passing attack to suit the Cannon's strengths.

Bend-Over scurried behind Coach Bamford, camera vest flapping and lenses jostling around his shoulders, as Bamford strode the field to meet Coach Magnusson, thinking there might be more front-page fireworks between the adversaries to shoot, but there weren't. The two coaches shook hands for a long time, patted each other on the shoulder, and stood talking for several minutes while players, students, and fans swirled around them.

❖ ❖ ❖

I asked Coach Bamford what he'd talked about with Coach Magnusson after the game, and he uncharacteristically opened up.

"First, I'm extremely proud of our football team. We've faced a lot of adversity, and we've overcome it, and this win puts us on our way to our goal. We're still improving, and our best football is yet to come.

"I told Coach Magnusson he's got a lot to be proud of as well. I always knew this, but to see the way his players reacted to that unfortunate outburst tells me a lot about the character he's instilling in them. Winning's important, it's why we're in this business, and you won't be in it for long if you don't, but developing young men of character is even more so."

For the first time, I sensed a little melancholy in Bamford, instead of the usual single-mindedness and gruffness and bluster and intimidation. It was as if he knew the win should feel really good, but it didn't feel as good as he thought it would. It was as if he wanted a little more of what Magnusson had, an intangible that couldn't be manufactured but had to emanate from deep within the soul.

DRABEN BOWL: THE WARRIOR WHACK

Bamford, to me, was the classic transactional coach, using his players as pawns for his own aggrandizement and advancement. Magnusson, on the other hand, was the epitome of a transformational coach, catering to his players' needs and filling a gaping void by providing mentoring in their progression from boys to men.

I had no idea if Bamford was getting more philosophical or reevaluating his approach; I only knew I had never heard him go out of his way to praise another coach or equate anything else with winning.

Magnusson also was passionate about winning and wanted to bring the Golden Manatee back to his principal for community pride. He was disappointed in the outcome but gratified by his program.

"I would have loved to bring the Golden Manatee back to East Grove for the bragging rights. That means a lot to the kids and the community. All credit to Dolphin, they outplayed us today, and Connor Crane is going to be something special. But we're still a play-off team. We're putting the Draben Bowl behind us and setting our sights on bigger goals.

"I think everyone saw today what our program is all about, on the field and off. We *are* men and boys of character. We *do* the right thing. If you don't know what the right thing is, you won't be a Calusa Warrior for long. I couldn't be more proud to be associated with any group of people.

"Hey, Jake," Coach Magnusson interjected. "Make sure you get this in the story:

"Football *games* are for the here and now. *Football* is for life. We're preparing for the game of life."

Life would have to wait for Magnusson. The here-and-now post-season march was starting in eight days as the calendar turned to December, and unfortunately for East Grove, it drew the 4A team with far and away the top player in the state, and maybe the nation, Elroy Jones, who had been virtually unstoppable for two years.

Dolphin was rapidly developing one of the top players in Florida of its own, The Cannon, and did not draw a world-beater in its regional game.

As the deep fryers were packed into the backs of pickups, elementary school children stripped off their feathered headdresses, and moms gathered up their clans to go home to watch NFL football and put finishing touches on oddly stuffed turkeys, the journey for the crown jewel of Florida high school sports began for real.

Hitting the Big Time

Shlomo received an unanticipated call at Le Château in early December from Citrus Coast Sea Nettles coach Storm Musselchamp. Power forward Melvin "Popeye" Boykin had been called up to the NBA, Darnell Stukes had failed a drug test, and starting center Deke Igwehigbo was out with an injury, leaving the Continental Basketball Association team with only three big men. Musselchamp needed two players immediately for the next night's game at the Dolphin Civic Center, and Shlomo was his second choice, as much because Musselchamp was reasonably sure Shlomo could be in uniform the next day as for his ability. Musselchamp's other potential call-ups already were committed to teams around the world—Israel, Italy, and Turkey were popular destinations for American players who didn't make the CBA—or working a real job far away.

Musselchamp offered Shlomo a ten-day contract. Shlomo responded that he'd check with his headmaster in the morning, and if Biff Scully approved, he would join the Sea Nettles for their afternoon run-through and be on the bench for the game against the Albany Patroons, coached by Zen master Phil Jackson before he went on to win eleven NBA championships with Michael Jordan and Kobe Bryant. Promoter extraordinaire Scully not only approved Shlomo's leave of absence but ordered and hung a huge banner outside the school on Hernandez Avenue that read: "Father Ignacio Our Savior: Home of Pro Basketball Player and Teacher/Coach Shlomo Grubner."

Unfortunately, Shlomo hadn't taken to heart Coach Musselchamp's advice about staying in shape and being ready for a call-up. Our two-on-two games on Conquista Island, which sometimes expanded to five-on-five when other weekend warriors showed up, were the only thing that prevented complete rustiness.

I sat next to Whalebait Wally of WFIN-AM at courtside to cover Shlomo's debut game. Knowing I had covered Shlomo's tryout, Wally arranged a pregame interview with me.

"Teacher by day, lumbering big man by night," Wally opened. "Dolphin County's own Shlomo Grubner, English teacher and basketball coach at Father Ignacio Our Savior Episcopal School in Drabenville, was just called up yesterday by Coach Musselchamp after impressing the coaching staff in his summer tryout. He's been called the Yarmulke Yeti. Tonight, I'm calling him Grubner the Grinder because he may get some lunch-pail work in the middle.

"Jake Yankelovich of the *Citrus Coast Daily Inquirer* has been following Grubner's career. Jake, what can you tell us about the Sea Nettles' new big man?"

"He's been working out on a regular basis with another former college player and some other top local talent," I said, referring to Spooner and misleadingly including Dieter and myself as "local talent."

"Coach Musselchamp told Grubner at the end of tryouts to be ready at a moment's notice because you never know what can happen during the CBA season, and Grubner has dedicated himself to staying in great basketball shape for just such an opportunity," I concluded, another vast overstatement.

Dieter and Spooner came to the game with a homemade sign that read, "Shlomo the Yarmulke Yeti...Yessss!" in deference to legendary New York Knicks broadcaster Marv Albert's signature call after a made basket. They sat in a section with dozens of Camelot Cay acquaintances, including Sweet Stephanie and Raunchy Rosie, who were regulars at Sea Nettles games, and Father Ignacio students, teachers, parents, and headmaster Biff

Scully, who brought a megaphone and shamelessly yelled, "Our Teacher Shlomo, Let's Go for Father Ignacio!"

❖ ❖ ❖

Shlomo came out for warm-ups in his white Sea Nettles warm-up suit with blue and green trim, and gave a fist pump to his rooting section, which responded with cowbells and horns. He looked jacked up during layup lines, springing for dunks with each hand and spinning in double-pump reverses to cheers from his section for each shot.

Shlomo was glued to the bench until 3:11 of the second quarter, when Axelrod picked up his third foul and Musselchamp motioned for Shlomo to check in to give Axelrod a breather and keep him out of further foul trouble. Shlomo tore off his warm-up, displaying the number nineteen jersey he requested in honor of his favorite player, Knicks' center Willis Reed.

The Patroons went at Shlomo right away, working the ball inside and scoring over him on two straight trips. "The Patroons are shlamming Shlomo, they're taking him for a shloth. Shlomo better show he's no shlouch or he'll be shlinking back to the bench," Wally announced in a shtick he must have rehearsed all day. "He's got to toughen up inside if he wants more playing time."

I could tell after two minutes of action that the fast pace of the professional game and adrenaline withdrawal had exhausted Shlomo. This was no Duffy Park Elementary School five-on-five with the local garbage men and bartenders; these were guys clawing to make the NBA.

On one Sea Nettles possession with less than a minute left, a missed three-point shot resulted in a long rebound and a break out for the Patroons. Shlomo was trailing the play badly and had barely made it past half court to play defense when an errant Patroons' pass was picked off. Now Shlomo was ahead of the field and Sea Nettles' point guard Carlos Brugera led him upcourt with a pass. Adrenaline must have kicked back in. Shlomo raced to catch up to the ball, took one dribble and two big steps and launched into the air. A Patroons defender flew in front of him as Shlomo shifted the ball from his left to his right hand and soared from the left side of the basket to the right for a one-handed reverse dunk that sprang Musselchamp and his assistants out of their chairs with fist pumps and brought the Civic Center crowd to its feet with chants of "Shloooo-mo, Shloooo-mo, Shloooo-mo!"

"Oh my! Cleared for takeoff!" Wally crowed. "Grubner the Grinder has become Shlomo the Shkywalker!"

Shlomo wasn't done. Again he found himself in the right place. The Patroons missed a shot with ten seconds left, and Brugera pushed it up court. Finding no open runners, he hit a wide-open Shlomo trailing the play at the top of the key. Shlomo set his feet and let fly a soft, arching, three-point shot with perfect backspin as I had seen him do countless times in our games of H-O-R-S-E and five-on-five at the Duffy court when he didn't feel like banging inside with hackers like Dieter and weekend warriors who, during the week, ride the Duffy Beach Refuse & Sanitation trucks. The shot ripped the net cords as the half expired, and the crowd exploded, sending Shlomo to the locker room with more chants.

Shlomo got in the game for one spell of Axelrod in the second half and produced two more plays for the highlight reel. He blocked one shot into the third row of seats. On offense, he swept across the lane and swished a feathery hook shot from nearly the foul line, bringing Whalebait out of his seat with more well-prepared, hyperbolic catch phrases.

"Sky hook by the Jewish Jabbar! Jewish Jabbar's bringing Lakers' Showtime to Nettles Land, Citrus Coast-style!"

The Sea Nettles won, and then the real fun started. Shlomo was indoctrinated into the perks and nightlife of the professional athlete.

❖ ❖ ❖

After I finished and transmitted my game story from the Civic Center, which was in DeVaca City, just over the Blue Fin River Bridge, I reunited with Shlomo at the Pirate's Ransom Lounge at the Drabenville Holiday

Inn Waterfront. The Pirate's Ransom, with its pulsating dance floors and bars on two levels, was the gathering place for Sea Nettles players, cheerleaders, groupies, and media after games. I had dropped in a couple of times around midnight during the young season to meet up with Bend-Over, who would rendezvous there with Wicked Juanita.

Several groupies surrounded Shlomo, beer in hand, when I hit the scene. Stephanie and Rosie, looking hot in heels and tight jeans and tossing their long hair back as they sipped umbrella drinks and chatted with players, were regulars at the Pirate's Ransom after games, I discovered. They casually dated several players, er, hooked up for one-night stands.

Then there were the drugs. Two players with dangling gold chains and strong cologne invited Shlomo to join them and three girls for lines of coke in a private back room. Shlomo declined that offer but accepted Axelrod's to go outside on the expansive deck overlooking the Blue Fin River to smoke high-grade hashish. It was there, while getting high, that Axelrod taught Shlomo to always keep a supply of clean urine samples acquired from other people in his refrigerator and bring at least one to every practice in a cooler, to be smuggled into the testing room and substituted for one's own sample in the event of a random drug test. Axelrod even gave Shlomo two samples from the cooler in his car, and for the next ten days, we always had three or four lab-supply clear cups with snug lids halfway-filled with what looked like lemon-lime Gatorade in the back of our Le Château fridge.

Shlomo went on a three-game road trip and played two more home games during his ten-day contract, averaging six minutes per game and becoming an instant crowd favorite at home, where he had a couple more rim-shaking dunks and, since he knew his playing time would be limited, earned a reputation for reckless dives on the floor and lunges over the scorers' table and into the stands going after loose balls, knocking fans over backward, sending Cokes and popcorns flying, and bringing raucous cheers from the locals.

Each home game ended by closing down the Pirate's Ransom, a drawn-out toke on the deck with Axelrod and hangers-on, and a late night back at Le Château with a random groupie met that evening. Axelrod's drug-testing strategy proved spot-on and saved Shlomo from an embarrassing release. CBA officials showed up unannounced at the Sea Nettles' practice facility one day to conduct the random drug test. Just as Axelrod had taught him, Shlomo had smuggled in a fraudulent sample inside a water bottle. Drug testers frisked players and checked their bags for fake samples but hadn't caught on to the water bottle trick. When it was Shlomo's time to pee, he surreptitiously stuck the sample inside his compression shorts, and came out clean.

He survived the urine test but couldn't outlast Boykin's return to the team after he was sent down from his NBA roster. Whalebait interviewed Shlomo after his last home game, after the news broke that Shlomo would be waived when Popeye rejoined the team.

"I have no regrets, Wally," Shlomo said after putting up goose eggs on the stat sheet but registering a nice floor burn in two minutes of action. "I lived the life of a professional athlete for however long it lasted, gave it my all, and lived it up. It was more than I ever thought it would be. But I'm a teacher and a coach, and I guess Coach Musselchamp is telling me it's time to get back to my kids. Mr. Scully, thanks for giving me my big break. I'm coming home."

This is Big, Really Big

Heading into the postseason, with two schools in the state tournament, Dolphin and East Grove, and DeVaca City and Great Bay just missing, I believed I had enough on the school board redistricting scandal to pitch the story to Skip and Paddy. I hoped to convince them to help me shepherd it up the chain of command. I knew we'd need a lot of evidence, confirmations, and persuasion if the story was going to see the light of day.

I met with Skip and Paddy and outlined the whole convoluted mess in high-level, broad strokes just to let them know what we were dealing with before, as Mahotie often said to me, getting down to brass tacks. I took them through the timeline and showed them the documentation—court filings against Big Papa's company, the bank statements from JJ, personal information and records on school board members—all the background and evidence that Monsieur and I had meticulously assembled. Then I told them about the key interviews with school board members Bunny Heavener, who was offered what seemed like a bribe but didn't accept it; and Clarence Walker, the Palmertown linchpin in the case, who could corroborate what all the data indicated but didn't prove; and I showed them my interview notes. And if they had doubts about Boots Walker's story and his motives, I told them I had the interviews with his Roma Rojo acquaintances to back up his claim.

Paddy took it all in, peering at my documentation over glasses nearly falling off the bridge of his nose, offering a few "hmmm-hmmms" and "uh-huhs" and "wows."

Predictably, Skip was initially more skittish about the allegations and potential consequences—for Coach Bamford and the *Dinqy* if we were either right or wrong, but especially if we were wrong.

"This is big, really big," Skip said. "Did you talk to enough people, talk to enough? If we even consider going w-w-with this—and that's a *huge* if…if—we got to make sure we cuh-call around to everyone, and I mean everyone, and lock this thing down airtight, ya know what I mean?"

Paddy said he needed more time to review everything and think about it, which is what I expected. But he added, "This looks like good work, kid. You know I took a big chance when I hired you right out of college; we usually wouldn't do that, but I thought you were capable of something like this. You're gonna make me look like a genius…or an asshole," he said and made his incongruent, high-pitched giggle.

Then he got serious again. "I'm going to look it over and get back to you soon, Jake. You know we're in a really delicate time to even consider coming out with a story like this, with Dolphin just starting their playoffs and just getting past all that controversy with the sexual assault case. It might be better if we wait until Dolphin's season is over before we even think about running anything, or we're going to look like we're sabotaging them." He paused for a moment. "Does the *T-D* have anything on this?"

"I don't think so, but it's hard to get a bead on what Reindollar is up to. He's a good poker player," I responded, adding that the school board payoffs and the charges against Sammons and Hilliard might all be tied together in a byzantine scheme I had not yet explained. "Even if Reindollar had the goods, I have my doubts whether the *T-D* would run it; they're so in bed with the whole Bamford family and Dolphin High that they fluff each other's pillows."

"I know what you're saying," Paddy said. "I'd love to beat those bastards on a story like this. Hard-hitting journalism, that's where Wellington and Chenault want to make a name. This could be it.

"You know this is going to be tough to get past Wellington and Chenault, don'tcha Jake? They're gonna be super careful before putting our reputation on the line. There have been too many journalistic fiascos and flimflammers that have given us all bad names, like that Janet Cooke woman up there at the *Washington Post* writing her uber story about an eight-year-old street-urchin heroin addict who never existed—remember that one, Skip?—just made all that shit up, gave us all black eyes.

"They're gonna want the i's dotted and the t's crossed and *your ass* baptized and sanctified," Paddy added, giggling again. "You ready to pitch the boardroom? You ready for that?"

"Yeah, Paddy. I haven't been here long enough to become a full-fledged homer yet, so might as well do it now." We both laughed.

Skip looked anxious, but I had to credit him for being open-minded and backing me so far, albeit with reservations and the chronic security-blanket advice to "just call around."

All I could do now was wait for the wheels of the *Dinqy* hierarchy, under the thumb of the parent company bureaucracy, to turn. Until then, it was back to the daily grind of football play-offs.

"So Jake," Paddy addressed me, preparing to return to routine and comfortable sports-talk territory, "do you think East Grove has any chance to stop that world-beater Elroy Jones…?"

The Mahotie Cringe

East Grove and Dolphin both opened their play-offs in Orlando, on a Friday and Saturday, respectively. Mahotie and I were to share a motel room. This would be a hoot.

We drove together in Mahotie's Matador, which reeked of his previous night's Taco Bell dinner, Burrito Grande wrappers and hot sauce packets covering the floor. Mahotie was a TV trivia freak and had a collection of *TV Guides* dating to 1968. So during the ride, we played his favorite time-killing game, TV tag, where one person named a show, then the next person named an associated character or actor from that show. Then players took turns naming someone else—character or actor—with a connection to that show or someone on another show who shared a first or last name, and on and on until someone was stumped. I documented this round to memorialize Mahotie's idiot savant-like talent.

Gilligan's Island—Skipper—Gilligan—Russell Johnson (Professor)—Russell Cosby (*Fat Albert*)—Fat Albert—Bill Cosby—Bill Bixby (*The Incredible Hulk*)—Lou Ferrigno (Hulk)—Lou Grant—Mary Tyler Moore—Ted Baxter—Ted Bessell (*That Girl*)—Marlo Thomas—Danny Thomas—Danny Bonaduce (*Partridge Family*)—Keith Partridge—Brian Keith (*Family Affair*)—Johnny Whitaker (Jody)—Billy Barty (Hollywood dwarf, *Sigmund and the Sea Monsters*, starring Whitaker)—Uncle Bill (*Family Affair* again)—Anissa Jones (Buffy, overdosed at eighteen)—Davy Jones (*The Monkees*)—Shirley Jones (*Partridge Family* again)—Shirley Hemphill (big waitress, *What's Happening!!*)—Fred Berry (Rerun)—Fred Mertz (*I Love Lucy*)—Freddie "Boom Boom" Washington (*Welcome*

THE MAHOTIE CRINGE

Back, Kotter)—Fred Flintstone—Barney Rubble—Barney Miller—Abe Vigoda—hmmm, Abe Vigoda, Abe Vigoda…STUMPED by fuckin' Abe Vigoda!

Hang-dogged, hump-backed, bushy-browed Abe Vigoda. I couldn't remember any other Barney Miller characters or Abe's name on the show (Phil Fish). The only Abe I could think of was Lincoln, and who could make a match with a fuckin' Vigoda!

Mahotie must have beaten me twenty-two consecutive times over two hours with his photographic recall of TV—which is saying something, because I knew my TV trivia—punctuating each win with an annoying, "How 'bout them apples!"

The first thing Mahotie did when we got to our low-budget Econo Lodge–Disney was don a pair of skintight red Speedo swimming briefs—the suave European Disney tourist look—and hit the miniature pool, flapping in humongous flip-flops that engulfed the ground like snowshoes. This pool was close quarters, more like a wishing well, and there were several little boys and girls with their mothers, and I shuddered at the thought of them making eye contact with Mahotie's bulging package. I cringed when I heard one girl exclaim to her mother, "Look, it's big!" while pointing toward Mahotie.

When alabaster Mahotie, spread-eagled on a chaise lounge and embalmed with a sheen of hideous white goo, was done sunbathing, we went out for an early dinner at Golden Corral, the ubiquitous compadre to cheap motels, to fuel up before the East Grove game. We arrived at four o'clock, Gold Rush Hour for the over-sixty-five early bird dinner special, and got in line behind a gaggle of septuagenarians.

Mahotie didn't even start eating until he had assembled four plates piled pyramid style with foundational elements like steak at the bottom and small pieces like corn on top, and lined them up in priority order in front of him—first salads, then grilled meats, potatoes, and succotash, followed by pasta and garlic bread, chased by the taco bar.

"Mitch, isn't that gonna make you sick for the game?" I asked incredulously.

"Jake, you never look a gift horse in the mouth," Mahotie replied. "The Golden Corral is the gift of abundance, extreme fecundity, my friend, and I choose to partake to the fullest for my ten ninety-nine, thank you very much."

With his gift for gab, Mahotie started up conversations with three tables of seniors around us, discovering one couple who had been married for sixty years, a man who had battled Nazis from a tank, and a brother and sister given up for adoption during the Great Depression. Mahotie topped off his dinner with the sundae bar and a pink cotton candy, saluting his new geezer friends on our way out: "Y'all enjoy the rest of your lives. You only live once, and y'all are doing a helluva job stretching it out and whatnot." The geezers hugged Mahotie good-bye like an adored grandson.

"You'll talk to anyone, won't you, Mitch?" I asked, after the WWII vet finally released Mahotie's hand from his two-palm grip.

"That's how you become a good reporter, Jake."

"What, by talking to Moses and his band of elders?"

"You got to be comfortable talking with everyone."

❖ ❖ ❖

At the stadium, Mahotie and I waited outside the locker room for the Calusa Warriors to emerge. This was a different feeling than the regular season. Back home, we always had to maintain dispassionate impartiality, because games usually involved two teams within the *Dinqy*'s coverage area. But in Orlando, I felt a real allegiance to my hometown school and wanted to see East Grove succeed. East Grove did things right and instilled values and character in their players. I didn't want to go overboard, but I offered, "Good game tonight," to Coaches Magnusson, Gamble, and Polansky as they jogged out of the locker room, trailing the players. They acknowledged me with a nod, a small sign of respect to someone they could just as easily demonize as the enemy, and Polansky exclaimed, "We're bringin' it home, baby," as he passed.

East Grove's skill in running the Sims option formation offense using the talent and speed of the Jenkins brothers and a swarming defense overwhelmed the Orlando opponent to produce a 33–16 win.

As was their custom, the East Grove coaches lined up outside the locker room, and like a wedding receiving line, greeted and talked to each player individually, sending them to the showers with a pat on the back, a process that took fifteen minutes.

Seeing East Grove and Dolphin play on back-to-back nights for the first time—the Fightin' Dorsals also cruised to a relatively easy first-round victory—I was struck by the difference in the way the respective coaching staffs responded to their players. While the East Grove coaches made a point of congratulating and saying something to each player individually about his game, or maybe his family or his character or even his school performance the previous week, no doubt instilling pride and closeness and maybe even love for many who'd have none otherwise, the Dolphin coaches huddled with each other on the sidelines after addressing the team en masse for a minute after their win, and the players walked unaccompanied by the adult leaders to their locker room. For all its talk about family, Dolphin operated more like a corporation, the players interchangeable parts deployed to achieve the mission; East Grove functioned more like a Young Life ministry, with football the backdrop to express belief in each individual and impart feelings of worth, meaning, and purpose.

❖ ❖ ❖

Rooming with Mahotie was awkward, bordering on cringe-worthy. After we filed our East Grove stories from the stadium and returned to the Econo Lodge, Mahotie took a shower. But he didn't dry off with a towel. Instead, he turned the window air-conditioning unit to full blast and stood buck naked in front of it, arms up high like a perp—or a perv—about to be arrested. He left the curtains wide open, oblivious to the family walking by, which made me hold my breath, anticipating their repulsion.

"Jesus Christ, Mitch, what the hell are you doing? This isn't Orlando's red-light district. You trying to get us arrested? Aren't there any towels in there?"

"Yeah, but I like to air dry, better for my pores. I have a history of acne. It's all about the clogged pores."

"Mitch, kids come here for Mickey, not dicky. Close the fuckin' curtain!"

"Don't be so uptight. The naked body's beautiful, man, if you overlook the acne. No need to hide it in our own living room."

"Mitch, this isn't our living…Forget it, just shut it!"

Then he moved on to the second phase of his nighttime ritual, emerging from the bathroom looking like he had sneezed on a pile of blow. Mahotie disperses handfuls of talcum powder in the air and stands under the cloud until he is covered with a thin veneer of white.

Finally, Mahotie's most ridiculous nightcapper: Mahotie ready for bed in a pair of lederhosen with suspenders.

"Mitch, what the fuck are those?"

"Lederhosen."

"Ladder what?"

"You know, what the dudes wear at Oktoberfest."

"Right, the dudes dancing with beer steins and schnitzel. But why, Mitch?"

"My folks are German, and I wore them growing up. It's my heritage, and this is the only time I can wear 'em except Oktoberfest. Besides, they're comfy. You know what they say, 'Whatever floats your boat.'"

"OK, Mitch, float it and whatnot. Good night."

Is Goofy a Dog?

THE NEXT DAY, before the Dolphin game, I let Mitch talk me into going to Disney World despite my abhorrence of theme parks. I soon discovered that Mahotie's main mission was to find Goofy and engage him in a debate about whether he was a dog. He had just seen *Stand by Me*, in which four Oregon preteens on an overnight wilderness adventure sit around a campfire at night and ponder why it's hard to identify Goofy when it's obvious that Mickey's a mouse, Donald's a duck, and Pluto's a dog.

Once Mahotie found Goofy, he wouldn't let him go. Goofy must have broken the Disney rules by talking. Unfortunately for Goofy, he didn't know what he was dealing with until it was too late.

"Goofy, what the hell are you?"

No response.

"Hey, Goofy, I'm talking to you." Mahotie nudged me. "Watch, this'll be funny."

"Hey Goofy, did you see *Stand by Me*?"

"What?" Goofy replied, his voice muffled.

"The movie, *Stand by Me*. The kid said you're not a dog because you drive a car and wear a hat. I want to know."

"What do you mean?"

"Are you a dog or not?"

"Why do you care?"

"I have a bet with my friend." (Oh, thanks, Mitch, for including me in your inanity.)

"Mister, I'm working here. Either give me a tip or get out of my face."

"Why won't you give me an answer?"

"Because you're absurd." Goofy clammed up and walked away, but Mahotie was shadowing him and cutting off his path. With shoes even bigger than Mahotie's, Goofy couldn't change direction quickly.

"Listen, creep, if you don't get out of my way, I'm going to get Disney police," Goofy growled through his buck-toothed grin.

"Goofy, be a sport and settle our bet."

"Whadya think? Goofy is a dog, jerk-off."

I couldn't believe my ears, a foul-mouthed Goofy.

"No, Pluto's a dog. You drive a car, Goofy. And I'm going to file a complaint with customer service for rudeness to a Disney guest," Mahotie threatened.

"I'm done with you," Goofy said and gestured for a yellow-jacketed security guard. As the Disney police approached, Mahotie ran—and I trailed him—laughing like Goofy until finding refuge in It's a Small World.

Sugar Plaines Ain't So Sweet

I spent the next two weeks crisscrossing Florida for play-off games with my ragtag team and bandwagons of East Grove and Dolphin fans.

One of those stops was East Grove's semifinal game in Sugar Plaines, a town in Huckerbee's neck of Florida, down Okeechobee way. It's a bastion of solid ground surrounded by vast plains of swamp and muck, which accounts for a large portion of the U.S. sugarcane production.

Another outsized crop in Sugar Plaines and nearby sugarcane towns was NFL players. This low-income agricultural community sent a staggeringly disproportionate number of players to the NFL. If Sugar Plaines kids didn't make that long-shot dream, they'd likely work in the sugar industry and its ancillary businesses like equipment, fertilization, and trucking, or slip into a lifestyle of drug trafficking, violence, and crime.

Sugar may have been the town's lifeblood, but the proliferation of other white substances and synthetic compounds rivaled it and held greater appeal and profit for many Sugar Plaines denizens. Sugar Plaines made a natural drug distribution hub—an off-the-grid swampland with undermanned law enforcement, yet close enough to major drug consumption centers like Miami, Fort Lauderdale, Palm Beach, and Orlando, and their transportation networks. Drug cartels along the Atlantic Coast and even as distant as South America found a large supply of willing mules in Sugar Plaines. Predictably, crime and violence followed, providing Sugar Plaines with the dubious distinction of being the city with the highest violent-crime rate in America per ten thousand residents.

By standards of legal and taxable income, Sugar Plaines was dirt poor, with an average income per household below $17,000 and 40 percent of residents living below the poverty line. The city had the look and feel of a Third World nation. It reminded me of the little Jamaican hilltop villages that I had run through with buddies on a college trip there—forlorn shacks with tin roofs, dusty roads roamed by unclaimed dogs, a scattering of nondescript bars, liquor stores, barber shops, convenience stores, flea markets, and Laundromats where languid people loitered day and night. It was the type of town in which pizza places didn't dare to deliver. Sugar Plaines broke down into thirds—hardworking citizens who kept the town alive, welfare recipients who sucked from its teat, and people involved in the drug trade, who threatened to annihilate it.

The evening I arrived, I had arranged an interview for a feature story on Sugar Plaines's all-state offensive and defensive lineman, William "Big Willie" Washington, a six-foot-six, 305-pound man-child who'd been earning buzz as an NFL prospect since his freshman year. I'll never forget my initial phone conversation with Big Willie, which he accepted from the school's athletic office because he didn't have a phone at home, where he lived with his grandmother. Big Willie had a reputation for being as humble and gracious off the field as he was ferocious on it. He was a straight-A student and an accomplished cello player, an instrument he couldn't afford to buy but had played on loan from the school since seventh grade when the Plantation school district went searching for a cellist to complete its orchestra for state competitions and Big Willie volunteered, intrigued by the bulk of the instrument.

"I'm just a proud country boy from the 'cane capital of the United States, a plowboy from the tall grass and muck and dirt," Big Willie told me when I asked about his background. "How can you get a big head when you come from here? You'll see. This place ain't nothin' but a dust bowl stickin' out of the swamp."

SUGAR PLAINES AIN'T SO SWEET

I asked how to find his house for our interview. His directions gave me a harbinger of the place I was about to visit.

"If you're coming from Orlando, take the 222 south for about fifty miles until you hit Swampgrass Highway heading east. That'll take you to Main Street in Sugar Plaines. Go through downtown and just keep on going out the other end. You'll pass a few burned-down barns, and you'll see a huge tree on your right with weeping willow and gnarly branches in every direction, where the drug dealers and winos and cards and domino players hang out 24-7. Then it's going to get dark, real dark, like you've gotten lost. Just keep going until you come to the flashing traffic light just past the railroad tracks, turn left on Sucrose Alley Road at the little trucker stop that says 'Girls, Girls Day and Night' and 'Breakfast All Day.' I'm the fifth house, when the road turns to dirt, a white shack about a mile back."

Just being there for three days, I felt overcome with lethargy and foreboding and hopelessness. I could not imagine living there for a lifetime, as many Sugar Plainesians did, acclimating to the rueful circumstances to the point of obliviousness. In fact, Sugar Plaines made East Drabenville, and even Palmertown, feel positively buoyant by comparison.

❖ ❖ ❖

All this is just to say the backdrop of the biggest game of the East Grove players' lives was not lost on Coach Magnusson. He granted my request to get inside the locker room before the semifinal, and the final if they made it, agreeing that such access might enable me to give readers more insight into what East Grove really stood for and dispel its countywide reputation as "the ghetto school."

"Coach, five minutes," said a Sugar Plaines High field attendant, popping his head into the visitors' locker room before the game.

The players were sitting on benches in the cramped, muggy locker room, nervously jiggling their legs, heads down, helmets dangling from their hands. Several were wrapping tape around fingers and retying cleats;

others were rifling through game plan notes or good-luck letters written by cheerleaders; one was reading a Bible passage to himself; and a few were heaving in bathroom stalls. Magnusson moved to the center of the room and turned a slow 360 degrees to take in the mood.

"Bring it in," he said, and players put their notes and letters and Bibles and tape back in their lockers, emerged from the stalls, stood, and gathered in a circle around Magnusson. Magnusson let silence permeate for thirty seconds. "Men," he opened, "I'm honored to be here with you. No matter what happens tonight, I'm proud of you and love you all. I know Coach Gamble and Coach Polansky feel the same," he said, glancing at his assistants, who nodded.

"You're going to have a severe physical challenge tonight." He paused to scan the ring of players with his intense blue eyes. "But even more than that, gentlemen, it's going to be mental. You think you got it tough. You think life's been unfair. Well, you live like princes compared to guys you're going to face tonight. This is all they've got. And they're hungry, men. Not just hungry—desperate.

"If you can't match their desire, their desperation, they're going to have us for breakfast, lunch, and dinner and send us home empty, I guarantee you that. Do you have that desire in your gut tonight? Is your mind focused? Are you determined to your core? Anything less, and we're going home for good, and I'm not ready for that, men. No, this means too much, too much for our school, for your families, for our community, for each one of us. Men, these are the moments we live for.

"All we need tonight, men, is all you've got. All you've got, there's no other way. It's the only way. Nothin' else good enough but all you've got. What have you got tonight, men, what have you got to give for your teammates next to you? For yourself? I see the hunger in your eyes. I know what you got. Do you?"

"Yes, Coach!"

"Do you?"

"Yes, Coach!"

"Now let's show the Glade Runners who's hungry! Hank, send us out!"

Defensive coordinator Hank Gamble joined Magnusson in the middle and dropped to one knee. Players held hands and bowed their heads as Gamble improvised a prayer, ending with, "When our work is done, let us leave Sugar Plaines tonight as a family, closer than ever, safe, healthy, and full of joy."

❖ ❖ ❖

A menacing crowd greeted East Grove as the players raced onto the field. Fans yelled epithets and hurled objects during warm-ups as field attendants looked the other way. Outside the fence appeared to be an open-air drug market, with one-on-one meetings taking place all around the asphalt basketball court and items being passed through the fence.

I chose to report on the game from the sidelines to experience the intensity. During the national anthem, I was pelted by ice cubes but didn't turn around, fearing I'd encourage more.

Magnusson had delivered the right message to his players, and as a nod to their allegiance to him, they had taken it to heart instead of tuning it out as coach's prattle. From the outset, the game was more violent than any I had seen all year, and to the Warriors' credit, they were rivaling Sugar Plaines's intensity. Sugar Plaines played helter-skelter with seeming disregard for their bodies, flying to ball carriers, laying out for extra yardage, and delivering blows to East Grove tacklers before going down with the ball.

The only 4A team all season with the speed and athleticism to contain East Grove's attack, the Glade Runners were holding the Warriors well below their thirty-seven-point average, leading 21–14 midway through the fourth quarter.

Big Willie was shedding two blockers on every play, clogging the running lanes, batting down throws, and forcing Ronnie Jenkins into hurried passes, but I could tell he was getting tired, pausing after every play to put his hands on his knees and shuffling slower back to the defensive huddle. Polansky noticed too, calling for a series of misdirection plays for the Zonk and screens to Renny Jenkins that relied on allowing Big Willie to penetrate the line unabated and then running to the spot he left. In the first quarter, the plays wouldn't have worked, because even with his girth, Big Willie had agility and could change direction, recover quickly, and swallow up any ball carrier within arm's reach with his strength. But now his determination was wilting after his first errant move, and East Grove's fleet of speedsters were occupying the Glade Runners' second-level defenders, leaving big gaps in the line.

East Grove had moved sixty-one yards to the Sugar Plaines twenty-four-yard line, with a minute forty-five left. Sugar Plaines called time-out to adjust its defense. Polansky gathered his offense.

"We got 'em set up for this. Fake Tampa Right, Spider 3 Wide Banana, Brown Set on 3. Got it?"

"Got it, Coach," Ronnie Jenkins answered.

"We execute, we score, men."

I knew what Polansky called when I saw it unfold. Ronnie Jenkins pump-faked a screen pass to his brother. Sugar Plaines was so concerned about screens and draws and misdirection runs that they left Big Willie at home to hold his gap. Without pressure from Big Willie, blockers doubled other rushers, giving Ronnie more time for the play to develop. East Grove had overloaded the right side with three receivers. One ran a fifteen-yard comeback route; another, a ten-yard out. The receiver split widest, Tyrus Taylor, ran the banana, bending the route all the way across the field toward the end zone back-corner pylon. The fake screen drew in the safeties, and nobody ran with Taylor until too late. Ronnie lofted the ball toward the pylon, and Taylor ran under it for the score.

With no hesitation, Magnusson called for the two-point conversion from the three-yard line to win or lose the game, rather than an extra-point kick for a tie. Polansky dialed up the play, which I learned had been determined in advance for just such an occasion: "We didn't come this far to play it safe, men. Fake Miami B, 2 Dog Left, Y Loop, Orange Set on 1."

"After we score, our D will seal the deal," Magnusson told the team, matter of fact.

It was a quick snap, a fake plunge to the Zonk. Ronnie reverse-pivoted and rolled to his left, bringing defenders not already piled on the Zonk in pursuit. Renny Jenkins came from his slot position, took a short pitch from his brother, and turned on the afterburners, heading in the other direction. East Grove blockers formed a wall, giving Renny Jenkins a path to the goal line for a 22–21 lead.

As a team, Sugar Plaines was a lot of things, but one thing it wasn't was poised. I could see Sugar Plaines deflate after the two-pointer—heads dipped, helmets dropped, eyes averted, hands clung to hips in disgusted poses. The coach ran the sidelines clapping and fist-pumping to exhort his players, but body language showed resignation. The Glade Runners were front-runners and good at it; their comeback prowess had never been tested, and with the stakes so high, their emotional fragility was exposed.

The Glade Runners' first two passes were off-target, causing receivers to pound the ground in frustration and the quarterback to look to the stars. The quarterback frantically motioned to the bench for substitutes, but they didn't have their helmets ready, causing a delay-of-game penalty. On third down, Sugar Plaines went for the Hail Mary desperation pass, the coach perhaps sensing that only an answered prayer could save them. East Grove, with two safeties playing deep, intercepted to ice the game.

Girls, Girls

I GOT QUICK quotes from Ronnie Jenkins and Magnusson on the way to the locker room because I didn't have time to wait for the wedding reception ritual. It was 9:45 p.m.; the bulldog edition story was due at 10:30 p.m., and the press box had no phones for me to transmit a story from my Radio Shack portable computer. I had written the framework of the story in real time from a sideline bench. All I needed to do was add quotes and stats from Halumka up in the press box and top it off with a lede. After talking with Magnusson, I shoved my Sparco Reporter's Notebook in my pocket, slung the Radio Shack across my shoulder, ran to the opposite stands, and bounded up the bleachers to the press box to get stats and the play-by-play log from Halumka. I told Halumka to get a quote from the Sugar Plaines coach, then work the East Grove locker room and call me at my motel by 11:30 p.m. with the material.

I didn't have time to finish the first-run story and make it to my motel by the 10:30 p.m. deadline. Having been advised that any Sugar Plaines motel was guaranteed to be an hourly rate drug-dealing and prostitution hub with front-desk attendants behind bulletproof glass, I booked my motel twenty miles south, off the nearest highway. The only pay phone I knew about was at the Girls, Girls truck stop near Big Willie's.

So I headed that way, hoping I was tracing Big Willie's directions correctly because it was too dark to read street signs, and remembering Big Willie's advice that when I passed the community hangout tree and it got so dark I'd swear I was lost, that's how I would know I was going the right way.

After a nervous mile when I debated turning around to find another route, it beckoned like the Cape Hatteras Lighthouse: Girls, Girls in neon red. I parked and got out the computer to finish the bulldog story when three rapid knocks on the Turdmobile window scared the shit out of me. A guy unfurled a baggie and pressed it against the window.

"Not me," I yelled through the glass, shaking my head. I started the car and moved to a darker, more remote corner of the parking lot, not knowing if it would be safer or more dangerous, but at least it was out of the main trafficking corridor.

I finished the story under the glow of the Turdmobile's interior light and carried the computer and plug-in acoustic couplers into the truck stop at 10:27 p.m. This was always the most nerve-wracking part of game nights. It was even more so that night because of the importance of the game, the prime space held for it in Saturday's *Dinqy*, and my unfamiliarity with my surroundings.

My first attempt was the diner, where an "Out of Order" sign was taped over the pay phone. I hustled next door to the go-go lounge, Sugar Plum Revue. Scantily clad women were gyrating on a platform to pulsating music above rumpled-looking truckers and blue-collar workers at the bar, while other girls in high heels, some topless and others in skimpy push-up bikini tops, worked the room with drink platters. I blocked out the distractions, called the transmission-dump number, got the high-pitched buzz, connected the acoustic couplers to the mouthpiece and earpiece, and prayed. Everything went smoothly for the first thirty seconds. From experience, I knew the transmission would take about one minute. I doubled down on prayer. A few seconds later, the dreaded hieroglyphics scrolled across the screen, meaning the transmission was broken. The words were clogged in the utility lines. It was 10:31 p.m. I called Skip Blintzer, who I knew would be spritzing a minute after deadline, to let him know the story was on the way as soon as I could get the 40 percent success rate couplers to work. If the fit wasn't snug, only God could complete the transmission, and I was summoning Yahweh now.

I reconnected. This time, it didn't get ten seconds through before the Morse code ran across the screen. The symbols might have helped me bomb the Nazis from a warship, but they weren't doing shit to calm Blintzer's Friday night freak-out. I slammed the phone on the receiver three times, clanging loud enough for the bar squatters to turn their attention from the dancers toward me, and tried to muffle a "Goddamn it!" but it came out much louder than I intended. A topless dancing girl with huge boobs and a drink platter approached me. She got real close, in my proverbial personal space bubble, so close her hair tickled my nose, and her hip rubbed my leg.

"Sounds like somebody's havin' a rough night, sweetie. What'r ya, some kind of FBI man? We've had y'all here before. Ya making a drug bust? D'you want a private room to help you relax? I can make you feel better."

The temptation was strong. How long would it take, ten minutes? Maybe I did need to relax to write better for the final edition. So maybe Blintzer would have less time to obsess over his copyediting, so what? It was probably better for him and the *Dinqy* anyway. I'd have to listen to him rant about being late and how it disrupts the integrity of the choreographed editing and layout process, but I calculated the trade-off would still be in my favor. I wondered what the private rooms in the back looked like. Curtained peep shows? Velvet couches? Mirrored walls and strobe lights? Beads and incense?

I got out a crisp twenty-dollar bill, figuring I'd fudge my expense report for payback. I stuck it in her garter, where it stood out among tattered ones and fives.

"Hold a room for ten minutes, I got some business, then I'll be back," I told her, doubting I'd take her up on her offer but wanting to buy enough time to stave off any bodyguard goons who might come after me for hanging around their strip club without compensating the entertainment.

I was down to my last resort—the outdoor pay phone, which would leave me exposed like a fugitive cowering in a dark corner to avoid the helicopter's spotlight. The booth was vacant, and as a bonus, the light worked. I hooked up the couplers and scanned the parking lot for trouble, like an undercover cop. The transmission completed as I heard an angry voice approaching.

"What the fuck, get the fuck out of there, mothafucka!" Obviously I was trespassing in a drug dealer's office, which was open for business. I jammed the computer and couplers into my bag and slapped my official-looking press pass against the glass, which was convincing enough to persuade the intruder that I might be an undercover cop and to veer in another direction as if looking for a lost dog. I bolted from the booth and floored the Turdmobile to the motel, where I capped off the full story by midnight.

Pitching Foghorn

After returning from Sugar Plaines, as I started preparing for the state finals, the O-Dog called me at the bureau. "We got a meeting with the muckamucks tomorrow at ten o'clock, kid, right after morning editorial. Bring all your stuff and get a good night's sleep."

For the first time since my job interview, I put on a blazer and tie and loafers. I wanted to look the part of a serious journalist, based on the examples of the county government reporter and editorial writer in my bureau office, who looked like they worked at a law firm, and distance myself in appearance from my true compatriots, Mahotie with his size-fifteen Hush Puppies with white socks and Halumka with his flannel shirts and floodwater Dickies.

We met in the executive conference room on the fourth-floor, the New Palm City headquarters' top floor, where all the people listed on the newspaper's masthead worked, executive vice-president of this and senior managing director of that, and where all of the newspaper's awards from the South Florida Society of Newspaper Editors or the Florida Organization of Investigative Reporters hung. Wellington and Chenault were joined by the "Quad County Today" metro editor and the op-ed page editor; Paddy, Skip, and Jean-Paul Boneau—I had to be careful not to refer to him as Monsieur in front of this crowd—accompanied me. I had lobbied to have Monsieur join us for his legal and investigatory expertise and because he knew so much background on the story, and I knew that he had advocated passionately and successfully to run controversial stories in the past.

"Thanks for joining us today in New Palm, Mr. Yankelovich," the debonair Chance Wellington greeted me. Every time I saw Wellington, tall with slicked-back white hair, a trim beard, and wire-frame glasses, he was impeccably dressed in a dark suit and a bow tie. Or he'd wear a necktie and have a matching handkerchief folded like a silk napkin at a five-star restaurant sticking out of his suit pocket. He reminded me of Alfred the butler from Batman's stately Wayne Manor. He had a refined Southern drawl that was a mix between a more intellectual Andy Griffith of Mayberry and a more refined Foghorn Leghorn. He had worked his way up from reporter in his hometown of Dothan, Alabama, the peanut capital of the world, to city editor in Birmingham, to managing editor in Atlanta, when the offer came from parent company, Stennett News Services, to be executive editor of a sleepy provincial paper in this booming Citrus Coast area and transform the *Daily Inquirer* into a regional powerhouse, and that's largely what he had done during his five-year swan song.

"We know you're terribly busy with the football play-offs, so we will certainly be as efficient as possible today so you can get back to your pressing work. High school football, as you know by now, is vitally important to our Dolphin County readers. Mr. O'Manahan has briefed me on the situation that you have investigated with the Dolphin County school board, and I believe you have been involved as well, Mr. Boneau?"

"That's right, Mr. Wellington, and I really think we got 'em nailed…I mean we've got all our ducks lined up in a row. We've done our due diligence, the facts speak for themselves, and if you don't mind my saying, sir, I think we got 'em dead to rights."

"Thank you, Mr. Boneau, I'm sure you've done excellent work and that's all well and good. But we can't go into this flippantly. When I was a young reporter, all full of vim and vigor like yourself, I also thought everything I did was foolproof and thought editors were the biggest fuddy-duddies in the world for making me check my work and check again and get more confirmation and ask more and more questions. But since I became an editor oh so many years ago, I have realized the value of cautiousness and circumspection. We cannot risk ruining lives and reputations, not to mention the reputation of this fine institution that Ms. Chenault and I and we all are building, without being 101 percent sure, and then we have to go back until we are 102 percent sure. Do you understand what I am saying, Mr. Boneau?"

"I do, Mr. Wellington, that's why I can feel confident in saying I am 110 percent sure, after working this story with Jake, and I think Jake agrees with me; is that right, Jake?"

Now I felt put on the spot, and I knew the spotlight would inevitably turn to me anyway. All of a sudden my confidence dropped. I had the disturbing vision of this stately, sophisticated, erudite, and grandfatherly Wellington dude bouncing me on his knee and, in the condescending voice you'd use with a five-year-old, telling me that I would not get a lollipop from Grampy if I didn't tell the truth.

Meanwhile, the young and glamorous Chenault was staying quiet and taking notes, letting Wellington take the lead.

"Do you agree with Mr. Boneau?" Wellington asked me. "Do we have this story right, zipped up, no holes or loose ends?"

I hesitated for a second. "Yes, Mr. Wellington, I think so."

"How old are you, son?" Wellington asked, suddenly becoming patronizing.

"I'm twenty-two."

"Well, I've been in this business for thirty-eight years, and I'm not staking my reputation on a twenty-two-year-old *sportswriter* who 'thinks so.' What are you hanging your story on?"

"Boots…Clarence Walker, Mr. Wellington, the school board member from DeVaca City. He told me on the record that he accepted bribe money from Augustus Papadopoulos, the school board chairman, in exchange for a vote and funneled it through his friends to develop the Praise Palmertown Athletic & Education Complex. I talked to the guys Walker laundered the money through. They weren't real sophisticated about it; they told me straight out about their financial connection with Walker and their donations for the complex. It's all on the record."

"That's one school board member. Gus needed at least two others. That's not enough. What else do you have?"

The O-Dog was right. The old man who was accustomed to being in control was making this a hard sell.

"Well, Jean-Paul and I found a lot of evidence through public records that Shelley Jochnowitz and Lenzell Langston's financial fortunes changed drastically for the better during this time, though there's no discernable reason for it other than money under the table. They voted with Gus, but they've declined to talk to me for an interview about the Palmertown redistricting decision. They want to keep that in the past, forget about it, I think for obvious reasons. But I do have Bunny Heavener, who confirmed that she was offered a bribe for her vote but rejected it. She said she'd consider going on record if it ever came to that.

"And this is the best—I have official bank statements from Sunshine State Bank & Trust showing regular transfers of large sums of money from a Bamford trust account to a business account owned by Papadopoulos."

"That's really hard to get, really impossible without a subpoena," Monsieur chimed in. "I don't even know how Jake got it, but that was great reporting work."

"Circumstantial. Too much circumstantial," Wellington said. "We need a second school board member to go on record and back up Mr. Walker's story. This story has got to be bulletproof, or our lawyers won't let it run—too much risk for libel that could cost us millions."

"We've got Heavener," I offered.

"No, not good enough," Wellington responded. "She didn't take a bribe. There's no money trail. It would be just her word against Gus's. Who is she? A schoolmarm? A housewife? You know what I'm getting at."

Now I was getting perturbed. All this hard work and digging and overtime and putting myself on the line—not to mention taking a physical beating—just to have this dinosaur put the kibosh on what I was sure would be the best story the Citrus Coast had seen in a generation with more legs than a Siamese octopus, all so he presumably could protect his first-rate reputation in the business and assure the bean counters in

Chicago's Stennett corporate headquarters that the advertising dollars would keep flowing without the potential disruption of a reported scandal that might anger a certain segment of readers, and so he could continue frequenting the high-society, elitist events with the Papadopouloses and Bamfords and other power brokers of the Citrus Coast so that one day soon he could be feted by them at his retirement gala and be bestowed with the title "emeritus," which would transmit an appropriate reverence to his being into perpetuity. A Bamford-Papadopoulos scandal might screw all of that up.

"Y'all remember Janet Cooke at *The Washington Post* and her fairy-tale eight-year-old heroin addict?" Wellington asked, addressing the room before turning his full attention to Chenault. Paddy and Skip glanced at each other and chuckled. "We don't know what this Mr. Walker's motive is. It may be impure. How do we know we can trust him? We don't, nosah, nosah.

"Find me a second school board member who will admit to taking this so-called bribe, and get it on the record, and then I will think about running your story, son."

Paddy and Skip knew when to be quiet, but I was feeling bolder than I should have. Now I was playing with a quick trip through the front revolving doors and a place in the unemployment line.

"Mr. Wellington, with all due respect, I don't think we can get a second member to give themselves up. Why would they? Jochnowitz got a new condo on the beach and Langston is building a ghetto economy empire out of the deal. Frankly, it's a miracle that Clarence Walker admitted what he did, and it's only because he's God-fearing and has a conscience. Once we go with the story, it's going to get law enforcement involved, and then it's going to have legs—Christie Brinkley legs—and we won't know how far it will reach.

"I understand your concerns, Mr. Wellington, I really do. But if Jean-Paul is confident we have the goods, that's good enough for me. Jean-Paul is the consummate professional and thorough as all get out, I believe you'd agree. I think we should hop on it soon and ride it hard, and make the *T-D* chase our ass on a blockbuster in *their own backyard,* if you don't mind me putting it bluntly like that, sir."

"I appreciate your passion, Mr. Yankelovich. I was hungry like you when I was a green reporter. An executive editor has more to consider. This story is dead unless you get a second board member like Walker for corroboration.

"Do you gentlemen have any other business you wish to discuss?" We looked at each other and shrugged. "In that case, y'all have a f-i-i-i-i-ne day now, y' hear?"

Office Porno

On the way out of the conference room, Chenault tapped me on the shoulder and asked me to come to her office. I obliged. I had only seen a few porno flicks in my horny young life, but I was pretty sure this was one of the common story lines. The mature, buttoned-up professional woman, with hair pinned up in a bun, cerebral glasses, and conservative skirt and blouse, invites the naïve younger man into her office, sizes him up from behind her desk, grabs him by the tie, and in short order, everything comes down and off, the desk becomes a surrogate bed, and major moaning and grunting ensue.

I couldn't help but think of Chenault in that way. She was hot as all hell; in fact, she was a Florida state runner-up beauty queen—nearly a Miss America Pageant contestant—as a collegiate at Florida State. She was tall, slim, and brunette, with high cheekbones, a dazzling, wide smile of ivory white teeth, and soulful brown eyes that could make you fall in love. I couldn't be sure, but she might not even have been thirty, which signaled a meteoric career rise—from college intern to city hall reporter to "Citrus Coast Today" editor to managing editor in six years—considering other news reporters and section editors had been at the paper for twenty years or more. The age difference between us was small enough that I could see Chenault as a contemporary and even a girlfriend if I aimed for the moon, but the gap in titular power, prestige, acumen, maturity in navigating within a corporate environment, social status, and comfort in associating with elites from business, philanthropy, medicine, academia, and just plain wealth made me feel more like a boy with an Oedipus complex than anywhere close to her equal.

I took a seat in front of Chenault's large, mahogany desk. As she checked a phone message, I waited for her to put her legs up on the desk and kick off her high heels, unpin her hair, lunge on top of the desk, and grab me by the tie, or announce how hot it was in the room and unbutton her blouse, and maybe even drop a few conveniently accessible ice cubes from her water glass down her bra. I pondered whether I should feel guilty for being such a chauvinistic, objectifying, dismissive sleazebag in the presence of a smart, accomplished, regal, and dignified woman, but I really didn't. It felt right, authentic. How mundane is life without some fantasy?

"Jake, I wanted to talk to you in private about the story you're working on."

My mind flashed, and my mouth must have opened wide for a split second. I was stunned. It was as if my brain put flashing neon lights around "IN PRIVATE." Whoa. Could my fantasy turn real? I saw myself climbing out of my body and smothering Chenault's equivalent avatar on top of the desk. Then she continued, and I beat back my shadow self; Carl Jung would have been proud.

"I believe in this story. I believe you've done the investigative work and verification, like Jean-Paul says, your due diligence, and I'm going to do everything in my power to put our best editors on it and get it in print. Mr. Wellington is being very cautious, and I understand that. He comes from a different era. There was more reverence and deference for authority and a more genteel approach, especially in the Deep South where Chancey— Mr. Wellington—cut his teeth. You know as well as I do it's not like that anymore. It's rough-and-tumble.

"Anyway, enough of the journalism history lesson. I could tell you were frustrated in there. I just want to encourage you to keep working the story. I know you're busy with football play-offs, but I want you to write this story as much as you can while you work your daily beat. When we get the green light—and I'm confident we're going to soon—we'll want to move on it quick."

I asked Chenault whether there was any room for negotiation on getting a second bribe-taking board member on the record, which I reemphasized would be extraordinarily unlikely and, in a persuasive Mahotie imitation—if she really wanted to get down to brass tacks—unrealistic.

"I'd go with it *if* we have Heavener on the record. Let me talk with Mr. Wellington about it. I may be able to convince him to walk on the edge a little more."

❖ ❖ ❖

I left Chenault's finely appointed, spacious office with bay and palm tree views and the professionally decorated fourth-floor executive suite to rejoin the sports slobs in a corner of the chaotic third-floor newsroom with its standard-issue maze of cubicle stations with protruding computer monitors, piles of printouts and newspapers, Associated Press style guides, and Blintzer's fish-platter condiments.

I told Paddy and Skip about my conversation with Chenault.

"That's not surprising. She has a lot of sway over the old Clark Gable, if you know what I mean," Paddy said.

"No. What do you mean?" I said.

"Let's just say it's not a well-kept secret they're something more than editorial colleagues."

My job interview. Way back then, I had had the intuition that there was something more than professionalism and the love of a good lede between those two.

I asked Paddy why he thought Chenault was much more eager to go with the story than the erstwhile journalistic stalwart Wellington. He obviously had pondered that already.

"I wouldn't be the least bit surprised if the Big Papa or Bamford—or probably both—have threatened Wellington with exposing his affair if he publishes anything damaging about them. Those families and their friends travel in the same circles as our execs. Hell, they're at some charity fund raiser or awards banquet or dedication ceremony together every weekend and twice a week. You think Wellington could hide his desire to play footsy that well? No way. The word is out. People just act like they don't know and everything is just business, of course."

"Yeah, I kind of felt like something was going on between them," I said.

"And not just that," Paddy said. "Think of this. Wellington has his dream retirement all set. He's got a beautiful house with his socialite Southern belle wife on Solo Calcetino Key, with all the other rich retirees. Between them, they have a ton of connections. All he has to do is collect a few more years' worth of big paychecks, then suck Stennett dry with a golden-parachute retirement package and his whopping pension, and he's living the Margaritaville dream until the day he croaks. Why would he want to mess with that by denigrating and enraging two of the most powerful families down here—and all their friends and loyalists and business partners? Why would he want to bring that cancer to his own private Margaritaville? Think about it. If you were getting up there and living in paradise, wouldn't you just put it on autopilot? It's just as likely that Wellington would be the one vilified and shunned instead of Big Papa and Bamford if this story gets out."

On the other hand, Paddy explained, Chenault was wildly ambitious, a real go-getter for whom everyone believed—she, most of all—that the sky was the limit. She was still carving out a name for herself in journalism, which was still an old-boy network where women were few in the boardroom. She was always on the lookout for a home run, the investigative story with depth and consequence that led to more and more layers of exposure; where readers did not just glance at the headlines out of habit but felt compelled to read the paper through jumps and sidebars for fear of missing out on new developments and fresh angles; where competing media dreaded what would come next; where people could point to the newspaper and say, "That newspaper had an impact; that newspaper caused things to change." It was clear, Paddy said: Wellington had a stake in easing his way into a cushy retirement; Chenault had a stake not only in becoming the next executive editor of the *Dinqy*, but also in garnering national attention from journalism's biggest hitters as a rising young star.

Before that day, I believed Wellington was the one I had to win over; then I learned he just had to be moved out of the way. I was glad that it appeared I had Chenault in my camp to do the heavy lifting. It might be that I'd never be groping her naked body atop her office desk, but there was a good chance she could help me reach an immensely satisfying climax nonetheless.

The Electric Company

The week before Christmas brought unbridled excitement to Drabenville. The city was accustomed to having local high schools in the state championship game but rarely two in the same year. The marquee outside Mudville Mike's, traditionally a Dolphin High haunt, gave grudging respect to Dolphin's poor, ragamuffin cousin:

"DRABENVILLE THE CITY OF CHAMPIONS
BRING IT HOME JIMBO & THE FINS!
Go East Grove"

East Grove was playing for the 4A championship at the Gator Bowl in Jacksonville on Friday, and Dolphin was gunning for the 5A title at the University of Florida in Gainesville on Saturday. My entire motley crew was to travel together in a *Dinqy* van to both games. Blintzer and I diagrammed assignments for the preview week and the games—opposing team features and analysis, a look back at past championship teams, a character study and comparison of Bamford and Magnusson, a revisit of the Sammons-Hilliard-Schlorf suspension situation, and a portrait of the Jenkins twins and their symbiotic relationship.

Blintzer gave us the pep talk at our Sunday night planning meeting after we returned from the semifinals. "We're going to cover the sh-sh-shit out of this, guys. There's no such thing as overkill. Drabenville can't get enough. Save your sleep for Christmas; your present will be the *Dinqy*'s b-buh-best high school football coverage ever. As soon as we get out of here, we all gotta just start to c-cuh-call around."

❖ ❖ ❖

Bend-Over had a brilliant idea for our road trip. Since the infamous Florida State Prison in Starke was en route between Jacksonville and Gainesville, Bend-Over pitched a photo essay to the Florida Associated Press on life inside the state's toughest prison, with a focus on death row. Starke whacks murderers the way the Bug Zapper annihilates flies, and the warden wanted to promote Florida's aggressive stance on violent crime. I got a credential as Bend-Over's writer, and we were able to pass off Mahotie and Halumka as a columnist and editorial writer. Starke would be our entertainment between games.

Accustomed to covering games in small-potatoes high school stadiums, it was awe-inspiring to experience the vastness and luxury of the Gator Bowl when I entered the press box on Friday evening. I quickly honed in on the sounds of Whalebait Wally, who had started his pregame chatter two hours before kickoff.

"Chummers, if you're a Dolphin County football fan, and you'd be a hammerhead if you're listening now and you aren't, you will be in subterranean heaven over the next twenty-eight hours. We have a chance for a double-dipper, and I don't know about you, but ol' Whalebait's as stoked as an electric eel in a tank of light bulbs.

"Speaking of electric, East Grove's going to have their hands full with Uncalachicola High's All-World running back and kick returner, Elroy "Electric Company" Jones. When the Electric Company turns out your lights, you know the party's over."

Elroy Jones was unanimously voted Florida's high school player of the year. He had a full scholarship to the University of Florida-Orlando (UFO), where he would go on to break NCAA rushing records and become a first-round NFL draft pick. Nobody had stopped him during the Uncalachicola Uprising's undefeated season, in which he gained more than 2,400 yards rushing, scored twenty-eight touchdowns, and added ten touchdowns on punt and kickoff returns. He was the second coming of

THE ELECTRIC COMPANY

Marcus DuPree, the Philadelphia, Mississippi, high school phenom who became legendary as a University of Oklahoma freshman in 1981 before his comet flamed out in an ill-fated United States Football League career.

Coach Magnusson let me into the pregame locker room again, which was like the Ritz Carlton compared with the Sugar Plaines locker room. Players were so keyed up, they were hardly talking. Too many were gagging in the toilet stalls, and even with much more bountiful accommodations, there was a line for toilet privileges. Legs everywhere were jiggling. Fingers flexed reflexively, as if players were warming up for harp rehearsal. Several players crossed themselves, pointing to the ceiling and raising their eyes. I could feel how bad the boys wanted it for themselves and their coaches, school, and community. It was the same sense I'd had since August during my tour of the East Drabenville Y with Johnny Littleman and my first sight of Magnusson lining his field with military precision. Two players got in a scuffle. That's when Magnusson took charge, summoning the players by using his thumb and index finger to make a commanding whistle, a specialized coaching skill. The players got down on one knee, resting a hand on their helmets. They looked at Coach Magnusson in anticipation, and he said nothing for a full minute, pacing between the points of the semicircle and scanning his players' eyes. Finally, one word:

"Relax."

Another thirty seconds of silence, this time without pacing.

"Relax."

Again, with eyes closed.

"Relax...Breathe...Envision...See yourselves at your best, barely touching the ground, soaring as if the laws of gravity don't apply to you, knowing exactly what to do without thinking, just reacting, creating. See yourselves free, unbound, joyful. Men, if we play that way tonight, we will triumph."

He paused and scanned; every eye was upon him, wide.

"Tonight, men, is not about being perfect. We won't be. We aren't. Tonight is not about getting...a championship, a trophy, praise, respect.

Tonight is about giving, giving more than you ever thought you could. Think of your family, your grandma, whoever helped you get here. What would you give to make them proud? Think of East Grove, the Ghetto School, Thug City. What would you give to bust that myth?

"And what will you give for yourself? This is all we've got, men. Right here, right now. That's all there is. As long as you live, you may never have another moment as special as this, another moment when you get to share greatness with brothers who love you. This is forever, and forever is now, forever is here. Tonight is *not* about winning, men. It's about giving. I promise you, if we give everything, we will be winners. You've given everything to me and Coach Gamble and Coach Polansky. We are honored and privileged to share now with you, to share forever with you.

"Lead us out, Hank!"

"Lord, we had a battle in Sugar Plaines, and you saw us through," Gamble began with such emotion that tears rolled from each clenched eye. "Tonight, we have another challenge. We look to you for strength; we're prepared and ready for whatever you have in store for us. Lord, we don't pretend to be so presumptuous as to ask you for a result, but we ask you to help each one of us be the best we can be for each other, and as always, to watch over us, and we trust the outcome will be what you will.

"Our Father, who art in heaven, hallowed be thy name. Thy kingdom come," Gamble recited the Lord's Prayer. "...For thine is the kingdom, and the power, and the glory, for ever and ever. Amen."

"Amen!" the players roared in unison and bounced to their feet.

If I felt like laying someone out with a full-bore hit at that moment, I can't imagine how much adrenaline was pumping through the Warriors.

❖ ❖ ❖

Elroy "Electric Company" Jones exceeded his hype, breaking loose on sweeps and bursts up the middle time and again. Uncalachicola fans accentuated the legend with signs like "Don't Mess With Electricity" and "When The Electric Company Knocks On Your Door You Will Pay."

East Grove had great athletes, but as with any sport, there are many different levels of great. The tennis player ranked three-hundred in the world is unquestionably a great player, yet he has virtually no chance to beat a player in the top thirty because they are several levels of greatness above him in some combination of physical ability, mental toughness, experience, or strategic knowledge. Similarly, a college running back drafted in the seventh round is a great player, but ninety-five times out of a hundred, he won't come near matching the performance of a first-round running back for the same reasons.

In this game, Electric Company was like a first-rounder playing against a bunch of seventh-rounders. He plowed through and around the East Grove defense on four first-half touchdown drives, scoring twice. The threat of Electric Company runs was enough to allow receivers to run open for two more scores. But East Grove held its own on offense, and when the Zonk bullied into the end zone to close the first half, the Warriors charged into the locker room inspired, trailing 27–21 and with the state championship within realistic grasp, if only they could find a way to impose a second-half blackout on Electric Company.

Elroy Jones was a lethal combination of speed, power, quickness, footwork, peripheral vision, and natural instinct. He displayed all those talents on the second-half kickoff, taking it to the house to return the Uprising to a two-score lead. Magnusson tried to prevent his troops from getting discouraged.

"I'm looking at the eyes right now," he said, facing the benches. "I'm looking at the body language. Don't give me frustrated; don't give me down. Give me ready; give me confident."

While Magnusson exerted a calming influence, the Zonk, who played middle linebacker and captained the defense, made a raw emotional appeal, daring to break Magnusson's rule against swearing.

"The Electric Company, bullshit! You buyin' into the hype, y'all!" he ranted, roaming the sideline like a caged lion on the scent of raw meat. He stole a line from *Rocky* when the Italian Stallion realized that Apollo Creed was human too. "Electric Company, he ain't so bad. He ain't so bad. Ain't nothin'! C'mon, y'all, what's wrong with y'all! He put his pants on just like us. He eat his Wheaties just like us. He ain't no Superman! He ain't wearin' no cape! We can't play scared. Electric Company got to go down! We gotta put him down! Let's go, goddamn it, let's go!"

Magnusson's approach may have been better. East Grove was forced to punt from midfield on its next possession, and despite Gamble's admonition to punt out of bounds to avoid a Jones return, East Grove's punter failed to clear the sideline. Jones caught it at the ten near the right sideline and cut toward the line. East Grove's coverage team was pressing too hard. Two players who could have made the tackle overran the play, and a third went to the turf grasping at air when Jones made his first move. Here is where Electric Company showed his supremacy. East Grove still could have had him pinned against the sideline for little gain, but he did a U-turn and reversed field. Overeager and undisciplined in their pursuit lanes, East Grove's players got trapped on one side of the field. Electric Company outran the coverage to the far sideline, picked up a convoy of blockers, and was gone, high-stepping to the end zone in an extended-arm, Heisman pose for the last twenty yards.

I could feel the East Grove sideline palpably deflate before Jones even started his high-step. Magnusson tried to preempt a collapse, slapping players on the shoulder pads, saying, "Head up," or "Let it go, next play."

Not enough. The game was over. East Grove would never recover from those two demoralizing Electric Company shocks. Electric Company scored twice more, for six in all, bringing out Uncalachicola's "Turn Out The Lights" signs in the stands and capping a 53–31 victory.

Before the game even ended, Coach Magnusson and his assistants were congratulating and encouraging the players, many of whom were crying with elbows on knees and towels over their heads.

"Heck of a ride, gentlemen, heck of a ride," Magnusson repeated down the line. "Hold your heads high. I couldn't be prouder, couldn't be prouder."

Old Sparky

Florida State Prison in Starke, a drab, sprawling complex in the middle of vast agricultural fields, has housed some of America's most notorious and prolific serial killers, including real-life movie subjects Ted Bundy, the most infamous of all for pure evil and depravity, and later, Aileen Wuornos, title character of *Monster*, who murdered at least seven prostitute-seeking men. Drifter and murderer John Spenkelink became a cause célèbre for celebrities who opposed capital punishment, including Alan Alda and Joan Baez. One fine day, all the Starke death row inmates would have an appointment with destiny known as Old Sparky, the electric chair.

As we entered the prison and approached the guard desk at the visitor's check-in station, Mahotie broke into his ridiculous B-9 Environmental Control Robot routine from the 1960s *Lost in Space* TV show.

"Danger Will Robinson, danger!" Mahotie said in a stern monotone, turning his body mechanically at ninety-degree angles and stiffly and alternately waving his arms, imitating the B-9 protecting young Will from alien beings. "Danger…"

"Mitch, you can't fool around here! These guards aren't gonna think your shit's funny, and I'm not staying here overnight to babysit you in General Pop," I said. I stopped the group from going any closer to the guard's desk to make sure Mahotie was listening.

He loosened from his robot pose, as if he heeded my warning. We started walking again. Then, from behind, I heard: "Does not compute!

Does not compute! Does not compute!" There was Mahotie, in the same spot, swiveling rigidly, rotating his head side-to-side.

"Mitch!"

An assistant warden and a Florida Department of Corrections public affairs officer took us on a tour of the maximum-security wing and death-row cellblock. In max, we faced a barrage of unruly and offensive hoots and hollers from inmates who rattled items against the bars. Halumka attracted the brunt of unwanted attention, as one inmate yelled, "Hey, Mutton Man, you be right at home in here, country-ass, bumfuck, honky, Aryan Brotherhood motherfucker!" We told Bert not to make eye contact, but he did, encouraging more abuse. "I want you to be my celly with them country-boy choppers. We be real good friends, Mutton Man!"

Meanwhile, Bend-Over was snapping like crazy, taking portraits of inmates who had provided permission and artistic shots when they had not, like hands sticking through bars and silhouettes in the yard.

We observed death row from a viewing area above the cellblock. We watched as several dead men walking were escorted in shackles to meet with lawyers or prison officials or for their one hour of daily exercise in isolation. Then we saw Ted Bundy shuffle out of his cell with a guard on each side. Despite being warned not to interact with the inmates in any way, Mahotie couldn't contain himself.

"Hey, Teddy, I hate to add insult to injury, but have you gotten friendly with Old Sparky yet? A word to the wise, Teddy, ya may want to give her a test drive to check the batteries and whatnot, you know, make sure it's firing on all cylinders. I'll come back for your big day. Wouldn't miss it for the world. Should be very stimulating, ya know, all's well that ends well. Ashes to ashes, dust to dust."

The warden had tried to silence Mahotie, but Mahotie talked right over him even as he was led away. In the middle of Mahotie's diatribe, I caught a glimpse of Bundy craning his head forward between the guards to check out the commotion. For a split second, my eyes locked with pure evil, beady, dark, and menacing eyes set in a hollow, ashen face. "If looks could kill" was apropos. I knew right then if Teddy could have pulled a Houdini, he would have strangled the life out of Mahotie or any one of us and relished every second. Jolted by the glance, I blurted out before I could censor myself, "Excuse my friend, Mr. Bundy. He's a big talker. Enjoy your workout. Have a good day."

"Who are those freaks?" I heard Bundy ask the guards as they escorted him to the exercise room.

Steve Blass Disease

Throughout the play-offs, the Cannon had been regressing to his erratic DeVaca City game form. The Fins relied on defense to eke out a 13–10 semifinal win. The Cannon had all the physical tools but obviously a serious case of the mental yips. The more the expectations increased and stakes rose and pressure grew, the poorer Crane performed. He threw wild, high balls prone to interception and brain-froze on decisions. He was the Steve Blass of Florida high school football, the Pittsburgh Pirates All-Star and 1971 World Series Game 7-winning pitcher, who, soon thereafter, developed an inexplicable and permanent condition that became known as "Steve Blass disease," which rendered him incapable of throwing a baseball anywhere near home plate and drove him out of the Major Leagues within one season.

During championship week, Bamford arranged to have Crane see a sports psychologist and a hypnotist at the Sergio Bonatelli Tennis Academy and Sports Performance Institute in hopes they would beat the neurotic anxiety out of his system, leaving only the supreme athletic ability and easy confidence unfettered by subconscious thought. Unfortunately for the naïve Bamford, distorted thinking doesn't change magically in one session.

"Chummers, one question will determine the Fightin' Dorsal Fins' season tonight," Whalebait Wally opened his monologue. "Will Connor 'the Cannon' Crane be the squid or the whale? You know, Trawlers, sperm whales and giant squids are known for having epic battles. I think that's what's going on inside the Cannon's head. We'll see who's victorious."

This enraged Donny Monday, who was nervously chain-smoking and fixing his comb-over before kickoff. He had spent the previous hour asking anyone associated with the Dolphin team—student trainers, boosters with special locker room privileges, equipment managers—how the quarterback was feeling, and got responses that included, "He appears to be searching for a ring in the toilet," "He's got the shakes like malaria," and "He looks like he hasn't slept in days."

"Wally, what the fuck does that mean, 'the squid or the whale?'" Monday asked with a sourpuss face on commercial break. "For Chrissakes, would you start making sense someday, shit for brains? I'm God damned tired of you reducing Dolphin football to Mrs. Paul's Fish Sticks, and so are your listeners, Jesus Mary God Almighty!"

"It's simple, Donny. He's either going to power through like a big 'ol sperm whale spouting a geyser through the blowhole or he's going to go 'pfffffftttt' like a squid discharging ink. I hate to break it to you, Donny, but from the trend I've seen the last few games? Pfffffftttt."

"Pfffffftttt my ass, and why do you have to bring sperm into the conversation—not gettin' any, Wal?" Donny countered. "Connor's got an All-American gun…Just a little…fragile ego, or whatever the hell the shrinks call it. Jimbo'll fix it, he knows kids…He'd better…Connor was great against…Yeah, maybe the guy's a fuckin' head case! A real Fruit Loop! Don't tell him I said that, Wally, or his dad, or I'll hang you by your whale balls like a pendulum. Jimbo better have Sammy ready…"

Wally laughed loudly at Monday's about face.

"Just in case," Monday finished, "but he probably won't need the rapist, so shut the fuck up and go back to pulling your pud and musing about sperm!"

Coach Bamford didn't allow me in the locker room before the championship game against the Fort Patton Beach Watchassee High Tornadoes. I reported from the Dolphin sideline. Halumka was the spotter in the press box.

THREE YARDS AND A PLATE OF MULLET

Wally was right about the Cannon—pfffffftttt for the first half. Total squid. He hesitated on pulling the trigger on open receivers and took sacks, missed reads and locked in on blanketed receivers, panicked and scrambled when he didn't have to, short-armed balls and rifled others with no arc or touch. He was horribly inaccurate, completing three of seventeen for twenty-eight yards and two interceptions. Watchassee jammed seven or eight defenders in the box and dared the Cannon to beat single-man coverage, and he couldn't. With each incompletion and sack, the blitzes became more ferocious and the Cannon more skittish.

"Didn't we work on this all week in practice, getting the ball out on quick-pop passes?" Bamford quizzed his assistants after an unsuccessful offensive series. "We knew we'd get bum-rushed."

"Yeah, we did, Coach," one answered.

"Doggone. Connor delivered the ball all week like a Meals on Wheels volunteer, set the table, dessert, everything. I thought he got fixed at Bonatelli's, but look at this. Just look at it! My word!" Bamford said, shaking his head and spitting simultaneously.

With Hobie Schlorf gone, Bamford corralled his offensive line coach on the way to the locker room, down 14–0 at halftime. "Time for some mullet ball. Tell the O-line and Sammy."

Coaching Genius

The move would cement Bamford's reputation as a coaching genius, burnish his legend to mythic proportions in Dolphin County and the greater Citrus Coast region, and punch his ticket to the college head-coaching ranks. Dolphin opened the second half with a completely different offensive look, changing from a spread offense with four receivers to a wishbone option formation popularized in the 1970s by college powerhouses Texas and Oklahoma, with three runners behind Sammy Sammons at quarterback. Mondo was the power fullback, and Nate Hilliard and Dexter Cartwright were the tailbacks, with Cartwright going in motion as a swing pass threat. Hilliard had played intermittently in the first half, mostly as a slot receiver, with few touches, as Mondo got most of the carries.

I knew the change might be coming: I had seen Dolphin practicing the wishbone with Sammons during the week as a contingency in case the Cannon's therapy didn't take. But obviously, Watchassee had no clue, preparing only for the Cannon and a high-octane passing attack. In the second half, the Tornadoes' defense looked confused; players were pointing at Dolphin's skill position players and shuffling to try to get assignments straight. Watchassee coaches were yelling at their players to change alignments; players were bumping into each other trying to get into position as Dolphin was snapping the ball.

Good defenses are able to make quick reads of plays from studying tendencies on tape. Watchassee had not read Dolphin's book because it hadn't been written. They were flat-footed because they could not diagnose plays and had no idea where the ball was going.

It was also the wrong day for Watchassee to face Sammons and Hilliard. Both ran with a fury and determination I had not seen all season, unleashing their pent up wrath and frustration on Tornadoes defenders, punishing them upon contact and fighting for extra yardage on every play. They bounced up from gang tackles as if they couldn't wait for more pounding. Sammons ran the wishbone as though he had been playing it all season, deftly faking up the middle to Mondo and running around edge, running along the line, and pitching to Hilliard a split-second before getting plastered, and connecting on quick hitches to Cartwright. Drives of eighty-two and ninety-one yards sandwiched around a Watchassee score brought Dolphin to within a touchdown, 21–14, early in the fourth quarter.

Sammons capped off Dolphin's next drive, another grinding ninety-yarder, with a thirty-yard score off a fake pitch, defenders bouncing off his shoulders and lunging at his heels, to close the gap to 21–20 with four minutes left. When Cal "Wide Right" Stimson trotted on to tie the game, Bamford turned his back on the play to watch the scoreboard at the opposite end zone. True to form, Wide Right shanked the extra point. For ten seconds after the miss, Wide Right stood motionless in the spot where he finished his follow through, head down and hands on his helmet, while teammates jogged by and tried to pick him up with a word or tap on the shoulder pads.

When Bamford heard the Dolphin section groan and saw the scoreboard stuck on 20, he took off his headset and hurled it at the ground. He wandered away for a moment, out of earshot of players, but I shadowed him. "God bless it, Cal! How many players do I have to send to shrinks? Cryin' out loud, I knew we should have gone for two."

Watchassee's drive stalled with two minutes fifteen left, and after a punt, Dolphin took over on its twenty-five-yard line with two time-outs left. Other than one strike to Cartwright, Sammons and Hilliard dominated the ball on runs and pitches, gouging the Tornadoes for ten and fifteen yards a pop and looking unstoppable. On third-and-four from Watchassee's nine, Sammons was hit just as he pitched to Hilliard, causing a wayward ball that Hilliard pounced upon for a big loss at the seventeen.

Bamford called his last time-out with thirty-two seconds left and huddled with his coaches for his biggest decision of the year, and probably his career. A thirty-four-yard field goal was well within Wide Right's range, but Bamford had no faith in him. On the other hand, Bamford had studied probabilities enough to know that the odds of picking up a first down or scoring on a fourth-and-twelve were less than one in five.

"We're going for it," Bamford announced. He gathered his offense and called a play. Wide Right sat alone on the bench, staring blankly into space. On the way back onto the field, I noticed Sammons, Hilliard, and Cartwright in conversation as they approached the huddle. Sammons took the snap, wheeled, and threw a line drive in the flat to Hilliard.

"What the hell's he doing?" Bamford groaned to the O-line coach. "Where's my skinny post? Who changed the play?"

Hilliard caught the ball perfectly—on one short-hop, like a shortstop gobbling up a grounder. Hilliard stood still with the ball, as did the rest of the Dolphin players, seemingly dejected about the last-gasp unsuccessful play and lost championship. Sammons and Cartwright walked toward Hilliard, as if to console for a bad break. Watchassee defenders started celebrating, and a few began running off the field. Just then, Hilliard bolted for the end zone, with Sammons and Cartwright running interference, knocking the few Watchassee defenders who realized what was happening off-balance and sprawling. Hilliard hurdled the last defender who dove to try to chop him at the knees and somersaulted into the end zone.

The three Palmertown players celebrated in the end zone, while the other unaware Dolphin players seemed stunned. Three officials held a quick conference, then one raised his arms, signaling touchdown. None had blown his whistle, meaning the play was never dead. Though Hilliard hadn't caught the pass cleanly, it actually wasn't a pass at all but a lateral thrown slightly backward. As a lateral, it was technically a fumble that could be recovered and advanced, and it had fooled Watchassee, which appeared unaware of the rule. I had seen the Palmertown friends practicing the play on their own during the week, Sammons working on throwing a clean-bounce one-hopper and Hilliard assuming his baseball infielder stance to envelop it—quite a feat with a spherical ball. Now they had executed it perfectly under pressure, obviously not telling anyone else but Cartwright of the play change, and it held up as the winning score when Watchassee failed to pull off a last-second miracle.

A bunch of Dolphin players grabbed the Gatorade bucket and sneaked up behind Bamford as he walked to greet the opposing coach, dousing him with Gatorade and ice as they had seen the New York Giants do to Coach Bill Parcells. Bamford stopped in his tracks, raised his arms, and grimaced under the frigid Gatorade shower before laughing and moving on.

While the Fightin' Dorsals were embracing and celebrating, I was able to pull Sammons and Hilliard aside for a quick interview before the hordes of reporters ensnared them in the locker room or monopolized the floor in the tightly controlled press conference.

"It's bittersweet, man, bittersweet," Sammons said, tears on his face. "After all me and Nate been through, it was sweet to show we stick together and do anything it takes to win. I never gave up hope. I said Sammy Sammons would be vindicated, as God is my witness, and today is the exclamation point. We champions, baby. We endured, and no one can take that from us."

Great quote, I thought. I congratulated and thanked Sammy and headed in search of the Cannon.

"Mr. Yankelovich, I got one more thing to tell you," Sammy called, summoning me back.

"Like you taught me back on my darkest day, I got something I want you to know off the record. That means it won't go in the paper, right?"

"You got my word, Sammy. What do you got?"

"You know I don't like to swear, Mr. Yankelovich, but fuck Coach Bamford, fuck Dolphin. Except for Coach Schlorf, he had our backs, and they hung him out to dry just like us. I did this for me and Nate. I did this for my mama. I did this for Palmertown, the Palmertown Six. For Coach Bamford? Fuck, no! If not for Palmertown pride, I'd take it all back just to fuck him! Excuse my bad language and please forgive me, I just wanted to get that out and thought you'd understand."

"I know what you mean, Sammy. Coach Bamford can be tough to deal with. Enjoy the moment…for yourself and Palmertown."

❖ ❖ ❖

I had never seen a locker room as jubilant as Dolphin's—hugs and shouts of unadulterated joy and tears and other displays of unfettered raw emotions that anyone would be lucky to feel and show just once in his life and bottle the memory forever. I was caught by surprise by feeling jealous. I was only five years older than some of these players were. Though I was now an adult and a professional and already had started to become hardened to the dreams and idolizations of youth in my new workaday world, it reminded me why and how much I loved sports. I had imagined such moments for myself countless times while shooting jumpers alone at the local park, sprinting along the chalk with the football, dodging imaginary tacklers on the elementary school field, and practicing high corner soccer shots at summer camp. My moment of pure joy, however, remained unexperienced except in my imagination, save for the occasional significant tennis win as a youth, which was a deeply personal and individual satisfaction and hard to share with anyone else. In contrast, this Dolphin achievement was magnified because it came out of five months of pain, sweat, grime, guts, and shared sacrifice, dedication, and camaraderie among fifty players who needed each other to make it happen.

Coach Bamford made sure to pump himself up during the postgame press conference, knowing how many college recruiters were at the game and that hordes more would see it on tape.

"Connor brought us this far. The kid's a major college talent, and with him at the helm we revolutionized into Air Coryell," Bamford explained to the throng of reporters from across Florida, *USA Today*, and scholastic

THREE YARDS AND A PLATE OF MULLET

sports publications, referring to the explosive, pass-happy San Diego Chargers of the late 1970s and early '80s under Coach Don Coryell.

"But today just wasn't Connor's day. Sometimes he struggles with his reads and decision-making. I had a gut feeling Sammy would ignite us in the second half, so I made the move to go back to our bread and butter, what we call 'three yards and a plate of mullet.' Only Sammy was so good today, it was more like fifteen yards. As a coach, you got to know your players and be willing to pull the trigger and adjust. That's what I did today, and it paid off."

Bamford was asked whether he expected to get any interest from colleges based on his back-to-back championships, and whether he would be interested.

"Let's not go so doggone fast. I'm going to enjoy this one tonight and for a long time. All I know is I have Dolphin in my blood, and there's no place else I'd rather be right now," Bamford answered. Then, curiously, he opened the door wider. "The future will take care of itself."

References to *right now* and *the future* were dead giveaways. I knew at that moment that Bamford, as he uttered those words, was mentally fielding offers that either had been proposed or he was anticipating.

Just like the first time I met Coach Bamford in his office on a ninety-seven-degree August day, he let me know in no uncertain terms that my time with him on this night was limited, as I attempted to get a more exclusive and personal quote after the press conference.

"You got two minutes, Jake. Our bus is running, and the kids want to get back to the hotel to celebrate. Whadya need?"

All I could think to ask in that short a time was the universal question: "How do you feel?"

I got the same cantankerous Bamford I had come to know and expect. "Is that all you got, Jake? Were you watching the game? Why don't you come down from your ivory tower and *learn something* about football. My goodness! How do I feel? How do you think I feel? This is what we work for all year, putting in new plays in spring practice, two-a-day puke-a-thons in summer, and grinding every goll-dang day of the season. It's what we live for, and tonight's the icing on the cake. It doesn't get any better."

I was able to parse his statement enough for a great quote that others wouldn't have. But it also occurred to me that Coach Bamford couldn't describe how he felt, perhaps because he didn't feel much except relief that he didn't fail and that he could check off another requisite box to further his own ambition and a temporary respite from his insatiable desire to dominate and win. He had respect from his kids, mostly derived from fear of disappointment or failure or weakness, but I don't think he had love, as Magnusson did. As for whether Bamford was truly happy for his kids, it was hard to tell. I think his narcissistic personality overwhelmed his empathy and ability to connect. But that's also what made him great at what he did, and what kept me at arm's length all season.

"Hurry up, Jake. Time's a wastin'," Bamford pressured me as I scribbled fast to get down the usable part of his quote. "You got anything else?"

I realized this might be my last minute with Coach Bamford in my career—I didn't know if he or I or both would be gone come spring practice. There were two other things I wanted to know. After a full season, I realized that being a wallflower wouldn't get me anywhere with Bamford. Being brazen also might not produce printable results, but it was the only way to earn respect, so I asked.

"Coach, I don't buy your answer about college coaching. I know you're itching to get back. What's the truth on your offers or interest in you?"

"You got some balls, Yank, always trying to stir something up. You heard me in there. I'm staying. I'm Dolphin's coach. That's all that's important. The rest is none of your business."

"One more thing, Coach. Did you have two guys rough me up after the Clear Vista game?"

Coach Bamford glowered at me without saying a word. He looked as though he was about to call me a pussy and a mama's boy and make me run into a blocking sled over and over, harder and harder, until I collapsed on the ground in tears. I locked eyes with him and didn't retreat, as I would have back in August. We stayed like that until Bamford broke for the bus. He turned back before stepping on.

"You know, Yank, you've made a lot of enemies in a short time here. Never underestimate the love for Dolphin football," he said, grinning, and then disappeared into the bus.

❖ ❖ ❖

I made it to the press box to meet Halumka for game stats just in time to catch Whalebait's close:

"The Dorsal Fins have proved they are the kings of the sea, devouring the rest of the field as so much cuttlefish in their wake. Coach Jimbo Bamford floats atop the flotsam and jetsam of the Florida high school football world again with a remarkable second straight Class 5A championship, despite the swarm of saltwater crocodiles aiming to make Dolphin its prey. Bamford is now firmly ensconced as the admiral of the high school ranks. The question all of us chummers are going to want to know is: will the admiral's ship sail to a new theater? Something tells me there's going to be plenty of bait cast to reel him in."

I was wondering the same thing, and how much I would miss Bamford the next season—despite his bullying and cold-shoulder treatment and the angst it produced in me—if he departed for greener pastures and bigger greenbacks. And whether my reporting on the Palmertown Six might effectively scuttle his plans to do so.

I soon found out. A week after school reopened from holiday break in January 1987, Dolphin High called a press conference for the announcement: Coach Bamford had been hired as the new head coach at Florida Agricultural and Technological University (Florida A&T), which boldly proclaimed it would be rivaling powerhouses Florida, Florida State, and the U—the University of Miami—for supremacy in the state—ergo, the nation—and would be leaving Dolphin immediately to begin recruiting.

Someone Else

Bamford's imminent departure only heightened my urgency to break the story. Based on Chenault's encouragement to keep grinding, I called at-large school board member Bunny Heavener, who had been approached by school board chairman Gus Papadopoulos with an offer to pay her son's tuition at an exclusive private school for children with learning disabilities in exchange for a vote. I told her that I had the confirmation I needed and was going ahead with writing the story about illicit activities by the board to influence a redistricting vote and needed her story on the record for corroboration.

"Bunny, remember when we talked before, you said to get back to you if I found wrongdoing, that you didn't want to go along with the status quo but you wanted to speak out if the public trust was violated? Well, Boots gave me his whole story about illegal activities—well, they sure seem illegal, but we'll have to leave that to the legal system once the story gets out—so this would be your time to go on record with the story you told me."

"Gosh, yes, I remember, that was quite disturbing," Bunny said. "I'd really love to help you, but now may not be the right time. Can you get the backup you need from someone else?"

No, no, no, fuck! What do you mean, not the right time? Someone else? Are you washing your hair today? Walking your dog? I was afraid of this, the moment of truth colliding with weakness of conviction. I had to go into salesman mode and talk her back onto the ledge. I had to think back to my Kabir-wear days.

"Bunny, this *is* the time. I've got everything I need to wrap this story up with a ribbon and a bow, except you. And it won't run *without you*. Were you serious about protecting the public trust? Because this is a huge chance for you to do that. You wouldn't want to look back with regret that you didn't step up when you had the opportunity."

I don't know if I consciously intended to, but I was laying the guilt on thick.

"It's just that I'm working on getting a new countywide program approved for students with learning disabilities, and I need Gus's support. He may propose it for next year's budget. You know it's a chairman's budget. That's the power of the chair. We can only cut or move funds around; we can't add more costs. You can get one of the other members, can't you?"

"No, Bunny. I've tried several times with Shelley and Lenzell; they're not going to talk, no reason to. I've gone as far as I can. You're the one."

"I'm really sorry I can't help you now. I thought about it, and I really think it's better if I don't. Good luck with your story."

"I really hope you'll reconsider. Call me back if you change your mind."

Power Play

I called Chenault to deliver the bad news.

"Don't give up," she told me. "Sources change their minds all the time. I can't tell you how many times people went back and forth on me when I covered city hall. Wait a little while, and then give her a call again. Things may change."

I didn't know it then, but Chenault was referring to more than just Heavener changing her mind. In mid-January, the entire *Dinqy* staff was called to a meeting at a church large enough to seat everyone a block from headquarters, where Wellington announced that it had been a great run and that the *Dinqy* was well positioned to challenge the *St. Pete Times* and *Miami Herald* for supremacy in Florida, and that he had love in his heart for the paper and everyone who worked for it and the community, which had welcomed him into its social and business circles so warmly, but that it was time to move on to a new chapter in his life, writing books, starting a philanthropy, and, who knows, perhaps becoming a visiting journalism lecturer at a university, and to spend more time with his wife and five grandchildren, and that effective February 1, Alize Chenault would be serving as interim executive editor while Stennett News Service conducted a national search for his replacement.

After the announcement, during drinks at Tangerine on New Palm City's Orchard Street, Paddy, who had his ear to the ground on such things, told me it wasn't as simple as Wellington just deciding to take his moneybags and surf off into the Gulf sunset. Rumor had it that the

Wellington-Chenault affair had gone cold after two years—at least from Chenault's perspective—but Wellington couldn't let it go, and in fact had become a downright lecherous scoundrel, contradictory to his public persona of the erudite and dignified Southern gentleman, and his behavior in Chenault's presence had been noticed in the newsroom and at community events as quite startling if not out-and-out deplorable. You couldn't blame the guy, Paddy said, not many men eligible for Social Security could have an elegant and dutiful wife at home while keeping a thing going with a breathtaking Equal Rights Amendment woman half his age who could still outclass all but the most dazzling beauty pageant competitors.

But now Chenault was showing Wellington that women, too, could have alter egos and had threatened to expose the affair and level sexual harassment charges against him. The word is, Paddy said, that Chenault held the cards as a single woman—look what happened to Democratic presidential candidate and married man Gary Hart when he took one too many sailing trips with the exhilarating Donna Rice; can you say, "career suicide"?—and she decided to play the royal flush. Sure, Chenault had beauty in spades, but that was only a means to an end. What she had even more of was smarts and ambition, and the end was a position of power and respect in a man's world. If she had to use every tool in her arsenal—sex appeal, included—to shatter the glass ceiling, by God, she would, said Paddy, who had seen her operate close up for six years. It just so happened that the most operative and precise tool at her disposal now was blackmail, and she wielded it against her former lover the way Braveheart brandished his sword against the English army.

Rather than risk humiliation, legal wrangling, and a scandal that his own paper would have to cover—not to mention the likely fallout in his marriage and the enormous divorce costs and diminished retirement that such a settlement might entail—Wellington in all likelihood admitted to himself that Chenault had gotten the best of him, but not until after he gave the best of himself to her, and that he had still enjoyed a hell of a ride for a relative fossil like himself and decided to swallow some pride and call it a career with his stellar reputation intact.

At least, that was Paddy's take on the sudden turn of events, and I believed it.

Do You Know Who I Am?

With the news of Wellington's imminent departure, I went after Heavener. She was still holding out for Chairman Gus to help her enact the educational program she so coveted, but I could tell that her resolve was starting to crack. If Gus was loyal to anyone, he was loyal to himself—even I could see that in my short time in Drabenville. Perhaps Heavener was coming to that realization as well.

"The budget comes out in two weeks," she told me. "Look, I haven't forgotten you. We're just so close to doing something great for so many kids in this county who are suffering in big classes without the attention they need. I just can't take the chance of ruining it now."

In the meantime, as Chenault had advised, I powered through the story, putting background, facts, research, and interviews together into a coherent narrative, forgoing Lucky Charms to start writing at 7:00 a.m., an ungodly hour for a sportswriter. I left placeholders to fill in the backstory and quotes from Heavener, in an act of faith that she would come through. In fact, the whole effort was predicated on that.

I saved calling Gus Papadopoulos and Coach Bamford for last; I didn't want to tip them off to what I had too early while the story was pending, or give them too much time to work behind the scenes to kill it. I anticipated being stonewalled, but it was essential to make the attempt. I spread all of my notes and documentation in front of me.

Big Papa was first, in case he mentioned something about Bamford. I called him at his office and identified myself as a reporter calling about school board business. I got him on the line. After introducing myself, I skipped right past the small talk and asked him directly about Clarence Walker's allegation that he was paid off to vote in favor of Palmertown's redistricting.

Silence. Then, "Who did you say you are?"

"Jake Yankelovich, sports reporter at the *Dinqy*."

"Why are you asking about school business?"

"Because there are indications that the redistricting was related to sending better athletes to Dolphin High, and that some board members were unduly influenced, and your name was mentioned."

"I don't know anything about that."

I knew I had to get tough, or act as if. "Did you offer a bribe to Boots Walker for him to vote for the Palmertown redistricting?"

"Son, do you know who you're talking to?" Papadopoulos asked. I expected the power play. This was a man used to controlling situations and getting his way.

"Yes, you're the school board chairman."

"That's not what I mean. Do you know who I am?"

"Did you pay off Clarence Walker?"

"I don't know what you're talking about. Who do you think you are?"

"Did you offer—"

"That's the end of this discussion." Click.

❖ ❖ ❖

Coach Bamford was next. I needed to get this interview before he left Dolphin and entered another universe entirely. I reached him as he was clearing out his office.

"I'm working on a story about the Palmertown redistricting."

"I thought we had an understanding on that, Yankelovich; it's ancient history."

"Not to me. It's relevant."

"We're state champions, that's what's relevant, and I'm going to Florida A&T, that's what's relevant. What's done is done. Time for you to move on, too."

I told him what I knew from Boots Walker and about his financial connections with Papadopoulos and the unusual economic gains made by other board members who voted yes.

"Yankelovich, I thought you learned. I told you to be careful about what you look into. A lot of people want to bring down Dolphin High any way they can. You covered our championship run, did an OK job. Why are you going back to this nonsense? I told you during training camp this talk about Palmertown was asinine, and it's still the most asinine thing I've ever heard. It's not worth my time."

"Do you have any comment on Boots Walker's allegation?"

"Not worth my time. Your editors are going to hear about this call. You better have your bags packed. I'm not sure how long you'll have a job, but I've got a new job to do. We're done."

❖ ❖ ❖

It could have been that a threat from Bamford against Wellington to expose his newsroom affair if a Palmertown redistricting story was published had as much to do with Wellington's retirement as Chenault's threat of a sexual harassment allegation. But now that was academic: Wellington was yesterday's news, Bamford was hitting the big time, and the story was green-lighted and awaiting the finishing touches, if Heavener came through.

The draft came out to 120 column inches without Heavener's information, and even then, it was only cut by ten inches after going through Skip and Paddy, the Quad Counties metro editor, and Chenault. By comparison, my average game story was fifteen to twenty inches. It had what it took to qualify as an exposé, which meant it would start on the front page and occupy at least two whole pages inside, along with Bend-Over's photos and graphics, including a flow chart showing the money trail. Now all I could do was wait.

GET READY FOR A FIRESTORM

I DIDN'T GIVE a crap about the Dolphin County education budget, except for the fact that my journalism career might be hinging on it. So I asked the bureau's education reporter, Diana Wrigglesworth, to let me know when it was made public, and told her about the minutiae I was interested in. Wrigglesworth was none too happy I was edging in on her beat, asking me condescendingly, "Don't you have enough to keep you busy in the Toy Department?"

On the day the budget came out, I mercilessly bugged Wrigglesworth, who was uptight anyway, to try to find some obscure new program for children with learning disabilities or attention deficit disorder or something similar buried somewhere in a special education or needs-based learning or Dolphin County differentiated-instruction category.

"You'll have to wait," Wrigglesworth snapped at me. "I'm on deadline. You see how thick this budget is? I've got to write about new school construction and teacher staffing and salaries and class sizes. Your thing is way down on my list, Jake."

A few days later, Wrigglesworth stopped by my desk. "I was a rookie once, too, so I'm cutting you a break," she said. "I looked for you. Couldn't find anything new for the Sped Kids. In fact, that budget was cut."

I called Heavener. No answer. Left a message. Didn't hear back. Called again the next week, same thing. It was looking like a lost cause.

The next Monday morning, as I was planning my stories and game coverage for the week, my phone rang. It was Heavener.

"Sorry I didn't get back to you, I was trying to work things out, but it's not going to happen, the bastard. I'm ready to talk. The election's in September and I'm done, fed up. What do you need from me?"

Heavener recounted her story, and I reread her quotes to her to make sure she was OK with the wording and could stand behind them. As soon as I hung up, I called Paddy, and he conferenced in Chenault.

"Get down here now and add in Heavener and go over it with a fine-tooth comb to see if anything else needs to be updated," Chenault said in businesslike manner. "I suggest you call Clarence Walker and let him know we're going with it. I'm having Legal review it one more time just to be sure. It's going to be the lead story on Wednesday. I'm having our design team work on a special layout package. Get ready for a firestorm. Oh, and Jake, good work."

❖ ❖ ❖

I went to our Conquista Island Circle K Wednesday morning to pick up a few copies. The headline blared in an oversized font:

DOLPHIN SCHOOL BOARD MEMBER: I TOOK MONEY FOR PALMERTOWN VOTE

Walker Alleges Bribe from Chairman to Boost Dolphin High Athletics

The fallout started immediately, as the Dolphin State attorney's office announced an investigation, leading to second- and third-day stories, and other media outlets began chasing the story, playing catch up. Though Boots Walker had mentioned his perception of Coach Bamford's involvement in the transactions, it was hearsay on his part. Walker's direct dealings, and therefore his only firsthand knowledge, lay with Papadopoulos, so the original story did not allude to Coach Bamford having any role; the coach was mentioned only insofar as his school gained a number of top-flight athletes from Palmertown, including the Palmertown Six football players, and his family's business relationship with Papadopoulos, a fact that loosely established the long chain of relationships that investigators could follow: from the Palmertown Athletic & Education Complex to Roma Rojo Tomatoes to Boots Walker to Gus Papadopoulos to Bamford & Sons Gulfcoast Development Services to Coach Bamford to the Palmertown Six.

But within ten days, when the State attorney's office announced that Coach Bamford and the Dolphin High Athletic Department were being investigated, the recently departed Bamford became part of the public record and fair game for coverage. Another audacious headline blared:

LEGENDARY DOLPHIN FOOTBALL COACH JIMBO BAMFORD INVESTIGATED
    FOR LINK TO PALMERTOWN REDISTRICTING SCANDAL
Former State Championship Coach Said to Covet Palmertown Athletes

❖ ❖ ❖

The day the story broke, I got a call from Florida A&T Athletic Director Lance Cundriff.

"Mr. Yankelovich, you covered the Dolphin High football program, correct?" Cundriff asked.

"Yes."

"And you investigated the controversy with the Palmertown Six and the school board?"

"I did. What are you looking for?"

"Listen, as you know, we just hired Coach Bamford. I was not aware of the situation reported by the *Daily Inquirer*, you know, the story mentioning Coach Bamford being investigated. I'd rather not discuss this over the phone, so I'd appreciate if you could come to campus and we could talk in person. I'm sure it's no big deal, just an unfortunate misunderstanding, a mistake—"

"Well, I wouldn't go that far, Mr. Cundriff. The verdict is still out."

"Yes, well, in any case, I can have interviews set up for you with your local athletes making a name for themselves at A&T to make the trip worthwhile."

❖ ❖ ❖

The story that had already shaken top brass at Florida A&T became all consuming for Chenault and the *Dinqy*. It was a readership bonanza, and by extension, an advertising and revenue driver. It was the must-read story that Chenault had hoped it would be throughout the Quad County region, creating a daily buzz in diners and hair salons and on golf courses. We were beating the pants off the *Drabenville Times-Democrat* in its own Dolphin County backyard, siphoning revenue and subscribers.

By this time, I had become merely one contributor among many to the mushrooming story, as the *Dinqy* flooded the story with resources to cover new developments, unearth new details, and find new sources, including Dolphin County cops-and-courts reporter Jean-Paul Boneau, business reporter Dieter Klingenmeier, education reporter Diana Wrigglesworth, and hotshot young investigative reporter Nick Erpenbeck. The paper's top editors and columnists—they even allowed the O-Dog into the inner circle—huddled with Chenault every morning at 9:30 a.m. before the routine 10:00 a.m. daily planning meeting to discuss the Palmertown scandal, a gathering that became known as the "Palmertown Vice Squad."

I never did reveal my brutish encounter with two hooligans disguised as Dolphin football players on a dark West Drabenville street outside Norville Haggard's house to authorities or my superiors at the paper. It was too late now, so I never will know whether they were dispatched by Coach Bamford or took a warped sense of justice or an overzealous approach to crisis management into their own hands. I'd like to think that Coach Bamford was above taking the stereotypical two-bit mobster knee-capping route of intimidation, but I wouldn't put such tactics beyond him.

You've Got to Take It

Curious about what the Florida A&T University athletic director wanted to know, I made the trip to Florida A&T in the Redneck Riviera. I met with Cundriff and fielded his questions for an hour. He had a PhD but was as naïve about Dolphin County high school football as I was when I took my first sightseeing tour in Johnny Littleman's Buick in July. By the end, I was sure that Cundriff had done a terrible job vetting Bamford and had just gift-wrapped the job for him because he was the hottest available property in the Florida coaching ranks, and Florida A&T needed a name that conjured promise as much as it needed a winner.

As a gracious Southern host, Cundriff took me on a tour of Florida A&T's athletic facilities. As we walked through the newly modernized weight room, I heard a familiar voice, then came eye to eye with Coach Bamford, who was overseeing a players' workout. After an uncomfortable minute when we ignored each other as Cundriff pointed out new exercise stations, Bamford came to greet me, motioned me to follow him to an attached coach's office, and shut the door.

"You won't win. You can't win. You should have learned that by now," Bamford opened bluntly.

"I'm not trying to win. Just reporting."

"What did Cundriff want?"

"What I know about the investigation of irregularities in the school board redistricting decision."

"What'd you tell him?"

"Nothing more than what's been published. I don't give away my work or my sources."

"You know they'll never pin anything on me, don't you?"

"I *don't* know. How does that work?"

"You met the State attorney?"

"Yes. I've talked to him."

"You know how far back the Bamfords go with his family?"

"No. Why? Does that matter?"

"Before your daddy was born, maybe your grandpa. In business together. You know my sister is an assistant State attorney?"

"Yes. So?"

"That's how it works. Don't be naïve."

"You know I've got bank records. You and Big Papa, questionable transactions."

"Just business. Doesn't mean shit."

"You can walk on water."

"Damn straight. In my town, I can. I do. Ever been to Mudville Mike's, the Rotary, the Chamber, the Knights of Columbus? Ask any of 'em; they'll tell you."

"I have. Did some of my reporting there."

"Besides, I'm clean as a whistle. You've been running around out there, making a mountain out of a molehill. I'm surprised Wellington's let that crap get out the door."

"He's gone. Beauty queen's in charge."

"That bitch? She's a real go-getter. She'd love to nail me, make a name fast. She's got some power; I've got more. Ain't gonna happen."

"I wouldn't be too sure. She'd crawl over hot coals naked for a good story."

"I'm sure. You still don't know how Dolphin County works, do you? We call the shots. I thought you were learning. No better teacher than me."

I reconsidered. Bamford was right. For all Chenault's ambition, if I had to bet, I would bet she wouldn't be bagging this big mackerel.

"I do, more...I see how it works. I learned a lot from you. You put me through the grinder."

"That's the only way you would have survived. If you learned anything, it should be this: The world doesn't owe you anything. You've got to take it. You're only, what, twenty-three, and now you're in on the secret. You should thank me. For all your highbrow education, funny you had to come to Drabenville to learn it."

"I see your point. Drabenville's definitely been an education. Good luck here, Coach."

I stuck out my hand, and Bamford shook it. I headed for the door. Before I could close it, and the Coach Bamford chapter of my life, he summoned me back.

"Hey, Jake."

"Yes, Coach," I said, stepping back into the doorway.

"You're a pain in the ass. You've been a thorn in my side since you got here, like no one before and I hope to hell no one again."

"It's not how I intended it, Coach, really."

"I'll give you your props. You're a persistent son of a bitch. You've done your job, put in the work, stood up, and faced adversity. I don't have to like you and what you do, but I can respect that in anyone. If you ever need a reference for a job or a college beat or anything, give me a call. I think I can have some influence."

"I will, Coach, I will."

Coach Bamford got up and followed me out. As I headed back to the athletic director's office, I overheard Bamford exhorting his new players in the weight room.

"We have a losing culture here, fellas. That's gonna change, and it starts right now, in this room. Weakness is for losers. I've seen your tapes. They're shit. None of your jobs are safe. We're weak. Losers. Losing football. I've never been part of losing football, and I won't be. That's the way it's going to be, so get your head right, lift hard, and toughen up. You better grow some rocks, 'cuz we're going three yards and a plate of mullet all year long."

I exited the facility chuckling. It hadn't fully registered until that moment—I was going to miss the shit out of Bamford.

I hit the gateway to the Redneck Riviera, Interstate 10, fifteen minutes out of campus along a boulevard of palms, glad to be headed back home to Drabenville.

Made in the USA
Middletown, DE
13 October 2015